THE SILICON DAGGER

The Legion of Space
*Darker Than You Think
The Green Girl
The Cometeers
One Against the Legion
Seetee Shock
Seetee Ship
Dragon's Island
The Legion of Time
Undersea Quest
   (with Frederik Pohl)
Dome Around America
StarBridge
   (with James Gunn)
Undersea Fleet
   (with Frederik Pohl)
Undersea City
   (with Frederik Pohl)
The Trial of Terra
Golden Blood
The Reefs of Space
   (with Frederik Pohl)
Starchild
   (with Frederik Pohl)
The Reign of Wizardry
Bright New Universe
Trapped in Space
The Pandora Effect
Rogue Star
   (with Frederik Pohl)
People Machines

The Moon Children
H.G. Wells: Critic of Progress
The Farthest Star
   (with Frederik Pohl)
The Early Williamson
The Power of Blackness
The Best of Jack Williamson
Brother to Demons, Brother to
   Gods
The Alien Intelligence
The Humanoid Touch
The Birth of a New Republic
   (with Miles J. Breuer)
Manseed
Wall Around a Star
   (with Frederik Pohl)
The Queen of the Legion
Wonder's Child: My Life in
   Science Fiction (memoir)
Lifeburst
*Firechild
*Land's End
   (with Frederik Pohl)
Mazeway
The Singers of Time
   (with Frederik Pohl)
*Beachhead
*The Humanoids
*Demon Moon
*The Black Sun
*The Silicon Dagger

*available from Tor Books

THE SILICON DAGGER

JACK WILLIAMSON

TOR®

A TOM DOHERTY ASSOCIATES BOOK

NEW YORK

This is a work of fiction. All the characters and events portrayed in this novel are either fictitious or are used fictitiously.

THE SILICON DAGGER

This book is printed on acid-free paper.

Design by Victoria Kuskowski

Edited by James Frenkel

A Tor Book
Published by Tom Doherty Associates, Inc.
175 Fifth Avenue
New York, NY 10010

Tor Books on the World Wide Web:
http://www.tor.com

Tor® is a registered trademark of Tom Doherty Associates, Inc.

Library of Congress Cataloging-in-Publication Data

Williamson, Jack.
    The silicon dagger / Jack Williamson.—1st ed.
        p.   cm.
    "A Tom Doherty Associates Book."
    ISBN 0-312-86540-6
    I. Title
PS3545.I557S55   1999
813'.52—dc21   98-47006
                                                    CIP

First Edition: April 1999

Printed in the United States of America

0   9   8   7   6   5   4   3   2   1

I WANT TO THANK MY EDITOR, JIM FRENKEL,
FOR HIS LASTING FAITH
AND ABLE AID.

"BEWARE THE UNEXPECTED—
IT STRIKES FROM THE DARK."

THE SILICON DAGGER

CHAPTER ONE

AFTER ALDEN'S BURIAL the funeral limo took us back to the old Georgetown house. Marion, the children, and I. Beyond tears, Marion sat erect, bleakly staring straight ahead. Little Angela was in her lap, quietly sobbing. Beside me, Tim let his fingers creep into mine. To break the silence, I asked about his school.

"A charter school," he said. "I like it a lot."

He glanced up at his mother and back at me.

"I think I'll be a surgeon. Dad said I could be, if I tried hard enough." He frowned. "If I could find the money. He said medical schools cost a lot."

"I'll help you," I told him. "If you try hard enough."

I felt his fingers tighten, and my own eyes blurred. Alden had been my half-brother, ten years older and almost a second father. Tim was only ten, less my nephew than a loyal kid brother. When the bomb exploded I had been away, hiking on the Appalachian Trail with college friends. Stunned by the news when we got home,

I had not long ago begun to feel Tim's loss, his mother's and sister's, their pain suddenly more real than my own.

At the house, Marion stopped for a moment on the sidewalk, staring at the bed of roses that had been Alden's latest hobby. I offered to take us all out for dinner, but the children wanted to stay home. While she was slicing cold roast for sandwiches, Tim led me upstairs to see his father's office.

Yellow tape was stretched across the room. The police had taken his laptop computer, but the big desktop machine lay mangled in the litter of books and papers under his shattered desk. A sheet was spread to cover the stains of his blood.

"The cops and the FBI are coming back tomorrow to look for more clues." Tim was very grave about it. "It was a plastic bomb, they say. Very hard to trace."

He caught my hand to lead me toward the tape.

"Dad was working on the printouts from his laptop." He gestured at the clean-swept floor around the sheet. "The pages were scattered everywhere. Mom picked them up, and the cops let her copy them before they took them away. But I don't think—"

He looked away to hide his tears, and spun the knob on the wall safe where Alden had kept his tax returns and the contracts with his publishers. Reaching inside, he found a worn brown leather wallet.

"Dad—Dad's." He tried to steady his voice. "Mom wants to keep it just like it was. To remember him."

I gave it back, and he locked it in the safe.

"The second bomb," he said. "The cops say the bombers were maybe the same, but the explosive was different. I don't—" His voice broke again. "I don't think they found anything."

The first bomb, only weeks before, had brought down the Federal Building at Frankfort. The building was considered well secured, but evidence suggested that the plotters had smuggled the explosive a little at a time into a paint shop across the street behind it and used a curved barrier of sandbags and concrete blocks to focus the blast.

"In a terrible way," Alden had told me at the time, "it clinched my point that that home-grown terror is a major menace to the nation. Now my agent wants to make it the springboard for another infonet documentary. He's calling it *Terror: The Rising Wave*. I don't much like the title, but it should make another book and help spread the word."

We sat in the kitchen. Marion had made hot cocoa for the children. Angela went to sleep with half her sandwich still in her hand, and Marion carried her up to bed. Tim answered the phone.

"Davey," he told me. "I'm going over to his place to catch up my math homework. If you don't mind."

He thanked me when I said I didn't mind, and came to shake my hand before he left. Marion lit the gas log in the living room when she came down, and brought a half-bottle of leftover wine.

Alden had found her on a Senate staff. My mother had called her plain. She wore glasses, and put her dark hair in a bun, but to him she had been beautiful. The kids adored her, and I ached for her now. When she and Alden were newly married, she used to tease me, calling me her baby brother. She still acted the elder sister, sometimes superior, but always kind and uncommonly wise. I loved and respected her enormously.

"I've been terribly worried since his book came out." I saw her pale lips set. "People who read it quit talking to him. Mad about what he'd said or afraid of what he might say. He'd had phone calls warning him to get out of Kentucky. He never admitted he was afraid, but I begged him not to go back."

She made a bitter face.

"He said he had to." She shrugged in wry resignation and looked into my eyes. "Alden had an old-fashioned love of his country. He said he saw a breakdown coming unless men of good will did something about it. He died for what he was trying to do."

She looked away to hide her eyes.

"Even here—" Her voice broke, and she stopped to pour the wine. "Even here I've had wicked phone calls. The worst was from a man with a snarly voice and an odd accent. 'Get the shit-sniffing wolf out of Kentucky, or we'll be shipping him back in a box.' "

The glasses trembled in her hand. She handed one to me.

"Clay, you know Alden was never a wolf. Sometimes a lamb in wolf skin, maybe, but nobody had any decent right to hurt him." She caught an unsteady breath. "I couldn't stop him from going back, but we tried to cope. He asked the cops to watch the house. I drove Tim to school. But the bombers—"

She flinched as if from actual pain.

"Cowardly bastards! I saw the thing when it came in the mail. The wrapper was printed to look like something from his publisher. The cops have found a scrap of it that shows a Kentucky postmark. Not much—" She shook her head. "Not much hope."

She sat frowning at the gas log till I asked about her plans.

"I'll carry on." She set her glass down on the coffee table and turned to me with a tight-lipped smile. "I always managed our finances. We'd saved some money. Alden had good insurance. I can keep the house. The kids need me here till Angela starts to school. I'll go back to work then, maybe part-time at first. I've kept up connections. A job should be no problem. But later, when the kids are ready for college—"

She bit her lip and turned to me. "Clay, I told the cops you'd been working in his office. They want to see you in the morning."

"Not much I can tell them." I sat groping dully through the emptiness of loss. "Alden kept his secrets, at least till he had them ready for print. The day he hired me for his research assistant, he told me not to ask too many questions." I recalled his bleak little grimace and words I couldn't repeat to Marion, not now. "Knowing too many answers could get you killed."

At the time I'd wondered if he only wanted to impress me, but now the recollection left me awkwardly silent till she asked about my own plans.

"Alden had promised to help me go back to law school." I had dropped out to take the research job with him. "Now I don't know."

"You're welcome here as long as you want to stay." She gave me a pale smile. "But that's about all—"

She stopped, her voice quivering.

"I'll be okay." I sipped the wine to thaw a lump in my throat, wishing for something I could do for her and the kids. A shock of hatred hit me, hatred for the makers of the bomb, hatred for all the other haters Alden had feared. "I have a few dollars in the bank. There's financial aid if I do go back to school."

"It's been a long day." She set her empty glass on the table. "I'm going up."

I asked to see her copy of Alden's laptop files.

"They were on a disk he brought home from Kentucky," she said. "Outlines for work in progress and notes on people he'd seen. Not many of them friendly. I had wicked phone calls while he was down there."

Her face twisted, she hugged me silently and went up the stairs.

I carried the printouts to the little apartment behind the garage that had been my room since I was old enough to want one of my own. I loved that place. Alden's artist-father had built it for a studio. His portraits of our mother and her parents still hung on the walls, along with an oak-framed photo of him standing beside them in front of the house.

He had done his own parents, his father a sternly starched and bearded gentleman with a gold watch chain across his chest, his mother in the frills of the time, her eyes cast demurely down. And my mother again, done as a forest nymph, discreetly nude, save for a luminous halo. The old man had imagination.

I sat down with the copied pages. They were raggedly marked where the blast had torn them, and splotched black with spatters of Alden's blood. A few were missing, but Marion had put the rest in order. I was soon lost in what they told me.

"Terror is a weapon," he began. "A weapon of the few against the many. It attacks democracy and the freedom of speech by seizing the channels of information to turn those principles against themselves. By killing the innocent, it alienates those it was meant to sway, and so defeats itself. The worst of crimes, it must be countered. True information is our best defense against misinformation. I look for truth, a search that has earned me enemies."

The term "muck-raker" had angered Alden, though in another age he might have worn it proudly. An investigative journalist, he had spent his career probing for dirty little secrets people were trying to keep and being hated for it.

"If nobody hates your story," he once told me, "it isn't news."

People enough had hated him for what he uncovered. The threats had begun with his infonet stories on anti-government dissidents: militant militias, religious extremists, hostile immigrants, unhappy special-interest factions, radical talk-show hosts and their converts. His book, *Terror in America*, summed up what he found.

It had brought a storm of angry denials, but also a generous contract for a new series to run in print and on the global infonet. The publishers had promised him an audience of eighty million on the infonet, scattered over forty nations.

"I'm going to call it *Powderhouse or Promise*, he told me. "I want to explore the springs of trouble and look for ways to make things better. I've picked out McAdam County for one typical social sample. Conflicts make news, and it's sure got big conflicts!" Emotion had quickened his voice. "Kentucky has had battles forever, beginning with the Shawnees and Daniel Boone, and then families split by the Civil War. These days there are a bunch of conflicts: the Feds hunting pot farmers, and pot farmers sniping at them; wealth against poverty; gangs in the schools; crooks in high office, militias on the march; infocrats—the masters of information science—against the idle ignorant. It's the nation on a microscope slide, playing out the story of our time." His jaws went tight. "Refugees from a dead past, trapped in the information age and slow to learn what it takes to survive."

Alden's head was angular and rugged under an untidy shag of black hair. Anger could put him into what Marion called his wolf skin. He wore it now, his lean face set hard and his black eyes shining.

"I've seen trouble brewing nearly everywhere, but that county frightens me. Its habits of violence date from the time of the first settlers. The pioneers got there with not much except their guns and the Scotch-Irish sense of honor they defended in their duels and their feuds. Their old folkways die hard. A lot of people, baffled and frightened by change they can't understand, their instinct is to fight. I heard lunatic hotheads quoting Jefferson and the Constitution, ranting for rebellion.

"Yet the county's still full of honest citizens." Suddenly rueful, he let his voice fall. "Good people in church every Sunday, working hard, paying their taxes, listening skeptically to all the liars on the infonet, wondering who to blame for putting America on the road to hell. They need the truth about the information revolution, even the hard truth I told in *Terror in America.*"

Hot with a helpless rage against his killers, I read the files and read them again, searching for any clue that might reveal his killers. The last file was headed simply McAdam.

"McAdam County," it began. "A little America, with everything from illiterate aliens to a fine liberal arts college. Old Calvin McAdam brought his wife and his wagons and his cattle and his slaves over the Cumberland Gap and up the Wilderness Road two hundred years ago. His descendants were big wheels in the county for generations, though their fortunes have fallen now.

"The current patriarch is Colin McAdam, a history professor till he retired. I found him in a white-columned Greek Revival mansion rebuilt rather shabbily after Civil War guerrillas burnt it to the ground. Though he's no longer a power in the county, he's still a gentleman. He served me a mint julep in a silver cup and showed me relics of the proud McAdam past. He's tradition and the past.

"He has two sons. Stuart is the black sheep. He organized the Kentucky Rifles, a local militia that's itching for any kind of trouble. He's in prison now on a narcotics charge. He's almost a living symbol of today's dilemmas.

"His older brother, Rob Roy, is their hope for a brighter future. A computer wizard, he dropped out of college with a couple of his fellow nerds to write software. They've set up an outfit they call CyberSoft. Their star product is an encryption system that's so secure the Justice Department is demanding a key.

"There's a daughter, Beth. Unmarried, she's a loyal McAdam. Still lives at home and teaches some of her father's history courses. I've asked to see her when she gets back from a summer in France, though she may not want to talk. The McAdams guard their privacy. Most of what I heard about them came from one Sam Katz, though I take him with a double pinch of salt.

"He says the Katz clan came down through the Gap a year ahead of the first McAdams. Says his people claimed the best bottom land in the valley. Says the McAdamses murdered old Gideon Katz and ran his family off their homestead. The feud went on for three generations. Colin McAdam snorted when I asked about that. He called Katz a worthless shyster, and firmly closed the subject.

"He is a lawyer. Perhaps he is a shyster; opinions seem to differ. I spent time with him because he knows county politics, but I never really understood him. He spoke freely about things past, but got nervous and clammed up when I tried to probe the here and now. He knows things he doesn't want aired on the infonet. Things he seemed afraid to say."

I went through the pages again, looking for answers. There were notes on a good many others who had willingly talked, and several who hadn't. Sheriff "Bull" Burleigh had ordered him out of the courthouse. The district attorney, Saul Hunn, advised him to get his dirty nose out of Kentucky. He had met Rocky Gottler, "the power behind Burleigh and Hunn."

I found a longer note.

"Juan Diego Gottler. Born in Argentina, son of a Kentucky horse breeder who went down there to raise Thoroughbreds on the pampas and married a local girl. The only horses, it turned out, were in the brochures he got up for investors here at home. He went bankrupt and disappeared.

"Rocky's uncle raised him. Like Katz, he's something of a mystery. He has money. I never learned where it comes from. He seldom shows it off, though he's president and principal owner of the Border State Bank. Uses his money to buy power. A big backer of Senator Madison Finn. I heard him referred to by various folks as the invisible king of McAdam County.

"When I called him to ask for an interview, he took me out to lunch and a round of golf. He's dark, heavyset, and he talks very fast in a high-pitched voice with a very faint Spanish accent. I thought he was surprisingly cordial, considering what I'd written about him in *Terror*. Turns out he'd read it, and he wanted to talk about the information age.

" 'Your infocrats may be about to inherit the earth,' he told me. 'But they don't scare me. Myself, I don't know scat about computers and your information age, but I do know who to hire. My uncle hired thugs to take out the pickets at his coal mines. I'll pick up your info experts when I need them.'

"Gottler has gripes of his own against the status quo, though I could never pin him down on exactly what they are. He's as keen as they come. He was wonderfully warm to me, so cordial he almost alarmed me. But he's a wild card. He cultivates dissidents. One is Stuart McAdam. When McAdam organized his militia, Gottler paid for uniforms and rifles, and after Stuart was convicted, he campaigned to get him out of prison.

"All that may make the county look like a madhouse, but I did meet one sane man. He's Cass Pepperlake, owner and editor of a little weekly, the *Freeman*. His masthead reads 'The Truth Can Make Men Free,' but he says he finds too few people ready for the truth. He warned me that my book had pretty well erased my welcome in the county.

"I trust him, but I met another man whose ambition troubled me. Kit Carson Moorhawk, a little man with big ideas. The son of a miner, he got his law degree and made a fortune when he helped a client get patent rights to a process for clean-burning high-sulfur coal. He lived high till his luck turned, built the Moorhawk Tower in the middle of town, married a beauty queen, bought a stable in the Blue Grass country, raced a winner at Churchill Downs.

"Till Gottler turned his luck, Gottler's bank owns a coal company that beat Moorhawk in a long patent fight. He lost everything: his stable and his tower and his mansion on the horse farm. Gottler lives in the mansion now. Moorhawk's wife went to Florida and sued for alimony he can't pay. The IRS is after him for back taxes. He hates them and hates the courts and hates the whole national establishment, big business and big government.

"Yet I like him, in spite of myself. His misfortunes are not entirely his own fault. He has charisma and aspirations to fit a bigger man. In the last election, he ran for the senate as a Libertarian. Defeated, of course, but he's not finished. He hates the past, and he has dreams that could make him dangerous. If our nation is a powder keg, Moorhawk is the match that could set it off."

Marion had pieced that much of the mangled printout back together.

". . . anomie." I found the words on the copy of another torn, black-spattered page. "Confusion, depression, despair, and a paradox that makes me wonder. The common man has always been at the mercy of the ruling few who commanded technology. It's been true from the stone axe down to the H-bomb, but it's a different story now, with information technology free to every man who can run a computer. That's the paradox. Suddenly we all have the means of power in our reach. It ought to set us free, but we're afraid of it, afraid other men will use it against us because they're afraid of us. It's a threat to the status quo, to the old world order, on a wider arena than McAdam County."

I frowned over that and the other mangled scraps till my head was aching. Finally I pushed them all aside and went to bed, wondering if I had overlooked some clue. Of all the men and maybe women in the county nursing private discontents or grudges, who might have feared my brother and been desperate enough to seek out the technology to build a letter bomb? I went to sleep with no idea.

CHAPTER TWO

THE POLICE CAME back next morning, a federal agent with them. They searched the crime scene again, photographed it, removed the yellow tape. Special Agent Botman was a tall gray man with shrewd black eyes in a pale hard face. He kept me in my own office, pausing now and then to answer the beep of a muffled pocket phone as he grilled me about Alden and my research job. His flat-voiced persistence finally vexed me.

"Alden never told me all that much," I protested. "He kept his secrets for his books or the infonet. Most of my own work was done right here in this room, reading proof on his manuscripts and handling correspondence. I did bits of background research for him at the university and in the Library of Congress, but I've never been to McAdam County. Or even to Kentucky, except for one summer vacation, when I cruised from the Falls of the Ohio down to Cairo in an outboard motorboat with a college friend."

He shrugged and kept me there with pointless inquiries about my life and my family and my schooling, till the police came to say they were through. Still in Alden's office, they gathered up their notes and prepared to go.

"Sorry we haven't got further," Sergeant Hammond told Marion. "But you can see the problems. We've found nothing promising. A few bomb fragments. Bits of a nine-volt battery. Pieces of plastic and aluminum foil. A scrap of paper with a possible Kentucky postmark. And one odd thing—"

He paused, with a puzzled frown.

"Something you'd never expect. Shreds of an unusual vegetable fiber mixed with the fragments. We've had the lab look at them. Bits of an oak acorn, so they say, shattered by the explosive. You say you knew about no acorns in the room." He stopped again, peering at her till she nodded. "Why would anybody put an acorn in a bomb?"

She shook her head.

"No sense to it." He shrugged and stood up. "That's about it. Nothing we can move on, except maybe the postmark. We'll send everything to the forensic lab and keep the file open."

While they were muttering their awkward words of sympathy and apology for troubling her, Botman drew me aside.

"Mr. Barstow, I must ask you to come downtown with me." His tone was civil enough, but also commanding. "Director Garlesh wants to see you."

That astonished me, but he gave me no time to ask why. In his car, he spoke briefly again on his shielded phone and drove in silence to the new FBI center on Constitution Avenue. A silent elevator shot us to the top floor. I waited with an armed guard in the anteroom till a sallow-faced male secretary called me into the director's big bare office and sat down at a silent keyboard in the corner of the room, looking poised to record everything we said.

Bella Garlesh was a thick-set, ham-faced woman with heavy jet-black eyebrows and a low-pitched gravel voice that might have been a man's. She sat stiffly erect behind a huge bare desk in front of a wall hung with enlarged photos of herself at official events.

"Clayton Barstow?"

I nodded.

"I regret your brother's death. For many reasons." Scanning me with narrow, steel-colored eyes, she left me wondering till her next words startled me. "Did you know he was reporting to us?"

"He wouldn't!" I blinked into her wide blank face. "That would have ruined him, if anybody knew."

"We agreed to keep it secret. He was never an official agent. Never took an oath or accepted funds. We can't give him public credit for his sacrifice, but he knew the cost and willingly took his risks." She paused with a solemn nod at the seal of the bureau on the wall across the room. "Your brother did perform a significant national service, Mr. Barstow. I think he died for it."

"I don't believe—" I shook my head. "His whole career depended on respect for his sources. He'd never break his word."

"Alden Kirk was a loyal American." She let the words float for a moment. "Loyal, and deeply troubled by all he was uncovering. His infonet articles revealed a disturbing state of affairs. His book was even more alarming. We asked him for confidential reports on matters he considered too sensitive for publication."

"You say he agreed?"

"A reluctant compromise." Her heavy shoulders twitched. "He never broke his word. I think not to anybody. Yet he did confirm that he was on the trail of something grave. Something that made him willing to bend his professional rules enough to give us useful help."

Shocked at that, trying to grasp it, I had time to trace the dark shadow of mustache across her lip. Her colorless eyes fastened on me, narrowed to unreadable slits.

"Did you know he had had wind of a group that was plotting actual armed insurrection?"

She waited, grimly silent, till I spoke.

"All I know is what he published. He didn't compromise his sources, even with me."

"He hadn't got to the bottom of it," she said. "All he ever reported was hints and hearsay, but they were enough to disturb him. And to alarm us, when we take them with the whole atmosphere of rebellion that worried him. Enough to concern the National Security Agency and President Higgins when our reports went on to them."

She paused to see how I was taking it,

"Something else." Her cold stare grew sharper. "Did he ever mention rumors of a weapon? Some group working to develop an actual super-weapon?"

"Something atomic?" I groped for something that might make sense. "Maybe stolen plutonium?"

"We discussed that." She shrugged off plutonium. "Your brother thought it was something new. Perhaps based on the new information technologies. He was never sure. And now—" Her lips set hard. "His death is a crippling loss."

A loss perhaps to the bureau, yet her blunt voice held no hint of personal regret.

"If you can give us any kind of clue—" She had paused again, her steely eyes as narrow and intent as if she were accusing me of mailing the bomb myself.

"I can't," I said. "He wouldn't have mentioned it to me. He never wanted to risk me or his family." I searched her wide poker face. "So you think these plotters killed him?"

"That could be." She shrugged, her dull voice suddenly harder. "We don't know. We do have other information that seems to confirm it: militia activities, anti-government sermons from a dissident pastor, infonet traffic in codes we haven't broken. There's also big money banked, from sources we can't trace. Rumors of secret research at CyberSoft that could shake up digital information technology. We were pressing your brother for more than he ever gave us. Names. Plans. Locations. Anything about an actual weapon." She bent closer toward me. "We were hoping you would know more than you've been able to tell us, but I believe there's still a role for you."

"For me?" That took my breath. "I don't see anything—"

She raised an imperative hand to stop me.

"As Mr. Botman reports of their last contact, your brother wanted to end his connection with the Bureau. He had picked up fresh hints of a criminal group—with no names for anybody he called it a shadow gang—organized to fund the would-be rebels. They were only hints, but he said McAdam County had got too hot for him since his book came out. Even the innocents, he said, were afraid to talk. Mr. Botman wanted him to send you there to carry on for him."

"Me? I've told you—"

She halted me again.

"Your brother refused. Indignantly, Botman says. He didn't want you there in what he saw as an ugly situation. The bomb seems to prove that his concerns were justified, but we've worked out something that ought to protect you."

I'd caught my breath to speak, but she waved her thick-fingered hand.

"Here's our strategy for you. The Barstow name will be your shield. In college, you had a history minor. We'll arrange your admission to McAdam College as a graduate student doing research for a thesis on the history of McAdam county. That will be an adequate cover that betrays no connection to Alden Kirk. It should allow you to move freely, meeting people and gathering facts.

"What do you think?"

What could I think? She had turned my whole world upside down. I sat there feeling dazed, staring blankly at her impatient face and the photos of her triumphs till she spoke again. She raised her voice.

"President Higgins has read your brother's book. Our briefings have left him deeply anxious for the safety of the nation. If those traitors are actually building a weapon and hatching rebellion, he wants them crushed.

" 'Now!' He's got a temper. He was yelling at us. 'Squash 'em! If it takes a nuke!' "

"Why me?" I asked her when I found wits enough to speak.

"I'm not Alden. I don't have his know-how or his experience or his contacts."

"The Bureau's got the know-how. God knows we've got the experience, though it has got us nowhere in McAdam County. People are hostile to our agents and too often able to spot them. Even the local lawmen aren't very helpful. That's why we're sending you."

"I've not agreed—"

"You will." Her voice had a flat finality. "Though not in any official way. You will work as your brother did, with nothing on paper to connect you to the Bureau. That ought to protect you, but it means we can give you no help or recognition if you run into trouble."

A spy mission was nothing I wanted. It had hit me too hard for any quick response. The secretary coughed discreetly. I shook my head and sat peering blankly around the big room, looking for any way out. All I saw was bookcases filled with dark-bound, gold-stamped legal volumes, an American flag on a staff standing beside them, the big photos of the director's bureaucratic victories.

"Think about it, Mr. Barstow." Her voice had sharpened. "Think about your country. Think about your brother. Mr. Botman will call you in the morning."

That was all. She waved a commanding hand at the secretary. He rose to show me out. Another agent drove me home.

I took a long bike ride that afternoon. I'd loved Alden. I knew the importance of his work, and the mission seemed a little less appalling as I rode. The autumn sky was brilliantly blue, with fallen leaves scattering the paths. Yet I had no eyes for the splendor of the turning trees. I came back feeling that my life had tilted. Suddenly I wanted no more of the comfortable sameness of the world I had known. My dread of the mission was fading into wondering expectations.

Marion was out, trying to settle her future with Alden's agents and editors. I spent the rest of the afternoon reviewing his laptop files. Most of them were pointless now, but I circled the names of people I might hope to meet. Trying to imagine anything I might do where the federal agents had failed, I drew a blank. She asked me in for dinner. Afterward, when Angela was in bed and Tim had gone up to study, she made fresh coffee and we sat in the den.

"What now?" she asked me. "Have they got anything?"

"A few bomb fragments. Part of a Kentucky postmark. No fingerprints. Nothing, really."

"What did you find in the file?"

"Nothing the cops didn't. Alden was turning over rocks, the way he always did. He found good citizens, and uncovered scorpions. Maybe one vicious enough to sting him, but there's nothing to tell us which one."

"So the case is closed." With a long sad sigh, she set her cup down. "His life gone for nothing."

"Not yet." That brought light back to her eyes. "Not quite."

I told her about his reports to the Bureau.

"Alden?" She seemed as deeply shocked as I had been. "He was no spy!"

"Not willingly. Garlesh said he'd felt he had to do it. For America."

"So he was a hero?" she whispered. "If it's true."

"Garlesh says it is. Not that she intends to tell anybody else."

Her head sank for half a minute, and then she looked back at me.

"So they want you to take his place?"

"Not in any official way. I swore no oath. They will cover certain essential expenses, but that's all. No badge, no papers, no pay."

"So you're all alone?" She made a quick little grimace of pain. "No support from anybody? No help if you run into trouble? They'll just disown you, leave you to the wolves?"

"I suppose so. It's no more than the risk Alden took."

"Why go?" Her voice was sharp with protest. "You can't bring him back."

"They want me to carry on his work. Reach his sources. Look

for the trouble spots that troubled him. Report whatever I can find. I don't like it, but I must try. For Alden's sake."

She wiped her eyes and looked at me. "You think you can finish this new book?"

"Later, maybe." I stopped to think about it. "He'd made a good start. I have his notes and drafts of the opening chapters. But all that's for later. The bureau thinks he was about to uncover some kind of plot he never really knew much about. They want me to finish his job."

"Clay, you shouldn't!" She was suddenly my older sister, giving wise advice in an anxious voice. "You aren't trained for it. I don't want you dead, Alden is enough."

"I want to know who killed him."

"If you must go." She shrugged, with a sad little grimace. "If you must."

CHAPTER THREE

THE TELEPHONE RANG the next morning while we were still eating breakfast. Marion answered and handed the instrument to me.

"Barstow?" Agent Botman's hard flat voice, with a note of emotionless authority. "I'll see you in your own office at nine, to discuss our preparations for your duty in McAdam County. Can you be there?"

It was more command than question. I said I'd be there. He knocked on my office door at nine, precisely. A tall gaunt man in a gray business suit, he wore a narrow black mustache in a narrow, sallow face.

"Thank you, Barstow." He gripped my hand briefly and seated himself as if he owned the place. "Director Garlesh is grateful for your service to the Bureau and the nation. She regrets that you can never be rewarded."

I sat down at my desk.

"I am going to Kentucky," I told him. "But not for the Bureau.

I want to know who killed my brother. If I do work for the Bureau, what can you do for me?"

"Nothing." He was crisply impatient. "Not for you as an individual. Of course we still have a very active interest in your brother's case, and in all the elements of unrest he was investigating in McAdam County. At the moment, unfortunately, we have few promising leads. That's why the director has asked you to undertake the mission."

"As if I'd had a choice." Muttering, I added, "I don't want a letter bomb."

"Better watch your mail." He spoke without humor, dark eyes shrewdly squinting. "There is risk. The risk your brother took. The director hopes to keep you safer. She has created a special high-security unit for you. We are arranging your admission to McAdam College as graduate student in history. That should give you adequate cover. Here are your instructions."

He laced his narrow fingers together and paused to let me listen.

"You may not see me again, but I will be your contact. You will report and receive further instructions on a secure telephone. I will identify myself with the code name Acorn One. You will be Acorn Two."

He gave me a scrambler and showed me how to use it.

"Keep it well concealed. It's our own encryption system. We don't want it compromised. We'll expect a report from you at twelve sharp every Friday night. And at midnight anytime when you have anything significant. If I'm not on the line, you will hear recorded instructions."

Waiting for word from the Bureau, I packed my bag, did what I could for Marion and played chess with Tim when he had time from his lessons. I heard no more from Botman, but the fax brought receipts for fees, meals, and housing at the Katz House for the fall semester at McAdam College.

Katz House! The name startled me a little when I recalled Alden's laptop note on Sam Katz. No connection, probably, but I had questions for him if this led me to him.

Marion gave me Alden's laptop and kissed me on the cheek. Tim shook my hand and hoped very gravely that I got home safe. I made the long drive down to McAdam City in a rental car with my books, bike, and baggage, and found the room the bureau had rented for me in a decayed mansion two blocks off the campus.

The house, itself a chapter of history, was a two-story brown brick set back behind a dying lawn. Faded letters on the dingy marble facade above a long verandah spelled KATZ HOTEL. The front door framed a stained-glass rainbow. A sagging swing hung on one side, with three battered white wicker rockers arrayed on the other.

Nobody answered the doorbell. Pushing inside, I found myself in a wide hall between a glass door lettered SAXON & KATZ, *Attorneys at Law*, and another door with the legend, KATZ GUNS AND AMMO. Ahead of me, at the end of the hall, a plump young woman with a pleasant round face and a towel wrapped like a turban around her hair faced me across a counter.

"Sorry, sir." She was shaking her head. "If you want a room, we're full up."

She brightened when I showed her my receipt.

"You're all okay, Mr. Barstow. Paid up in full for the whole semester. We've put you in Number One. It's here on the first floor, back at the end of the hall." She pushed a key across the counter. "We keep the back door locked, but your room key works it. What you do in the room may be your own business, but we do have rules."

She nodded at a sign behind her.

NO LIQUOR!   NO KIDS!   NO PETS!

"No problem," I said. She stood waiting, and I asked about the history of the house.

"It's old." My interest in it seemed to please her. "Built by a Dr. Kerry McAdam, way back in the 1830s. His son went bankrupt trying to build a railroad, and Tim Katz bid it in at the auction. My husband's people have owned it ever since. It was a button factory, a hospital in the Civil War, later a hotel. We're proud of the place. My husband has his office here. The second floor rooms rent to college students only."

"He's a lawyer?" I glanced back at the door lettered *Saxon & Katz.*

Nodding happily, she gave me a card.

SAMUEL KATZ, ATTORNEY AT LAW

Tax Attorney
Patent Law
Confidential Investigations

I thanked her and inquired about Mr. Saxon.

"Dead." Trouble furrowed her smooth pink face. "A tragic accident. Right here in the office. He was cleaning a gun. He and Sam had had a problem over their retainer in a big drug case. Saul Hunn—he's the city-county prosecutor. A sneaky snake! He tried to nail Sam for the killing. Pure spite. We showed him up for the fool he is. Sam and I were out at a bar when the maid heard the gunshot, with witnesses to prove it."

"An interesting story." I wondered how much of it Alden had known. "I'd like to meet your husband."

"He's out of town," she said. "Clean sheets and towels once a week. No maid service. You keep the room yourself. Trash cans out in the hall by seven Monday mornings. House rules are on your honor, but the maid has orders to report beer cans and empty bottles."

I promised to be careful and asked when Mr. Katz would be back.

"Hard to say." She turned impatiently. "He's up at Lexington on a case."

I drove around to the back door, moved into the room, returned the rented car, and walked back across the campus. Old Calvin McAdam, the family pioneer, had left a thousand dollars "to establish a Presbyterian seminary." Not enough then, but his son Scott became a banker and invested it well. Bruce McAdam, a grandson and perhaps not so devout, took a Harvard degree and came home to become the first president of the McAdam Academy.

The original building, small and rather shabby now in spite of the ivied sandstone walls and the white Greek columns, still stood at the center of the campus, a mile from the downtown center. I stood in line next morning to show my transcripts to a counselor. He sent me to the history department.

"See Professor McAdam. In Liberal Arts."

Liberal Arts was an old red brick with neither ivy nor marble, dwarfed by the Moorhawk School of Technology, an impressive pile of silvery metal and mirror glass built in the halcyon days before Moorhawk lost his patent battles.

Wandering down the hall, I found an open door beside a sign that read *Elizabeth McAdam.* A young woman sat at a computer inside. A student assistant, perhaps. My eye was caught by three large portraits hung on the opposite wall: A handsome blue-eyed boy happily smiling at a squirrel perched on his extended hand; A lean youth with both hands raised in wonder, his grave face smiling into sunlight; An older man with thick black hair and a flowing black mustache, his fine-boned features caught in a quizzical smile. All three were simply done, yet caught with verve and a sense of character.

"Are they McAdams?"

"My brothers and my father." The girl turned from her computer as I spoke. "Done in a freshman art class, before I found I'd never be an artist."

She had taken my breath with the clear ring of her voice, her sleek sheaf of honey-colored hair, the way she filled out a neat tan sweater. It took me a moment to ask, "You're Professor McAdam?"

"I'm McAdam. And you?"

"Clay Barstow."

"Barstow?" She studied me in a puzzled way with intense blue eyes. "Have we met?"

"I don't think so." I was certain we hadn't; she was nobody I'd ever forget. "I'm down from Washington. A grad student in history."

She frowned again. "I really thought you were someone I'd known."

She tapped her keys and studied the monitor.

"Clayton Barstow." She nodded as she read. "B.A. at Georgetown. *Summa cum laude.* History major, journalism minor." She looked up at me, her eyes more violet than blue, and piercingly keen. "A nice record, Mr., Barstow, from a great school. What brings you to McAdam?"

That struck me silent. I wanted her to like me. The truth would do nothing for that.

"I want to work toward a masters in history."

"Why here?"

"I had a school friend from Kentucky." Actual fact, but then I was forced to invention. "His people had been pioneers. I was fascinated with all he told me about his family and the state."

"Kentucky history has been done." She gestured at the full shelves behind her. "Again and again."

"New history keeps happening."

"Too fast." She nodded soberly. "In ways that sometimes sadden me. Ways too complex to be explored in a graduate thesis."

"I know, but I have a limited topic in mind." I began to quote from Alden. "We're in transition from the industrial age to the information age. I want to study the process as it affects one small group."

"What has that to do with Kentucky?"

"I'm looking for a test-tube specimen of America." More from Alden. "I hope to find it here. Kentucky is a border state, neither North nor South, East nor West. Bits of the past still hang on in the hills. Moorhawk funded the school of technology here. New futures keep drowning the past."

"Sit down, Mr. Barstow." I loved her voice, but her tone was still formal, coolly skeptical. "Do you know computer science?"

"My brother gave me a Nintendo set when I was five years old." Bits of fact when they might fit. "I'm no scientist, but I use computers. I see them changing the world." Another bit from Alden. "I want to look at the destination of the information highway."

"Why liberal arts?" She frowned again. "If your interest is information science, perhaps you should register in the school of technology."

"The technology is moving beyond me. I find people more interesting."

"So do I." She tapped her keys. "Do you have some specific area in mind?"

"To limit the study, I want to look at the impacts on a single county. Perhaps on a single family." In spite of her lifted eyebrows, I decided to take a risk. "Perhaps the McAdam family."

"No." She spoke instantly. "I don't think so."

"I never expected to be meeting you." That brought only a gravely attentive nod. I went on, hoping for something warmer. "My friend had lived here. He spoke of the McAdams. I've looked them up in the Georgetown library." Actually, I had. "Calvin McAdam followed Daniel Boone out of Virginia. Two centuries of McAdams have been bankers and lawyers and scholars. Rob Roy McAdam is the computer wizard at CyberSoft now. Your brother, I believe?"

"He is." Her fine eyes had narrowed, scanning me again. "I'm proud of Rob. Proud of my family, Mr. Barstow, but we value our privacy."

"Which I will respect." She looked so firm about it that I quoted another point of Alden's. "Though preserving anybody's privacy is becoming a pretty difficult problem in this information age."

"Whose problem?" She was sharply ironic. "I think it's worth defending. Sometimes it is defended. You may have heard of a Washington reporter recently killed by his own curiosity?"

"You mean Alden Kirk?" I tried to hold an even tone and a poker face. "Are you suggesting that his inquiries here led to his death?"

"Federal agents seem to think so." She shrugged. "Down here, Mr. Barstow, we dislike prying outsiders."

She glanced at the door as if ready to be rid of me, but I kept my seat and asked if she didn't have another brother.

"Stuart?" I heard her breath catch. "What about Stuart?"

"His name came up in my library research."

"So you know he's been in prison." Her face was suddenly flushed. "He's out now. I want you to know, Mr. Barstow, that he's still my brother, and I'm still proud of him. Stuart does stand up for his rights, if you think that's a problem. We Kentuckians have always done that."

I'd touched a tender spot. Watching her flash of emotion, I waited for her to continue.

"It was a drug charge, Mr. Barstow." Her voice had quickened. "Perhaps you know that hemp was once a cash crop here. Rope was made from hemp. It's a hardy plant, now called marijuana. It still thrives, a weed in our woods and danger to our farmers. Letting wild hemp grow on your land is a federal offense. Did you know that?"

I shook my head and sat admiring the glow of her indignation.

"My brother had a law practice himself before his troubles began, specializing in drug cases. He says the drug laws are racist. Whites use alcohol and drive cars till they kill themselves. Blacks and Hispanics use marijuana, which he considers less addictive and less harmful than nicotine, and go to prison for it."

"Stuart did?"

"Politics, Mr. Barstow." Her face set hard. "It's a rough game here. We play it for keeps. Stuart plays to win. He has friends like Senator Finn, who pressed for his freedom. Friends also in the militia he's organized.

"A lot of his members are farmers who were arrested when a few wild hemp plants were found on their land. He kept his office open, defending them in court, till his enemies got him arrested and railroaded into prison. The sheriff claimed he'd laundered drug money and claimed they'd found marijuana in his home.

"He was the innocent victim—"

She caught herself and flashed me a momentary smile.

"Please forgive my heat, Mr. Barstow, but I love Stuart. I don't want him maligned." The smile gone, she was suddenly severe. "I believe the FBI tried to connect him with the letter bomb. Fortunately, he was still in prison when it was mailed."

"It was sent from here?"

"I know nothing about that." Her voice had gone hard. "I don't want to know. Perhaps that Washington reporter was on the trail. He was looking for American terrorists. The federal investigators seem to think he found more than he was looking for."

With another glance at the door, she waited with visible impatience.

"One of my profs was a sociologist." Not ready to go, I invented him out of Alden. "He used to talk about a wave of terror spreading through the world. Looking for causes, he believed he had found them in a wave of an anarchy created by the new information technologies as they began to erode the old systems of authority."

"Maybe." The borrowed words seemed to have won me a moment of respect. "But anarchy is nothing new. The pioneers built Kentucky out of a frontier anarchy. Guerrilla anarchy ravaged the state after the Civil War. I hope that doesn't happen again."

"My prof was afraid it could. He wanted to write a book on the social impact of information technology. He suggested the study I want to undertake."

"An interesting topic." That moment of respect had passed. Distant again, she glanced at her desk-top monitor and sharply back at me. "But I don't advise you to follow it here. Better forget the McAdams and look for another set of victims. In any case, you aren't ready for any formal research."

She frowned at something on her monitor.

"I see twenty graduate hours you can transfer." Her voice was crisply decisive. "We'll require a full semester here before you can submit any research proposal."

Another student had appeared at the door, and I had to leave. Walking back toward my room, I was in no mood to enjoy the bright morning sun or share the cheer of incoming students calling greetings to one another. Certainly no bomber herself, Professor McAdam had balked me and the Bureau. I longed to know her better, but she'd clearly had enough of me.

Just off the campus, wondering about Stuart and searching for another move, I stopped at the Jay Eye See, which sported a sign with a racing Thoroughbred outlined in green neon. A few chatting students sat round a long table, ignoring a video tour of the Mammoth Cave that was running on a wall screen at the back of the room.

I ordered a beer. A heavy man in a McAdam Rebs T-shirt sat a few stools down at the bar. When he grinned companionably at me, I asked about the red-white-and-blue band around his brawny arm.

"Our campus uniform." His voice had a flat Appalachian twang. "The Kentucky Rifles."

I told him I was new on the campus, and asked what the Rifles were.

"The county militia." He moved to the stool beside me. "I been in the National Guard. Quit because the governor could mobilize it and turn it on the people. The Rifles are free, standing by for our own defense if we ever need them. Under our own command. Right here in the county, with no shit to take from anybody."

He eyed me speculatively.

"I'm Ben Coon. Reb lineman last year." He offered a muscular hand. "You might want to join us."

I shook his hand, ordered another round, and asked why I should.

"Are you a loyal American?"

"I think so."

"We need every good man we can get, because the liberal

crazies in Washington and the international bankers are scheming to put the army under UN command. They're plotting to let the UN enslave the nation. All the world if they can. Yammering about trying to outlaw our Constitutional right to bear arms and make us into slaves."

I asked him why he thought so.

"Several reasons." He gave a vague shrug. "But the bombs at Frankfort and now in Washington ought to be a hint that somebody ain't taking no more crap. If the Army comes, under orders from the UN or Higgins or anybody else, we'll teach 'em how to fight. Fall back in the woods and give the bastards hell. Get me?"

I said I got him.

"We've got a march coming up, through town and on out to the rally. Better be there if you want to hear Captain McAdam. That's Stuart McAdam. A damn fine man, leading the fight to save our God-given rights from the chicken shit idiots like that damn Yankee reporter that got blown to Hell by the last letter he ever saw."

He scowled ferociously.

"Get what I mean?"

I said I did.

"Hey, Ben." A fat girl in a red sweat suit was calling from the table. "What's with the Rebs?"

He nodded at me, picked up his beer, and went to join them. I sat listening as I finished my own. Loud talk of vacations and classes and Rebel prospects, with no more about the Rifles or martial law. My own thoughts, however, had gone back to Georgetown and my little nephew showing me the clean white sheet spread over my brother's blood spattered on the floor.

CHAPTER FOUR

THAT WAS A Friday. At midnight I looked out to see that the corridor was empty, locked my door, and plugged my phone into Botman's scrambler.

"Acorn Two." I recited the code name he had given me.

"Acorn One." His brittle recorded voice asked for a progress report. I had no progress to report. After half a minute of silence, his natural voice came on the line.

"Get this, Barstow. Your mission has now become more critical than ever. Stuart McAdam is emerging as a strong suspect, but we've got to have solid evidence. Continue every effort. Report further action and hard information with no delay. That is all."

Continue? How?

I recalled Alden's comment on the weekly *Freeman* and its editor, "one sane man." Next morning I rode my bike downtown and found FREEMAN in time-dimmed letters on the age-stained brick of an old two-story between a parking lot and the vacant front of what had been a furniture store, a block off the courthouse square.

The front office was almost a museum, with wooden roll-top desks standing along the walls and ancient manual typewriters collecting dust. A chime had rung when I opened the door. The man who stood up to greet me had aged with the building.

"Good day, sir."

A thin little man with a neat little tuft of iron-gray chin whiskers blinked at me through bright-rimmed glasses. In shirt sleeves, he wore wide green suspenders and a battered black hat on a lean old head. Spry enough, he came to offer a blue-veined hand.

"I'm Cass Pepperlake. Glad to see you, sir."

"Clay Barstow."

He waited to see what I wanted.

"I'm a graduate student out at McAdam," I told him. "I took communication courses at Georgetown University and worked on the student infonet desk. I'm looking for a part-time job."

"Sit down, Mr. Barstow." He nodded at a chair. "Let's hear your problems."

I sat down, a little uneasy. I had problems enough, but few I was free to talk about. I told him I was a history major, planning to write a thesis on the county. He spent half a minute looking me over before he asked what brought me to McAdam County.

"That book, really." I had seen a red-jacketed copy of Alden's *Terror in America* on the corner of his desk. "You've read it?"

"Twice." His gaze sharpened. "What's your interest here?"

"The history in that book." I couldn't tell him much of the truth. "History happening today, right here in the county."

"Disturbing history." Frowning soberly, he picked it up and riffled through the pages. "I met Alden Kirk. Got him to sign the book." His lips pursed ruefully. "I suppose he'd dug too deep into something ugly."

"Something that killed him?"

"Maybe." Noncommittally, he shrugged. "Maybe not. He was looking at violence coming to a boil all over America. He certainly found it simmering here, but I'm afraid the investigation has come to nothing."

"That's what I want for my thesis," I said. "The culture of violence. Causes and effects, if I can pick them out. A newspaper job should let me meet local people, listen to their feelings, pick up background. If you have any sort of opening—"

"I wish I did." Shaking his head, he seemed to see my disappointment. "We're a small paper. Little weeklies like the *Freeman* have become an endangered species, if you understand?"

I looked around the room and said I understood.

"People today watch the tube; scan the infonet if they read any print at all. Kids don't learn to read, not really." He stopped to study me again. "There's one possibility, if you're interested. We do take on a few interns from the college."

"I'm certainly interested."

"There's an unfortunate drawback. We can't pay in actual dollars. All you get is experience and credit hours."

"No matter. I'd be grateful for the opportunity."

And I wanted to know who killed my brother. He was frowning thoughtfully through the steel-rimmed lenses.

"Okay." He finally nodded. "We'll give you a trial, if your professor approves."

He offered his hand when I thanked him, and got up again to show me around the office.

"The *Freeman* has a proud past, Mr. Barstow. It dates from 1855, another time of danger to the Union. The founder was Cassius Pepperlake, a Congregationalist minister who preached against slavery. The cellar under the back room is said to have been a station on the Underground Railroad. Morgan's raiders wrecked the press and set fire to the building in 1862. Cassius fought for the Union. He died at Perryville.

"His son Caleb revived the paper after the war. Tried to patch up wounds and push for something better. Exposed graft in Grant's administration and right here at home. We Pepperlakes have kept the paper alive, fighting for what we thought was good, though I guess our greatest days are gone."

He paused to sigh.

"I was teaching out at the college when my father died. Journalism and philosophy. When nobody wanted to buy the paper, I retired to keep it alive. Times are hard for us—and getting harder— but I think the *Freeman* is needed now as much as it was in Abolition days."

In the back room, he showed me a rusting Linotype machine, a massive press gone to rust and dust, an antique desk under a lithographed pin-up girl on a calendar many years out of date. The Masons had met in the empty hall upstairs, he said, before they built new quarters.

"Victims." He shook his head as if in pity for the ancient equipment. "Victims of the new technologies."

Trying to size him up, I waited for more.

"It's what we used to call progress." His shoulders twitched to a small wry shrug. "All the dawning wonders of the electronic revolution and the information age. Not so wonderful for the *Freeman*. We've lost half our circulation. That press hasn't run since my father died. Now we make the paper up on the computer and pay the *Messenger* to print it. That's the *McAdam Messenger*. Now owned by a big media chain. Their national ads and most of their editorial content come down from a satellite."

I followed him back toward the front room.

"America's trapped in a sort of battlefield—if you can excuse a few words from the column I'm composing. A battlefield at night, where lost and leaderless men are firing at the flashes of one another's guns, never knowing who or what the actual enemy is. As I see the danger—"

He checked himself, blinking critically at me through the steel-rimmed glasses.

"Do you think I'm some kind of nut?"

"No sir. Not at all."

I wanted the job. I had my orders from the bureau, and a more urgent mission of my own. And he was making sense. Thinking of Alden, I asked what enemy he saw.

"Information technology." Nodding at the computer on his

desk, he paused for words and went on in a tone of sober emphasis. "The African slavers three hundred years ago had no concern about the seed of conflict they were sowing. Our information engineers today are just as blind to consequences, but they're enslaving us just as surely.

"Splitting us into classes. The elite classes that can master and control the technology. The underclass that can't. Brains, you might say, at war with brawn. In the hands of the masters, information technology becomes what I like to call the silicon dagger. A weapon of stealth. Its masters slip up behind us to strike out of the dark."

A stooped old man in suspenders and shirt sleeves, shuffling across the creaky floor. His voice was slow and raspy, but the drama in the quiet words made me peer at him in astonishment.

"I keep alert for trouble, Mr. Barstow. That's the business of the *Freeman.* I lived through the Cold War. The balance of terror was terrible enough, but we thought we knew who the enemy was. We did defend ourselves, but times have changed. Kirk's book alarmed me. His murder frightens me now, because of what he had revealed: enemies here among us, a more insidious threat than the Soviet empire ever was, armed with this silicon dagger.

"All the new technologies of storing information, transmitting it, using it for a weapon, they're killing the world where I grew up. Killing the values I love. Killing individual freedom. Killing privacy."

I thought of Elizabeth McAdam.

"How do computers enslave us?" He paused for an instant, but not for any answer I might offer. "They know everything about us. They squirrel away endless bits of fact from tax rolls and credit agencies, police records and subscription lists and mail orders, from charitable donations, even the cash register in the supermarket. All those bits—each harmless in itself—are shared, combined, analyzed, forged into their blades against the helpless underclass.

"The computer masters—I call them the infomasters—they control the media: newsprint and radio, TV and the infonet, books and lecture circuits. They strike the rest of us in a thousand ways you never notice, the sound bites on the news, the appeals to kids on cereal boxes, the subliminal overtones in infomercials. You've probably never stopped to notice how they rule the way you vote, what you buy, what you eat, what you believe. They've created an invisible empire."

Perhaps. I shook my head.

"The infomasters may think they rule us all, but they've enslaved themselves just as surely. The computer and its electronic kin are melding us into a single amorphous mental mass. They're erasing the whole culture that used to shape our lives. So subtly that most of us never know we're being had.

"Or what do you think?"

With a shrug at the intensity of his own emotion, he sat back in his chair, poured coffee in plastic cups, and looked inquiringly at me. I accepted a cup and waited till he went on. "Alden Kirk listened to me. He made notes."

"On this silicon dagger?" I tried to veil my interest. "Did it kill him?"

"A figure of speech." He shrugged dismissively. "He asked what it had to do with our problems here. I tried to tell him. We're a poor county in a poor state, with a long history of stubborn individuals inclined to violent action. Most of our former leader class moved away long ago, to bigger cities, wider avenues of power. We're the underclass left behind: confused and bitter people blaming one another for problems we seldom understand.

"Kirk said he was working on another book, about how we're trapped. I'm trying to do the same thing right here in my own small way, with a column I call 'Cassandra Says.' You know what happened to Cassandra. I'm more cautious than Kirk was. The *Freeman,* after all, is a pretty feeble reed. I don't want to get my own letter bomb."

"Nor do I." This looked like an opening. "Do you know what other people Kirk talked to while he was down here?"

"I know who he was asking about." He pushed up his glasses

to squint at me, shaking his head. "A gallery of local rogues, and a few better men. The Feds believe the bomb was mailed from here. I've wondered, naturally, who could have mailed it."

"Do you have suspects in mind?"

"Frankly, I'd be afraid to guess."

I tried another angle.

"If I get this job—"

"The internship? It's yours if we get on."

"I think we will," I said. "Though I have to think of my own skin. Could you give me any pointers on people I ought to avoid?"

"Maybe." He squinted again, weighing me. "If you'll keep my comments to yourself?"

I nodded.

"Let's begin with the courthouse ring. Kentucky has a hundred and twenty counties. Each has always been a little kingdom, with its own little king and his cronies. Sheriff Bull Burleigh is the reigning king of McAdam County—or at least he tries to play the role. The man who made him king is Saul Hunn, the acting county attorney—the city and county governments were merged when they both went bankrupt. They run the county, or think they do. They can be nasty about it, yet they're puppets themselves, running things for Gottler—Rocky Gottler, who owns the bank and half the county.

"They all belong to Senator Finn's statewide machine, if you want to look one step higher in our master class. And they're all at odds with the McAdams, the founders of the town and kings of the county for the first hundred years. Old Colin McAdam is a dethroned patriarch. Recently he retired as a history prof at the college. He was something of a firebrand when he was younger, hoping to restore the McAdams to their old position in the county, but he's harmless now.

"Stuart, his older son, is another story. Bitter about nearly everything. About his own hard luck. About the misfortunes of the family and the loss of all he'd hoped to inherit. He was a lawyer, at war with Hunn and Burleigh over his clients in the marijuana trade. He's recently back from a year in prison and sick of the law that put him there. Don't cross him.

"There's a younger son and a daughter. Rob Roy is in computer software with a little firm he calls CyberSoft. It could elevate him into the master class if he can keep it alive, but the federal courts are trying to put him out of business."

As innocently as I could, I asked about the daughter.

"Elizabeth," he said. "A college teacher but better looking than you might expect." He grinned at me. "You ought to meet her."

"I did. She's my new professor. I'd like to know her better, but she doesn't want me digging into McAdam history."

"She wouldn't." His grin was gone. "We've never liked nosy outsiders."

Trying to push her violet-eyed image out of my mind, I asked if there was anybody else I ought to know. He squinted, reflecting.

"There's Kit Moorhawk. A local kid. He rode for his father as a jockey before he had a bad fall and quit the track to get his law degree. He's had his share of ups and downs. With a college friend, he got patents on a process for clean-burning coal. They set up Coal Combustion Corporation and flew high for a time. Kit married his high school sweetheart, funded the tech school out at the college, served in the state legislature. Defeated when he ran for governor as a Libertarian.

"High times till his Coal Combustion Corporation lost the patent suits and went bankrupt. Kit's hard up now, in tax trouble with the IRS. Hunn and Burleigh spread rumors that killed him in politics and broke up his marriage. The ex-wife's gone to Hollywood. But he's still a friend. Kirk wanted to meet him, but he was out of town, appealing a case for Rob Roy's CyberSoft.

" 'Father' Joel Garron is a very different customer, a fire-breathing infonet evangelist. He calls his church the Temple of the Sword, and now he's spurring his followers to draw the sword of God against the abortionists. He has them sniping at our local clinic. Bullets through the windows. A Molotov cocktail tossed at the doctor's car. There are suspects enough, but Burleigh and Hunn have made no arrests."

He sat scowling unhappily till I asked about others.

"There's a woman Kirk inquired about. A local girl who once worked here on the *Freeman*. Stuart McAdam picked her up in a Louisville night club and brought her back home with a promise to marry her. They lived together till he beat her up. She's at the TV station now."

He was draining his coffee when his phone rang. Listening, he clucked sympathetically and finally grinned.

"A rural correspondent," he said when he hung up. "Sheriff Burleigh jugged her husband on a marijuana charge. Stuart Mc-Adam has him out on bond, but she's going to be late with her copy."

I asked for more about the internship.

"It will run though the semester. The contract calls for twenty hours a week. You'll be working twice that, for six hours of graduate credit. I wish we could pay in coin of the realm, but we're literally a nonprofit enterprise."

He stood up to see me out.

"You'll be meeting the rest of the staff. Tom Hobbs, our ad man, works on commission. Cal Hazard sells real estate and works half days for us, handling circulation—which keeps dwindling in spite of everything we do. We go to press on Thursday afternoons. Be here Wednesday morning at eight."

I shook his hand and thanked him for the opportunity.

Elizabeth McAdam had an advisee in her office when I got there next morning. The trim tan sweater had been replaced by a snug green jacket. Waiting at the door, I stood admiring her for her brisk professional concern for the student's problem and the warmth of her sympathetic chuckle when they had it solved. Desire thrilled through me, but faded fast as she dismissed the student and turned more coldly to me.

"Mr. Barstow?"

She listened while I told her about the internship and laid the contract on her desk.

"Not yet, Mr. Barstow." Lips tight, she shook her head at it. "Not till I sign."

"It's all set up," I insisted. "Mr. Pepperlake made the offer. It's approved by Professor Atwood in Communication Science. All I need is your signature."

"Sit down, Mr. Barstow." Sternly frowning, she nodded at the chair. "We need to talk."

I sat down and waited uneasily.

"Yesterday I thought I recognized you." Fixed on me, her eyes were glacial. "Your close resemblance to Alden Kirk struck me after you were gone—I'd seen him on TV when that book came out. I emailed an inquiry to a colleague at Georgetown. He confirms that Kirk had a half-brother named Clayton Barstow. That's you?"

"True," I had to say. "May I explain?"

"I don't see how you can." Her straight bright hair was short and pushed back, bound with a band the color of gold. Her fair face was flushed, the violet eyes defiant. Anger became her. "You've come sneaking here on false pretenses. To spy on my own family. Can you invent an excuse for that?"

"Please," I begged her. "You know my brother's dead. That postmark seems to show the bomb was mailed from here. The authorities haven't been able to do much about it. I want to find out anything I can."

"I regret the tragedy." She nodded soberly. "I believe he left a family?"

"A wife and two kids."

"I'm sorry." She seemed to mean it, yet her face set hard again. "He should have known he was intruding where he wasn't wanted. And you—" Her voice flattened. "Do you really expect to break a case the FBI can't?"

"I have to try. And there's something bigger."

That caught at least a flash of interest.

"It isn't just McAdam County." I borrowed again from Alden's notes. "My brother was troubled by what he called a national breakdown. A loss of social order. A return to tribal mores. Suspicion of government, business, science. Hatred of every other country and every other faith and race. A national sickness that he thought could kill us unless we found a cure."

"Go make a speech." She was not impressed. "If you have a magic panacea to cure the world."

"I don't. Alden didn't. He was simply trying to diagnose the sickness. I was hoping to pick up what he hadn't finished."

"Not here, Mr. Barstow." Her voice had sharpened. "I don't care what you want to write about Kentucky or even about the country, but I don't want your meddling into my own family. We McAdams may sometimes soil our laundry, but we wash it ourselves. If you want my advice, forget the McAdams and get out of town."

"Thanks. But I can't do that."

"You're a fool if you don't."

"I'm fool enough to stay."

"Listen to this." She bent toward me. "Last night, when I was wondering what to do about you, I called my brother Stuart. He's a hard man, Mr. Barstow. He does hold grudges against a lot of people. Against Alden Kirk, because of something about him and his militia in *Terror in America*. He thinks Kirk's infonet series helped his enemies send him to prison."

She must have seen me flinch from her determined face.

"I didn't tell Stuart who you are, Mr. Barstow." I saw a brief sardonic smile. "I don't want your blood on my hands."

"Are you saying he'd kill me?"

I met her icy eyes. *The way, I thought, that he killed my brother?*

"He's not a murderer." She flushed as if I had slapped her face. "But he does have friends. I'm simply suggesting that you might be on guard if you happen to meet the friends or his clients."

I sat wondering what she meant.

"Mr. Barstow, you've got my advice." She pushed the unsigned contract at me. "Withdraw from the college and get out of the county."

I pushed it back.

"God damn you, Mr. Barstow." Violence quivered in her voice. "You'll be sorry."

Yet then she signed the contract.

Next morning, curious about Stuart McAdam, I pedaled out to the Kentucky Rifle headquarters. The shabby old building had been a furniture store. Two new metal poles stood in front, an American flag flying from one, a red-starred Rifle banner from the other. Ben Coon bustled out to welcome me with a genial grin.

"Mr. Barstow, come on in and meet the captain."

I followed him into a huge, bare, barn-like room, with rifles racked along the wall behind a bare metal desk where Stuart was rising to his feet. Standing lean and very straight, he wore a red jacket that had a military cut and a gold rifle emblem pinned over his heart. What struck me was his likeness to his sister, the even features of her beauty hardened into a striking male distinction.

"Clay here's a new grad student out at the college," Coon was bumbling. "I told him about the Rifles. Let's sign him up."

Smiling affably, Stuart came to take my hand in a vigorous grip.

"Yes, sir?" Even his voice had overtones of Beth's. They might have been twins. His smile was appealing; I wanted to like him. "What can I tell you about the Rifles?"

"I'm interested." Which was true. "I'm new here, learning what I can."

"If you want to join up—"

"Probably not." That dimmed his smile. "I'm an intern on the *Freeman.* I was looking for a story."

A story I knew he was unlikely to tell, but I felt anxious for anything I might learn.

"That yellow rag of Pepperlake's." Beneath a thin brown mustache, his lip curled in comtempt. "He doesn't like us. He won't want your story."

"Maybe not." Coon caught my arm and appealed to Stuart. "Listen, sir. Here's a man we need. Fit enough and smart enough. Give him a pitch."

"About the Rifles—" Stuart took a moment to eye me, and his tone grew warmer. "We aren't outlaws, no matter what you hear. We're just old-style Americans, the same sort that fought the Revolution to win our independence. We're organized now to take it back again."

I glanced at the rifles on the rack. "To fight for it?"

"If we must." His chin thrust out. "I'm afraid we must."

"Who would be your enemy?"

"The system." The words came fast, as if he had spoken them before. "A federal system rotten to the heart, run by power-mad politicos and bureaucrats that have bought the media. They're taxing us to death, squandering our good money on idiotic projects, stuffing their own pockets, running us to ruin. They've got to be stopped.' "

"That's the Rifles." Coon grinned with approval and gestured at a ledger-like book lying on the desk. "Let's sign you up."

"We're for real," Stuart pressed on when I shook my head. "A little band of good men and a few brave women unhappy with the system, looking for recruits with cause enough to join us. We find them everywhere. I've been a victim—"

"The captain's a martyr." Coon spoke up with a kind of devotion in his tone. "But fighting back."

Stuart shrugged. Silent for a moment, he burst out. "Fighting the drug laws! Laws enacted by self-righteous bigots who claim the right to regulate the private lives of everybody else. They're wrong. They're racist. They're killing the country. They killed me."

I must have stared. I was astonished by his sudden vehemence.

"I was a lawyer," he went on more quietly but still grimly earnest. "A good one, I think, trying to do right for my clients. Some of them had planted pot when they lost their tobacco quotas—if you want to make a difference between cannabis and nicotine. The Feds did. And did me in for defending my clients." He shook his head, his voice gone bitter. "The justice system—they call it justice—got me disbarred. Revoked my license. Put me in prison."

Stabbed with sympathy in spite of myself, I wished Alden could have met him.

"A stinkin' system, but now we've got the captain back to carry on the fight." Hopefully, Coon gestured again at the open book. "We need you in the ranks, Mr. Barstow—"

"Barstow?" Stuart stiffened. "That's your name?"

"It is," I had to say. "Clayton Barstow."

"My sister spoke about you, Mr. Barstow." He stepped back from me, his face suddenly hard. "I don't want you in the Rifles."

Coon gaped and waved me toward the door.

CHAPTER FIVE

"*ACORN ONE,*" *BOTMAN'S* recorded voice answered when I called his scrambled phone at midnight. I gave my code name. After a moment I heard his live Brooklyn voice, sharply impatient. "Okay, Barstow, let's have your report."

"Nothing to report," I said. "Worse, my cover's broken. My academic adviser has recognized me. She dislikes me. I don't know her intentions. She may expose me—"

"You can't quit now. We have bad news from field agents on the site. They are convinced that an underground group in McAdam County is near success in developing a new and deadly weapon, possibly intended for terrorist attacks on federal agencies. The nature of it is still unknown, but we have to give the report some credence. The Moorhawk Institute has made the county a center for high-tech research. Unfortunately, our field agents say their sources have been unable or unwilling to reveal names or other specifics. Your own mission is now more critical than ever."

"Maybe," I said. "But I don't have a clue about what to do next."

"Just get with it."

"Can't you give me something to go on? Possible sources? Possible problems or dangers?"

"Sorry." He was sharply abrupt. "We're already compromised. You're on your own. Report progress as you make it."

Progress was hard to make. All I got from Professor McAdam was a cold look when I happened to cross her path on the campus. I'd dropped her seminar in Confederate history and enrolled in Atwood's information theory. At the *Freeman*, I answered the phone and keyboarded copy from the rural correspondents. Working with Tom Hobbs, I took the photos and wrote the stories for a series we were running on local business. He sold the ads to run beside them.

I had a letter from my little nephew back in Georgetown. He was writing his own game programs on a wonderful new computer his mother had given him for his birthday. Angela had got over a cold; she and their mother were well. They all missed me. He told me to take care and come home when I could.

And Cass Pepperlake took me to Rotary.

"Senator Finn will be speaking," he said. "He's here on a campaign swing. A prince of the Beltway, but not very popular here in the county. His law of life is tax, spend, and please the special interests that pay him off. A lot of us locals are sick of him."

"Madison Finn? Didn't Kirk mention some funny business with campaign funds?"

Pepperlake shrugged without concern.

"If he's crooked as a double-jointed snake, what's new? Under our wonderful system, I doubt that any really honest man can be elected to high public office."

My eyebrows must have lifted.

"Look at the cost of a winning campaign. To raise the millions, you've got to make promises you know you'll never keep. Which means common honesty is no longer so common. What does matter is the spin you put on the facts—or what the media report as facts. Finn has an instinctive gift for spin control."

Rotary met at noon on Fridays at the Bluegrass Inn. We filed by a counter to fill our plates and looked for a table. The long room was filled with well-dressed men and women shouting greetings, shaking hands, cracking jokes, bending over their meals. Community leaders. Pepperlake called them the local elite.

"Clayton Barstow, our new intern at the *Freeman.*" Pepperlake introduced me to the little group around our table. "He'll be calling some of you about our new business series."

Cordially enough, they shook my hand as he identified them. Merchant, horseman, home builder, optometrist, soft drink canner, a woman who owned a hillbilly museum, a mortician who was also a captain in the National Guard. Good American citizens by the look of them, jovially prosperous and law-abiding.

Yet I had begun to wonder.

"Our senator." Pepperlake nodded toward three men at the head table, on a low stage at the side of the room. I knew Finn from the infonet. With a bulldog jaw and an artful wave in his thick shag of iron-gray hair, he looked statesmanlike enough.

"Sheriff Bull Burleigh on his left," Pepperlake murmured. "The manager of his county machine."

Burleigh was a beefy man with a badge on his breast and a pistol at his hip. He and Finn sat with heads close together, Burleigh nodding to whatever Finn was saying.

The other man had leaned in to listen.

"Rocky Gottler." Pepperlake nodded toward him. "He owns the ballot box and tells the senator how to keep his seat."

He turned to introduce a youthful latecomer who had brought his plate to our table and slipped quietly into the vacant chair beside me.

"Rob Roy McAdam. Our own computer wizard."

"When the magic works." Modestly, he grinned. "Sometimes it doesn't."

The other brother of my beautiful professor. Dressed in unpressed chinos and a dark T-shirt, he had her blue eyes and high cheekbones, with a stronger chin. A silver shield on the T-shirt was printed

CYBERSOFT
CRYPTOPHONE

He shook my hand with no hint that his sister had said anything about me. I told him about the business articles I was doing for the *Freeman* and asked if I might see him for a piece on CyberSoft and the cryptophone. Hesitating, he looked at Pepperlake.

"Why not?" Pepperlake asked him. "It'll give you a chance to tell your side of the story."

"Okay." He nodded. "Call me."

Acting City-County Attorney Saul Hunn was president of the club. A tall thin man with sharp fox features under a heavy mane of silky white hair. He rang a bell, called us to order in his formal courtroom voice, had us stand and face the flag for the pledge of allegiance.

"An old tradition," Pepperlake murmured. "No longer taken as seriously as it used to be."

Hunn recognized a few visiting Rotarians from other clubs. We sang "America" and "My Old Kentucky Home." Burleigh rose to introduce our distinguished guest.

"Our man in the Senate." He paused for a lukewarm patter of applause, "He got us the new post office. The new armory. The new airport. He saved our tobacco quota. He stands for law and order. America for Americans! Senator Madison Finn!"

At the podium, Finn apologized for his voice, rusty from speaking in thirty counties in three days. He thanked the citizens of McAdam County for their loyal support, and praised Sheriff Burleigh for his war on crime.

"Can we win it?" A jeer from the back of the room. "What about the gangs in grade school? Drugs on the campus? The abortion mill and Father Garron. The jail running over. Sex maniacs let loose. The Frankfort bomb?"

"The FBI works under wraps, but they tell me they're on top of the bomb cases."

Were they, really? I didn't ask.

Pepperlake raised his hand. "What about the marijuana farmers reported to be shooting at the Feds?"

Burleigh stood up when Finn turned to him.

"A tough problem, Senator." He paused to inflate his chest and raise his nasal Appalachian voice to fill the hall. "Crime's always tough to fight, but we've working hand in glove with the Feds. We've picked up a dozen suspects. They all stand together, swearing to their alibis, but we've got three of 'em still in the cooler."

And delayed one of our correspondents, I recalled, with her column for the *Freeman.*

"Senator?" A cocky little man with no coat and a bright green vest stood up. "Where do you stand on the Fair Tax Plan?"

"Kit Moorhawk," Pepperlake murmured. "His tax plan would abolish the IRS."

"Taxes, sir—" Finn had to clear his scratchy throat. "Taxes are one of my major concerns. You know I've always fought waste and fraud. I always will. But we're all Americans." He gestured at the flag. "I just heard your pledge of allegiance."

Burleigh clapped once, but subsided when nobody followed.

"Allegiance," Finn repeated, "to our great American democracy, which now stands as it has always done on a foundation of fair taxation. The Internal Revenue Service is that firm foundation. Some of you may be unhappy—"

"We are!" I heard that shout and a volley of applause. A raucous voice rose higher. "We pay taxes with our own good money. You Beltway bandits steal it. You buy votes with it and fly around the world on your luxury junkets. Your reformed welfare system is grinding us into the mud and squandering our money to feed a generation of whores and their bastard babies."

Finn looked hurt.

"Sir, please!" He raised a protesting hand. "Don't forget that America is a great democracy—the greatest that ever was. Democracy includes everybody. I won't balance the budget on the backs of starving mothers and their crying babies."

"On our broken backs?" A derisive snort.

"Look at what your taxes buy!" Finn scanned the room, searching in vain for any show of support. "Your precious freedom and the national power to preserve it. We are still the world's single superpower. I'll be holding hearings on national defense. I intend to keep our splendid military machine the mightiest on Earth."

Not impressed, the mortician waved to get his attention.

"Senator, I hear talk of martial law if there's more trouble here. Will you turn that war machine against us?"

"Against McAdam County?" Finn looked startled. "You just heard me swear my own allegiance to our sacred nation. I'll defend it to my last drop of blood. I trust, however, that we'll never need to put down another armed insurrection." He looked at Burleigh. "Sheriff, do you care to comment?"

"No problem, sir. Not here in McAdam City." Burleigh grinned with a show of yellow teeth and his hand on his heart. "We do have a few bad apples, but most of them are already in the jug or on their way there. If I ever need the National Guard to help defend our county or our Constitution, I'll ask for it."

"Senator, I hope you never need to." Pepperlake had raised his hand. "But I am concerned. More than one of my subscribers have said we ought to follow the example of our revered forefathers who rebelled against the oppressive tyranny of George the Third."

"Rebellion? Actual talk of rebellion?" Flushed with anger, Finn goggled at him. "High treason!" He turned to Burleigh. "Get their names."

Burleigh rose to approach our table.

"No names. Not from the *Freeman.*" Pepperlake waved him down. "My readers may be unhappy with the state of the country, but they aren't idiots. When they talk of armed resistance, they don't want their names in print."

Burleigh glowered.

"Unsigned letters can be traced. I want them for the FBI."

"Signed or not, they're no danger to the union." Finn waved him back to his chair. "The writers are likely backwoods hicks. If they knew the unhappy history of Kentucky in the Civil War, they'd hold their peace and pray to keep it."

He looked at his watch and said he must leave for an afternoon rally in the next county. A few loyal supporters rose to begin a standing ovation, but sat down again when nobody joined them. Burleigh escorted him out of the room.

"An independent county!" The soft-drink canner at our table spoke to Pepperlake. "What kind of fool would talk of that?"

"Fools or not," Pepperlake told him, "people do."

Burleigh came to the the *Freeman* office that afternoon with a federal agent to demand those seditious letters for the FBI. Grumbling because Pepperlake hadn't saved the envelopes, they stayed to question him about his finances, his editorial policy, his rural correspondents, his infonet edition.

"Finn's one of our Beltway overlords," Pepperlake said when they had finally gone. "At least as long as his magic holds. He takes money from Gottler, hires the best in the business to whet his daggers, and recruits the likes of Burleigh and his bullies to do the actual stabbing." His eyebrows lifted. "Today's great American statesman."

Three women burst into the office an hour later. A strange trio. One was lean as a skeleton, taller than I, robed and shawled in black. She was waving a brown manila folder. Another, cloaked in crimson and muscled like a wrestler, carried a heavy wooden cross that towered over her red-cowled head. Its long staff was carved into a blade and painted silver.

The third was a slim pretty girl in her early teens. She wore a plain white gown, and her long bright hair fell over a sleeping baby cradled in one arm. Her free hand held a glass fruit jar that contained something red.

Together, the three advanced on Pepperlake's desk.

"Martha!" With a startled smile, he rose to greet them. "Mrs. Watson. Lily Rose."

I recognized the names. They were three of our rural correspondents.

"Welcome, ladies!" He blinked in puzzlement and started around his desk to meet them. "How can I help you?"

"We come from God." The one in black intoned the words in a sepulchral tone, and waved her folder. "We bring a you a sacred commandment."

He stared at them, a gold tooth gleaming in his open mouth. The girl with the baby stepped slowly forward and set the fruit jar very gently on his desk.

CHAPTER SIX

''*WE COME FROM* the Temple of the Sword, the fortress of God on earth.'' The woman in black spoke again in that hollow doomsday voice. ''We are sent by Father Joel Garron, high commander of His hosts on earth.''

Marching on to meet Pepperlake, she flourished the manila folder.

''His message to you, Mr. Pepperlake.''

The afternoon before, I had ridden my bike out to the edge of town for a look at Garron's temple. A sprawling building of red-striped stucco in the middle of a wide parking lot, it had a silver-painted steeple that tapered into a sword thrust into the sky.

''Martha?'' Pepperlake blinked at the fruit jar on his desk and back at her, his hands raised in baffled dismay. She was Martha Korn, who wrote her column from the strip-mined hills across the county line. ''What's this all about?''

''Salvation.'' Her foghorn voice rolled again. ''The salvation of the nation. The salvation of your own trembling soul.''

He turned to the others as if appealing for help. The girl with the baby was Lily Rose Mayfair, who had been mailing us a weekly column from the Henry Clay Middle School. With a look of sad reproach, she pushed the fruit jar with its red contents farther across his desk.

"Mr. Pepperlake, we bring you a sign from God." Her voice was sweet and high. "We bring you a body of a murdered baby."

"Why?" He shrank back from it. "Lily Rose, what do you mean."

"Mrs. Korn will tell you."

"We bring you a proclamation." Martha Korn found a page in her folder. "It comes to you from Father Garron, who is the Lord's anointed voice." She waved the page and began to chant. "They that shed the blood of unborn infants shall die the death of the damned. So sayeth the Lord, and His will be done.

"Whereas Dr. Stuben Ryke has maintained a notorious slaughterhouse for the unborn here in McAdam City, and whereas he has hardened his Satanic heart against God's warnings to cease and desist from the killing, and whereas he has appealed to the laws of the world for shelter from the servants of God:

"Father Garron proclaims him to be an agent of Satan, lost beyond the laws of God and all hope of salvation. He is therefore expelled from the society of God-fearing men, who are hereby forbidden all contact and commerce with him on pain of eternal damnation.

"Furthermore, Father Garron now announces that he has been guided to choose Colonel Stuart McAdam of the Kentucky Rifles as his candidate for city-county manager and mayor in the coming election. Colonel McAdam has pledged his righteous determination to end this abominable baby-killing and run Dr. Ryke out of the county."

She waved the page high and laid it on the desk beside the fruit jar.

"Read it," she commanded him. "Take it to your heart. It is signed by Father Garron, and sealed with the blood of an unborn baby."

"Gretchen, I don't understand." Gretchen Watson's sword had

sunk as if its weight was tiring her arm, but he retreated from it. She was the correspondent whose husband had been arrested. "What has this to do with me?"

"We want you to print it." All three spoke in well-rehearsed unison. "In bold black type on the front page of tomorrow's *Freeman.*"

"Ladies, please!" He spread his hand in protest. "You know we can't do that."

"Find a way." Watson looked at Martha Korn, who nodded support. "Or face the judgment of God."

"No way." He looked into their stony faces and made a helpless shrug. "This week's edition is already made up and gone to the printer. If the Reverend Garron wants to run a political ad next week, Jim Hobbs is the man to see."

"Next week is too late," Martha Korn told him. "The Rifles are marching to a rally at the temple tomorrow. Colonel McAdam will be making his announcement on our infonet program, speaking to all the world. The election is just two weeks from Tuesday."

She gestured, and they all turned to march away.

"Ladies, wait!" Pepperlake followed them. "Don't go off mad. I hope you'll try to understand. What you ask is simply impossible. I want you to know how much we value your columns. Please keep them coming—"

The baby had begun to cry. Seeming uncomfortable with it, Lily Rose held it up toward Martha Korn. She scowled and turned away. The baby screamed louder. They filed out of the office and tried to slam the door behind them.

"Phew!" Pepperlake sank into the chair behind his desk, with a rueful grin at me. "Quite a show! Old Joe Garron! I knew him before he found the faith. Failed farmer, failed actor, failed broker. Arrested once for posing as an MD, peddling his own miracle cure for asthma and the common cold."

He picked up the fruit jar to study the contents.

"I grew up on a farm," he said. "I don't think this thing's human. Clay, take it out to the college. Get somebody in biology to look at it."

"For a story?"

"No story. Not for the *Freeman.*"

I asked why not.

"Stuart." He made a face. "A troubled kid who lost his early promise, gone rotten now and making bigger trouble every year. His militia's full of hotheads, all gone dangerously crazy since he went to prison. The mayor refused to grant the permit for their march till Gottler and Finn told him to think again. Finn doesn't care for any kind of confrontation in the middle of his own campaign."

"I wish we could cover it."

He looked uncomfortable.

"We're sitting on the fence, at least for now. Stuart knows I don't trust him, but he is a McAdam. I knew his dad back in grade school. Rob Roy's a friend of mine. You know his sister out at the college. Her students love her."

He stopped to wink at me.

"A beautiful woman." I hoped I hadn't colored. "But not one for romance. Certainly not with me."

"I guess you think the *Freeman* ought to stand for something." He was grave again. "It should, but we have to pick our issues. I'm holding what little fire we have till the dust begins to settle."

"And we do nothing on the militia march?"

"We ran a little notice last week. That's enough. Ride your bike out to the rally if you want to see the Garron show, but I'm lying low."

That afternoon I carried the jar out to Dr. Chatterji in the college biology lab. He peered at it, unscrewed the lid, recoiled from the odor, and screwed it hastily back.

"Pig," he said. "With no formaldehyde. Male, three weeks along. Might have made a prize boar."

Pepperlake and Cal Hazard, the part-time circulation manager, stood with me outside the *Freeman* office next morning to watch the

Kentucky Rifles march down McAdam Avenue, around the courthouse, and out South Main toward Garron's Temple of the Sword.

A police car came ahead to clear the street. With a drummer
in the lead, the Rifles came lustily singing "The Battle Hymn of the
Republic." Neatly uniformed in white military hats, red shirts, and
royal blue pants, the men in the front ranks carried shouldered rifles
and marched with a well-drilled precision.

Stuart McAdam led them, riding a bay Thoroughbred. He sat
the horse well, bowing and waving to friends. Spatters of applause
came from farmers and business people standing with us.

"Rifles made for the Chinese Army," Pepperlake nodded at the
weapons. "Bought from Sam Katz before the new gun laws put a
crimp in his business. Gun control!" A sardonic sniff. "That's their
hottest gripe. They want guns to fight the government."

Hazard was clapping vigorously.

"Give 'em a hand," he urged me. "They're us. The army of the
people, ready to defend us from the the whole damn Army if they
have to. I'd join up myself, if I wasn't so old."

The last ranks, most of them in overalls, carried hunting
rifles, pump guns, double-barreled shotguns. A fat man in grimy
yellow coveralls brought up the rear, holding a pitchfork at a
jaunty tilt, bawling the song and grinning happily at us as he swag-
gered by.

"Buzz Hamp." Pepperlake grinned. "The town comic."

"See you." Hazard turned to leave us. "I'm on my way to the
rally."

"You see what troubles me." Pepperlake shrugged unhappily
when he was gone. "It troubled Alden Kirk. I remember a comment
of Kirk's about storm clouds rising. Decent men like Cal ready to
believe Stuart McAdam when he calls our government the enemy."

"But still we're lying low?"

"The *Freeman* is. We're only a weekly, remember. Anything
we could run would be stale before we got it out. And think about
it, Barstow. Feelings run high, and I have to live here."

I had to say I understood.

"If you want a story, call Rob Roy McAdam about CyberSoft and his cryptophone, That's all the controversy I want right now."

A second police car came after the column, and then a parade of private cars. I followed on my bike. The parking lot was almost full, but space enough was left in the sanctuary beneath the sword-shaped steeple. Ben Coon met me at the door, trimly military in his Rifle red-white-and-blue. He grinned and grasped my hand.

"Glad to see you here, Mr. Barstow. I'm sorry how the colonel brushed you off. He was out of sorts, but we need you in the Rifles. I can talk him around." He ushered me in and sat with me.

"Sister Korn! Sister Watson!"

He murmured the greeting to the two women seated beside us, whom I had failed to recognize without their black and crimson robes. They smiled at him, nodded very stiffly at me, and turned back toward the tall wooden cross that towered over the pulpit, the shaft shaped into a silver-painted blade. Stuart McAdam sat on the bench behind it, beside a long-beaked rawboned man with black-dyed hair.

"Father Garron," Coon whispered. "A crazy windbag, but he does stand with the Rifles."

The hall was soon filled, people standing in the doorway. Silence fell when Garron walked into the pulpit and raised his hands. Half-chanting in the same slow and hollow tone that Martha Korn must have learned from him, he prayed God Almighty to slow the ruthless slaughter of the innocent unborn, to receive their souls with mercy, and visit His just vengeance upon their killers.

"Sadly, my dear brethren, this unholy abomination has been allowed to flower here in our own home county. The Devil's dirtiest work! It corrupts the morals of the young, destroys good families, consigns countless souls to everlasting Hell. It must be stopped. It can be stopped. By the infinite grace of God, we have with us one who can stop it."

He gestured at Stuart McAdam, who bowed and then sat straighter in his crimson jacket.

"I give you a man you know. A man who bears a most respected name and shares our time-proven values and our trust in God. A man of high achievement, who has served us well as a devoted Rifleman and now pledges his sacred honor to serve us even better."

He gestured for Stuart McAdam to stand. Applause rippled through the hall.

"I am happy to announce that he is now a candidate for our city-county mayor and manager in next week's election. He promises to bring back the law of God, to stop the Satanic slaughter of the unborn, and to defend our sacred freedoms. I pray the blessing of Almighty God upon him and all his future works."

He stopped aside, waving McAdam onto the pulpit.

"Good friends, good neighbors, fellow patriots!" McAdam made a striking figure in his tall yellow cowboy boots and the trim crimson jacket. When the footlights caught his face, I saw the likeness to his sister in her coldest, most official mode. It stabbed me with the question: *Did she know or suspect that he was the killer?*

He spoke well, sliding fluidly between ringing old-time oratory and the intimate ease of an infonet sex confession. "I may have made my own mistakes, but I've always honored the family name. We McAdams have always fought for freedom. Back on the highlands of Scotland, we fought British tyrants for it. We came to Virginia when they overwhelmed us. We fought them to liberate the thirteen colonies. We fought their Yankee heirs for the freedom of the states.

"That inborn instinct for freedom made America great. Our democracy has become a model for all the world. But now, my friends—" His voice fell, and he paused to shake his head. "Sadly, we have forgotten what we were. We have let our liberties die and rot for the lack of heroes' blood to feed their roots. We let the fat-cat bureaucrats in Washington pour our tax dollars into UN rat holes all around the world, stifle honest business, pamper special interests, deny the sacred rights our forefathers shed their blood for.

"My friends, am I a fool?"

With an appealing smile, he bowed to his audience and got a chorus of *No's*.

"What can I do?" Modestly, he spread his hands. "As mayor and manager of McAdam County? Not much, perhaps. I make no promises to move mountains. The best I can do is to help you re-kindle the precious spark of freedom. To gather the few embers still alive and begin our sacred mission when and where we can.

"The task is forbidding, as all of you know, but our cause is far from hopeless. Others across the nation will surely follow our lead. Noble men and women everywhere have seen their faith mocked, their children seduced into drugs and crime, their jobs sent over-seas, their earnings taxed away.

"If you don't like that, pray God to let you see the light! Listen to my warning. Watch the infonet. Read between the lines of all the clever double-talk that comes from Washington. Look at the crime and corruption right here at home. Our noble sheriff and even our courts have allied themselves with the federal forces swarming in to threaten our last spark of liberty."

He spread his arms and raised his eyes to the sword-shaped silver cross.

"Remember Waco!" His voice pealed louder. "Remember Ruby Ridge! Remember the new breed of martyrs pledging their lives to freedom all across the nation. Remember all that you your-selves are suffering under government gone mad. I beg for your votes, and pray Almighty God to let the holy flame of freedom spread from McAdam County all around the world.

"Here is my platform, one I share with all who love our sacred heritage of liberty. We stand for the right to life. We stand for our Constitution. We stand for our freedom to worship God and speak our minds. We stand for a righteous America, where we live as the fathers of our nation hoped, free of aggression, safe from foreign or domestic tyranny."

"Praise the Lord!" Garron was on his feet. "Praise Him for blessing us with Brother McAdam and his campaign for a more sacred city and a consecrated nation. Let us pray for his victory on election Tuesday. Let God Almighty and our own eternal Temple bless his battle to recover our lost liberties and abolish this hellish abomination of slaughtering the unborn—"

The roar of applause drowned his voice. People all around me were rising. Martha Korn and Gretchen Watson had come to their feet, clapping hard.

"A great day!" Grinning with enthusiasm, Coon turned to shake my hand again when the crowd began to scatter. "But we've got hard fights ahead. Barstow, we need you in the Rifles."

"Not me," I said. "I'm not hungry for any kind of fight."

"Hungry or not, we've got a war ahead." His grin was gone. "A war to save our liberty. We've got to take sides. I hope you take God's side." His hard voice followed as I turned away. "Think about it, Barstow. Think about it."

Thinking about it as I pedaled back to the *Freeman* office, I thought Botman would want my report on Stuart McAdam and Garron, who were certainly no friends of the bureau. And I added Garron to my own list of suspects. Had Alden's sardonic comments on his past and his Temple of the Sword given him motive enough to mail the bomb? The incident of the pig fetus led me to wonder.

"A bad day for McAdam county," Pepperlake muttered when I reported to him. "Maybe for America. Stuart frightens me. Likely he frightens his family."

"Can we somehow oppose him?"

"Not me." He was emphatic. "Not the *Freeman*. Not here in the county. You've felt his charisma. And he is a McAdam. Even a black sheep McAdam can still be a local hero." He tried to ease my disappointment. "Why don't you call Rob Roy? A saner McAdam. Get his reaction to Stuart if you can. And ask again if he'll let you do the CyberSoft story."

I placed the call. A secretary promised to get Mr. McAdam back to me, but never did. That midnight I dialed Botman's number.

"Acorn Three." A strange voice answered, shrill with an edgy impatience. It paused for an instant. "Order number?"

Without speaking, I hung up.

Late one night I heard a noise at the locked front door of the *Freeman.* I had stayed to remake the back page to include a puff on a car dealership to run with a half-page ad Tom Hobbs had sold for a special promotion. I turned on the outside light and found a woman slapping the rain-streaked glass with her open hand.

I unlocked the door.

"Let me in!" She was bare-headed, with no raincoat. Wet blond hair plastered her cheeks. She looked about my age, and temptingly modeled in the cling of her wet blue blouse. She was breathing hard. "I've come to warn them."

"Warn who?"

"Mr. Moorhawk and his congress. They're meeting upstairs in the old lodge hall."

"Who are you?"

"Lydia Starker. Just let me in."

Pepperlake had cautioned me about readers who came in to complain about what we had printed or failed to print, sometimes violently. I'd even encountered two or three, but never one at night.

"I know Mr. Moorhawk." She looked desperate. "I know Cass Pepperlake and Rob McAdam. I've come to warn them."

"Warn them?" Was she mad? "About what?"

"No time for talk." She moved to push past me. "Just let me upstairs."

I blocked her way. "If you can explain—"

"They'll be here any minute." She was breathing hard. "The sheriff and his deputies. A federal agent. They're at the TV station now, just waiting for a camera crew. Burleigh wants a sensation on the infonet."

Still unbelieving, I stepped back and let her in.

CHAPTER SEVEN

SHE RAN PAST me into the dark back room. I grabbed a camera and followed. She flipped a light switch and darted around the old Linotype. The rest rooms were in the far corner, opposite a little space I had taken for a storage closet. She ran to that, wrenched the door open, and snapped on the light in a narrow stair well. I followed her to the top. She battered on another door there till Cass Pepperlake opened it and goggled in astonishment.

"Miss Lydia, what do you want?"

She slipped past him into a dim and dusty-smelling hall. A dozen men sat around a long table in the middle of the empty floor, Kit Moorhawk at the head. I recognized Rob Roy McAdam and a florist and the soft-drink canner from the Rotary lunch.

"Kit!" She ran to Moorhawk. "Burleigh's coming to bust you."

"Bust us?" He scrambled to his feet. "For what?"

"Anything he can. Sedition. Plotting armed rebellion."

"That's absurd!"

"Burleigh and Hunn saw red when they heard about the Rifle

rally." She turned to the others. "They got wind of the meeting tonight, maybe from Gottler—he has contacts everywhere. They're on their way here now with the Feds and a TV crew."

The startled canner was on his feet. "How do you know?"

"I work at the station. I was on the phone when he called for the camera crew. Slipped out the back and ran in the rain."

Rob Roy was still calmly seated at the end of the table while most of the others crowded around her in a clamor of dismay.

"Let's not panic," he called to Moorhawk. "Stuart may be my outlaw brother, but you know I'm not involved with his Rifles or his politics. He's his own man. He does his own thing. He always has. He'd never take orders from Gottler and his gang."

"They believe you are involved," Lydia said. "Stuart has let them think so."

"Stuart!" He made a face. "He's always making problems, but we're honest people here. The Citizens Congress is a private discussion group. We've broken no laws."

"Burleigh and Hunn!" The canner scowled. "I don't want to tangle with them."

"Nasty brutes!" The florist had started for the door but hesitated uncertainly, looking back at Moorhawk. "We've got to get out."

"Hold it, Mack." Moorhawk spread his hands, palms down. "Bugging out, we'd look guilty of all they say we're doing. Let's sit tight and tell the truth."

"Whose truth? They'll make up their own, and screw us with it."

"They're at it already." Lydia raised her breathless voice. "They're parked at the TV station, waiting for cameras. Burleigh wants to tape the bust and make it an infonet circus."

The florist muttered something and vanished down the stairwell. Pepperlake shrugged and turned back to the others.

"If you want to get out, there's a safer way." He pointed at a stack of chairs and tables in the back of the hall. "The fire escape, just behind that junk. A steel stair outside takes you down to the alley."

"Most of us are parked in the lot just across it." The canner led the way. "Make it quiet. Make it quick."

Pepperlake guided them out.

"We're caught!" The florist came trembling back from the stairwell before they were gone. "They're already here. Two squad cars parked out front."

Pepperlake pointed. He scuttled after the others, and Pepperlake closed the fire escape door.

Still sitting, Rob Roy was filling a plastic cup from a water pitcher on the table.

"Cool head, Lyd."

"Not all that cool."

Still breathing hard, Lydia pushed the wet hair off her face and collapsed into the chair beside him. She started back to her feet when we heard a crash and shouts below. Pepperlake listened at the stairwell door and closed it quietly.

"You're the intern?" Rob Roy waited for me to nod. "Calling for the CyberSoft story?"

"I told him to." Pepperlake brought an open bottle of Jim Beam from a filing cabinet. "We need the story, so long as it's something local and safe to print. And need your ads, whenever you get back in business."

"Whenever." Rob Roy shrugged. "But here they come."

Whistling "Dixie" under his breath, Pepperlake sloshed whiskey into plastic cups and pushed them around the table. Feet came pounding up the stair. I got my camera ready and heard hammering on the door.

"Open up!" Bull Burleigh's bawl. "Open to the law!"

Rob Roy beckoned Lydia back into her chair.

"Breathe easy, Lyd," he murmured. "Just sit still."

The door flew open, splinters exploding from the lock. Burleigh burst into the room, a man with a shouldered video camera just behind him.

"Freeze!" Burleigh bellowed. "Freeze where you are."

Police crowded after them and spread to cover us with drawn

guns. I raised my camera to get a shot of his fat red face. Light blinded me. Burleigh lunged at me, snatched my camera, hurled it at the wall, and stepped aside to let the TV camera sweep the room.

"Why, Bull! Saul!" The plastic cup still in his hand, Pepperlake pushed up his glasses and looked up at them, his eyebrows lifted in the image of mild astonishment. "Can you tell us what this is all about?"

The purring camera stopped at last. The dazzling light went out. When I could see again, Burleigh stood glaring at Pepperlake.

"Where are they?" He turned to scowl at Rob Roy and Lydia. "We were informed that others would be here."

"Just us." Pepperlake shrugged. "Who do you want?"

"A gang of troublemakers that call themselves the Citizens Congress, if you don't know." Burleigh stalked closer, shouting triumphantly at the camera. "A nest of terrorists trapped in their conspiracy."

Pepperlake peered into Hunn's narrow, sharp-chinned face with an expression of innocent bewilderment.

"Saul, I think you owe us some kind of explanation—"

"Any explaining is yours to do." Hunn pursed his thin lips and turned to Moorhawk with an air of stern authority. "Your slick little crew face charges of sedition. Obstruction of justice. Even murder."

"Murder?" Moorhawk blinked at Hunn with shrewd gray eyes. A small man with pale untidy hair and a neat little rust-colored moustache, Moorhawk wore a bright purple vest, a bright green tie, and the look of a startled child. "Who's been murdered?"

Alden, for one.

"A dozen people," Hunn snapped. "Killed two weeks ago by that bomb at the Frankfort Federal Building."

"You don't suspect—"

"We want to know." Burleigh was looking hard at Lydia, and she cringed from his gaze. "We intend to find the facts."

"We have evidence," Hunn plowed on. "Hard evidence linking that bomb to this so-called congress. We were informed that they were meeting here."

"Look for yourselves."

Hunn glared into the corners of the empty room and turned back to huddle with Burleigh and a tall man behind them. Still wet from the rain, Lydia was shivering. Rob Roy put his arm around her. We sat waiting till they broke out of the huddle and Burleigh strode toward us.

"Gentlemen, have a seat." Pepperlake gestured at the chairs around the table. "If you don't mind, I'd like an apology for this uncivil intrusion."

"Apology?" Burleigh snorted. "I want answers." He shook his head at the empty chairs. "What was going on here."

"Our business." Pepperlake shrugged amiably. "Private business, unless you can show us a search warrant." He gestured at the tall man. "Who's your friend?"

"United States Marshall Harrison Creighton."

Creighton came on toward the table, Hunn and Burleigh beside him.

"Rob McAdam." Hunn nodded at Rob Roy and turned to Creighton. "The man you came to look for."

"R. R. McAdam?" Creighton came to stand over him. "Head of CyberSoft Corporation?"

"Yes, sir." He waved at the Jim Beam bottle. "May we offer you a drink?"

Stiffly, Creighton shook his head.

"McAdam, we have something to discuss." He scowled and raised his voice. "I'm an officer of the federal court. You and your corporation have been enjoined to cease and desist from the production or distribution of a device known as a cryptophone. The court has received no reply."

"Mr. Moorhawk is my attorney." Rob Roy nodded at him. "We met here tonight to frame our response."

Burleigh stepped aside, growling something to Hunn.

"Cass Pepperlake, publisher of the *Freeman.*" Rob Roy gestured at him and then at me. "Clayton Barstow, a staff writer. The *Freeman* will publish our reply."

"A newspaper squib?" Creighton sniffed. "That's no legal answer."

"Mr. Creighton, please." Moorhawk stood up, protesting mildly. "If you have a moment to listen, I can state our case here and now. In our opinion, the federal action against CyberSoft is an unfair and illegal restraint of trade. We expect to carry our defense to the highest court."

"Do as you like," Creighton snapped. "As you know, however, your crytophone has been found to be a threat to the national security. External enemies or criminal gangs here in America could employ it for the transmission of secret messages detrimental to the public peace and safety. The court has forbidden any manufacture or use of it until such time as you choose to provide our national defense agencies with complete algorithms for the decryption of cryptophone messages."

"My client is aware of your demand." Moorhawk shrugged. "But he is also aware that the value of the cryptophone system derives from its absolute integrity. The court is demanding that we destroy that integrity. The order amounts to the illegal expropriation of our property."

Creighton turned to Rob Roy, something close to a snarl in the twist of his lips.

"McAdam, we aren't playing games." His flat raspy voice was almost a snarl. "I came here to bring you a warning from the court. If you continue to promote this prohibited technology, you will find your buildings padlocked and yourself in a federal prison."

"Thank you, sir." Rob Roy grinned at Moorhawk. "Your advice will be considered."

"Laugh if you like," Creighton sneered. "But the court has found your cryptophone to be a weapon of war, which you have supplied to potential enemies both here and abroad. The government will act accordingly."

"We stand for the freedom of speech." Rob Roy grinned. "We'll act according."

"You damn McAdams!" Burleigh's voice dropped to a threatening growl. "You ain't the lords you used to be. We are the law of the county and the law of the nation. We're going to put you and your chickenshit corporation out of business."

"I am a McAdam, and proud of the name." Rob Roy nodded cheerfully. "But don't confuse me with my dear brother Stuart. I don't command any militia army. I assure you that we aren't here to hatch insurrection."

"We have evidence you are."

"Just four of us?" He made a sardonic shrug toward Pepperlake, Lydia, and me. "Do you think we came here to declare our independence? To make war on the United States of America?"

"No matter what I think, you skulking McAdams are done for."

Nodding for Creighton and his deputies to follow, he stalked toward the door.

"Something else before you go," Pepperlake called after them. "I'll be billing McAdam county for what you did to my door downstairs. And for any damage to Mr. Barstow's camera."

Burleigh turned back to shake a black-haired fist.

"Talk to your cocksucker lawyer. Let him sue."

Pepperlake followed them down the stairwell. I picked up my cameras. The flash was knocked askew and the shutter didn't work, but I found Burleigh's fat red face still in the digital memory, yellowed teeth shining through a dark bristle of unshaven beard as his big mouth yawned to shout.

CHAPTER EIGHT

WE WAITED AROUND the table. Rob Roy poured a little whiskey into his cup and offered the bottle. Lydia shook her head. Moorhawk helped himself, added water, and sat without tasting it. Pepperlake came back up the stairs at last. Softly whistling "Dixie," he sat down at the table and pushed the bottle away.

"About Mr. Barstow?" Moorhawk nodded inquiringly at me. "Is he here by chance? Or one of us?"

"A college kid from D.C." Pepperlake shrugged, with an amiable grin. "An intern on the paper."

I told them how I had let Lydia into the building.

"Something else you ought to know." Rob Roy studied me soberly and spoke to the others. "Mr. Barstow isn't just any college kid. My sister says he's a half-brother of Alden Kirk, author of *Terror in America.* He claims to be down here looking for his brother's killer."

Startled at that, I felt a flash of resentment at Elizabeth McAdam. I thought she had promised not to expose me. "True," I said.

"I was Alden's research assistant. I want to know who mailed the bomb."

"So what?" Moorhawk looked doubtfully at Pepperlake. "I don't want us on the infonet."

"I'm not reporting for the infonet," I said. "Or to anybody except the *Freeman.*" That, I told myself, was true. My arrangement with Botman had very definitely broken down when "Acorn Three" asked for my order number. I didn't intend to call again.

"We McAdams don't cut throats," Rob Roy was saying, "but my sister disapproves of spies."

"So do I." Moorhawk looked at me rather grimly. "The raid seems to show that we already have a mole here in the congress. We don't need another."

"But we must consider Mr. Barstow." Rob Roy sipped his drink and eyed me judicially. "He may be here by accident, but I think better with us than against us."

They all studied me.

"I came here to take up my brother's work," I said. "I hope to finish the new book he meant to write. And to do whatever I can to identify his killer."

"A tall order." Moorhawk studied me again, shaking his head.

"I have to try." Waiting under their critical eyes, I took a nervous sip from my cup. "I don't expect Burleigh and company to do much about the letter bomb. Not since I've met them."

Moorhawk nodded at last, and Lydia gave me a slight pale smile.

"Okay." Pepperlake seemed relieved. "I think your brother would have been our friend. I had intended to sound him out when he got back from Washington. Do you have questions?"

"What is the Citizens Congress?"

Pepperlake shrugged. "We began after a few of us had met your brother, a little group of concerned citizens discussing the sorry state of the nation as it looked to Alden Kirk. No dues or membership cards, though you must agree to keep our secrets."

"Agreed," I said, and they all rose very solemnly to shake my hand.

"Tonight—" Still on his feet, Pepperlake turned to Moorhawk and waited for his nod. "We weren't exactly plotting sedition, but Stuart McAdam and his militia have alarmed us. We met to hear an announcement from Kit."

Moorhawk rose and turned to Rob Roy.

"Your brother Stuart and his Rifles—" Wryly, he shook his head. "They've become a threat to the peace of the county."

"I don't control Stuart." Rob Roy shrugged. "Nobody does." He waited inquiringly. "The announcement?"

"Won't shake the earth," Moorhawk said. "Call it one small step. Maybe enough to jolt Hunn and Burleigh. I'm going to run against your brother for city-county mayor and manager."

"Have you thought about the cost?" Pepperlake squinted at him. "County politics can be nasty."

"I should know." Moorhawk nodded, and added deliberately, "The campaign may get rough, but the county's sick for something better than we'd ever get from Stuart and his Rifles. Or Burleigh and Hunn. Or even Finn and Gottler, if you want to reach that high." His eyes narrowed. "Can the *Freeman*—"

Pepperlake had to hesitate.

"We'll do what we can," he said. "But we have to stay alive."

"All I can ask for."

Moorhawk turned to study me with the fixed intensity of a poker master.

"Okay, Barstow." He nodded at last, and spoke with a sudden force, his voice as loud as the hues of his tie and vest. "If you're with us, here's where I stand. I read your brother's book. I wish I'd known him better, because I share his concern for our future.

"We are breeding barbarians. Kids who grow up without families, without discipline, without God, with no culture except violence, no belief except in themselves, no loyalty except to their gangs. They are ignorant of history, of science, of everything except the streets. They can take us down the way Rome went down."

"Can you stop them?" Pepperlake seemed sardonic.

"Who could?" He shrugged. "A lot of us have seen trouble

coming. When I had money and expected more, I planned to endow McAdam College into an island of culture, where a few dedicated men and women might do what they could to shelter some spark of our civilization the way the church did through the Dark Ages."

"A noble dream." Wistfully, Pepperlake nodded. "I wish you'd made the money."

He put his bottle back in the filing cabinet, and we followed him down the stairwell. A thin cold rain was still falling when we came out of the building. Rob Roy's pickup was on the lot behind it. He let me load my bike, and we drove Lydia back to the TV station where she had left her car.

When she got out, I asked to see her again.

"Why not?" She smiled and gave me her telephone number. "We've had an interesting evening."

"A good kid," he said as we watched her drive away. "I've known her since grade school. She's had a hard life. Rough times as a nightclub hostess. An affair with Stuart McAdam that went very sour. But now I think she's getting herself back together."

He dropped me and the bike off at my room.

"Come by the plant tomorrow," he invited me. "Let's talk about the cryptophone."

I located CyberSoft in what had been Moorhawk's Coal Combustion Corporation, a long low green metal building off the Lexington highway. The parking lot was empty when I got there next morning, but half a dozen bicycles were racked out in front. A short fat man with thick glasses and a lot of hair came to the door. I introduced myself and asked to see Mr. McAdam.

"Rob Roy?" He nodded and shook my hand. "We're free and easy here. I'm Mike Densky. Rob said you'd be here. Come on in."

The big room inside was almost as empty as the parking lot, though I saw a few people busy at computers. Rob Roy came to beckon me genially to a chair in front of his desk and poured coffee for us before he asked how I got on with Beth.

"I don't."

"I know." He grinned as if amused. "She's another McAdam, but you'll find her okay when you get to know her."

"If I could—"

His grin spurred me to ask about the cryptophone. He reached across his desk for a wallet-sized device cased in slick brown plastic. A thin metal antenna and a thin-stemmed microphone snapped out when he clicked a switch and coiled back into place when he clicked again.

"Wireless," he said. "Linked to the infonet system through digital relays and the global satellites. They're trying to break my encryption algorithms. Trying reverse engineering on my hardware. Trying to break us. Threatening to throw me into prison." He shrugged and gave it to me. "Hold it to your ear. The pressure switch turns it on."

It hummed faintly for a moment and went silent.

"Yes?" Elizabeth McAdam's voice startled me. "Mode?"

I knew nothing to say.

"Open mode." Her cool voice grew crisper. "Who are you calling?"

"Nobody," I said.

"Voice unknown." I realized that I was really speaking to nobody. "Identify destination if you wish to continue in open mode. If you wish to use secure mode, give your name or ID number and repeat the alphabet as initial voice sample."

I handed the instrument back to Rob Roy.

"It's really private?"

"Too private to suit the government." Amusement flashed in his eyes. "It's based on a new wrinkle in physics we're keeping to ourselves. It fits a very real need for total security. Hackers are breaking the best systems in use, though nobody likes to admit it."

"It can beat the hackers?"

"And rile the FBI and the National Security Agency. It's an educated telephone. In the open mode, it gives you an ordinary infonet link. In the secure mode, it recognizes voices and encrypts signals into secure digital strings that can travel safely on any public channel. It can save the last two hours of talk, still protected. Messages can be decrypted only by another cryptophone, and only after it has matched instructions with the voice track of an authorized receiver."

"You won't give it up?" I said. "And the justice department calls you disloyal?"

"Maybe I am." He nodded cheerfully. "But the cryptophone is our own creation. Potentially a very valuable property. Revealing the algorithms would destroy it." His jaw set. "I won't give them up."

"So they're trying to close you down?"

"They've done that." His face tightened. "When we had a market—only a very small beginning—most of it was overseas. They've shut that off. Customs has been ordered to seize our exports and arrest anyone trying to take a cryptophone out of the country. We've had to stop shipments and shut production down."

He pushed his coffee aside and sat gazing at nothing, stubborn defiance on his face.

"What next?" I asked.

"Moorhawk left for Washington this morning, under subpoena to testify before Senator Finn's National Defense Committee. They want to know which criminal groups or foreign powers could have received cryptophones. There's not much we can say. If we'd interrogated or recorded the buyers, we'd have had no sales." He scowled at the empty desks, lips set hard. "They're determined to put me out of business. To get my secrets if they can."

"Don't they have a point?" I thought of Botman. "Couldn't terrorists use your cryptophone?"

"Perhaps." He nodded soberly. "That alarms the feds, maybe with good reason, though in the end they'll have to admit that technological advances have left them in the dust. Information science has grown beyond control. As for your unlucky brother, I think he should have been more concerned with why the FBI and the CIA are so desperate to seize my technology for themselves."

"Is your defiance worth the cost?" I had to ask. "To you?"

He paused to consider that. I was struck by the clean grace of his bones and his likeness to his sister—and to Stuart. A family mask that changed immensely with the wearer.

"Moorhawk sees it as a matter of principle." His eyes came back to me, as keen as Beth's but more blue than violet. "He wants to defend the right of privacy, the right of the individual against the crowd. So does Pepperlake—at least as far as he can with his struggling weekly. For me, it's more personal. CyberSoft's my life. I grew up with computers. I saw the need for stronger security while I was still a college sophomore. Dropped out to work in it. Worked nights and weekends till Moorhawk came up with the venture capital to finish it."

His voice dropped.

"It's ours now. I won't give it up. Not to the infonet managers. Not to the Department of Justice. Not to anybody, though offers have run in the hundreds of millions. Creighton, our pal in the FBI, is accusing me of every crime in his book. The courts have given us an ultimatum. We don't intend to blink."

"What if they don't blink?"

"If they don't—" He gave me another piercing look. "Barstow, are you really one of us now?"

"I am," I said. "Cross my heart. Though I'd like to know more about who we are."

"Your brother set us on the road," he said, "with *Terror in America*. Pepperlake talks about what he calls the temper of the time. He remembers World War II and the way the country was united then. A man in uniform could hitch half across the country, counting on good citizens to get him back to base on time. He wouldn't get far now.

"Your brother was asking how we lost the unity that made us a nation." He gave me a twisted grin. "But I guess you know the book."

"Alden saw the problems," I said. "I don't think he knew the answers."

"Does anybody?" He shrugged soberly. "Our little group has never found a cure for the sort of thing that killed your brother." He paused again to study my face, and finally shook his head. "I don't know who tipped Hunn and Creighton off, but you may be standing where he was."

"I've considered the risks," I told him. "They do concern me. But I'm wondering about you and your congress. You seem to have the local courthouse gang against you as well as the federal government. Can't they smash you?"

"Maybe they can." His lean shoulders squared. "Maybe they can't. We have an ace to play."

I didn't ask what it was, but he let me stay another hour, talking about his life.

"We McAdams were sometimes a very happy family." Recollection warmed his face. "Our father is an easy-going guy who loves history. Taught it till he retired. He likes good stories and good bourbon. He has his double shot every evening, collects antiques, works now and then on a history of slavery he'll never finish.

"But our mother—" His smile disappeared. "She was a shrill-voiced Christian fundamentalist who hated him for frittering away the last of the family fortune. Always calling him a good-for-nothing sot and nagging him to give his soul to Jesus. I think she was bad for Stuart." He made a wry face. "The youngest sibling. Beth calls him a rebel soul. In trouble with his parents or his teachers or the law all his life. He got expelled from VMI, got a dishonorable discharge from the Army, did his year in prison in spite of all the old man and Beth could do to save him. Free again now, on a pardon Gottler must have paid for, he's back in command of the Rifles.

"He could be an angel when he tried, but he used to play dirty tricks on me when I made him jealous. He brought Lydia home from a hard life in Louisville with a promise to marry her then beat her half to death before she left him. Yet I've put up with him. Most people like him. He's clever. He can show a sort of charm.

"And you know Beth."

"Only slightly."

Amusement crinkled his eyes.

"The best of us, Clay. Don't give her up before you get to know her. She kept the house after our mother died. Still lives at home and looks after our father. Stuart has always been her poor little baby brother. He's never been nicer to her than to anybody else, but she always forgives him for anything. Tries to bail him out when he needs her.

"She is okay," he told me again. "You ought to know her better."

With no easy answer for that, I thanked him for the interview and got up to leave. He nodded at the cryptophone.

"Yours," he said. "If you want it."

Surprised, I thanked him again.

"Careful," he warned me. "The National Security Agency has experts working to break my algorithms. It has a little security kink of my own that ought to keep them scratching their heads for a long time to come, but they can detect the encrypted signal. You could be in hot water for mere possession of the instrument, even if you never try to use it."

I dropped the little instrument into my shirt pocket.

"I gave your brother one," He shook his head as I rose to go. "I hope that's not what did him in."

He walked with me to the door. Turning back when he smiled and offered his hand, I glanced at the glass-walled cubicles around the long room, most of them empty.

"For all you have done, you seem to have a small staff."

"Once it was larger. We depend more on AIs now."

"Artificial intelligences?"

"If you call them intelligent."

"If not?"

"They're systems of algorithms that use their own sort of logic. They can store a lot of data and process it faster than a human brain can, but they lack intuition. Call them the foot soldiers of the computer revolution."

"So they didn't invent the cryptophone?"

"They helped." His shrug seemed enigmatic. "I have to give them credit."

"You aren't afraid they'll get out of control?"

"They'll never have my brother's ambition." He laughed, perhaps a little ruefully, and grew more sober. "They won't take the world over, but there's no predicting what could be done by those with know-how to create and use them."

I wasn't sure what he meant by that, but his face had become so grim that I decided not to ask.

CHAPTER NINE

THE CRYPTOPHONE'S CHIME startled me next morning.

"Mr. Barstow?" Beth McAdam's actual voice, cool and official. "Can you come to my office this morning?"

I caught my breath and said I could.

"Be here at ten. Something urgent."

Walking in five minutes early, tense with a mix of hope and trouble, I found her already at her desk. She looked warmly fresh and desirable in the same tan sweater, but she gave me no smile. Nodding for me to sit, she closed the office door and sat scanning me with stern disapproval. I waited uneasily till she spoke.

"Mr. Barstow, you're ignoring my advice." Her manner brought back long-past scoldings from my stepfather. "I warned you to stop your meddling here. To get out of town."

"So?" I gave way to resentment. "Why should I care?"

"Remember your brother."

That hurt.

"I'm sorry." She had seen me flinch. Her tone softened, though only for a moment. "I'm not your enemy, but you will have serious enemies when they learn your business here."

"A risk I have to take."

"If you feel that way—" She gave me a searching frown and abruptly went on, "Perhaps we can help each other."

"How?"

My breath came faster, with the fleeting hope for some sort of friendship.

"I can keep quiet about who you are and your business here." *But not,* I remembered, *with Rob Roy.* Her narrowed eyes were sharp as blades. "You can answer questions for me. How about it?"

I heard nothing warmer in her voice.

"Okay," I muttered, wondering what answers she wanted.

"So we've agreed."

She was absently fingering a paperweight on her desk, a racing Thoroughbred in bright black glass mounted on an oval silver base.

"I'll keep quiet, but others may not." She pushed the horse away and fixed those intense ultra-blue eyes on me. "I must warn you again, Barstow. My advice still stands. I can't protect you from others who won't want you here."

"Thanks," I said. "Understood."

Still intently watching me, she touched the horse again.

"Last night you attended a meeting of this so-called Citizens Congress? I believe you became a member? Right?"

How did she know? Had Rob Roy told her? Baffled, I had to admit that I'd been at the meeting.

"Who was there?"

"I recognized Mr. Pepperlake and his attorney. The others were strangers."

"I want the truth." Her face set harder. "I think you know my brother Rob."

"Slightly. I met him at Rotary."

"You know him better than that." My stepfather couldn't have been more severe, yet I felt, or wanted to feel, a generous human warmth beneath her stern official shell. "You saw him at the meeting. Yesterday morning you visited him at CyberSoft. He gave you a cryptophone. Right?"

I had to nod.

"Mr. Barstow—" She paused to frown forbiddingly. "I want your full cooperation, because I'm concerned for my brothers. You heard Stuart making his political announcement at the rally?"

She waited for another uneasy nod.

"He's not a bad man." She was sharply defensive. "Sometimes impulsive, often reckless, trouble-prone since he was a baby, but never really evil." Her baby brother, Pepperlake had said. Forever in need of her protection, now far beyond her control. What could she expect me to do about him?

"Not that he's stupid." Tight-lipped, she shook her head. "Maybe too smart. He wants too much, reaches too far. He's surrounded now by all the trigger-happy thugs in his militia, talking open rebellion. They're asking for trouble."

"They could get it," I said. "The rally made a splash on the infonet. Washington must be listening."

"I've begged Stuart to back off." Nervously, she picked up the little glass horse and set it down again. "So has his father. He won't listen. I think I know why. He expects help from Rob."

She must have caught my startled look.

"Rob's never been close to me. Secure in himself and always independent." Her gaze grew keener. "Did he mention a weapon?"

"He spoke of an ace he could play."

"He does have something." I saw her disappointment. "Something he hinted at once, back before trouble seemed so close. Only an idea then—he called it a bit of serendipity he'd hit on in his search for information security. It may have come to nothing. Stuart thinks it didn't.

"My brothers—"

She stopped for a moment, looking up with a wistful half-smile at her own portraits of them and her father on the wall behind me.

"Rob's a genius. Or so our mother used to say. That always

made Stuart furious. They've never got on, and I don't like what might happen now."

She looked back at me, a somber shadow in her eyes.

"The Silicon Shell. That was a name he had for the weapon he'd imagined if it was to be a weapon. Designed for defense, he said, not for aggression. He'd picked the name to hide the actual idea. He doesn't talk about it now. He's too stubborn to listen, even when I've begged him to make some reasonable deal with the government on his cryptophone."

"So you expect some kind of showdown?"

"It could be something—" She stopped, with a wry twist of her lips. "I love Stuart, but he frightens me. Back from prison now, he's harder than ever. Bitter against the government and not afraid to talk of treason. He's got a lot of fools around him. They could start a crazy little war and get a lot of people killed.

"And there's another player. Kit Moorhawk—I think you've met."

I nodded, wondering how much she knew about the Citizens Congress.

"Rob's business partner back when he had money and his attorney now. A political opponent of Stuart and Burleigh. Each man with his own agenda. The government is crowding them all into a mix that can turn deadly. Maybe deadlier, if that weapon does exist and Stuart gets control."

Unconsciously, she had pushed the tiny horse toward me, frowning at it as if she were moving a chessman in a very serious game.

"Take a look at the group. Rob's fighting the Feds for the cryptophone. Moorhawk's afraid of prison for fraud or tax evasion. As for Stuart, the infonet stories on his rally have sparked a new move in Congress to disarm the militias. And now—"

She pushed the horse abruptly aside, as if she had lost it in the game.

"Subpoenas were served on Rob yesterday afternoon, demanding his lab notes and business papers. Though the courts are only after the cryptophone, the documents could give them the weapon too, if any weapon does exist. I'm afraid Rob's bitter enough to let Stuart and Moorhawk lead him into trouble.

"Moorhawk's the most alarming."

She saw my puzzled look.

"Maybe you like him. A lot of people do. A natural leader, with too much ambition for a man his size. He could con my brothers into some tragic blunder. I don't mean just county politics, though that's already explosive enough. He and my brothers—"

Staring at the black horse, she cringed as if she had seen sheer disaster riding it.

"I'm concerned, Mr. Barstow. Terribly concerned, and not just for my own family." Her eyes rose to me, the widened pupils dark with dread. "I'm a historian, a student of change. We face a historic event now. As great, I think, as the invention of fire or planting crops or the use of metals. That's information technology."

"Alden talked about it," I said. "He called it the taproot of terror."

"Because a new world is growing from it. A hostile world to those who don't or can't adapt. It rewards the few who learn its laws and hurts the millions who don't. Terror's their weapon of rebellion." She nodded, and I caught a fleeting smile. "I read your brother's book. I wish I'd known him. He had a real insight when he called America a powder keg, waiting for a match. I'd say the whole world is waiting."

Frowning, she reached for the horse again.

"That's why I called you in, Mr. Barstow. If Kit Moorhawk does enlist my brothers, if Rob has really invented some potential weapon, they could be about to touch a match to the powder. I want to stop them."

Sharply, she rapped the desk with the silver base of the horse. Her widened eyes were violet, and I heard the ring of determination in her voice.

"I want your help."

She was sincere and beautiful and altogether admirable, but still no friend. I waited uneasily for her to say more and finally asked what she expected me to do.

"Keep up your membership in Pepperlake's congress." Her sharp commands came as if she had made a list. "Watch him and Rob and Moorhawk. Listen to their plans. Pick up anything you can about this Silicon Shell, whatever it is or could be, about Kit's plans and ambitions, about Stuart and his Rifles. Watch Cass Pepperlake. Keep an eye on Garron and his mob. Get word to me about anything you think might lead to open violence.

"Agreed?"

"Agreed," I said. "On one condition. That you'll inform me about anything that could help me find who killed my brother."

"I'm sorry about him." A flash of genuine sympathy. "The case looks hopeless. I will pass along anything I learn, but that's yesterday. Our problem is tomorrow."

I asked what she meant to do about tomorrow.

"Anything I can."

That was all she said. It left me wondering. How far would she go to help her baby brother? What did she feel toward Rob Roy? How could she hope to intervene in whatever they planned? On the personal level, how did she feel toward me? Why had she told me so much? Was she aware of her sexual allure? Her power over me, if she chose to use it?

"Do your best, Mr. Barstow." On her feet, she gave me a smile that seemed for a moment to show the trust I longed for, and offered her hand. "We've got a lot at stake."

Leaving her office, I carried problems of my own. Botman, the Bureau, "Acorn Three." I'd promised Rob Roy and Pepperlake to keep their secrets. I'd agreed to cooperate with her. I'd kept quiet about Director Garlesh and the Bureau. My own first goal was still to identify the bomber. I had conflicts enough to give me a headache, but I found myself haunted by her fear of some secret weapon and the powder keg it might ignite.

At midnight, on an impulse of patriotic loyalty that overcame my qualms, I dialed Botman's number again. His phone rang forever. I hung up at last, relieved that nobody had answered, not even Acorn Three.

Most of next morning I spent digging into the *Freeman* files and writing a feature story about Rob Roy McAdam and the rise and fall of CyberSoft. Pepperlake made me redo it twice, cutting everything about the cryptophone and signal security, before he found it safe to print. Though he allowed no mention of Lydia Starker, the story brought her back as I had first seen her in the pelting rain outside our door, breathing hard from her run to warn her friends of the raid. Captured by her image in my memory, boldly heroic, desperate, vulnerable, her rain-soaked hair and clothing plastered to her body, I tried to call her on the infonet.

She was out, her office said. I found L. Starker in the audio directory. The phone rang a long time before a sharp-voiced woman answered. I asked for Lydia.

"Who are you?"

"A friend." Hoping it might prove true, I gave my name and said we had met at the *Freeman.*

"Freeman!" She spoke it like an oath. "Nosing into honest people's lives."

I caught my breath and asked again for Lydia.

"Maybe she's here. Maybe she ain't."

All I heard for half a minute was a loud clock ticking, but then Lydia was on the line, seeming startled till she recognized my name. I asked if we might meet for dinner.

"This evening?" I liked the ring of pleasure in her voice. "I have a car. Let me pick you up."

I was waiting in the Katz House lobby when she came in, temptingly trim in a blue denim skirt and a bright flowered blouse, her sleek hair combed back and fairer than I recalled it. She stood a moment searching almost as if we were strangers, but then her face lit as if we were already friends.

"I've endured a bad week." Even with a frown her face was still enchanting. "I'm glad to get away."

New in town, I let her pick the restaurant. She drove me to a small Italian place in an old house that once had been a private dwelling. Seated in a quiet back room, we shared a bottle of wine.

"I'm sorry about your brother," she said. "Mr. Pepperlake introduced us when he wanted background on the McAdam brothers. I think Pepperlake was his best friend here." A shadow crossed her face. "Perhaps the only friend."

She refused more wine. We ordered veal scallopine. I felt happy with her. She seemed eager to hear about my life in Georgetown and my work with Alden. Listening to her talk about McAdam City and the music program she hosted on KRIF infonet, I almost forgot to eat. She said nothing about the McAdams or the cryptophone or Sheriff Burleigh's raid, and I didn't want to spoil the evening with unwelcome questions. In the parking lot as we left, she paused to ask me, "Where?"

It took me a moment to get my breath and meet her eyes. I whispered, "Anywhere."

She drove us north on the Lexington road to a motel across the county line. The kid at the desk took my money, grinned enviously at Lydia, gave me a key and a wink. I don't recall the room itself, but nothing will ever erase our few hours there. With hardly a word, we stripped and stepped into the shower. We soaped and scrubbed each other. She was laughing at a moon-faced birthmark on my belly when I carried her, slick and dripping, to the bed. Eagerly passionate there, she woke emotions I had never felt.

By midnight, passions spent, we lay in bed together, naked and relaxed. I recall a hint of the lilac perfume left in her hair, her sweeter body scent, the even rhythm of her breath, her playful fingers tracing my face. Drowsily relaxed, she talked more freely about the McAdams.

"I've known them since grade school. McAdams were royalty

and I was nobody, but they were good to me. Rob used to look out for me like an elder brother. Other kids used to pick on me. For being the preacher's brat. For wearing Goodwill garments. Because my eyes used to cross when I was tired. He beat up bullies who wouldn't stop. And Stuart—"

She lay still, remembering him. Her voice had softened when she went on.

"I adored Stuart. Puppy love, I guess you'd call it. He was a smartass, always in trouble for trying to be the best, the brightest, the strongest, the bravest. He would fight anybody who said he wasn't, but he never hurt me. He let me walk with him to school and wanted to give me his lunch money when my folks were too proud to let me take the free lunch. Years later, after we were grown—"

She stopped, remembering again.

"He looked me up in Louisville." Her voice had slowed and I heard a tremor in it. "He found me in a night club—that's what they called it. I'd used up the little luck I ever had. Hooked on coke. Down and desperate. I owe him a lot. He saved my life. Brought me home to McAdam. Helped me break the habit. I think—I really think—"

Her body tense, she lay breathing fast. I waited till she went on, almost whispering.

"He said he loved me. I think he really did. We lived together. He helped me finish business school and find a job. We were going to be married when his got his problems solved, but—"

I felt her tremble.

"Trouble happened. He never got them solved."

I asked about the trouble.

"A lot of it." She paused till I thought she had no more to say. "For one thing," she went on at last, "he was still a lawyer then. His best clients were marijuana farmers. I guess he went too far for them, because the federal narcs got after him instead of them. They woke a devil in him."

I heard her grit her teeth.

"An ugly devil." Her voice had a bitter edge. "He was ugly to me, yet I can't hate him. Pity him, perhaps. I've tried to understand him. Sometimes he was almost paranoid." He accused me of spying for the FBI. I felt her shake her head. "I guess he was born what he is. A mix of good and bad. Like we all are, maybe, but not to such extremes. But I'm still afraid—"

She caught a long breath and sat up on the side of the bed.

"Thank you, Clay." She leaned to kiss me as I sat up beside her. "I needed this! Needed it terribly."

I couldn't ask why, but I held her close till she shivered and stood up.

"I've got to go." She gave me a wryly painful grin. "You've spoken to my mother. I live with her because she needs what I pay for room and board, but she can be difficult." Soberly, her voice fell. "About Stuart, there's something I told your brother when he asked about him. Stuart has a past. Things he wants forgotten."

She caught my shoulders to push me away and let me stand there for a moment longing to take her back to bed. Her hair was long and fair, almost a garment, falling free around her pink-nippled breasts. I tried to pull her closer. She shook her head and pushed me firmly back.

"I like you, Clay," she whispered. "A lot. I wish life had been simpler, but I've really got to go. Let's get dressed."

I asked for another date.

"When I can," she promised. "When I can."

Beth McAdam smiled next day when I passed her on a campus path, but my mind was full of Lydia, her laughter at the birthmark, the way she cut her scallopine, her recollections of Stuart McAdam. I longed to know her problems, to shelter her from trouble, to hold her close again. I tried to call her at the infonet office. She was out again, but I felt happy just to be here in the same city with her.

I spent the afternoon at the *Freeman,* reading proofs of my feature story and making up inside pages for the next edition. Early next morning, while I was boiling coffee water on the hot plate in my room and peeling a banana to go with bran flakes, my crypto-phone purred.

"Clay!" Calling in open mode, Lydia was hoarse and breathless. "If you want to know who mailed the bomb that killed your brother, get out here now. I live with my mother in a red-tiled house on the corner of Fourth and Walnut. For God's sake make it quick."

CHAPTER TEN

I UNPLUGGED THE hotplate and pedaled fast to Fourth and Walnut. The red-tiled house sat on the corner across from a dark brick Church of Christ. Leaves were falling from the actual walnuts that overhung the house, but the lawn had been mowed clean. I leaned my bike against the post that supported a weathered cast-metal sign lettered STARKER and crossed a wide verandah to ring the doorbell. After an endless minute, a woman opened the door.

"Yes, sir?" She looked a little like Lydia, but darker, shorter, stouter, gone sour with time. She wore a red-checked kitchen apron, her hair in a thick knot on top of her head. One cold eye was wide, the other squinted at me sharply. "What do you want?"

"I want to see Lydia. She just called me."

"She did?" A suspicious snort. "Why?"

"Really, I don't know. I came to find out."

"What's your name?"

I gave her my *Freeman* press card. The narrowed eye squinted at it and back at me.

"Barstow, huh? I never heard her say any such name. Are you dating her?"

"No." I only wished I were.

"Where did you meet her?"

"At the *Freeman.*"

"Why was she there?"

"She wanted to see Mr. Pepperlake."

"What about?"

"Please, Mrs. Starker—you are Mrs. Starker?"

"I am. But I don't like anybody bustin' into my home at this time of day." She peered at my bike, where I had left it against the post. "What do you want with Lydia?"

"Ma'am, I don't really know." Respectfully, I took off my Rebs cap. "She called like I told you. She wanted me to get here fast—"

"Mister, I don't know what this is all about." She scowled at me doubtfully. "My daughter ain't up for breakfast and I don't like funny business. Get back on your bike and ride away before I call the cops."

"Please, Mrs. Starker. She does want to see me. Won't you let me wait?"

She studied me again, studied the press card, finally stepped back to let me into a dark living room that looked empty of luxury or even common comfort. A tall grandfather clock ticked loudly in the corner. A big red-letter Bible lay open on a library table that stood like an altar under a gold-framed print of a bleeding Jesus on the cross.

"Sit there if you want to wait." She waved me to a threadbare sofa. "And explain how come you've got such an interest in my daughter."

She stood glowering while I searched for a safe evasion.

"A story for the paper," I said. "She said she had important information for me."

"About what?"

"That's all confidential till the story breaks."

"Is she in trouble?"

"I hope not, but I do need to see her."

"Lydia has always got in trouble." She shook her head, raising her mismatched eyes to the crucified Christ. "Even back in school. More when she went off to sing in Louisville—if singing was all she did. Worse trouble when she got tangled up with that Stuart McAdam. I don't want people talking about her again—"

I heard a crash of breaking china in a room behind us.

"That damn cat!" She hurried out. I heard a hiss and a slam. She came back muttering. "I thought it was Lydia, here to speak for herself. I don't know why she ain't in here for breakfast, but sometimes she does sleep late."

Sighing, she wiped her hands on the red-checked apron and sat down in a straight-backed chair across the room, her head cocked to listen. All I heard was the clock's slow tick. Looking around the dark and barren room, found my eyes fixed on a white-bearded man in a photo on the table beside the heavy Bible.

"That Lydia!" She burst out again in the same tone of resigned frustration. "Warren and I sweated our lives away to make her a good Christian home, with a better chance than we ever had, but she grew up—"

The cat had meowed. She paused to listen again.

"Grew up wild." Her voice sank into weary despair. "Mr. Starker did punish her when he had to, but he baptized her the day she was three. He preached to her and prayed over her, but she never found Christ. Run away from home before she turned thirteen. The cops brought her back, but she run away again. And look at her now."

"Is she all that bad?"

"If you don't know—" She squinted the good eye again, trying to measure me. "You're sure she did call this morning?"

"Half an hour ago."

With a skeptical shrug, she looked at the clock.

"I got her breakfast ready. Biscuits hot. Grapefruit cut the way she likes it. Bacon fried and eggs ready to scramble. The only decent meal she ever gets. She ought to be here."

She pointed at the photo by the Bible.

"That's Mr. Starker." Her voice sank reverently. "A man of God. He was a missionary back from Africa when I met him. He run an honest business till his heart went bad, and served Christ all his life. He preached against the Devil-brained baby-killers in Washington and right here in the county. He prayed for the right to worship God and teach His worship in the schools. He struggled every way he knew to save our daughter from the black mouth of Hell.

"And now she dishonors his name."

I had no answer for that. The clock kept counting its slow seconds till at last I saw her shift impatiently.

"Can't you call her?" I asked. "She seemed so anxious to see me."

"Maybe she thought better of it. You can see she just ain't here."

"Maybe you ought to find out why."

She bristled.

"Mister, I don't need no damn fool advice from you. Lydia don't like to be bothered, not since I found the condoms and smelled marijuana smoke in her room. It's back of the house in what used to be a garage. She keeps her door locked and says what she does there ain't no business of mine."

The old clock began to toll the hour.

"Six." Decisively, she stood up. "You're wasting your time. If she was ever up, she's gone back to sleep."

"Won't you knock on her door? She said she had something important—"

"Good-bye, Mr. Barstow." She waved me out. "She never liked nosy reporters. I doubt she likes you."

———

On the walk outside, I saw a car parked on the drive in front of what must once have been a garage. The old doorway had been bricked up, the new wall broken by a window and new entrance. The window blind was drawn. The new door hung open. Burst open, I saw, the lock splintered out of the frame.

A telephone was ringing inside.

I stepped closer and stopped to listen. Silence, except for the impatient phone. I walked to the shattered door, called Lydia's name, heard no answer. I walked inside.

One narrow room, an unmade sofa bed on one side, shelves of well-worn books and a kitchen counter on the other. Coffee perking on the counter. Two doors at the back of the room were open. One showed a narrow closet, clothing hung on a rack, the other a basin and toilet.

And two naked legs sprawled on the floor.

Lydia lay in the doorway, staring blindly at the ceiling. A blue terry cloth robe had been ripped half off her, one arm still in the sleeve. The hilt of a heavy kitchen knife thrust up between her breasts. Blood made a crimson sash around her torso and soaked the robe beneath her. She had been drying her hair. The broken dryer lay beside her. Three oak acorns were spaced around her head on the golden fan of her loose, blood-spattered hair.

I stared down at her, racked with shock and pity. Her eyes were wide, her mouth slightly open, fine teeth shining. Pale from loss of blood, her face seemed strangely composed, almost as if she slept. It still held some faint ghost of the life and charm I recalled. I stood there sick with shock till the ringing phone broke into my daze. I picked it up.

"Acorn Five?" a male voice asked. I thought it had a slight foreign accent. "Acorn Five."

I hung up. Back beside Lydia, I called her name. She didn't move. I bent to feel for a pulse. Her wrist was lax and dead, but I found a cryptophone in her hand. I put it to my ear. There was only silence, till I heard Mrs. Starker's hoarse scream close behind me.

"Murder! He's killed my daughter!"

She shrieked and fled when I turned.

Running for my bike, I found the cryptophone still in my hand, sticky with Lydia's blood. I dropped it into my shirt pocket, wheeled the bike across the sidewalk, and pedaled up Walnut as fast as I could.

Police cars were soon howling behind me.

CHAPTER ELEVEN

BLIND TERROR . . .

My heart thudding, I pedaled frantically. Lydia's image filled my mind, the blade between her pale-nippled breasts, the blood-freckled fan of her hair. Her mother's shriek echoed in my ears, louder than the sirens.

At six, the town was only waking. I heard a whining lawn mower. Far off, a rooster crowed. A dog barked. A battered pickup roared past, loaded with an upright refrigerator, a mattress and a motorcycle, all anchored with ropes. The sirens came closer. Two blocks up Walnut, I turned into Sixth. Three blocks farther, I wheeled into an empty alley and stopped to think.

The stupidity of flight broke over me. Mrs. Starker had seen me standing over Lydia's body, her blood on my hand. My fingerprints would be found on the telephone. Lydia's bloodstained cryptophone was still in my shirt pocket, where I had dropped it on the chance of some clue to the killing.

I couldn't go back to my room. Not since I'd left my *Freeman*

press card with Mrs. Starker. Bull Burleigh was chief of police as
well as sheriff since the city-county union. He and Hunn would be
as skeptical as Lydia's mother had been about anything I could say.
Call a lawyer? Kit Moorhawk was the only one I knew. Even as a
fellow member of the Citizens Congress, he would have little reason
to defend me.

Yet, even with nowhere to go, I had to move. Still breathing
hard and shaken with the nausea of terror, I was about to mount
my bike again when a cryptophone beeped. Lydia's? It was my own,
snapped to my belt. I put it to my ear and heard Beth's voice.

"Clay, you've got a problem."

"You're telling me!"

"Where are you?"

"In the alley off Sixth, between Hazel and Pecan."

"Stay there till I can pick you up."

I leaned my bike against a dumpster and stood waiting, listening to the sirens. A dog came by, sniffed at my shoes, ran on. A
moving van crept down Sixth, the driver craning to find house numbers. He glanced at me. Beth was suddenly beside me in the alley,
leaning out of a quiet electric sedan.

"Leave your bike," she said. "Get in the back. Down out of
sight."

I left the bike and crouched down in the back of the car, feeling
stunned and utterly bewildered, this miraculous rescue as hard to
believe as was the sight of Lydia with the knife in her heart. Beth
drove carefully, stopping for signs or lights. The last stop was in a
garage. Light dimmed and I heard the door closing.

"Okay, Mr. Barstow. Come on in."

I followed her into a big kitchen and stood looking around,
grateful but hardly daring to relax. The walls were hung with historic antiques: a double-bitted axe, a powder horn, a bullet mold,
rusty implements I didn't recognize. An enlarged Matthew Brady
battlefield photograph hung over a fieldstone fireplace at the end of
the room, flanked by long-barreled Civil War rifles that must have
fired Minié balls. A breakfast table was set for two. An aging black

woman in a white apron and a prim white cap stood beside the stove, staring at me in silent astonishment.

"Orinda," Beth said. "This is Mr. Barstow. Set a place for him."

"Yes, ma'am."

Orinda nodded at me and turned to get dishes from the cabinet.

"My father's in the garden," Beth said. "I'll call him in."

"I heard about you on the infonet." Calmly curious, Orinda looked at me when she was gone. "They say you murdered Miss Lydia Starker and ran away."

"I did run. I didn't kill anybody."

"I never said you did." She was staring at my hands. "Do you want to wash?"

In my daze, I'd forgotten the blood. She showed me to a bathroom and handed me a clean towel. When I came out, Beth had returned with her father, Colin McAdam, in brown chinos and a white sweat shirt. I knew him from the portrait in her office, though time had stooped his thin shoulders and silvered his flowing hair. He had brought a basket of ripe tomatoes and summer squash. Handing them to Orinda, he turned to look at me.

"Mr. Clay Barstow." She introduced me rather formally. "Alden Kirk's brother and research assistant. He came to investigate his brother's death and stayed here in spite of my advice."

"I met your brother." He gave me a vigorous hand. "Rather liked him, but I think he found more terror than he came to look for."

"About Lydia Starker?" I turned to Beth. "And how you came to pick me up? I never expected—" I looked at her father and back at her. "I did see Lydia dead. It knocked me out."

She turned to her father. "Dad, are you in touch with Stuart?"

"Stuart?" He shrugged, with an uneasy laugh. "Always Stuart. His rally was on the infonet, I don't know why. A mad world! Breakfast might help us think a little straighter."

Orinda had set another plate. He waved us toward the table

and we bowed our heads while he murmured grace. Orinda poured coffee, passed hot biscuits and bacon. He ate a bowl of oatmeal and asked her to slice his fresh tomatoes. Beth buttered a biscuit, took a slice of bacon, and left them untasted on her plate. Her coffee cup quivered and almost splashed when she lifted it. I drank a little coffee and sat trying to recover myself till McAdam grinned at me, wryly sympathetic.

"You're in quite a deep hole, Barstow."

"Which he dug himself," Beth said. "In spite of me."

"Now she wants to pull you out."

"I don't want his blood on my hands, if I gave his little game away."

"In that case," he said, "I'll stand by. Relax and eat your breakfast."

He asked Orinda to pass the food again and bring a jar of her apricot preserves. The tomatoes were temptingly red and juicy, tangily sweet when I tasted a slice. The biscuits were thin and brown and crusty. The butter was real. When he urged me to try the jam it had the flavor of summer. Suddenly ravenous, I was the last to push my plate away. Orinda cleared the table and refilled our coffee cups.

"Now, about your guest?" Colin turned from Beth to me. "You are a fugitive from justice?"

"But not the killer." I looked into his time-seamed face, trying to see if he believed me. "Lydia Starker was dead when I got to her room. Her mother saw me standing over her body, blood on my hands. I heard the cops coming and panicked."

He studied me intently.

"Do you want to surrender?"

"I think I need a lawyer."

"That might not save you." Beth shook her head. "Hunn and Burleigh are running hard for reelection. They seemed to feel that your brother was asking for what he got. They'd love a juicy infonet sensation for the campaign. With Mrs. Starker for a witness, they could nail you."

"Mr. Barstow," her father said slowly, "you're in quite a pickle."

Miserably, I nodded. "Mrs. Starker has my press card. I can't go home. Or anywhere."

"What made you go there?"

"Lydia called me. Promised to tell me who mailed the bomb to my brother. She sounded desperate. Urged for me to hurry. Do you think—" I looked at him and then at Beth. "Could my brother's killers have got her too?"

"If they did—" He gave me a probing glance. "They'll assume that she did tell you. I'd say you're in the same danger she and your brother were."

Beth nodded. "That's why I picked him up."

"Not a pretty picture." McAdam shook his head, absently holding his cup for Orinda to fill it again. "So many people hate the government, hate private capitalism, hate our whole system. Some of them are longing for their own Red October, their own Nazi *putsch.*"

Remembering that he had been a historian with a habit of analysis, I tried to listen patiently.

"Yet they're never evil in their own minds. Nobody is. A point your brother made when he was here for dinner. They're concerned about the same problems that bother everybody, but they're convinced that their answers are the only answers. That's what makes them dangerous. A kind of contagious insanity. Even good people catch it."

"You and Alden Kirk," Beth said to her father, shaking her head. "Professional pessimists. Always looking for troubles that seldom come. I think you've brooded too long on the evils of slavery."

"Long enough to see new shapes of slavery all around us. The evil heritage keeps coming down to every new generation." He shrugged and sipped his coffee, frowning at her. "You knew Lydia. Do you remember anything that might give us a clue?"

"Nothing that connects." Her face was pinched with pain. "Though I was on the phone with her till the moment she died."

"You were?" Astonishment sharpened his voice. "Why?"

"She called me after she called Clay." She looked sick, her voice hushed and quivering. "Called on a cryptophone Rob had given her. I heard her die. It was dreadful."

"Yes?" He waited.

"Nothing I could do." A helpless shrug. "She was begging for help. Trying to tell me anything she could, but it happened too fast. All over in just a few seconds. She had no time to say much of anything."

She shivered, her hands clenched tight, and sat a long time staring into her empty coffee cup before she looked up and went on.

"She was just out of the shower, drying her hair, when she heard them. She had me call the cops, and tried to describe them. Two big men in ski masks. One she thought she'd seen marching with the militia, but she gave me no name.

"She screamed for her mother, but nothing stopped them. One had a gun. The other told him not to shoot. He grabbed a knife off the kitchen shelf and came at her with that. She was screaming again when her voice changed to a bubble. One of them muttered something I'm not sure I got. It sounded like 'Score one more for Shadow Man.' The other snapped at him, 'Shut up and come on.' I heard them tramping out. That was all.

"Lydia Starker." Orinda was offering the biscuits and bacon again. Beth shook her head and went on, her voice hushed almost to a whisper. "In first grade she was my best friend. She was always begging to stay the night with me, to get away from her folks. I never blamed her, not since I stayed once with her."

She made a face.

"Cold people. Cruel as their cruel God. Her mother scolded her about her homework and made her mop the kitchen twice because she'd left a dry spot. We couldn't play outside or watch TV. Before breakfast, her father made us sit straight with our heads bowed while he read a chapter from the Bible and prayed a long time in a dismal voice. We had to eat oatmeal, and Lydia hated oatmeal."

She grinned at her father.

"I never went back, but I admired her. A free spirit. She used to run away from home. The first time I let her hide in our barn till the Starkers got here with the cops. The last time she rode a bus to Louisville to be a singer. She had ambition and looks I used to envy, but never had much luck. Never got beyond the nightclub gigs.

"She told me she'd tried life as a call girl. Not bad, she said, so long as you picked the right johns. I was glad when Stuart found her and brought her home. He said he was going to marry her, but he never did. She finally left him. Went back to college till her money ran out. Moorhawk's secretary for a year or so. Worked for Pepperlake on the *Freeman*. Lately she'd been on the infonet desk at KRIF. We always kept in touch, but there must have been a lot she never told me."

"So you're involved," her father said. "If the cops find a record of the call."

"They won't." I pulled Lydia's cryptophone out of my shirt pocket. "It was still in her hand. I'd picked it up. I found it still with me when I got to my bike."

Uneasily, he frowned at the smear of drying blood and then at Beth.

"So you're obstructing justice," he told her. "Harboring a fugitive. Concealing evidence." He nodded soberly at me. "What are you going to do with Mr. Barstow?"

"Hide him here," she said.

CHAPTER TWELVE

"*I CAN'T ASK* you to do that," I tried to protest. "If you'll just drive me somewhere out of town—"

"Where would you go?"

I didn't know.

"You can't go home to Georgetown." Beth was crisply decisive. "Or even call. The police will be warning travel facilities, putting up road blocks, tapping phones."

I sat dumb, feeling sick, remembering how Marion had begged me not to come here and how Tim had taken my hand with his grave wish that I got back safe. Orinda was offering coffee. I shook my head and pulled out my wallet. Two fives and a one, besides the credit cards.

"Get rid of the plastic," Beth said. "Better get rid of the wallet. You can't write a check. You can't buy a ticket. You can't show your face. They'll have your photo on the infonet."

"You're all in danger if you try to keep me here."

"In danger if we don't." McAdam let Orinda fill his cup. He

started to sip, set it down and looked sharply at me. "I've lived with problems. My wife was a difficult woman. Always too hard on Stuart, made him the rebel he is." He gave Beth a quizzical glance. "My children have conditioned me to surprises, but this is a bigger shock than most."

"I saw no choice," Beth told him. "I was already in it up to my neck. They know I was Lydia's friend. They'll have records of my calls to her and the cops. And—" She caught herself, frowning. "That's not all."

After a moment of silence, her father cast her a sharp look. He asked, "Was there any witness to your dramatic rescue?"

"Who knows?"

"Desperate people." With a philosophic shrug, he sipped his coffee. "Desperate times."

"Maybe not that desperate." A little relaxed, Beth turned to me. "I hope nobody saw me pick you up. You can trust Orinda. All you have to do is keep out of sight."

"For how long?" McAdam asked.

"Till we can manage something better."

"I was desperate enough," I said. "I don't know how to thank you."

"No thanks due." Beth's quick smile cheered me a little. I did need cheer. "I'm not in your fix, but I don't want questions. Certainly not from Burleigh and his crew. They have it in for us McAdams."

"What's done is done. Maybe overdone." McAdam sat back in his chair and asked Orinda to pass the breakfast again. Beth accepted her plate. I stirred cream in my coffee.

"I used to smoke cigars," he told me. "Beth cut me off when she was still a kid. I could use a good Havana now."

He pushed his cup away and wanted to know about my life and my work with my brother.

"I reviewed his book for one of the infonet history journals," he told me. "It struck me as a penetrating look at unrest in America."

When we left the table, he told Orinda to settle me in. She showed me to a room walled with shelves full of old law books, their spines stamped in faded gold. His father had been a lawyer, she said, who built it for an office. It had a private bath and a door to the walk outside. The cold air had a dry bite of dust and stagnation.

Stuart had taken the room when his grandfather died. The walls above the bookcases were hung with images of his boyhood heroes. A dusty print of Hannibal in Carthaginian armor, riding an elephant through an icy gorge in the Alps. An amateurish oil painting of John Hunt Morgan, the Confederate guerrilla leader, charging up a hill on a great black horse, his red saber held high. Neil Armstrong climbing down to the Moon.

Stuart had come home to stay through the trial before he went to prison. Clothing of his still hung in the closet. In a little drawer in the bedside table, I found a nine-millimeter automatic with a full clip and a cartridge in the chamber. An empty clip and a box of ammunition lay beside it. I left it where it was, thinking I might need it.

He had also left a good infotel set. Eager for news, I found financial channels, sports channels, foreign channels, too many channels. Most of them were interactive, begging me to click for footnotes, video clips, references, data I didn't want, more than enough to keep me at the monitor through my long days there following reports on the Starker case and wondering which to believe.

The stated sources were commonly "backgrounders" from nameless "high officials." Most of them evoked indignant denials from actual high officials, but they kept me puzzled and appalled. Lydia had been a cunning terrorist, so one story ran, the head of a secret cell. Searching her apartment, the FBI had found papers confirming the existence of her underground gang, which called itself Shadow Hand.

The first mission of her cell had been to eliminate Alden Kirk, who had learned too much about the group. A typed note signed Shadow King read *Congrats on K. disposal.* The other known member was Kirk's half-brother, Clayton Barstow. Authorities believed that he had infiltrated the group and killed Lydia to avenge Kirk's death.

Director Garlesh had refused to comment on the story, but Barstow was a fugitive now, on the most-wanted list. The FBI was circulating his description and a photo Pepperlake had taken when he joined the *Freeman* staff. The Bureau wanted him not only for the Starker murder but for what he might know about the Shadow gang. If captured, he was expected to testify in return for a plea bargain to save his life.

Those were strange days. Beth went to her college job. McAdam spent the mornings in his gardens, most of the afternoons at work on his history of slavery. I stayed in my room, alone with the infonet, jumping in startlement at every unexpected sound, trying to make some sense of the stories and my predicament.

Staring day after day of contradictory news reports and sage comments on the unrest in middle America, I tried and failed to make sense of what I heard. I left the monitor for the bathroom, for coffee I didn't want, or to pace the room like a rat in a trap. I skimmed McAdam's books about Kentucky pioneers and African slavers till I was sick of history. I thought of Marion and Tim, longing for something like Rob's cryptophones, for any way to have word reach them safely.

Beth and her father gave me a few hours of relief when they were at home for meals. Her desperate tension was only half concealed, but he seemed philosophical.

"Don't sweat it." He made mint juleps before dinner, generous with the bourbon. "We've placed our bets. All we can do is wait for the draw."

Waiting was hard. I was numb from the shock and pain of Lydia's death, and haunted with the riddles of it. Who had slaughtered her? How had she really known who killed Alden? Was that knowledge, or some suspicion of it, the trouble she had hinted at, and the reason she died? I pondered those confusing speculations on the infonet and pressed Beth and her father for clues they were never able to give me.

"The world's an ugly mess," he muttered one evening over his julep. "I call myself a historian. I ought to understand our crisis better than I do, but I try to blame it on a shift of paradigms due to the information revolution."

I asked what he meant.

"When something baffles me, I go back to basics." He contemplated his julep, took a solemn sip, and nodded in appreciation before he went on. "Quoting myself, I like to say we're all born naked screaming individuals with no concerns except ourselves, but trapped in the eternal human dilemma. The species is gregarious. We can't survive outside the social group, the family, the tribe, the nation—or often now the corporation or the street gang or the outlaw militia.

"That's the new paradigm. In our information age, the group has gone global, and we individuals have to fight multiplied pressures and controls. The American worker has to compete with a hungry peasant in China. A master terrorist can work his puppets to plant a car bomb anywhere. Our own bureaucrats have shut Roy's company down because they're blind to change."

I had to ask if his new paradigm had murdered my brother or Lydia.

"Who knows?" He shrugged and thought about it. "The old war goes on, the private self against society, but information science is a brand new weapon in the hands of restless insurgents against the past. We're herd animals. Instinct drives us to follow our leaders, now the new electronic overlords. The old power kings are all in danger from any malcontent who can grasp the information blade."

"So what?" Beth frowned. "What do you expect?"

"All your brother feared." With a glance at me, he raised his glass as if to toast Alden's memory. "New power brokers will be springing up everywhere, driven by a thousand conflicting interests and agendas, attacking every old authority. It could mean—" He paused to shake his head. "Revolution."

"Revolution?" Her voice quickened. "Here?"

"Everywhere. We're global now." He gestured at the wall. "An alarming word when you recall the Bastille or Red October, but our own American Revolution was rather civilized. This new one will be quite a different game. I hope not so bloody."

"You expect disorder?"

"I'm afraid. We have the information dagger, forged by men like Roy but lost beyond control. We have those who will use it, and those who would kill to stop its use. The old order is in terror of the new. I'd expect disorder in between." He looked at me. "Your brother's killers, and Lydia's, might be found among those electronic rebels, if you knew where to look."

But of course I didn't know.

Trying, perhaps, to ease our strain, he talked about his history of slavery, The first volume, on slavery in the Old World, was finished and ready for the printer. The second, on the slave trade, had gone to his editors. He was spending his afternoons on the third, slavery in America.

"On a damn computer," he muttered. "Because I can't find anybody able to take dictation."

Orinda had served the juleps with straws, the glasses cradled in bowls of ice. He sucked at his, with an appreciative nod for her, and turned to me.

"I've spent a lot of my life on the project. It has changed me. I believed in human progress, back when I began. I thought we'd put the worst of our history behind us. I was wrong." Moodily, he shook his head. "When you know the absolute inhumanity of the slave hunters, the slave ships, the slave markets, the slave drivers—" His face twisted. "It haunts me. It has soured my view of humankind. I know too much history to expect anything better to come."

The hunch of his lean old shoulders was almost a shudder, but after a brief silence he gave Beth an affectionate nod.

"Being younger, my kids have brighter views. Beth wrote a thesis on American utopias. Rob has always dreamed of some new gadget that would transform our unhappy Earth to an instant paradise. Stuart would lead a new revolution if he could."

He paused to peer sharply at me.

"Your brother Alden fell somewhere in between, neither a crazy optimist nor the pessimist I've become. He saw terror growing, but wrote his book to spur us toward escape. His death seems to show some coming social breakdown nearer and more dreadful than anything Stuart could hope to stop. As for myself—"

He sighed and pulled again on the julep.

"In spite of Rob and all his new technologies, I can't help expecting a future darker than the past."

He left to guide a tour of Civil War battlegrounds. Beth went to her classes. Orinda and I were alone when they were gone. She cleaned the house and made lunch for me. We ate at the kitchen table, sitting together when I insisted. As we got to know each other, she talked about her life. The earliest ancestors she knew about had come over the Cumberlands with old Calvin McAdam. Two generations later, one had learned to read and write and then gone to Harvard with his owner as a McAdam house boy.

The plantation had been divided, she said, back before the War between the States. Josh and Marcus were McAdam twins. Josh had freed his slaves before Fort Sumter, and fought for the Union. Marcus left his wife to care for an infant son and went to join the Rebs; he died in Pickett's charge. Orinda's folks were still on the plantation, working for Josh's widow, when he got home from Appomatox to put his world back together.

"I'm the last of my people," she said. "The last here where we belong."

She drank hot black tea at lunch, and I shared it with her.

"A bad time for blacks." She offered lemon or sugar. "I guess there never was a good time for us, but in a way I think it's harder now. Except maybe for the fat cat Uncle Toms. I had a son named

Luke. Drafted to Viet Nam and come home crazy with drugs. In jail and out the rest of his life. Finally died of an overdose.

"He left a girl and a boy. The girl got to be a whore in Lexington. Sent me a thousand dollars once. Ten stiff new hundred-dollar bills. They made me vomit when I thought how she got them. My letters after that all came back. A pencil scrawl on the back of the last one said *Dead of Aids*.

"Jake was her brother. Two years younger. He come to live with me when Luke and his woman split. A good kid then. I loved him and tried to do my best, but he went bad in spite of me, just like his Daddy done. A lifer now in the Frankfort pen. It all goes to show your brother was right."

She saw my surprise.

"He was here for dinner. Talked to me. Asked about blacks here in the county, and wrote his name in the book for me. He seen our troubles." Her voice took on a bitter edge. "Did you watch the militia march?"

I nodded. "What about it?"

"If you never noticed, they's all white. They never say a word about us, but I know what they think. Law and order!" She sniffed. "They carry their guns and talk about law and order. It's their law. White law—if you don't mind."

She waited for my headshake.

"Stuart." She shook her head. "I've known him since he was born. I used to trot him on my knee and sing songs he liked. He was always after me when he got a little older, begging me to tell about the old McAdams back when they were the big men in the county. He was nice to me, mostly, but now—"

Lips pursed, she paused.

"He's head of them Kentucky Rifles. They load their guns and wait for trouble. Ready for black trouble, in some bad time when the anger breaks out. Maybe when blacks with no jobs and no money but drug money riot in the streets. Stuart and his Rifles are all set to move then, and show the world what they mean with their precious law and order. They want to wash down the streets with our black blood."

Somberly, she frowned at me.

"Mr. Barstow, I'm afraid of Stuart now."

A strange time, but not always dark. Beth made it wonderful. No longer hostile, she was now a warm and thoughtful companion who helped me deal with Lydia's death. Though I had to hide by day, at night I could walk outside in the big back yard, protected by a high cinderblock wall and brush and trees on the slopes beyond it.

Sometimes she walked with me. When my eyes had adjusted to the dark I could see her lean grace and the clean oval of her face. The night air carried the mild scent she wore. Sometimes she caught my arm when I might have stumbled over something in the dark. I felt her warmth, came to love her touch and her voice and just being with her. Sometimes we talked. I told her about my concern for Marion and Tim, and for little Angela, whose eyes had filled with tears when I kissed her good-bye.

"I know they must feel sick about you," she said. "I wish we could let them know you're safe, but that's a risk we just can't take."

Sometimes she spoke of herself.

"When I was a girl I used to feel trapped here in the old house and with all the generations of past McAdams. I wanted to get away. I loved to draw. Teachers said I had talent. I used to dream I could be an artist with a studio in New York or Paris."

"You could have been," I said. "I saw the portraits in your office."

"Some talent." Her shoulder had touched me in the dark; I felt her shrug. "Not enough. Out of high school, I went to Lexington to major in art. At the end of the first semester, my major professor set me straight about genius and talent. I felt terribly hurt, till I realized that he was saving me from a wasted life. I've always loved history the way my father does. I've been happy here, teaching it.

"Until this—"

She stopped and walked on in silence.

No longer enemies, we were strangers still, exploring each other with a mix of caution and delight. We walked a lot in silence, never quite certain what to ask or how to answer. We were silent, hand in hand, on that night when it was her turn to stumble. I caught her, held her closer than I meant to. She was electric in my arms, her mouth searching suddenly for mine. We needed no words till she moved to catch her breath and lead me back to the house.

I drew her toward my door.

"Not yet." Her whisper was hushed and breathless. "Not here. Not now." She tried to laugh. "It's no moment for romance. Not when the game can end any minute."

She caught my body hard against her, kissed me again, briefly but fiercely, and ran for her door.

I lay a long time that night. Thinking of her, thinking sadly of Lydia. Feeling almost safe, I'd locked the outside door and finally gone to sleep. I don't know what woke me. I sat up in bed knowing I was not alone. A cruel glare blinded me. Dazing pain exploded at the back of my skull. Rough hands seized my arms. Before I could get breath to yell for help, a hard palm sealed my mouth.

CHAPTER THIRTEEN

I WOKE SLOWLY from an endless, dreadful dream in which I was running naked through a bitter blizzard, bloodhounds behind me. I lay somewhere in the dark, shivering, pain drumming in my head. Listening, I heard wind in trees and a cricket chirping. Nothing else.

A surge of pain knocked me back when I tried to sit up. Nausea wrenched me. I vomited twice and lay there a long time, weak and trembling and miserably cold. The trees were dense black barriers around me, but a strip of sky overhead was lit with the stars of Orion, which Alden had taught me to recognize.

Fumbling with numb fingers, I found the hair on the back of my head sodden and damp with blood. I was still in the thin pajamas Stuart McAdam had left in his room. Drying blood had stuck them to my chest. Fallen leaves rustled under me when I tried to huddle against an icy wind.

In want of any shelter, I tried to stand. Pain exploded in my head, and I had to sink back. Crouching on all fours, I was sick again. I wiped my mouth on the pajama sleeve and squatted there a long time, numbed and aching, hopeless. Somehow I must have slept, because the treetops overhead were suddenly blazing with yellow sunlight.

The pounding in my head no longer quite so hard, I pushed to sit up. Something like a pebble turned under my palm: a large oak acorn, when I looked. It lay with two others around the leaves stained with blood from my head. I gathered them up and stared at them stupidly. Three acorns.

Acorn Three?

Peering around, I found the muddy ruts of a narrow, unpaved road walled with dense underbrush. Taller trees towered out of it here and there, but I saw no oaks. I recalled the acorn fragments left in the debris of the letter bomb, and the three acorns left in the blood around Lydia Stalker's head. Had they been a terrorist signature? Had Acorn Three planted a mole in the bureau? Botman, perhaps? Had he betrayed me to hide the way he betrayed my brother? I knew too little even to guess.

Too weak and sick to wonder, I reeled to my feet and limped to the road. It wound crookedly down a slope through rubble hills the strip-miners had left. I had no notion where it might lead, or what to do if it took me anywhere. Rocks and clods hurt my bare feet, and the mere act of walking took all my will.

I blundered on, too cold to stop moving, till a horn honked close behind me. My first thought was to dive into the underbrush and hide, but I had no strength for that, no time. I stumbled out of the ruts. A red pickup truck lurched to a stop beside me, the bed piled with hay. A black-stubbled man leaned out of the window, spat his cud of tobacco on the ground at my feet.

"Who the hell?" he shouted at me. "Who the hell are you?"

"Fred Rafton, from Baltimore." I groped for some believable lie. "Can you give me a lift?"

He spat again, squinting at me searchingly.

"What happened to you?"

"I was robbed." Desperate invention. "I had to stop for a truck parked across both lanes in an underpass. Two men ran up behind me. Dragged me out of the car, beat me up, took my clothes. Finally dumped me back there in the woods."

"Rough customers." He reached for his telephone. "I'll call the cops."

"Not yet," I said. "I'm sick and freezing. Can't you get help for me first?"

Shrewd eyes narrowed under thick black brows, he studied me again.

"Look at me," I begged him. "You can see the fix I'm in."

"What do you do?"

"I'm an accountant for a tax attorney back in Baltimore."

"Have you got money?"

"Not on me. They took my wallet, everything. I do have a bank account, a couple thousand in it, when I get back home."

"You are in sad shape." He leaned abruptly to open the pickup door. "Get in. I'll drive you to my place and let you wash up." His hard gray eyes measured me. "Near enough my size. I've got something you can wear. Pay me when you can."

I scrambled inside. He turned the heater up, and I huddled gratefully into its warmth. He drove on down the bumpy road, winding through the wilderness grown up since the strip-miners stopped. The radio was reporting a fire in McAdam. I caught a few words.

". . . under arrest. Pastor Garron of the Temple of the Sword calls him a heroic soldier of God, now in the red hands of Satan."

He snapped it off.

"That damned abortion clinic in McAdam. Burnt to the ground last night. Arson, Burleigh says. The firebug left a barrel of gasoline in a pickup parked against the building. Blowed up before he got away. Blast knocked him out and scorched the hair off his head. Firemen picked him up."

Out of the woods, we turned into a busy highway. I asked where we were.

"Lexington road." He jerked his head. "McAdam's ten miles behind us."

A few miles farther, he pulled off and parked on a gravel drive in front of a gray-painted farmhouse that looked a century old. A thickset woman in a yellow robe came out on the stoop and pushed up her steel-rimmed glasses to glare at me suspiciously.

"Who you got?"

"Poor guy beat up." He walked past her, with a nod for me to follow into the house. The pickup keys clinked as he dropped them beside a flower pot on a little table at the door. "In bad shape. I said we'd give him a hand."

"Let the cops—"

"He don't want the cops. No money on him, but he says he'll mail me a check when he gets back to Baltimore. Let him clean up. Look for things of mine he can wear."

Muttering under her breath, she jerked her head for me to follow and showed me through a cluttered living room into a bedroom with a bath beyond it.

"Git outa them bloody rags. Throw 'em in the trash."

She gave me a towel and a thin sliver of soap, and slammed the bedroom door.

I stripped the pajamas off, used the toilet, and ran the shower hot. The water burned the wound in my scalp and streamed pink down my torso. The heat of it stopped the shivering and restored a little life. I was out on the bath mat, toweling down, when I heard the woman's angry voice:

"—damn fool! Are you crazy?"

The man said something I didn't hear.

"He could cut our throats! Get him out of here!"

I tiptoed to the door and put my ear against it.

"Quiet, Marcy!" He was shushing her softly. "Don't you tip him off. I know he's desperate, but the radio says he's worth a hundred thousand dollars. The cops are on the way."

"Load the shotgun!" She was hardly quieted. "Call the cops again."

I dressed as fast as I could. They had left a shirt and khaki trousers on the bed, but no socks or underwear. The faded denim shirt was nearly too tight to button, the trousers hung loose. I snatched a belt off a hook to hold them up, a pair of filthy sneakers off the closet floor. They pinched my toes, but I got them on and eased the door open.

They were in the kitchen when I came out, the angry woman on the telephone.

"Give 'em time." Whispering hoarsely, he tried again to silence her. "He'll be hungry. Make him some breakfast."

"The hell I will! He could butcher us like pigs—"

The front door was open. I snatched the keys and ran toward the pickup. She was still ranting, but he heard the motor start and dashed out of the house, yelling at me. She came behind him with the shotgun. It took me two tries to get the cranky stick shift in gear, and bird shot peppered the cab before I reached the highway. Waiting there for space in a stream of heavy trucks and vacationers hauling boats, I heard the shotgun boom again.

On the pavement at last, I turned toward Lexington and kept the pickup well below the legal limit. A few miles down the road, I pulled into a rest area where a dozen vehicles had stopped. A man in boots and a wide-brimmed western hat was walking toward the toilet from a Jeep with an empty horse trailer in tow.

I parked the pickup beside it, climbed into the trailer, kicked a pile of manure out of the way and lay flat on the floor. The driver took an eternity in the toilet. Police sirens were wailing back toward McAdam before I heard the starter whine. The motor finally coughed, and we lurched back toward the Lexington road.

CHAPTER FOURTEEN

EARLY ONE NIGHT five days later, I limped up the alley behind the old Georgetown house. The cops and the Feds had probably staked it out, I thought, on the chance that I might come home, but I had nowhere else to go, nor way or will to go any farther.

Five days of desperate flight, desperate survival. One night I had slept in a barn. Another night, invited by rolled-up newspapers on the lawn, I had broken into an empty house, raided the kitchen, slept a few hours, and stolen a jacket. My feet were blistered in those pinching sneakers, the scalp wound had not healed, I felt faint and light-headed from hunger. But fortune had sometimes favored me. I was alive and free.

I found the footholds in the cinderblock wall that Alden had helped me chisel. Used up as I was, they were harder to climb than they had been when I was five years old, but they got me over the top. The house was dark. Nobody came when I knocked and shouted and rattled the kitchen door, but the key was still where Alden had kept it, in a little magnetic box struck under the steel shelf of the barbecue grill.

The house was hushed and cold when I got inside. I yelled and yelled again, and heard no sound. My hand was on a light switch, before I caught myself and blundered through the gloom to the kitchen sink. Water had been hard to find. I gulped too much, threw it up, leaned on the counter till I could drink again.

My eyes were adjusting to the dim little night lights Marion had bought when the threats to Alden had begun to haunt her. Whistling against the dead silence, I walked through the empty front room and the den, climbed the stair. Everything was neat and clean as she had always kept it, beds made, fresh towels in the bath. No hint of violence or disorder. She and the children were simply gone.

Where?

Perhaps to her sister's? The older sister, my Aunt Julia, was a retired nurse now, with a home on the shore of Puget Sound. The two were still close in spite of the distance, visiting nearly every Sunday by phone or infonet. Perhaps she had offered refuge when Marion wanted to escape the police and the media.

Perhaps. I dared not risk a call to ask.

In my own room, I found a flashlight and used it cautiously. Marion must have cleaned the floor, but everything was just as I had left it. I shucked off that tight shirt and the baggy pants and took a long hot shower. The scalp wound stung from the soap. I found antibiotic ointment for it, got into wonderfully clean clothing, and went back to the kitchen.

Ravenous, I found a feast in the refrigerator. Most of a cold rump roast. A leftover broccoli casserole. A glass of cold milk and a slab of pound cake. Bloated with it, I got back to my room and slept till the phone woke me. Nearly noon next day, when I looked at the clock.

Marion calling?

I reached for it with a groggy eagerness, but checked myself before I touched it. Who would hear me? Cops staking out the house? Agent Botman? Acorn Three? Julia, concerned about her sister? Or only a subscription solicitor? In any case a wiretap was surely on the line.

The blinds and curtains were tightly drawn, but the gray daylight seeping through let me explore the house again. Marion's car was still in the garage—Alden, away so much and using rental cars, had sold his own. Upstairs again, I found a bit of order restored to his office. His blood was gone from the floor. A new desk stood where his had been, neatly stacked with the notes and drafts the bomb had scattered, all in new manila folders.

Unlocking the wall safe, I found its contents undisturbed. His wallet lay in the wall safe were Tim had left it. Behind it, I discovered a brown-cased cryptophone. No doubt the one Rob McAdam had given him. Eagerly, I clicked the stud to extend the tiny microphone.

I could call Beth! Find if she and her father had been harmed by the men who shanghaied me. Ask if she knew who they were. Let her know I was still alive. Tell her about the three acorns I'd found in the mud by my head. Most of all, I wanted simply to hear her voice, to know that she was safe.

But of course I couldn't. I clicked the stud again and put the little instrument back in the safe. Even though the content of its signals might be secure, they would be transmitted through commercial satellite. Wiretappers would surely recognize the cryptophone code, locate the source, descend upon me.

Downstairs again, I found a new infotel set in the den. Bought, perhaps, because Marion wanted more news from McAdam County than had come over the single infonet channel on the old TV. I found the Washington headline channel.

"—McAdam County crisis." The anchor was Tex Horn, an ex-model who had made his name as an infonet actor. He affected a West Texas drawl and wore a white Western hat tipped far back. "Washintel WebWatch One brings you a special update from Ramona Del Rio, our observer on the spot—a hot spot now."

Ramona Del Rio was a lithe, doll-faced brunette with a stylish snow-white strand through her sleek black hair.

"Actual rebellion!" Her voice and look and words seemed a bit too theatrical. I wondered if she wrote her own copy, but her delivery was briskly professional. "The social historian Alden Kirk had spent the last few weeks of his life in McAdam County, documenting the sources of conflict and unrest for his infonet series and a book he never finished.

"The simmering tensions here began boiling over just a week ago, with the burning of an abortion clinic, an act of defiance against a woman's legal right to choose. Differences run deep, with threats of outright violence. Listen to Joel Garron—he calls himself 'Father Garron'—head of a militant sect, the Temple of the Sword."

She showed a brief clip of Garron on his pulpit, shaking his rawboned fist and calling the wrath of God down upon Dr. Stuben Ryke, "a red-handed baby-killer" engaged in the "Satanic slaughter of the innocent unborn."

Her sardonic tone grew serious.

"The alleged arsonist—"

She showed a clip of Sheriff Burleigh and District Attorney Hunn, seated with another man at a table in the county jail, steel-barred cell walls behind them. The third man wore yellow-striped prison coveralls. His hands lay on the table in front of him, linked with steel cuffs. A white bandage covered the top of his head.

"Benjamin Coon." He shrugged and gave the lens a carefree grin.

"A clear case of arson." Hunn's hard fox-face wore a slight smile; clearly he relished the camera. "The arsonist backed a pickup truck loaded with three barrels of gasoline into the front door of the clinic. He touched it off and ran, but the blast of a premature explosion caught him only a few yards away. He was blown off his feet and knocked unconscious. Firemen arrived in time to save his life.

"We have him here."

Smiling wider, Hunn gestured at Coon.

"Thank you Mr. Hunn." On the screen again, Del Rio nodded brightly and spoke to the camera. "That's the police story, but listen to Colonel Stuart McAdam, commander of a local militia unit, the Kentucky Rifles."

The lens caught Stuart on his horse, lean and dramatic, gleaming with the gold braid and bright gold buttons on that trim crimson jacket. It zoomed to his face. Beth's high-cheeked oval face, somehow transformed into a supercilious mask.

"A flimsy accusation." He bowed to the camera, with a shrug at the charge. "My good friends Burleigh and Hunn are running for reelection." He smiled with bland disdain. "They seem willing, unfortunately, to sacrifice an innocent man on the altar of their ambitions. Our county knows Coon. I knew his good father. I've cheered his touchdown passes. He is no arsonist. Certainly no murderer."

The word arsonist was a highlighted hot link. I clicked on it and saw the clinic as it had been, a modest brick building, the glass door lettered in black.

STUBEN RYKE, MD

Obstetrics and Gynecology

That dissolved into a close shot of a stout little man in a white jacket, lips primly pursed, smiling rather diffidently into the camera.

". . . victim of the blast," Del Rio's vibrant news voice came back. "Ironically, Ryke had returned to the building to place an order for a new security system. Repeated threats from militant fanatics had become too alarming to be ignored. Burned beyond recognition, his body was identified by his dentist."

His image faded.

". . . injustice rampant!" Stuart was back, standing now in Garron's pulpit, the silver sword towering over him. "Coon is no firebug, but in fact a hero, as his attorney promises to prove. He was driving past the clinic when he saw the fire. He parked his car near the clinic. He was running toward the burning clinic, attempting to rescue Dr. Ryke when the explosion caught him. As it happens, he saw the actual arsonist in flight from the scene."

My own picture flashed across the monitor.

". . . Clayton Barstow." Del Rio again. "Already wanted for the murder of Lydia Starker. A McAdam county farmer, Cyrus Kryer, has identified him as the fugitive he found on the morning after the fire, hiding in a strip-mined area near his home. Probably caught by his own firebomb, he was clad in charred and bloodstained rags. The Kryers gave him clean clothing and offered him food. He robbed them, seized their pickup, and fled."

Kryer and his wife were on the screen for a moment, she crimson in the face and shaking a knobby fist, he holding her arm to restrain her.

". . . happened a week ago," Del Rio's crisp news voice came back. "The object of a nationwide hunt, Barstow is still at large. Charged with the murder of Lydia Starker, he is wanted by the FBI for interrogation in connection with the unexplained disappearance of Special Agent Monty Botman. With the addition of funds raised by the Kentucky Rifles and the Border Bank, the rewards for his apprehension now total two hundred thousand dollars.

"As for the other suspect, Coon, he is still in the McAdam county jail, held on charge of arson and the murder. Bond has been denied, but he belongs to an influential militia unit that is demanding his immediate release."

The tube flickered and I saw Del Rio standing on a McAdam street corner. The county courthouse rose in the background, several stories of age-faded brick under a white-painted dome. The camera zoomed to a crowd gathered on the steps below the concrete Doric columns that framed the front door. It picked up a squad of uniformed Kentucky Riflemen waving red-white-and-blue banners printed *Free the Martyr! Free Ben Today!*

". . . explosive situation." The camera came back to her pert doll-face and white-streaked coif. "Judge Winter has ordered the

sheriff to hold him in protective custody because of the high tide
of sentiment, pro and con. His militia supporters are demanding
his freedom, promising their own protection if he needs protection.
The judge, however, may need protection more. Militia members
have threatened to drag him out of his chambers and read him a
lesson out of the Constitution."

The screen went black for an instant. The courthouse was gone.
Del Rio sat at her newsroom desk, dark-lined eyes and crimson lips
smiling vividly into the camera.

"That was a few hours ago. Burleigh and Hunn came out of the
courthouse to face the crowd—it was almost a mob. Hunn urged
them to disperse, promising to call for the National Guard if any
violence took place. That brought defiant hoots. The militia supporters did not scatter until Burleigh and his deputies fired tear gas
grenades."

". . . no actual resolution." Tex Horn was at his own news desk,
tipping his wide white hat even farther back and beaming cheerily
with his sun-browned or more likely makeup-dyed Texas charisma.
"Ramona Del Rio will be standing by with fresh updates on that
troubled Kentucky county as events occur. For the freshest infofax,
keep your mind's eye on Washintel WebWatch One."

A specialist in cosmetic surgery came on the monitor with an info-
mercial for his penile reconstruction clinic. I tried a dozen other
channels, but McAdam county was only one tiny spot on a world
vexed with multitudes of more newsworthy problems. Crisis in the
Balkans, famine in the sub-Sahara, strikes in China. Drought in
Canada, flood in Florida, a hurricane sweeping Japan.

World-vexing troubles, but the infonet also offered sports, com-
edy, hobbies, travel, faith, soap operas, interactive sex. After an
hour or two, I snapped it off and roamed the gloomy house. Upstairs,
in Tim's room, I found a narrow slit beneath a window blind that
let me peer across the street. Afternoon traffic was slow. A police
car crawled past, the driver's head turned toward the house. Later,

a brown sedan with two men in it was parked for half an hour at the end of the block, facing the house.

Abram Koster came strolling along the sidewalk, walking his Dalmatian. Once an Olympic wrestler, he now was retired from the CIA and somewhat gone to fat. He owned a home in the next block, and his wife had played bridge with Marion back in easier times. Little Angela had made friends with the dog, and I had interviewed him for Alden, asking for the little he felt free to say about infonet censorship. Then friendly enough, cheerfully willing to agree that the infonet had outgrown its would-be censors, he had become a hazard to me now.

I drew back from my lookout slit when he stopped to stare at the house. He was still there when I looked again, the Dalmatian sniffing the grass. He let it pull him a dozen paces on, and paused to peer again. Merely wondering, as I was wondering, why and where his neighbors were gone? Or searching for any sign of me?

I felt better when he spoke to the dog and sauntered on.

I took another long shower and put more antibiotic ointment on the scalp wound. In the kitchen again, I finished the leftover roast and casserole. Fatigue overwhelmed me before I had my dishes washed, but I looked again from Tim's window before I went back to bed. The brown sedan was gone. Night had fallen when I woke.

Back on the infotel, I found McAdam County still lost in the sea of more compelling sensations. A prime minister shot. A tour liner aground and on fire in the Indian Ocean. Fraud on Wall Street, crime on Main Street, sex scandal on a floating casino. Mars Magellan gone silent, more cities predicted to drown when global warming thawed the ice caps, a killer virus spreading across Brazil.

I ran a search on the C-Net file of the week with the key-words *McAdam* and *crisis*. It brought up a Senate committee in session. An infonet journal had published notes Alden had sent his agent for a never-written update on the merchants of terror. Alerted by the threats of disorder in his own home state, Senator Finn had called Director Garlesh to testify.

She raised a thick-fingered hand to take the oath and assured him that Kirk's *Terror in America* and his tragic death from a letter bomb had created needless alarm about the temper of the nation. Unfortunately, the letter-bomber had not been identified. Agent Botman, the leader of the unit assigned to the case, was still missing. She had put able new men on the case, however, and she was confident of an early resolution.

Kirk's killer had probably been some isolated fanatic, afraid of what might be written. Benjamin Coon, the suspected militiaman, was still held in the McAdam jail. A credible witness, however, had named Kirk's fugitive brother, Clayton Barstow, as the killer of both Ryke and Lydia Starker. Barstow had been traced toward the Washington area, and his capture was only a matter of time. She said nothing about acorns of any number.

"We're never complacent," she concluded. "We deplore Alden Kirk's tragic death, but the Bureau didn't need his sensational journalism to inform us of the state of the nation—a state far less alarming than his book has led the public to believe. Such reckless alarmists as Kirk are the actual terrorists, a far more frightening threat to the peace of the nation."

I slept well that night and woke almost myself. I made coffee, worked out in the basement on Marion's Total Toner, fried eggs and bacon for breakfast. The brown sedan was nowhere in sight when I looked out of Tim's window slit, but its gray twin was parked on the other side of the street, down near the end of the block and facing toward me. McAdam County was back at the top of the news when I got to the infotel. Ramona Del Rio was on the monitor, a brighter crimson on her lips and a fresh burnish on that streak of silver hair.

"A mob!" She was breathless with an excitement that seemed

more real than assumed. "An outlaw gang! A traitor militia! That's what Kentucky Governor Harlow Train has called the Kentucky Rifles. Led by an ex-convict, Stuart McAdam, they surrounded the McAdam County jail last night, demanding the release of accused arsonist and killer Benjamin Coon.

"Coon is a militia member. Claiming his innocence, McAdam threatened to storm the jail. Outraged local authorities appealed to Governor Train, who ordered the local guard unit to help them disperse the mob. That tactic failed. The guardsmen deserted in mass, surrendering the armory and their weapons to McAdam.

"Many, it appears, had been secret militia members. Others joined on the spot. The jailer released Coon and promised to sign up himself. The angered governor had ordered the mobilization of the entire Kentucky National Guard. Defying him, McAdam has declared the independence of the county, calling it the Free State of America. The militia is now drilling in the streets, while the townsfolk wait in apprehensive uncertainly for the arrival of the state guard and possible action by the federal government.

"That's the action here, up to now."

She waved into the lens with an intimate little wink.

"Until the next news break—and it's breaking fast—I'm Ramona Del Rio, on special assignment here in this tiny Kentucky county which is daring to take the epic but perilous road that led the Confederate states to defeat and catastrophic ruin a century and a half ago. A madman's gesture, on the face of it. The odds are too obvious to bear discussion, but the declaration has been enough to terrify the town and concern national authority.

"Governor Train has broadcast an appeal to the outlaw militiamen, begging them to shed no innocent blood. McAdam has made no public response, but his men are setting up an old antiaircraft gun on the town square. The streets are almost deserted now, though earlier I saw a few vehicles loaded with household goods leaving town on the Lexington road. State guard units will soon be arriving.

"A moment of historic drama here in McAdam City."

CHAPTER FIFTEEN

RAMONA DEL RIO was gone, replaced by a black-bearded man in an astrakhan cap, the flakes of an early Russian snow swirling round him.

"Crisis in the Hermitage!" He gestured across the flat black Neva at the long skyline of the old museum, roofs rimmed with white. "Three Georgian terrorists armed with machine guns have forced their way inside. Gunfire has been heard. A few tourists have escaped, but scores are still held. An unidentified woman was carried out on a stretcher. The men are now said to be demanding ten million new rubles in gold, and an airplane to carry them to Iran. They threaten to burn the museum and its precious contents unless their demands are met. Iran has denied asylum."

Another channel was showing the devastation from a giant tsunami that had redoubled the hurricane damage in Hokkaido. A Force 7 quake in Siberia had left a hundred coal miners buried alive. Twice as many were dead from a train collision in the Punjab.

Yet most of the world showed little concern for any disaster. I found football games on half a dozen American channels, cricket in England, soccer in the Ukraine, opera in Milan, high fashion in Paris and Tokyo, cosmology from Caltech. Nothing at all from McAdam County.

The sedans had vanished when I looked through my peephole, but a moving van was parked across the street in front of a house that had been for sale. The sign was gone, but the house still looked empty. I knelt to watch it till my knees were aching, and saw no motion about the van though I thought watchers inside must be waiting for me.

As long as nobody got into the house, I felt almost safe. I worked out again, showered, and ran a search for *McAdam* and *crisis* on the daysnews index. When that brought nothing new, I added Alden's name to the search string and found an academic symposium on "The Information Crisis: Panic or Panacea?"

". . . Kirk said so." A gray-haired academic touched a copy of Alden's book on the table in front of him. "Information is a great leveler, the ultimate equalizer. The new information technology is eroding the past. It questions old beliefs, displaces old elites, undermines old authorities. Look at the Soviet collapse, the fate of Red China, Cuba yesterday. The McAdam affair prefigures revolution here in America."

"Maybe." The black journalist was younger, his tone cheerier. "Maybe not. Information has always been the key to power. Look back at the invention of the alphabet, printing, the telegraph. Advancing technology will crumble the old power systems, spread new freedoms to all who can learn. It can inspire a more humane faith, create a more creative elite, give us a more just and intelligent authority."

"In McAdam County?" the gray man snorted. "Is terror authority?"

"Sometimes." The black man shrugged. "It can be the first phase of a new authority emerging, a new elite discovering itself."

"What new authority are you expecting?"

"I'm waiting." The black man grinned. "The infonet is recasting history, in much the same way that gold and silver from the new mines in the Americas recast it four centuries ago. What new elite will be taking the reins of authority? I want to see."

They were gone. Ramona Del Rio's vivid Cupid face filled the screen again.

"That symposium was recorded last night at the New Futures Foundation in Washington. President Higgins will speak to the nation at seven. He is expected to ask the rebels to negotiate with Senator Finn, who is on his way to McAdam as a special official emissary to the rebels. Will they refuse to see him?"

She smirked into the lens.

"Ramona Del Rio with Washintel WebWatch One."

The moving van was gone when I looked again, but I saw a cherry picker stopped at the light pole at the end of the block. The workman on the platform seemed to be doing something to the light, but he kept looking down the street toward me.

That afternoon I made a stew from meat and vegetables Marion had left in the freezer. I ate a full bowl of it, searched the daysnews channel again, and spent another hour on her Total Toner. I was waiting in front of the infotel at seven.

Higgins spoke from the Oval Office, a flag draped behind him. His staff had denied rumors that his childhood leukemia was recurring, but I thought he looked haggard under the makeup. Speaking to "dear friends, good neighbors, and fellow citizens of the oldest and greatest republic on Earth," he recalled a great-great-great-grandfather who had served as a private in the Union army under General Grant, had been captured at Shiloh, died at Andersonville.

"My fellow Americans, I have come to you to share a terrible concern." He stopped, his gaunt head bent. The camera zoomed close. I saw tears in his watery eyes and thought for a moment that he meant to speak of his health. "Forgive me, please." He gulped and went on. "My most profound concern is for my fellow citizens in the great state of Kentucky, but I beg all loyal Americans, wherever you are, to stand beside me in this national ordeal." He turned to face the flag, his hand on his heart. "I beg you all to join me now as we renew our most sacred pledge."

Huskily, he intoned the pledge of allegiance.

"I honor that pledge." Swaying on his feet, he swung back to face the camera. "I have sworn a solemn oath to defend our Constitution and the unity of our nation. I intend to do so with all the sovereign power vested in me and with whatever means that noble duty may require. But I want no violence. Our nations needs no violence. I pray to Almighty God that no blood is shed."

His graying, thin-haired head was bent for half a minute. I saw a large brown mole on a patch of pink bald scalp.

"Remember with me." Hoarse with emotion, he drew himself unsteadily straight. "Remember the heroic history of all the toil and blood and sacrifice that went into the building of America. I know that some of you feel unhappy with the state of things as they are. So do I. Many of you have suffered misfortune; that's our common human destiny. Some of you may feel threatened by the claims and deeds of others, but don't forget that your own deeds and claims may sometimes seem to threaten them. I beg you to understand, to compromise, to reason together.

"A final a word to my unhappy friends in Kentucky: I have asked Madison Finn, a faithful patriot and your own able senator, to undertake a vital mission. He is now on his way to that troubled state. I beg its leaders to sit down with him, listen to his proposals, and seek a path to peace. American blood has always been sacred. Let's not waste it now."

Tex Horn came on the screen, the wide white hat pulled aggressively low. He echoed Higgins's words with somewhat less feeling and effect, and then repeated a public statement from the President's Bethesda doctors that they had found his health superb, with no basis whatever for the rumored recurrence of any childhood malady.

"And that's the scat for now." He relaxed into his trademark drawl, pushing the hat to the side of his head and grinning engag-

ingly into the lens. "For the hottest hype on every happening, watch
Washintel WebWatch One."

"Look at the rebels!" Ramona Del Rio smiled from the tube with
the delight of a child about to open an unexpected gift. "They've
seized the county courthouse. Scattered the local officials. Civil
authority has been assumed by a group now called the Liberation
Congress."

The camera shifted from her to sweep the conference room at
the McAdam city hall—I'd been there with Pepperlake, covering a
city-county council meeting for the *Freeman.* I recognized Kit Moorhawk at the head of the long table, Cass Pepperlake and Rob Roy
McAdam sitting beside him.

"The Haven," Del Rio trilled. "That's what they've named their
new nation. It's to be a fortress of freedom and a safe refuge for its
defenders when times of trouble come. So they say." Her tone was
lightly sardonic. "Here you see Provisional President Kit Moorhawk, seated with the two other members of their executive council.
I am speaking with Stuart McAdam, their military commander."

She turned to Stuart, who stood close to her, lean and ramrod
straight in a new green jacket.

"Freedom—"

His voice fell. Solemnly, he shook his head.

"Sadly, my fellow friends of liberty, I had to stand silent through
the president's pledge today, because the great America I once
loved has failed us. It was established as a true democracy, its laws
to be enacted and its government administered by citizens selected
for integrity, education, and intelligence. It was designed to guarantee our most precious rights—life, liberty, and the pursuit of
happiness. But look at us today!"

Grimly scowling, he slapped the table.

"Generations of fools have squandered those sacred rights. We
walk in terror on our crime-ridden streets, our lives in danger every
day. Our individual liberties have been surrendered to tyrannical

majorities, ignorant idiots whose vacant minds change with every infonet broadcast. I'm sick of federal meddling—"

"Really, sir?" Del Rio broke into his tirade with a spirit that surprised me. "Does our government do nothing good? What about the federal marshals just sent here to defend the rights of a woman to her own body?"

He scowled at her impatiently.

"What about the Ryke clinic?" she demanded, with an impudent wink at the camera. "What about that Rifleman of yours, arrested for burning the building with Dr. Ryke inside? Why did your own men storm the jail to set him free."

"Ben Coon?" He blinked as if in astonishment. "Ben, trying to rescue the unfortunate doctor, was trapped in the blast. No criminal, he's a wounded hero. Our action to set him free was forced by the idiot judge who denied his bond. So what's your point?"

"Innocent?" Her perfect eyebrows rose. "The firemen swear they caught him in the act of arson, crashing the fire-car into the clinic and tossing a flaming torch back at it before he fled. You spoke of federal meddling. Is it meddling when the courts send federal marshals to protect a woman's rights?"

"The right to murder an unborn child?"

The camera caught Moorhawk's impatient glance.

"Your own opinion, Stuart." Pepperlake raised his hand with an air of deferential protest. "Kit and I have ours. But we aren't here to disagree."

Stuart was turning pink, glowering at him. "Let me tell you—"

The camera swung.

"Liberator Pepperlake?" Del Rio turned to him hopefully. "Can you tell us where you do agree?"

"We both beg for liberty."

"Thank you, sir." She nodded brightly. "That's what the world wants to hear about. Your revolt is hard for many of us to justify." She frowned demurely and touched her shining hair as if briefly puzzled. "It has troubled the nation. Any resistance from you seems doomed to certain defeat, perhaps with tragic bloodshed. Can you give us some sane sense of your position?"

"If you want the sad history—"

"We do," she said. "If you can make it brief."

"We want to save our skins," he said. "If you want it brief."

"Not that brief."

"Then here's a little more." Thoughtfully, Pepperlake pushed up his wire-rimmed glasses. "For Kit and me, it begins with Alden Kirk's visit here when he was at work on *Terror in America*. We got to know him. He shared his concern about the shadow of trouble over the nation. Living here in McAdam City, a very typical American town, we had only been dimly aware of the germs of terror already infecting us.

"A handful of us gathered to talk about how we might get the drug-dealing gangs off our streets and their fat-cat agents out of the courthouse. County politics has always been a life-or-death sport here in Kentucky, right next to racing Thoroughbreds. Kirk's inquiries had alarmed some of our local kingpins. When they needed a sacrifice for a coming election, they picked us. Our meetings were spied on. We were raided. Somebody seems to have persuaded the FBI that we were involved with the letter bomb that killed Kirk."

He paused to grin into the lens.

"Director Garlesh, I hope you're listening. I don't know all your people have done, but I think they got too close to some of our county officials. At the *Freeman*, our circulation manager found several pounds of marijuana stashed in his filing cabinet. He dropped it into a dumpster down the block before anything happened, but I think the county bosses meant to bust us and shut the paper down. Liberator Moorhawk was harassed on trumped-up charges of tax fraud. And Liberator McAdam has a brother—"

"Rob Roy." Stuart was loud and bitter. "He's invented a new telephone. The Feds tried to confiscate it. They put his CyberSoft Corporation out of business when he wouldn't give it up, and threatened him with prison."

Pepperlake lifted his hand. "Stuart, please—"

"They never stopped." Stuart was on his feet. "Not just the feds, but the state and the county. We have means to deal with the court-house gang, but the state has declared war on us. Governor Train is mobilizing the National Guard. Senator Finn is on his way here now, with an ultimatum from the president. They give us no choice—"

"Excuse me, Liberator McAdam." Del Rio checked him. "If the senator does deliver an ultimatum, what will your answer be?"

"If he wants war—"

"Cool it, Stuart. Please!" Pepperlake waved to halt him. "Let me answer."

Grumbling under his breath, he sat down.

"Miss Del Rio, I want to thank you for this opportunity to state our case." Pepperlake bent his head toward her with the courtesy of an older generation. "That's a hard indictment you've just heard from Liberator McAdam. I don't want you and your audience to get us wrong.

"Speaking for myself, I have a deep respect for President Higgins, an honest and able man, caught now in a tragic dilemma. I'm sure most of those around him are men and women of good will. Unfortunately, they're all trapped in a corrupt and perverted system which frustrates every effort to do what they know they should.

"But we want no war." He smiled disarmingly at Stuart. "Liberator McAdam lets his own eloquence carry him away. We are not aggressors. We stand ready to negotiate with Senator Finn when he arrives. All we ask is to be left alone."

"Really, sir." Del Rio's dark-lined eyes widened in innocent surprise. "Do you really think the national authorities can afford to leave you alone?"

"We'll see." He shrugged, with no visible concern. "We'll see."

When I looked out again, the cherry picker had moved to the light pole at the other end of the block. The man on the platform was busy with the light, but in a moment he straightened to stretch himself and scratch his hip while he stood gazing up the street toward me. He shrugged at last, turning back to the light. I took a shower and ate a bowl of cold stew. Del Rio was back on the infonet a few hours later, as chipper as ever.

"An epic unfolding!" It seemed to delight her. "WebWatch One is hot on the spot, with the hyperest hype. The rebel militia surrounded the McAdam County courthouse when officials refused to swear allegiance to their Liberation movement. The siege is now over. Sheriff Burleigh lowered his flag this afternoon and surrendered the building."

The camera swung from her bright child-face to pick up Burleigh's black-jowled scowl. He come down the courthouse steps, his deputies behind him. They all wore holstered pistols. One carried a flag. Another had his arm in a sling. Hunn followed, and a score of others I didn't know.

"Deputy Franks was wounded in an exchange of fire when he tried to leave the building," she said. "I'm told that there were no fatalities, no other injuries."

Stuart met them at the bottom of the steps, a Rifle unit standing at attention behind him. The deputy gave up his flag. They all dropped their weapons in a pile in front of Stuart. The camera followed them to a waiting school bus and returned to Del Rio's delighted smile.

"Under the terms of surrender they were granted amnesty and free passage out of the county if they want to go. Family members will allowed to follow, with their household possessions. Sheriff Burleigh and a few others have chosen to accept a compromise that lets them remain in the county."

The camera picked up a police car flying the Haven flag, a single white star on a green field. It swung in front of the bus and led it off the square, a train of cars and loaded pickups behind.

"An instant of history!" The lens picked up her vivid face again, excited emotion pealing in her voice. "Join me as we follow the refugees out of town on the Lexington Road. Exiles from all they knew and loved. Here is where we have to leave them, at the county line."

The camera zoomed through a haze of sunlit dust to the road ahead of the convoy. It picked up the white-starred flag on a police car stopped beside the pavement, and paused again on the stars and stripes flown on a troop carrier parked beyond a yellow-striped barricade.

"Our new frontier!" She gestured at the barrier. "The county line. The National Guard stopped us there. The convoy was allowed to go on, but the guard refused to let us take our cameras into their staging area."

"Top scat from where it's at." Tex Horn was on the tube, his big white hat tilted raffishly. "Ramona Del Rio is still on the spot, watching the rebels for Washintel WebWatch One, ready to pick up the poop when it pops."

His nasal drawl quickened to a graver tone.

"A White House bulletin, in the meantime, has released an update on Senator Finn. The senator's private jet arrived over the outlaw county an hour ago. He found the McAdam municipal airport closed, the runways blocked with captured guard vehicles. Unable to land, the senator's aircraft returned to Lexington. He says he will try again tomorrow."

CHAPTER SIXTEEN

THE CHERRY PICKER was gone when I looked out, but the moving van was parked in front of the vacant house across the street. I worked out again on Marion's Total Toner, ate the last of my stew, and went back to the infonet. The rebels had sealed off the county roads. The guard perimeter was under a security blackout, but newshawks had met the refugee convoy on the road beyond it.

"A turd on a stick!"

Deputy Sheriff Cornwall came on the monitor, dirty, unshaven, and seething with fury. "If Stuart McAdam thinks he's gonna be a king of the county, like his great-granddaddy was a hundred years ago, we'll be back to squash him like the cockroach he is."

On the salvation channel was Father Garron, a long-beaked bird of prey perched in the pulpit beneath his tall silver sword, preaching to the multimillion-soul infonet congregation he claimed.

"Soldiers of the sword, strike for God!" The hall must have been empty; his voice made a hollow boom. "Stand with Liberator McAdam against the baby-killing snakes of Satan who had tried to

frame a God-loving Christian for arson and murder. Ben Coon never
killed Dr. Ryke. Never needed to. No matter who drove the gasoline
truck, that fire in that murder mill was an act of an angry God."

An infonet reporter had found a wild-bearded militia leader
haranguing his followers somewhere in Arizona. They voted to rally
with their pickups and hunting guns to form a freedom caravan to
reinforce Stuart McAdam and his heroic Kentucky Rifles.

"Heroes of freedom!" He flourished a six-gun. "Don't let them
die alone!"

Alden startled me when I found him on the tube. C-Net was rerunning an interview taped the week before his death. He spoke about
the unrest he had found in McAdam County and tried to answer
critics who called his book a moneygrabbing slander on the peace-
loving people of small-town America.

A panel of wise old heads followed him, pontificating on "American Malcontents." Beginning with the Whiskey Rebellion in 1794,
which had melted away when Washington sent thousands of troops
against it, the tape skipped past Aaron Burr and the Civil War,
down to Waco and Ruby Ridge and the Montana Freemen.

"In spite of his critics," the chairman concluded, "Kirk's lesson
is clear enough. The blaze of treason is burning America. We must
put it out, as Washington and Lincoln did when they had to. President Higgins promises to follow their example. Whatever the cost
in money or pain or blood, the Union has to be preserved."

Somebody at Bethesda had leaked the president's medical records, which showed that he was suffering from an inoperable pancreatic cancer. Against the advice of his personal physician, he had
insisted on an experimental genetic treatment. The outcome was
still uncertain, but a recent physical had found no improvement. In
a top secret memo, his surgeon reported the prognosis dim and
advised him to prepare for the inevitable.

"A barefaced hoax," a White House spokesman answered.
"Lies invented by his political enemies to destroy his administration

on the eve of the November election. In actual fact, the doctors found the president in excellent health, with the body of a far younger man. Now in the midst of this national crisis, these malicious rumors amount to high treason. The FBI has been ordered to track down the sources."

Tex Horn was back with a final roundup on the rebellion. A spy satellite had found the airport runways still blocked. Though the county line was closed, even to outside journalists, Ramona Del Rio remained on the spot for WebWatch One, ready for the hype when it happened.

"That's the scam where I am." He tipped the white Stetson. "Senator Finn is spending the night at a Lexington hotel, awaiting permission to cross the county line. Will the rebels let him in? Will they listen to his plea from the president? Or do we face a second Civil War? Keep your eye on the WebWatch sky. Exclusive views of all the news!"

The moving van was gone next morning. The street looked empty till I saw the big Dalmatian leading Abram Koster down the sidewalk. He hauled the dog to a stop, stood a long time idly scanning Alden's frost-crisped rose garden and glancing sharply now and then at the front of the house. He bent at last to dig a rolled-up newspaper out of the fallen leaves on the untended lawn, peered into the end of the roll as if examining something hidden there, and buried it again before he let the dog lead him on.

The phone rang again while I knelt at the window. A dozen rings, and still it kept on. Botman, still searching for me? Someone else in the bureau? Acorn Three? Or simply some troubled friend of Marion? I was on my feet, almost ready to risk an answer, before it stopped.

Cleaning out the refrigerator, I fried the last two slices of bacon, scrambled the last egg, peeled the last orange, made coffee and toast, and sat down to one more breakfast before I went back to search the daysnews channels. The first thing I found was my own face. I was wanted for arson, murder, flight to escape justice, interrogation about the fate of a missing federal agent. The rewards required me to be taken alive. Feeling desperate enough, though I had no arms and looked harmless enough in Pepperlake's photo for the *Freeman,* I sat staring till my image was gone.

"Tex Horn on Washintel WebWatch One." He greeted me when I found the will to touch the keys again. He stood on newly sheared grass on the grounds of the state capital at Frankfort, the big hat tipped to shade his eyes from the sun rising over the lantern dome. "On tap with the scat from Senator Finn and Governor Train."

The camera shifted to a makeshift platform of unpainted boards. Finn and Train climbed the steps to it and shook hands with ceremonial smiles for the lens. A svelte honey-blonde in green and gold stood close behind Finn, her eyes shifting from him to the screen of a tiny palmtop. A heavy bear of a man in an olive-green safari suit shambled to Finn's side, touched his sleeve, and breathed something into his ear. It took me a moment to place him.

"Rocky Gottler," Horn was murmuring. "A McAdam banker. Friend and political backer of the senator."

Finn nodded his thanks to Gottler and stepped to a lectern flanked with the flag of Kentucky and the stars and stripes.

"Fellow Americans—"

Suddenly very grave, he paused to let the camera zoom to his head. A wasted moment. His eyes hollowed and shadowed, he looked as if he hadn't slept or shaved.

"We face a threat to the nation. A group of misguided men and women, here in our own great state of Kentucky, have embarked on a reckless act of rebellion. President Higgins doesn't want a second Chechnya or another Bosnia here in Kentucky. He sent us down to negotiate a fair and peaceful resolution. The rebels have shut him out of McAdam County and refused to talk.

"We spent most of the night in conference calls with President Higgins and members of his cabinet. We conferred with the leaders of Congress, the National Security Agency, the chiefs of staff, Director Garlesh of the FBI. We found a strong consensus. They are all as anxious as we are to avoid any needless waste of American blood.

"Early this morning, we agreed on an offer of amnesty to the these misguided rebels. Our terms are generous. The airport and the roads must be opened. The insurgent militia must lay down their arms and register their identities with the FBI. The leaders of this ill-named Liberation movement must submit to interrogation and swear allegiance to our national government. This malicious mockery of creating a new and independent nation must be forgotten.

"In return, we have agreed to press no charges of treason or any other offense, not even against the individuals who fired on the county courthouse and wounded a county official. Two hours ago, this offer was transmitted to the rebels. Their reply was a bitter disappointment.

"They don't want amnesty." Voice falling, he shook his head. "They demand the recognition of total independence for their Free State or the Haven—they seem to disagree on what to call their new utopia, but they swear that they'll give their lives to defend it."

He stepped aside and beckoned Train to the lectern.

"My fellow Kentuckians, most of you know me." A quick little bird of a man, he had won his first distinction riding an unlikely winner at Churchill Downs. Unsmiling, he had the face of a loser now. "I have relatives and friends in McAdam County. The tragic crisis there wrings my soul, but it has forced me to support a terrible decision.

"Sadly, sadly, these outlaws have left us no choice. As they are already informed, I have mobilized the Kentucky National Guard. President Higgins has dispatched a unit of heavy armor from Fort Knox to support the guard. The combined strike force is now assembled on the McAdam County line, ready to go.

"Yet, one more time, we are repeating our offer of amnesty. We are still waiting—and I pray Almighty God that He may chasten the stubborn hearts of the rebels and lead them to see their way to sanity and peace. The alternative will be the swift and severe punishment they have been fools enough to ask for."

He paused to shake his head.

"I beg them—I beg you, my good friends in McAdam County— to think of the cost of any continued defiance. A tragic cost, not only to you but to your neighbors and your own families, perhaps to hundreds or thousands of innocent people. President Higgins made his resolution clear. He is prepared to act at once, with whatever force may be required to save the nation."

He looked at his watch.

"It is now 7:56. Our strike force has orders to move at nine, unless the rebels have informed us by that time they accept amnesty. Our offer is too generous to be repeated."

"Stay tuned to the tube for the news while it's new." Tex Horn was back on the monitor, his hat pulled low. "Ramona Del Rio is still on top of the spot in the rebel county. You'll get the hype when it it's ripe, hot from the top of WebWatch One."

The camera picked up the white-starred flag flying from the courthouse and panned to Ramona Del Rio standing beside her car at the curb. Her sleek black hair looked freshly done, the silver streak as bright as new metal, though stress and fatigue had begun to wear through her makeup.

"WebWatch One, fact and fun!" She chanted it like a mantra. "The newborn nation will live or die today. The tiny rebel army, a former militia group, is dug in on the county line. Colonel Stuart McAdam, its commander, stands facing a force that seems overwhelming. The deadline is near. I'm Ramona Del Rio, now driving out to the front to show you the showdown."

Her camera man shooting from the car, she rounded the courthouse square and drove out of town on the Lexington road. The lens lingered on a busy mall, swept a used car lot, a farmer's market, an empty-looking warehouse. Here and there it zoomed to a homemade rebel flag flown from a building or a fence post, the white star raggedly stitched.

A road block stopped her: two police cars parked off the road and flying the rebel banner. Half a dozen men in red Kentucky Rifle shirts stood around them, wearing blue-and-white arm bands as Liberation uniforms. One stepped out to the side of her car.

"Sorry, Ma'am." His voice was hoarse and anxious, and I saw dark spots of nervous perspiration under his armpits. "For your own safety, we have to halt you here." He listened to her protest and finally nodded. "Pull off the pavement if you want the risk. Your own funeral, lady. I'd advise you to head back to town and get under cover."

She drove down narrow back roads and parked at last on a hill. Her camera man caught a farm pickup, following fast. The driver tumbled out and marched toward her, shouting angry demands for money. Though green-and-white ribbons fluttered from his radio antenna, he refused her check on a McAdam bank. He wanted no rebel money, if they had any, but American cash.

"Okay." With a satisfied grin, he folded her bills into his wallet. "Stay as long as you want. Me, I'm outta here."

He departed under a plume of yellow dust.

Back on the monitor, Tex Horn reran the appeals from Train and Finn on the statehouse lawn and followed with glimpses of Director Garlesh, the attorney general, finally the president.

"Zero hour—" Sitting in the Oval Office, Higgins looked drawn and puffy around the eyes. His hand quivered when he glanced at the watch on his wrist. "Our forces are poised and ready, but I have delayed the strike order for another fifteen minutes to allow this last plea to my troubled fellow citizens in McAdam county. My good friends—" Pale eyes watering, he blinked into the camera. "I beg you one more time to inform us that you will open the roads and accept the thanks of your nation and the forgiveness of Almighty God—"

He gulped and bent his head. His image gave way to the face of a clock, the hands creeping toward bright red numerals: 9:15. They faded back to Horn's big hat.

"—Watch One." His voice had quickened, the drawl almost forgotten. "The rebels have given no hint that they will knuckle under. The security blackout allows us no facts about the strike force. Friends of the rebels have extended their night-long candle-light appeal to the White House, but sources there confirm that the deadline will not be extended again."

The clock face was on the screen again. Dead silence. Then the slow tick of the clock. A ruffle of martial music.

"Seven minutes!" Horn intoned. "We're waiting to know the fate of the county, perhaps for the fate of the president in November. For hoots and scoops, watch WebWatch One!"

A montage of the stars and stripes, the white-starred banner, the clock, the McAdam courthouse and the statehouse dome, the clock, Burleigh shaking a furious fist at Stuart, the bleak-faced president, the rebel officials at their table in the McAdam city hall, and again the clock.

"Five minutes . . . Four . . . Three! We return you now to our Ramona Del Rio, on the battle beat for WebWatch One."

The camera caught her facing the wind from her hilltop, lean and bold in her trim black slacks and sweater, a hand camera aimed into the distance.

"Two minutes!" She picked upon the count. "Ramona Del Rio standing by on the McAdam battlefield, if there is to be a battle."

Her long lens found another rebel flag on a pole trimmed from a tree beside the road. It dropped to a barrier across it, a rough timber striped green and white, laid on saw horses. Closer, a double line of road-worn cars and pickups were parked to block the pavement. Men with rebel arm bands crouched behind them, rifles ready.

"Tanks! I see tanks advancing!" Del Rio seemed breathless. "In their camouflage paint, they look like prehistoric monsters. Thundering to crush this daring American rebellion."

Her microphone picked up no thunder but the tanks did look monstrous enough. Long and squat, splotched with dirty green and brown, they came down the road in single file, guns trained on the barricade. The camera swept the huddled defenders, caught an officer standing on the hood of a pickup, shouting silently.

Swelling in the monitor, the lead tank lumbered implacably forward. It splintered the flimsy barricade, crushed its path through the line of vehicles. Ahead of it, the riflemen scattered.

"The tank!" Del Rio's voice suddenly sharpened. "The rebels are running like scared rabbits. But the tank—"

The monitor went blank. Her voice was cut off.

CHAPTER SEVENTEEN

THE STREET SEEMED empty again next morning till I saw the Dalmatian leading Abram Koster into view. Carrying a rolled newspaper under his arm, he halted the dog in front of the house and stood a long time scanning Alden's roses before he glanced around him and bent to dig in the yellowed leaves for the paper he had left. He buried the one he had brought, glanced idly around, and followed the dog out of my sight.

"No news, good news!"

Tex Horn's mellow bellow greeted me on the infonet. The white Stetson a little askew, he was grinning so broadly that a gold tooth shone, but I saw tension in the set of his jutting jaw.

"The McAdam strike force is still under security blackout, but Pentagon officials report General Zeider's pacification force advancing as planned. Our satellite service has not yet been able to correct the technical glitch that has interrupted transmissions from the rebel county. Ramona Del Rio is still there, however, squatting on the hot spot for WebWatch One.

"That's hype from the hip. Hold for the top of the pop from Hopper Horn on WebWatch one."

The phone rang again while I was mixing pancake batter from a box in Marion's pantry cabinet. Botman? Acorn Three? The bureau or some city cop? Surely I was wanted more than ever, not just for Ryke's death and Lydia Starker's, but now because I was Alden's brother and linked to the rebels through Pepperlake and his *Freeman*. I let the phone ring till it stopped.

"—newsbreak!"

Horn was back on the infonet, looking flushed and elated.

"Exclusive from WebWatch One. We bring you Jess Koplovik, the first eyewitness to escape the McAdam battlefield."

Koplovik was a gangling youth in frayed blue jeans and a Reb T-shirt, his Reb cap turned backward. He seemed ill at ease in this moment of sudden fame. Sweating under the studio lights, he kept shifting in his chair, peering apprehensively aside, reminding himself to look back at the camera.

"Relax, Jess," Horn cajoled him. "You're safe here under the WebWatch wing, with a tale that can shake the nation. For a start, just tell the world something about yourself and how you escaped with your exclusive story of the rebel victory."

"I don't know—" He gulped and blinked. "I don't know if it is a victory."

"Don't fret about military tactics. Just say what you saw and how you got to see it."

"Okay, sir." He pushed the Reb cap farther back and squinted against the lights. "My folks live out of Baker Run. That's east of town, just off the Lexington road. Dad was a tobacco farmer till the market broke. We're trying to get into alternative crops. I was an ag major at McAdam College till the trouble began and I went home to be with my folks."

He wiped his forehead with the back of his hand and stopped to blink at Horn.

"Great!" Horn told him. "You're going great. Just tell about the battle."

"Not much of a battle."

"The tanks, Jess. About the tanks."

"I never knew they had tanks at Fort Knox, but somebody said they come from there. Big caterpillar tanks, splotched with funny paint jobs. They come in to park on our east field without asking and posted men with guns to keep us out. One man promised the Army would pay us a hundred bucks when Dad finally got to see him, but I don't know."

He squirmed and licked his lips.

"Go on. What did you see?"

"The guards kept everybody out of what they call their perimeter, but I had the infonet news on my laptop. We've got a big oak in our hill pasture. I built a spy nest in it when I was a kid—just two boards nailed to a fork in a high branch. It's still there. I climbed back to it, up to where I could see the road to the county line and the rebel roadblock. That was just their flag on a pole and a painted board propped across the pavement. The rebs had parked a few trucks and cars on the road behind it, but nothing big enough to stop a tank. I thought they were fu—"

He turned red, choking back the word.

"That's okay." Horn shrugged. "Just say what you saw."

"I thought the rebs had gone crazy." He caught a long breath and wiped his forehead. "I've got an old spyglass my uncle gave me. I had it with me in the tree when the tanks came. Snorting and rumbling, they came out of our east field one at a time and crawled on down the McAdam road in a single line.

"I had the glass on the front tank when it came to the road block. It never fired a gun, not that I could see. It just smashed through the painted timber and knocked the flagpole down and ran over the cars and pickups on the pavement. The rebs scattered back to their cars like scared rats. But the tanks—"

He scratched his head and blinked against the lights.

"The front tank stopped. Dad thinks it run over a land mine, but I never seen no flash or smoke. Not till men began tumbling out of it. I hope they all got out, because it finally caught fire and stood there a long time, burning. I think what hit it was more than any land mine."

"Why, Jess?" Horn asked him. "Why do you think so?"

"Sir, the tanks all stopped. The whole damn line. The others didn't burn, but something stalled them. I stayed up there in the tree till an Army jeep came down the bar ditch, a man in the back yelling at the tanks through a bull horn. I couldn't make out what he was yelling. Something stalled the jeep. He got out and ran on toward the county line, hammering on the tanks. The lids opened and the crews crawled out. A few stayed on guard around the tanks. The others walked back to where I couldn't see."

"You don't know what stopped the tanks?"

"No, sir." He frowned and licked his lips. "But it stopped more than the tanks. I could see into the camp they'd set up beyond our field. Tents and jeeps and trucks and big guns. Big trucks had been coming out to the road, ready to follow the tanks. They all stopped when the tanks did. I can't say why."

"Anything else, Jess? Anything at all?"

"I guess that's all I seen." He squirmed and squinted at Horn. "Men started walking back toward the camp from the stalled tanks. I climbed down out of the tree. Our phone was dead when I got back to the house. The TV, the lights, my laptop—everything was dead.

"Mom was scared when I told her what I'd seen. She was afraid the rebs had fired some secret weapon that might of killed all the world. She made me a sandwich and I walked out to my Uncle Ben's place. He lives four miles back from the county line. His phone and his power were okay. He was watching the infonet, but there hadn't been anything about the battle. He said what I seen from the tree might be important."

He turned uneasily to Horn.

"Sir, what do you think?"

"What will Higgins think?" Horn whistled and took off the Western hat, revealing a lot of bald pink scalp before he clapped it back. "What will the Pentagon think?"

"Do you think I'll be in trouble?" He mopped his wet forehead. "Should I have kept my mouth shut, like Dad told me?"

"You're okay, Jess." Horn grinned a little too heartily. "So long as you're telling the truth."

"It's all true, sir." He put his hand over his heart on the sweat-drenched T-shirt. "It's what I seen."

He vanished from the tube, and Horn spoke alone.

"That was Jess Koplovik of Baker Run, here on WebWatch One with his startling story of the first military encounter of the McAdam County War. Stay with us for anticipated reactions from the White House or the Pentagon."

Searching for those reactions, I found bits of Jess Koplovik's story on a dozen channels. Another was running a hypertext history of "The American Malaise" that began with any hot key you happened to click and never ended anywhere. I found my own face, still atop the wanted list. Finally, I got a contemptuous White House spokesman dismissing the foolish rumors of any military reverse in Kentucky.

Some public confusion, he admitted, had been caused by an unexplained power loss from the Moorhawk plant, which served a wide area in central Kentucky. Probably an act of sabotage by rebel sympathizers. In any case, the strike force had its own generators. It had not been affected.

Traffic was increasing when I peeked out of Tim's front window, but nobody was obviously watching the house. I worked out and showered. Marion's pantry cabinet was nearly bare; I had corn flakes for breakfast, with canned tomatoes.

Tex Horn was back on the monitor when I looked again. Bareheaded, in a khaki jump suit, he looked younger and softer without the big hat. The bald scalp was covered now with a mat of short-cut ginger-red hair. Grinning affably into the lens, he was picking his fine white teeth.

"Ramona Del Rio remains in McAdam." He tossed the toothpick aside. "Still standing by on the top spot for WebWatch One, ready with the pop when it's hot." He made a solemn face. "Unfortunately, however, all wire and satellite contact with the rebel county is still cut off by unexplained technical difficulties."

He paused for a brief montage of Del Rio watching from the hill, the wind molding a vividly crimson blouse becomingly against her. The tank rolling through the rebel barricade and over the rebel flagpole. Jess Koplovik sweating under the studio lights as he told about the tanks.

"Tex Horn here for WebWatch One." He was back on the monitor, with a shrug of innocent amazement. "Clearly, General Zeider's advance into the county has run into more trouble than the Pentagon cares to admit. If you want the hype while it's hyper, WebWatch One is going to open an eye in the sky.

"We have chartered an airplane. Within the next few minutes, I'm taking off from Lexington Municipal for an observation flight as close as I can get to the battle front. The authorities have warned us to avoid restricted areas round McAdam County, but I'll bring you all I can."

A total-globe crisis roundup followed, broken by Horn's radio bulletins. Though his pilot had orders to steer clear of the restrictions, haze filters for his long lens let him see far across the county line.

"The airstrips are still blocked," his last report began. "I see no unusual movement on the Lexington highway. Farm machines are raising dust in the fields and normal traffic is moving on rural roads. Cattle and horses are grazing peacefully. We are now turning north around the military perimeter. I can make out the tank column stopped at the county line, with no apparent motion anywhere around it—"

His voice was cut off. After long seconds of silence, an announcer spoke.

"That was Tex Horn on his observation flight around the rebel county. His last reported position was an estimated four miles northeast of the village of Baker Run. All contact with him and his flight crew has been interrupted. Further facts will be relayed as we receive them. In the meantime, we resume our daysnews summary."

That summary began with the howl of savage winds and glimpses of half-naked refugees fighting through angry waves and floating wreckage to reach the hull of a capsized boat.

"Hurricane in Bangladesh," the announcer droned, "reported to daysnews by Ishmael Singh."

Horn's radio bulletins were not resumed. A WebWatch military analyst speculated that his plane had been shot down. A Pentagon spokesman read a press release from General Zeider.

"We have no information about the fate of the missing journalist, Tex Horn. Although air traffic has been excluded from the McAdam County area at the request of Senator Finn, he had received a special clearance for an observation flight. He was told to remain clear of the military perimeter. He seems to have done so. I confirm that no military action was taken against him. Nothing else is known."

A Pentagon spokesman repeated the official line that the campaign against the insurgent county was still proceeding as planned. WebWatch One was still unable to restore contact with Ramona Del Rio. I worked out on the Total Toner. When I went back to Tim's window, Abram Koster was walking the big Dalmatian. Very deliberate, he paused to study the fallen leaves on the yard before he let the dog lead him on. For an early dinner, I made waffles made with the rest of the pancake mix, and ate them with what Tim had left of a jar of peanut butter.

Tex Horn was on WebWatch One when I got back to it. His shirt was torn, the Reb cap gone. His bronzed grin seemed painfully stiff, marred by livid bruises and plastic patches.

"Your eye in the sky," he mocked himself. "Till somebody stuck a stick in it. We were flying at five thousand feet over the Lexington highway, crossing it north of the military perimeter, when the radio failed. The navigation instruments went out. Both motors died, from no cause the pilot could determine. He glided us down to a rough landing on an abandoned road. The photographer had a leg injury, and we waited for the ambulance to pick us up. They were running us to the hospital, but I made them drop me off for this update. I'm Tex Horn for WebWatch One. Back with the scam as quick as I can."

Late that afternoon Abram Koster came strolling once more down the sidewalk, holding back the eager Dalmatian and carrying a rolled-up paper under his arm. He stopped in front of the house, glanced quickly up and down the street, and deftly exchanged the paper for the one he had hidden under the leaves.

A motion detector? Metal detector? Infrared detector? Geiger counter? Or what else?

I eased away from the window and went back downstairs. The phone was ringing when I passed the kitchen. I felt sick of the strain, sick of watching the infonet and waiting for nothing. With the refrigerator and the pantry cabinet empty, I must soon move on. I picked up the phone and listened silently, my heart thumping.

"Marion?" My Aunt Julia's anxious voice. "Marion?" She spoke again before I found the wit to answer. "Marion, are you there?"

"It's Clay."

"Clay?" She echoed my name. "Where have you been?"

"Hiding. Here in the house. She and the kids were gone when I got here."

"She was frantic about you. On her way to Kentucky, to do what she could. I offered to come and stay with the kids, but Tim was determined to go with her and she said she couldn't leave little Angela. Not even with me."

"So she's there in the county?"

"I haven't heard, and I'm worried sick. Clay, is there any-thing—Do you want to come out here?"

"I'm wanted. I can't travel. I'm afraid to say any more. I've got to hang up and get out of the house."

I ran back upstairs. In Alden's vacant office, I spun the dial of the wall safe to get his wallet, the cryptophone, the spare car keys. Five minutes later, I was backing Marion's car out of the garage.

CHAPTER EIGHTEEN

DRIVING AS FAST as I dared, I watched the rearview mirrors. At last, when no flashing lights had come up behind me, I felt relaxed enough to switch the satellite mapper to the HotBit channel. A Pentagon spokesman was laughing off "that bragging hillbilly kid" and his crazy tale of General Zeider's tanks in trouble on the McAdam county line. The general had reported no unexpected resistance. He was advancing into the troubled county with due deliberation.

The Washintel channel was rerunning Tex Horn's interview with Jess Koplovik. That was followed with his own story of the crash of his observation plane when he flew too near General Zeider's halted tank column on the county line.

"The old spin game!"

Horn himself came back on the tiny screen, sitting propped up in a hospital bed, plastic patches on his face, wearing a white bandage instead of the hat.

"Listen to Higgins and the Pentagon. Listen to Washintel

WebWatch One. Believe what you please—and hold the hoop for the high-test hype."

Stopping only when I had to for gas and coffee, I was somewhere in West Virginia when another news report jolted me wide awake. The cops and the FBI had Clayton Barstow on the run. Wanted for murder and thought to be a secret agent of the McAdams rebels, Barstow had fled his Washington hideout just minutes ahead of a police raid. My photo was on the screen, along with the license plate number of Marion's car.

Outside the next town, I pulled into a run-down motel where the VACANCY sign still flickered. The yawning night clerk took the cash I offered from Alden's wallet, shoved a key across the counter, and jabbed his pen at a map to show me my room. Behind the building, nothing was moving in the half-lit space between the parked cars and a wall of trees and underbrush. I pulled into a gap beside a long gas-guzzler with a Tennessee plate. Five minutes later, grateful for the pliers and screwdriver Marion kept in the glove box, I was back on the highway with the traded plate.

By sunrise, I was in Kentucky. Hungry and groggy for sleep, I found a counter seat at a roadside diner, ordered bacon and eggs, and listened to a refugee who sat beside me with his pregnant wife. He looked jittery, as tired as I was, and he wanted to talk.

"Ain't it a bitch of a thing? Nothing nobody wanted. Folks like us caught between a pack of idiots back in McAdam and bigger idiots in the White House." He slurped his coffee and shrugged at the woman. "Could be we were fools to leave the farm, but I was worried sick for Mandy Ann. God knows what will happen to the farm before we get back. If we ever do get back."

"I was scairt." His wife shivered.

"It's tough on her." He put his arm around her. She snuggled against him with a hollow-eyed smile. "We got held up for hours at the line. Had to drive all night, but she has a sister in Columbus. I guess I can leave her there till the baby comes. I've got to get home to look after the place.

"Who the heck knows what to believe?" He patted her shoulder and looked back at me. "We heard Stuart McAdam on KRIF, claiming the Rebs stopped Zeider dead, but now Higgins claims Zeider's just taking his own sweet time to pacify the county. Things looked peaceful as ever when we left, but we had to take a side road around dozens of tanks stalled on the county line, one of them on fire. I never trusted Stuart, not since he got to be a high-priced lawyer for marijuana dealers, but now I just don't know."

His wife had sagged against him. He paused to croon something in her ear before he turned again to me.

"Our place is off the Lexington road, just ahead of Zeider's army. We heard warnings for civilians to get out of his way. I thought I could get Mandy Ann to Columbus and get back to look after things, but now—"

He blinked unhappily at me.

"This damn rainbow. You heard about the rainbow?"

I hadn't heard.

"We seen it after sundown yesterday. Behind us in the sky when we looked back. God knows what it is. I asked a state cop. He crossed himself and said we'd better drive on."

I asked for more about it.

"Not much like the one God put in the sky after the flood, that's for sure. The colors are all squeezed together in a narrow bright streak, with a dark line on one side of it. I thought the sky looked brighter under it. It was over McAdam County. God knows what it is or what it means."

I filled the gas tank and drove on. Fifty miles farther, I saw people standing in the parking lot outside a convenience store, gazing up into the west. A small boy ran to the side of the car when I stopped.

"Mister, there it is!" He pointed. "Easy to see if you just shade your eyes and look high enough."

I got out of the car. Shading my eyes and looking high, I soon found a faint dark arch across the cloudless blue, a thin bright streak drawn beside it, the rainbow lines nearly too narrow to see.

"You know Father Garron?" the excited boy demanded. "He calls it Satan's seal. His sign that the Rebs are damned to die for all the babies they've sent to hell."

I used the toilet, bought doughnuts and a plastic cup of coffee to go, drove on again. On the mapper's little monitor, I found Tex Horn now back in his studio. He had makeup over the patches and the hair piece on his head instead of the bandage or the hat, but he looked as if he should have been back in his hospital bed.

"Hop to the hype with Washintel One!" His trademark grin seemed to hurt. "A time you'll never forget, and still the mysteries multiply! Zeider's tanks are still stalled on the Lexington road. The Pentagon still refuses to admit any military setback. Our Ramona Del Rio is still in rebel territory, sealed off from the world with no chance to air her inside tales of the rebellion. And now—"

He was silent for a moment, catching breath to boom again.

"Now we have another phenomenon. Phenomenon! A word I never understood, but I guess this thing's queer enough to fit the bill."

The monitor showed scattered buildings in black silhouette against a fading sunset. A streak of darker darkness with a thin bright line at its edge arched across the sky above the rosy glow where the sun had set.

"What is it? Maybe the secret weapon that enabled the rebels to defy Zeider and his tanks? For answers, Washintel One has gathered a panel of men who know as much as anybody."

They sat across the table: a physicist from MIT, a colonel from the Pentagon, the editor of the Louisville *KyNet*. The physicist, Victor Gueria, was a lively little man with a neat goatee and an impish smile.

"This shell over McAdam County?" Horn asked him. "What is it?"

"A shell? Exactly." He had a slight French accent. "The term I was seeking. It covers the rebels like an inverted bowl."

"Bowl of what?"

"Does anybody know?" He spread his arms. "Not much."

"Give us an educated guess."

"I've no basis for a guess. Here's the little I can say, based on media reports and sheer speculation. It's an arc of a perfect circle, cut off where it touches the Earth. It appears to refract transmitted light into a very narrow band of spectral color. It ignites explosives, perhaps through some electronic effect yet to be explained. It can be made opaque to selected radio frequencies, interrupting communication. Beyond that—" He shrugged, his smile ironic. "I think it's startling enough to refute the notion that science is done."

"Done what?"

"Done exploring our infinite universe." He bent forward, happy to have an audience. "You find cynics who claim we've already laid out all the big principles of the ordered universe. Left us nothing but chinks to fill in. Right now, I'm rather happy to say that I don't see any chink wide enough to admit this effect—whatever it is. Future science, I believe, will continue to astonish us with dazzling paradigm shifts—and new chances to dazzle the world with such unexpected and exciting forward leaps into an endless unknown."

"Thank you sir, and good luck to you!" Horn turned to the editor. "You're the media. What can you add?"

"Not much." The editor shrugged. "People are puzzled by this rebel weapon, sometimes terrified. One fanatic has called it the sign of Armageddon and warned the world to pray. Myself, if Dr. Gueria will forgive me, I'm pretty confident that the science already has the answer. I think, in fact, that I know who to ask."

They looked at him, waiting.

"A man named Rob Roy McAdam. I've tried to interview him, but somebody at his company said he was not available. Not to anybody. He's a native of the county and founder of a failed firm called CyberSoft. He and his colleagues have a habit of asking hard questions and keeping the answers to themselves. One example is a device for communication security he calls a cryptophone, which I believe has resisted federal efforts at reverse engineering. True, sir?"

He looked inquiringly at the colonel, a beefy man with ribbons on his uniform, who merely scowled.

"Comment, sir?" Horn asked him. "Your security wizards have really failed to break his encryption algorithm?"

"No comment!" the colonel turned pink. "I've never met this McAdam."

"Not many have." The editor nodded. "He dislikes publicity."

"I've seen his cryptophone," Gueria said. "It baffles my computer friends, but I can offer one comment on his works." He looked at Horn, "When we tried to identify the source of this barrier effect, it appeared to be centered in McAdam City. As nearly we can determine, in the precise location of the CyberSoft building."

" 'Barrier effect.' " Horn grinned stiffly at the colonel. "An effective barrier, would you agree, sir? If it has halted the advance of General Zeider's tank corps?"

"Poppycock!" The colonel grew redder. "General Zeider's mission was simply to probe the rebel defenses. He did so, and returned with his report for President Higgins." He looked at his watch. "I can tell you that the President will be on the air within the hour, reporting to the nation."

"To the nation?" The editor fumbled a laplink out of his pocket and turned to the colonel. "What will he say?"

"What do you expect?" The colonel stiffened. "No big surprises. None that I expect. The rebels have left him no alternative. He says he was not elected to preside over the disintegration of the Union."

Higgins was a tiny figure on the tiny mapper screen when I caught him shuffling to the lectern in the White House press room, his pale jaw grimly set.

"Fellow Americans—" His voice was hoarse and husky. "We're all Americans, even those misguided insurgents who are trying now to deny their own precious birthright. Twice I have sent Senator Finn to Kentucky with my own urgent appeal to them. They refused to let his airplane land.

"They puzzle me." He shook his haggard head. "Somehow, they

have willingly cut themselves off from rail service and mail service, from telephone and telegraph service, even from the infonet. I don't know whether these remarks can reach them, but I am speaking now to inform them—if they are listening—and to inform the whole American nation, that we have made our last best effort at peaceful reconciliation. All in vain. We have been rejected and ignored.

"I had hoped—" He paused, leaning on the lectern, his thin old voice quavering with emotion. "I would have given what life may be left to me to avoid this tragic moment. In spite of every appeal, however, and only after desperate discussion with my cabinet, the leaders of congress, and the chiefs of staff, our decision has been made. The rebellion—"

He stopped, hollowed eyes blankly staring, and took a long gasp for breath.

"The rebellion will be crushed."

That arch of shadow with its narrow rainbow lining climbed above the sinking sun, as far beyond my own understanding as it had been for the man from MIT. What did it mean for the nation? The world? If one county could drop out of the union, another might. If Rob Roy revealed his secret—or the secrets of his AIs—might America dissolve? Was the age of nationhood doomed to end. What then?

These were larger issues than I wanted to think about. I felt a sharper anxiety for Marion and the kids. They had gone to the county to help me. Were they trapped there now, faced with dangers I didn't know how to explore? If the county was really sealed away from all contact, how could I hope to reach them?

And Beth? Though Lydia was still a dark and painful riddle to me, Beth's image haunted my dreams. She had seemed half in love with me, but her baby brother was probably still closer to her heart. Did she know how I had been escorted out of the county? If she did, how did she feel about it? I longed to see her.

I met increasing traffic for a time. Cars with baggage or bicycles or now and then a mattress tied on top. Pickups loaded with household goods. The stream slowed and ceased. I came at last to a wooden barrier and a boldly painted sign planted in the middle of the pavement:

DANGER!
MILITARY ZONE
KEEP OUT!

I turned the car and used the mapper to locate a farm road that ran east, almost parallel to the county line. A dozen miles along it, another road took me south again, around the end of the county and finally to a similar splash of bold black ink:

DANGER!
EVACUATION ZONE
KEEP OUT!

The land looked empty beyond it: naked rock and scrub timber on hills strip-mined long ago and never restored. Wondering if anybody had still lived here to be evacuated, I pulled around the sign and drove on till the car stopped and refused to start again. The mapper was dead. So was my watch. When I tried the cryptophone, all I heard was silence.

I left the car and walked a few miles down the empty road toward the county line till something stopped me. Nothing I could see. Nothing I felt, except a sudden resistance like the feel of water to a wader. I pushed against it till a flash of heat and a wave of weakness forced me back.

Experimenting when I had breath again, I found a broken branch and probed with that. It met the same resistance. I pushed with all my strength till I felt heat on my arm. A splinter at the tip was charred and smoking when I drew it back. Gunpowder would have exploded.

I climbed a little hill that gave me a view of a bluegrass pasture in a shallow valley beyond the barrier. A few horses were grazing across it. Beyond them a yellow pickup was turning off a road. It stopped in front of a white-painted farmhouse. A little girl ran out to meet the driver. He picked her up to hug her, set her down to get a bag out of the cab. She followed him into the house. Not half a mile away, they seemed as distant as the moon.

I felt helpless. Defeated at least for the moment, I walked back to the dead car, ate my last doughnut, drank the last of the cold coffee, and crawled into the back seat to sleep.

Toward midnight, something like thunder woke me.

CHAPTER NINETEEN

STILL HALF ASLEEP, I stumbled out of the car and stood clinging to the open door. I had taken off my shoes, and sharp rocks hurt my feet. It took me a moment to remember where I was, but the rumble in the sky was aircraft engines, no normal thunder. The moonless sky was black. I saw no lights anywhere till something flashed high above me.

Not normal lightning. It lit no clouds, but something flashed again, and yet again. Listening dazedly for thunder, I heard a crash that seemed to jolt the ground, another and another, a roar in the sky that grew louder than the engine drone. The night was suddenly blazing with a Niagara of fire pouring down the curve of the barrier all across the north and east.

I knew in a moment that Zeider's assault had begun. His aircraft and missiles were exploding against the rebel shield, whatever it was that had made the rainbow that was no rainbow, baffled Gueria's science, stopped me with that flash of heat, charred my probing stick—and detonated anything explosive.

Blazing debris was sliding down, tracing the shape of that invisible bowl inverted over the county. I stood there shivering, staring up at the terrible splendor of it, till a nearer blast almost overhead scattered flaming stuff that seemed to fall straight toward me.

I tried to run. Dazzled by the fire in the sky, I tripped over something I didn't see. I fell and lay there aching and gasping for breath till another blast shook the ground and nerved me to my feet. Limping back to the dead car, I saw flames licking high where the falling stuff had come down, not a hundred yards away.

Relieved to be alive, I got back in the car and sat watching the flicker of those thundering concussions and the burning debris that kept raining down, sometimes so close I had to flinch. Remnants of missiles and shells, of bombs and bombers; the funeral pyres of unlucky airmen.

Pity for them took hold of me, and a deeper dread. Was this what Alden had foreseen when he wrote *Terror in America?* If a single county could defy a superpower, what new shocks might now shake the world? How many more brave men would be ordered to death by officers trying to win another war with the weapons and tactics of the last?

The assault must have lasted an hour. New explosions boomed and echoed from the dark hills behind me. The sky flashed and dimmed, burned and flickered and dimmed again as Higgins and Zeider did their desperate best to wipe the stubborn rebels off the map.

That dreadful half-dome of fire darkened and died at last, though smoky fires still burned all along the curve where the shell touched the earth. Silence fell. The night was black again. I sat there in the car, cold and achingly alone, wondering what might come now to Marion and the children, to Beth. They seemed to matter more than the rebels and the world.

I knew no answers and had nowhere to look for them unless I could somehow get inside the shell. I was thirsty and hungry. At last I must have slept. What roused me was the drone of small aircraft far off in the north, and later the thump-thump-thump of helicopters. Searchlights stabbed out of them, scanning the smoldering wreckage. Zeider was counting his losses.

The aircraft departed, at least from anywhere near me. Still I sat there, waiting for dawn, for hope, for anything, till something jarred me wide awake. Sunlight flooded the car. Something rapped the glass. I sat up and opened the door to a man with a pitchfork.

"Who the hell are you?"

I stared at him, too startled to speak. He was bareheaded, naked to the waist, chewing on a straw. His face and torso were blistered, his eyes inflamed and rimmed with grime. Blood had soaked through a crude bandage on his hand. Stepping warily back from the car, he leveled the pitchfork at me and snarled again:

"Who the hell—"

Without thinking, I gave him my name.

"Damn firebug!" He spat out the straw and jabbed the pitchfork toward me. "You torched my place last night."

"Not me." I shrank from the shining tines.

"Somebody did." His red eyes narrowed. "Blew up my propane tank."

"It must have been the rebel's weapon." I gestured toward the barrier. "It makes some kind of wall around the county. I don't know how, but it sets off explosions. It stopped General Zeider. It stopped my car. Stopped me when I tried to walk through it. It must have hit your propane tank. I'm no firebug."

"Just a federal agent!" He turned savagely sardonic. "Setting fires as you go, to clear the way for Zeider?"

"Didn't you see the sky last night?" He backed away when I climbed out of the car, but still clutched the pitchfork. "Missiles and bombs and airplanes blew up when they hit the barrier. Everything they threw against it."

"Bombs?" He shook his head in dazed disbelief. "I did see one hell of a storm, but I was trying to save my barn."

"The barrier explodes things," I said. "Ammunition. Fumes in gas tanks—"

"Ammunition in a gun?" He frowned at the red-stained bandage. "I ran out with a pistol when I heard the noise. It misfired. I was trying to tie my hand up when the propane exploded and I saw the barn on fire."

He dropped the pitchfork and grimaced at the bandage.

"A hell of a night!" he muttered. "Burnt my house. Burnt my barn. Like to got me when the roof fell in. "Hell of a night!"

He sat down on the hood of the car and wiped at his face with a grimy rag. His harsh hostility had melted away, and his forlorn face gave me a pang of sympathy.

"Lost everything I had," he muttered again. "Even my wife." His voice caught. "She's caught inside—inside whatever it is." He spread his arms in desperate appeal. "Will I ever see her again?"

"I've got relatives trapped there," I told him. "I was trying to get through to them, but who knows?"

"Hey!" His black-rimmed eyes blinked as if they had just discovered me. "You said your name's Barstow! You're Clayton Barstow? Wanted by the FBI?"

He hardly seemed to care, and I simply nodded.

"So you're on the run?" He paused to contemplate me, and finally shook his head. "Good luck. You'll need it."

I sat there staring at nothing till he spoke again.

"Tell me why—"

His voice caught again. Bare shoulders shaking, he sat for a time slumped down on the hood of the car before he went on.

"My wife and I." He nodded toward the barrier. "We're Christians. I was baptized into the Church of Christ when I was seven years old. I've tried to live right, the best a man can. I never thought God would let such hell happen. I don't know why—"

He blinked dully at me.

"Things change."

I knew nothing better to say, and he went on as if he hadn't heard. "You've heard of Father Garron?"

"I've seen him."

"Who hasn't? He's on TV every day. Martha listened to him on KRIF and tried to take me with her into his temple. He wanted us to tithe half what we made and give our lives to his crazy Kingdom of Christ. His God ain't mine, but Martha went mad for him. Hell-bent on saving every unborn baby.

"I asked who was going to love 'em and feed 'em and teach 'em anything. She said the Lord will provide. I told her to look at the gangs shooting drugs and shooting up the streets, and she'd see He had left 'em for the Devil to provide. That made her mad. She never paid no mind to common sense. Gave Garron's temple every penny she could get her hands on, and she's been spending every minute she could at his phone bank, selling salvation. Begging suckers to shell out all they have for tickets to Garron's crazy paradise.

"She was there the morning Stuart McAdam promoted himself to colonel and said he and his pals had declared their independence. Called me to get to the temple as quick as I could, because Garron said Armageddon had broke out. The final war between God and Satan. The baby-killing minions of Satan would find that their judgment day had come, and his Legion of the Sword would prevail.

"He was declaring a golden jubilee. McAdam County had become his Kingdom of Christ. The Holy Spirit had anointed him to rule it as the Viceroy of Christ. He was giving command of his Legion to Stuart McAdam, who would be marching out to conquer the rest of the world for the new age of the Apocalypse.

"She was still talking when the phone went dead. I never knew what happened, but my pickup wouldn't start. The power went off. The TV died. I started out to the paddock to look after the horses and ran into a wall I never seen. It scared me, Mister. It still scares me. I don't what to think. Martha don't know Stuart the way I do, and I don't trust Garron or his God.

"But still—" He made a hopeless gesture toward the smoke still drifting around the foot of the barrier. "I just don't know. Maybe Martha was right. Maybe Garron has set the Devil loose to scourge evil out of the world. Let me show you what they've done to me."

He slid off the hood of the car and limped stiffly up a side road to what was left where his farmhouse had stood: A pickup with the paint and tires burnt off, standing in the tangled steel and tumbled concrete blocks that had been a garage; a naked foundation, littered with burnt bed springs and appliances. He bent to pick up a little mass of twisted brass.

"A Seth Thomas clock. In the family for five generations."

He tossed it away and nodded toward a white-painted fence.

"I had horses. A young stallion sired by Rocket Dust. A Thoroughbred mare out of Final Friday, with a fine foal she'd throwed this summer."

"Caught in the fire?"

"Just as bad." He shook his head forlornly. "We ain't inside the county. That damn wall don't follow county lines. Cuts right across my place. The horses were caught on the other side." He waved his empty hands. "I'm cleaned out. Nothing to eat. Nowhere to sleep. Nothing to wear but the rags I've got on."

I reached for Alden's wallet.

"Thank you, Mister." He shook his head. "I ain't begging."

"So what will you do?"

"I don't know." He stood there half a minute, lips quivering, shaking his head at the charred relics of his life. "I guess I'll just start walking."

Wondering what I myself could do, I stared after him. A hundred yards up the road, he stopped and turned back, pointing into the sky. I heard the drone of an aircraft engine and saw a small plane diving out of the west.

"The wall!" Pointing again, he was hoarsely shouting. "It's down! They're coming out." He was suddenly running back to me. "Get out of sight till we know what they want."

We scrambled into the car. The plane came low up the road.

It circled twice to survey the wreckage along the wall, passing close over us, and climbed a little as it went on east.

"Now what the hell?" He stared at it in sick bewilderment. "If devils claimed the county, has God let them out?"

We sat in the car till the plane turned in the distance and came back along the road, flying a little higher, and finally vanished in the direction of McAdam City.

"Our chance to get inside!" I told him. "Let's go."

"Whatever you say." He shrugged, with a bleak grimace. "I guess they've done what they can to me." We got out of the car and started for the highway. "There's a short cut." He gestured. "Through the paddock."

I followed him down a side road. We had to leave it twice to skirt craters where bombs or missiles had fallen, but it led us along the white-painted paddock fence. The horses were gone. Dismally, he stopped to point at a gap they must have broken out when the assault terrified them. A mile or so farther we heard traffic and climbed a wooded ridge that let us look out to the highway.

"Garron!" He turned to me in glum-faced wonderment. "Garron and his soldiers of the sword."

A long line of cars and pickups was creeping slowly from McAdam City. It was led by a silver-painted pickup filled with men in Kentucky Rifle uniform, who held a huge silver-painted sword pointing into the sky. Loudspeakers were blaring out "The Battle Hymn of the Republic."

> *Mine eyes have seen the glory of*
> *the coming of the Lord.*
> *He is trampling out the vintage where*
> *the grapes of wrath are stored.*

CHAPTER TWENTY

"*GARRON'S HOLY LEGION!*" Whispering, he shrank back into the shadows of the trees behind us, and we stood watching till the loudspeaker faded and the silver pickup had gone on beyond where the barrier had been. "The saints of the sword, marching out to save the world."

He turned to me with a bleak ironic grin.

"Or has Garron turned them all to devils?"

Devils was the better word, I thought, but he cried out before I could speak.

"Martha!" His face was twisted with emotion. "Likely with them, coming home. When she sees what happened to our place—"

He stood still for a moment, and plunged headlong down the slope toward the highway. I went back down the other way and walked on behind the ridge till I reached a disused road that came through a gap to a woodlot stacked with drying firewood.

The highway was empty when I looked through the gap. I

stopped under the cover of a leaning tree, sat down on a rock, and tried the cryptophone. After a moment, I heard Beth's brisk recorded voice.

"Caller not identified. Please repeat the alphabet for voice match." That took my breath, and it took me a moment to begin. "Clay!" Her actual voice broke in. "Where are you?"

I saw her in my mind, recalled the warmth of her lithe body against me and the light scent she had worn that night in the garden when we stumbled together in the dark. Trembling, I had to catch another breath.

"Hiding under a tree," I said. "At the end of a ridge near the west highway—"

"Here?" She cut me off. "Inside the county?"

"A stroke of luck. I got through the barrier."

"Bad luck." Her voice went flat. "You shouldn't be here."

"I'm hunted. Nowhere else to go."

"You'll be hunted here. Nowhere to hide, unless you have a plan."

That dimmed my elation.

"No plan," I confessed. "I've been living on the run. No way to make a plan."

"What do you want me to do?"

I yearned for her sympathy, even if I had no right to it, but all I heard was a crisp detachment. I felt afraid she might hang up. She owed me nothing, after all.

"I don't know," I said. "With the county sealed off, I don't know what to expect."

"Nothing good." Her voice was slow and grave. "We seem to have won our battle with America, but we have wars of our own right here in the county. Just as bitter. Outcomes yet to be decided."

She seemed absorbed with them.

"I watched the bombardment." I tried to hold her. "Incredible fireworks. Did anything get through?"

"Through Rob Roy's screen? He calls it the silicon shell. It was magnificent." Pride lifted her voice. "Nobody here got a scratch, not that I've heard about. But you?" I heard a sudden concern. "You were outside?"

"And close," I said. "Burning junk fell all around me."

"You were lucky." A new concern edged her voice. "Clay, why did you come back?"

Because of her, more than anything, but I couldn't say that.

"To look for Marion Kirk. My brother's widow and her kids. She'd heard of my troubles and came back here hoping to help me. Do you know anything—"

"Not much." She stopped as if impatient with the question, but in a moment she went on. "Pepperlake called to tell me that Mrs. Kirk was here, asking about you. I had lunch with her and the children." Her voice softened. "I fell in love with your little nephew. So anxious about you, and doing his best to be the man of the house. Of course there was nothing I could tell them, except that you had disappeared."

"Are they still here?"

"In this madhouse?" Her voice sharpened. "Who knows? They'd come on the last commuter flight. Finally, when you weren't here, they wanted to rent a car to get out of the county, but it must have been too late for that. Too many people scrambling to escape Zeider's tanks."

"I've got to find them."

"Forget it." I imagined her forbidding frown. "You can't show your face. You know my brother Stuart?"

"Too well. He doesn't like me."

"He hates you, Clay." Her voice fell, I thought with regret. "His Kentucky Rifles are the army now. He controls the police. He's had your picture on KRIF a dozen times a day."

Her voice stopped as if she had no more to say. Sitting there under that storm-battered tree, I felt a wave of weakness and defeat. Getting through the barrier had seemed a victory, Beth's voice a benediction. All for naught. My finger was on the button to snap the microphone back into the slick plastic case of the cryptophone, when I heard her voice again.

"Has anybody seen you here?"

I put the little instrument back to my ear. "One man, but he's gone now with Garron's convoy."

"They've closed the shell again. He won't be back." She was silent so long that I thought she had hung up. "Wait." She was crisply decisive. "Wait where you are."

I waited, wondering what I was waiting for. My watch was running again. I set it by guess, listened, watched. Twice I heard the engine of a small airplane. Cawing crows cruised over the woodlot. A pebble in my dry mouth did nothing for my thirst. I moved to the cover of another tree where I could watch the road. Traffic on it had ceased. It must have been near noon when I saw a lone car coming fast from the direction of McAdam City.

It slowed, turned off the highway, stopped finally in the gap not a hundred yards below where I hid. The driver rolled a window down to look out. A man, I thought, till she took off a Reb cap and the sun caught her face.

Beth!

I ran to meet her. In the same tan sweater I remembered, she looked as lovely as she had been in my dreams. Her eyes really violet, her hair the hue of polished amber. Eager for her, I opened my arms as she slipped out of the car, but she stepped back to study me as critically as if I had been a stranger.

"You look used up."

Her feelings were hard to read. "Hungry," I said. "Thirsty."

"Wait a few minutes." She turned to look around us. "What's beyond the ridge?"

"A woodlot. Stacked firewood. Young trees that cut off the view of anything beyond."

"Good enough. Get in the car."

My anxiety was lost in the clean shape of her body, the glow of her skin, her slight but haunting scent, her fine-boned face, but she scarcely looked at me. Driving on through the gap, she parked in the shadow of the leaning tree.

"Okay. Let's talk."

She turned, waiting expectantly.

"I'm pretty desperate. It's wonderful to see you again, but—" I had to hesitate. "I don't know the situation here."

"Nobody does." She frowned. "An ugly muddle."

"I've no right to put you in danger."

"It isn't just you." She shook her head, staring across the stacks of drying firewood. "My brothers have put the world in danger. Rob Roy's new science promises consequences he never took time to think about. Stuart wants to conquer the world with it. America, anyhow. As for you—"

She turned back to frown very soberly at me.

"You've got yourself involved, but that's not all. You're a threat to my father and me. Even to Stuart. I don't want him forced to kill you."

"Neither do I."

I saw the fleeting ghost of a smile, but her tone was grim.

"Do you know it was his men who took you out of the house? Carried you out of the county."

"And beat me up on the way? I thought so."

"My own brother." She flinched from the pain of it. "I can't help what he is. I've always tried to save him from himself, but now—"

Gloomily, she shook her head.

"Stuart may dislike me," I said. "But I don't see how I'm any threat to him."

"He thinks you are." She nodded, her lips set tight. "He told me so when I tried to confront him. Made an ugly scene. He does hate you, Clay."

"He has no reason—"

"He hated your brother. He blames you both for his time in prison."

I wondered again if Stuart or his friends had mailed the letter bomb, but the FBI had turned up no evidence of that. Neither had I.

"Because of the book?" I asked. "He did expose a lot of people who didn't want to be exposed, but I don't think he ever made Stuart a special target."

"Or did he?" Her fine eyes narrowed, searching me. "Alden wasn't a witness at the trial that sent him to prison, but Stuart still blames him. He thinks your brother came here as a secret agent of the FBI. He thinks you were sent to take his place."

That hit me hard. It recalled Bella Garlesh and Agent Botman and Acorn Three. She must have seen me wince.

"Is that true?"

I wanted to deny it.

"Partly true." Looking into her face, I had to nod. "The FBI was investigating Alden's death, with no sign of success. An agent took me to meet Director Garlesh. She told me Alden had agreed to make secret reports to them."

Beth was nodding, her face set hard.

"I didn't want to believe her," I said. "Alden had ethics, but he was desperately concerned about the future of America. Garlesh said his love of the country persuaded him. And—" I had to hesitate. "She wanted me to report anything I learned."

"I suspected something of the sort," she murmured, "the day you turned up in my office. Go on."

"I'm no great spy," I told her. "They gave me a phone number for the contact agent, but I never had much to report. And then— I don't know what happened, but my calls were somehow intercepted. I quit calling, and heard no more from them."

"That's all?"

I nodded. I said nothing of the acorn fragments identified in the remnants of the bomb that killed my brother, nothing of the three acorns I found in the blood around Lydia Starker's head, nothing of those I found by my own head when I woke up in the mud. A grim enigma I had no answers for.

"I'm glad you told me," she said, "though the fact could make you harder to defend." A moment of sober silence. "I'm taking you back to our place."

That took my breath, and she saw my concern.

"A hard choice," she said. "I don't like the risk from Stuart and his police—he's made the city cops take an oath of loyalty to him. He wants to be president of the Free State—or whatever they name their new nation. I talked your problem over with my father. We didn't come up with anything better."

I was still reluctant.

"I think we can keep you safe. Stuart is out of the family now, after a bitter fight with my father. I've always loved him, or tried to, though he has often made it difficult. Sometimes impossible. He's crazy now." Her voice had sharpened, and I felt the pain of her regret. "Gone crazy with his sense of power. He had this mad dream of sharing Rob Roy's weapon with other militias. Uniting them to conquer the continent."

She shook her head and sat silent, staring moodily across the woodlot through the cracked windshield. Rousing herself at last, she turned back to me.

"He was mocking President Higgins for his concern for the needless loss of life. To justify his stand, he quoted Thomas Jefferson. I think I recall the words. After Shay's Rebellion in 1787, Jefferson wrote, 'God forbid we ever be 20 years without such a rebellion. . . . The tree of liberty must be refreshed from time to time with the blood of patriots and tyrants. It is its natural manure.'

"Our father came back at him with a different Jefferson, writing at another time with a more humane philosophy. I had to side with him. Other matters came up. Stuart got violent. He struck our father. They've always fought, but never with fists. This is the final break. Stuart won't be back in the house. We've had the locks changed since you disappeared."

"But if he runs the county—"

"So far." She nodded gravely, staring away into the trees, and finally shrugged. "Maybe not forever."

"I must get a message to Marion," I told her. "At the hotel if she's still there, or at home if she was able to get out."

"No message." Beth was very firm. "There's risk enough already. I'm driving Orinda's car instead of my own. We'll stay here till dark." She moved to get out of the car. "She fixed a lunch box for us. Let's eat."

CHAPTER TWENTY-ONE

WE GOT INTO the back seat, the lunch box between us. Saliva already wetting my dry mouth, I waited while she opened the box and poured ice tea out of a thermos. I drained two cups of it. Orinda had packed roast beef sandwiches, fried chicken, a couple of apples. Beth nibbled at an apple while I attacked a cold drumstick.

"You're like a famished wolf." She grinned at my appetite. "Tell me where you've been."

I told her how I'd gotten to Georgetown and something about my stay in Marion's house, and I asked for more about Stuart.

"He's gone mad." Pain shadowed her face. "Even before Zeider attacked, he was fighting a war of his own with Joel Garron. Garron wanted to make the free county the capital of his infonet empire."

"Garron won?" I asked. "I saw his holy army on the road, singing their battle hymn."

"He is on the march." She shook her head. "But only because Stuart drove him out."

Digging in the basket for another sandwich, I stopped to listen.

"Stuart wants to unite the militia groups scattered across the country into an empire of his own. Some of their leaders were already here with reinforcements for the Kentucky Rifles. The showdown came when the shell cut Garron off from his electronic congregation. He wanted the council to open it for his broadcasts and let him build a powerful new station of his own here in the county."

"The council?"

"That's the three-man executive body. Rob Roy, Cass Pepperlake, and Kit Moorhawk. You know Kit?"

"He's hard to know."

She frowned. "Stuart calls him a 'hollow man.' Says he's ashamed of his size, and forever trying to make up for it. He did for a time, with millions coming in from his coal combustion patents. He married a Miss Kentucky, built her a mansion, bought a stable of Thoroughbreds, endowed the tech center at the college. He paid Rob Roy's way though MIT and funded CyberSoft.

"But he lost the patents and the millions. Lost his wife. Lost a long war in the courts. He was robbed, he feels, by the coal interests and power companies, the justice system, the whole political machine. They've broken him. He's lost his nerve.

"I saw him at the Council meeting Ramona Del Rio covered for KRIF, back before Zeider's assault. He still puts up a front. Talks too loud, wears his rainbow vests, caves in when once he would have fought. Stuart was there to scare off Garron, talking war, bragging that his militia could take care of any Feds that got through the shell.

"Kit was afraid. You could hear it in his voice, read it in what he didn't say. Afraid of Stuart. Afraid the shell might fail. Afraid Garron would sell us out to President Higgins, even if they gave him what he wanted."

I had finished my sandwich. She grinned and handed me another.

"Rob Roy?" I asked. "If the shell is his, where did he stand?"

"He does own the shell—and guards it like his heart. But he

lives in his own ivory tower, content to play with his own new math
and happy with how well it fits the universe. He wants freedom to
think. Freedom for others to think and say what they think. That's
the why of his cryptophone. He wants an open road past all the
meddlers and censors.

"He and Kit might have offered Garron some kind of compromise. Kit out of fear, Rob Roy because he didn't care, but Stuart
won't have any kind of deal. He's not on the council, of course, but
he does command the Rifles. Kit was giving way to his bluster till
Cass Pepperlake spoke.

"In the end, it was Cass who made the difference. He has his
own dream of the future, but it's not carved in stone like Garron's
or Stuart's. No Kingdom of Christ, nor any militia empire. He just
wants to keep us really free, free to find our own future however we
can.

"Garron tried to bribe the council. With his new station built,
he said, he'd have millions coming in from his legion of saints, with
no guff from the IRS about his tax-exempt status. He offered to split
his loot. His flock was big and growing fast, all they owned gifts
from the Lord and due back to him. Their tithes would be a national
income no blockade could stop.

"The three finally met behind closed doors and came out with
a deal Cass had engineered. They opened a gate in the shell just
long enough to let Garron and his people out of the county. It had
to be quick, before Zeider could close the roads. Garron threatened
the wrath of Jehovah, but Stuart held the high card. I think Garron
plans to set up new headquarters and build his own infonet station
at his branch temple in Tennessee. Anyhow, he's out." She made
a face. "Good riddance!"

"But there's still Stuart."

"Stuart."

She nodded unhappily and said no more about him. The sandwich was gone, and another piece of chicken. She gave me a bright
red apple. I settled back in the seat happy just to be with her, feeling
no need to talk. Stuart didn't know I was here; he might never know.

I remember nodding off and murmuring some apology. When I woke dusk had fallen.

I lay sprawled in the seat. Beth was in front, starting the engine. She waited for me to climb in beside her, and had me wear her Reb cap, pulled low to hide my face. Driving without lights, she got us back to the empty highway and drove by moonlight till we saw lights ahead.

When she stopped, we were in her garage. Orinda met us at the kitchen door with a quiet brown smile. Colin McAdam got stiffly out of his chair to shake my hand. A gracious host, he offered drinks nobody accepted and murmured a blessing over a hot dinner, beef roast and vegetables out of his garden, but he ate almost in silence. He looked older, I thought, thinner and anxious. When Orinda offered coffee he excused himself and left the table.

"He's worried sick about my brothers." Beth dropped her voice. "He's never even tried to understand Rob Roy's science, but now he's afraid of what may come of it. He's tried to reason with Stuart, but Stuart never did listen to reason. I think he never will."

We sat over the coffee a few minutes longer, but Beth soon said goodnight. Orinda gave me the new keys to my room and brought fresh towels. The closets were empty, and the childhood mementos that Stuart had left were gone from the walls. When I looked in the little drawer in the bedside table, the gun and box of ammunition were gone. I found the empty clip still there, however, and a dozen oak acorns.

They set me to wondering again about the acorn fragments left by the bomb that killed my brother, the acorns I had found by Lydia Starker's head and my own, and Agent Monty Botman. What did the acorns mean? Was Stuart the Frankfort bomber and my brother's killer? Not likely; he had been in prison. What had become of Botman? Recalling McAdam's talk of an unsettling new paradigm, of new leaders rising to fight for the power of new technologies, I was glad to see the new deadbolt on the outside door.

———

The infotel set was still in the room.

". . . facts to the max." I heard Tex Horn's mellow boom when I turned it on. Sitting again at his studio news desk, he pushed the big white hat farther back and winked at the lens. "Washintel One is happy to report the channels clear in time for President Higgins and a new appeal to the Kentucky rebels."

On the monitor, Higgins was seated in the Oval Office, a flag draped beside him. Makeup had given his sunken cheeks a rosy glow, but failed to hide his illness.

"Fellow citizens—" His voice rasped hoarsely, and he started over. "My fellow Americans, citizens of McAdam County and citizens of every county in every state, I appeal to you in desperation. I love our nation. So, I know, do most of you. I am sad to say that recent events have left our national unity in the gravest disarray, but I'm not ready to write it off.

"But forget the rhetoric." He shrugged, with a feeble try at a smile. "I've no strength for empty wind, and our tragic situation leaves no time for waste. I can be very brief, very simple.

"As all of you know, McAdam County has declared its independence. The reasons for that rash act can be left for history, but it is one that no government can tolerate. Our forces under General Zeider were ordered to put the insurrection down. He reports that his action has resulted in a stalemate. His forces are now standing down, awaiting further orders.

"Our previous offers of negotiation or arbitration have been rejected or ignored. Tonight, after due consultation with the cabinet and congressional leaders, and out of our sacred obligation to the nation, I am making one last attempt. Let me remind you that one battle is not the war. Even if your defenses are impregnable—for all I know they may be—they can never make you truly independent. At best, you can only shut yourselves up in a prison of your own making.

"For the sake of your people, I beg you to consider the costs of your small victory. Can you grow food enough? Can you pump your own oil and refine your own gasoline? Can you generate power to light and heat your homes? Can you manufacture medicines? Won't your people want sugar, coffee, a thousand everyday necessities you don't produce?

"We aren't asking for your souls, or even threatening you with starvation. The chiefs of staff and the congressional leaders have approved very generous terms. First, you must withdraw your claim to national independence. The Union is indivisible; the Civil War established that. Second, your defensive weapon must be surrendered.

"In return, we offer a general amnesty to every inhabitant of your so-called Haven, with total immunity against any charges of treason or sedition. We propose the establishment of a neutral international commission to arbitrate your differences with the Union. We will compensate the inventor or inventors of your weapon with an award to be determined by the commission.

"We await your response, which we expect within twenty-four hours."

Higgins's quivery voice faded out. His haggard features dimmed and vanished.

"Fisherman Higgins back at the pond," Tex Horn rumbled heartily from the monitor. "Dangling the same old bait. Will the Rebs jump for it? I don't think so, but here's Ramona Del Rio, who has been trapped behind the lines until today. Washintel One is happy to welcome her back. Always on tap with her tips for tomorrow, she has asked Reb Commander Stuart McAdams for an early answer to the president."

His image faded into hers.

"Hiya, Tex." She touched her lips with her fingertips and waved the kiss into the lens. "I spent most of the morning with Commander McAdam, scouting the rebel perimeter. He left no doubt about his own plans. They don't include surrender."

The camera had caught her waving from the window of a pickup truck jolting over rough country. Beside her, sitting straight at the wheel, Stuart was stopping and stopping again to lift binoculars and scan the wreckage that had fallen along the foot of the invisible barrier. He paused to study a group of men outside the shell who were stabbing at it with rods, flashing red and green lasers at it, frowning at the dials of their machines.

"That was earlier today." She spoke again. "We saw half a dozen teams probing for the secret of the rebel defense, but no sign they were learning anything. While we wait for any answer to the president, here is a brief update on the conflict as I see it from here inside the rebels' wonder wall." Gracefully, she stroked the silver streak in her sleek back hair. "General Zeider's all-out assault failed to penetrate what they call a 'silicon shell' though there's no evidence that actual silicon is any part of it. It stopped him in his tracks.

"It has not been used, however, in any offensive way. It simply halted his assault. Tanks and other attacking vehicles were stalled and often burned. Attacking aircraft burst into flames and fell out of the sky. Bombs and missiles exploded in the air. Machine-gun and small arms fire had no effect. Troops threw their weapons away and fled in panic. The rebels have offered no explanation of how this shell deflects or destroys everything thrown against it."

The monitor went dark, then lit again with Stuart standing on the cab of his pickup truck, parked on the highway just inside the rebel checkpoint I remembered. Beyond him, searchlights bathed a fire-scarred hillside littered with all the burned and broken metal that had fallen out of the sky.

"A word about the commander," her voice went on, "while we wait for his remarks. He comes from what might be called the first family of the insurgent county and he has survived clashes of his own with the law. Once on trial for illegal traffic in arms and high explosives, he was acquitted by a jury of his local peers. More recently, he served a year in the Frankfort prison on a narcotics conviction. When I inquired today about his goals for the future, here is what he said."

Sitting with her in the studio, Stuart bowed to the lens.

"I will liberate America." His public voice rang confident and clear. "Our forefathers came here to find their freedom. They fought a bitter war to keep it, wrote the Constitution and the Bill of Rights to guarantee it. But now . . ."

Voice falling, he paused to shake his head.

"We have let foolish men squander our precious heritage in their greedy scramble for money and political advantage. Our property rights are gone. If my pasture floods too often, it becomes a wetland, no longer mine. If I am accused of a narcotics offense, the feds can seize my car or my home or my bank account before I am ever convicted—that happened to me."

Grinning, with a glint of defiance in eyes as blue as Beth's, he faded from the monitor and returned standing now on the pickup cab. A striking figure in his new green jacket, gold-braided pants, and white rebel hat, he paused for a moment, gazing soberly into the lens, then turned slowly to look out across the litter of ruined weaponry while the searchlight roved across it.

"A glimpse of McAdam as he is." The voice of Ramona Del Rio. His arm rising to sweep the new craters, the dead armor, the shattered aircraft, he turned slowly back. "Washintel WebWatch One brings him to you live, with his reply to the President."

"The poor old man!" Stuart laughed. "I heard his blithering. He's as sick as his dying country. Tell him we've had too many of his silly ultimata. Does he take us for idiots? How many dollars would your arbitrators set as the fair value of a weapon that can conquer the world?"

He swung back to mock the lens.

"Tell him good night."

Tex Horn blandly repeated Higgins, gravely echoed Stuart, and appealed to a panel of experts, who speculated on all they hadn't said.

"McAdam boasts like a winner," the sage from *Gunlaw* concluded, "but he'll be a loser in the end. When Higgins blockades him, what can he do but seal himself up his magical silicon cell and let the world roll on without him?"

"Think so?" The *Infax* pundit frowned. "His brother's the man to watch. Rob Roy McAdam. We were classmates at MIT, though I never knew him well. A genius who knows computers better than people. A master of the encryption game. The government shut his CyberSoft down when they couldn't break his cryptophone algorithms. This silicon shell is his answer. What Higgins needs is a second Rob Roy McAdam."

"If there is another." Tex Horn had turned to the *Hotwire* savant. "Your opinion, sir?"

"I'm alarmed." A grizzled and grim-featured former secretary of state, he shook his head gloomily. "If the secret of McAdam's weapon gets out, it could mean the end of the imperial nation. Maybe the end of history."

Horn seemed awed. "Sir, do you really mean that?"

"Every nation, every individual depends on every other in a system so complex that any glitch can break it down. McAdam's barrier weapon is that glitch. Without some kind of international law and discipline, civilization can't survive."

CHAPTER TWENTY-TWO

I SLEPT TILL Orinda called me to breakfast. An early riser, McAdam was back from his garden with the last fresh tomatoes of the season. He ate half a dozen sweet red slices before he attacked his oatmeal. Orinda had made ham and grits for me, because, she said, I'd looked so hungry. Beth sat motionless over her coffee and a bowl of oats, absorbed in all she had to think about. Her problems and her nearness filled me with a bitter longing.

"You'll see an old friend tonight," McAdam told me as we left the table. "Cass Pepperlake. Higgins and Garron and Stuart have left him no happier than I am with their conflicting schemes for the future. He wants to talk about his own ideas."

"A man you can trust," Beth told me.

She went away to her college classes. McAdam excused himself and retired to his study. Staying inside, I tried the infotel for news. The shell had been closed again, even to satellite signals. All I got was a local broadcast from a KRIF announcer. Federal forces were arrayed all along the foot of the barrier, he said, searching for bodies and hauling away equipment they could salvage. Meeting to hear President Higgins, the council had adjourned with no comment on his demands.

Orinda had set two plates for a light lunch, cold ham sandwiches and a stew of McAdam's garden vegetables. When she said he was asleep in his chair, I had her sit with me and asked what she thought of the war.

"No good in it." Her face turned bleak. "Not for anybody. I've been okay for most of my life, here with the McAdams, but I listened to the President last night. I don't want no amnesty, whatever amnesty is. But I've knowed Mr. Stuart all his life. I don't want to be nowhere with him for a king. And poor Mr. McAdam. He's sick about it, with all three kids involved."

She shook her head and ladled me another bowl of her stew.

When I heard Beth's car in the garage I came out of my room, but she didn't stay to talk. Laden with cheese and crackers and wine, she left them with Orinda and disappeared to take a shower. I was still in the kitchen, listening to Orinda's tales of her unfortunate progeny, when Pepperlake arrived.

I'd never seen him except in shirt sleeves, but tonight he had put on a neat tweed jacket and well-creased trousers. He shook my hand with no sign of surprise and accepted a glass of wine.

"We heard Higgins," I told him, "and Stuart. Does the council have any official answer?"

"Nothing for the media. Senator Finn called while the shell was down, speaking for the President. Moorhawk was with us on the line for most of an hour. We tried to tell him we can't give up our freedom. Surrendering the shell would leave us defenseless. Finn got angry, ranting till we had Rob Roy close the shell and shut him off."

He sipped his wine and asked about my adventures, chuckling when he heard about the observers on the street and Abram Koster strolling past with his rolled newspaper and the big Dalmatian.

"So they were waiting for you?"

"They'd searched the house before I got in. The cleaning woman had orders not to touch my room, but I found my reference books lined up more neatly than I ever left them. The waste basket had been emptied and set back on the wrong side of the desk."

He kissed Beth when she came out, adorable in a pink blouse and blue denim skirt. She sipped at a glass of wine and talked about the college till her father appeared. The shell had trapped out-of-state students, and frantic calls were coming in from distressed parents till the closing shell cut them off. Dinner was baked chicken and corn bread dressing.

"Thanks for remembering how I like it," Pepperlake told Orinda. "My wife won't fix it any more."

McAdam inquired about the *Freeman.*

"Doomed." Gloomily, he shook his head. "Unless we get the shell open to stay. No more news or features from out of the county. Not even newsprint, either, after we use up the little we have."

Yet he was soon smiling again, asking Orinda for another helping of her dressing, with an extra spoon of gravy. The meal finished, we sat around the table as Orinda cleared it. Beth offered more wine. Her father said we'd better stay sober, and asked Pepperlake what he had in mind.

"I heard Stuart last night. I need to know how you stand on his imperial dreams."

"My son." With a wry face, McAdam shook his head. "He's always been difficult. He's impossible now."

"You don't support him?"

"He's gone mad. I told him so."

"I've been bailing him out of trouble since he was born." Beth frowned unhappily when Pepperlake turned to her. "But this is the end. I'll never be the princess of his militia kingdom."

"And you?" McAdam turned to Pepperlake. "More to the point, you're on the council. What do you want?"

"Let me answer with another question." He looked at Beth and back at McAdam. "You're both historians. As honestly as you can, tell me what future you see for America. For the world?"

JACK WILLIAMSON

"Honestly?" Beth paused as if to ponder the word and glanced at me. "Your brother selected McAdam county as a fair sample slice of America. I think it is, and infected with what he called the spores of terror. A kind of mental pathogen spread by instant electronic technology that swallows the thinking individual into a mindless mob acting on the impulse of the moment. I've come to share Kirk's fear of a total breakdown."

She made a hard face.

"That seems believable enough, and I thank you." Pepperlake made a wry little nod, and turned to McAdam. "Colin?"

"Nothing brighter, if you want my view of the world." Dourly, McAdam shrugged. "I've studied the inhumanities of mankind far too long."

"Can you clarify the cause?"

"Progress, if you want one word. It's changed the rules. We spent a million years of evolution fighting to survive, fighting famine, fighting wild beasts, fighting one another, breeding fast to replace the dead. Now we can fight with deadlier weapons that still don't kill enough to keep the balance even."

"So what's the answer?"

"I see no near solution. In the long run nature will correct the problem, but not in any pleasant way. Finishing our ecological cycle, I'm afraid we'll keep on breeding like the animals we are till war and disease wipe out most of us, and leave a few to begin the old game again." Somberly, he shook his head. "Nothing I like to think about."

"You may be right." Pepperlake drew a long breath, and sat straighter at the table. "That's why I'm here. I want to talk about our own individual survival."

"Yes?" Beth and McAdam brightened a little, waiting.

"If we have to predict a new dark age, I want no new empire. No warring militias. No robber barons in silicon shells of their own. No Kingdom of Christ. Instead, I see the Haven as a kind of time capsule that can keep at least a spark of civilization alive. I want to make it a safe repository for the vital records and most precious artifacts of our culture. A little island of refuge for misfits with ideas that might help ensure the survival of our species."

"Perhaps—" McAdam nodded, smiling uncertainly. "Perhaps we can."

"But there's Stuart." Unhappily, Beth shook her head. "I love my little brother dearly, but he's a hot-headed egoist, I'm afraid, with no great devotion to civilization."

"I've spoken to both your brothers." Pepperlake nodded somberly. "Stuart hoots at any danger that we can't survive. Rob Roy calls me an idealistic dreamer. His problems with the Feds have made him a cynic. He doubts that we'll find anybody who cares all that much about tomorrow."

"Closer to home, we'd better look to the survival of the Haven." McAdam turned to Pepperlake. "Can you cope with Stuart? He's in command of the army and the police. He has political connections and militia friends all over the country." He sighed, with a sad little smile. "I used to be proud of him. He's got a good brain, a fine speaking voice, a contagious charisma. But he frightens me now. Suppose he got himself elected to your congress?"

"Nobody's elected. We choose our own members."

"You do?" Beth spoke sharply. "You few? You expect to rule the country?"

"Undemocratic?" Pepperlake shrugged. "Elitist? Maybe, but if you've read Kirk's book, I think you've got to admit that American democracy has failed."

"Do we?" McAdam frowned. "Can't your council be corrupted?"

"Perhaps, if we had planned the Haven to be some kind of ideal utopia, but our mission is something else. Maybe more ambitious. A benign aristocracy, if you look at the Greek roots of the word." Again he glanced at me. "It began when a little group of us had dinner with Alden Kirk.

"We called ourselves a congress, but it was nothing formal, not at first. Only that handful of us groping for escape from the age of terror Alden had foreseen. We had no actual hope of doing anything till Rob Roy began testing his silicon shell. That was when we organized and, finally dared declare our independence. We accept no new members until we are certain of their allegiance to our goal. Stuart fails our test."

"He is a problem." Wryly, McAdam nodded. "I don't know how you'll deal with him."

"Even if you did," Beth was shaking her head, "and even if the shell holds General Zeider out, the best you can do is to cut us off from everything we need. Even from the civilization you say you want to save. It looks to me like suicide."

We finished the wine. Pepperlake made his farewell. I retired to my room and slept through dreams where Beth kept changing into Lydia, dead on her bathroom floor. The power was off when I woke. The lights flickered and came on again while I was dressing in the dark.

"We're lucky, at least for now," McAdam said at breakfast. "I've spoken to Rob Roy. He'd kept the shell open for power transmission till the government cut us off the interstate net. The council found a couple of retired engineers with the know-how to start the old station out west of town. It's running now, but in poor repair. They don't know how long they can keep it going."

Later that day, KRIF rebroadcast a recorded appeal for public calm in the face of crisis. Pepperlake, Moorhawk, and the McAdam brothers sat at a long table in the old county courtroom, the green-and-white Haven flag on a staff behind them. They seemed united for the moment, though I saw no smiles.

Pepperlake began on a sober note. Though the attack had been halted, the county was surrounded. Vital supplies and contacts were shut off. Negotiations with Washington were in progress, but the outcome was still uncertain—

"But we don't want panic." Moorhawk interrupted, speaking too fast and too loud. "We don't want riots. We don't want famine. We don't want bloodshed."

"No danger of that!" Stuart sat erect in his neat green jacket, his voice ringing boldly. "The shell is invincible. Zeider couldn't touch us. Tomorrow is ours. We can conquer America. We can conquer the world."

"Please!" Roy lifted his hand. "We can defend ourselves, but I don't want to conquer anybody."

"Thank you, Roy. You have given us a great power and a great responsibility." Pepperlake looked back to the lens. "A duty that will demand the best of us. As Stuart says, we're in no danger— except from ourselves. That's the reason for this appeal."

"An appeal for sanity." Moorhawk spoke again, still urgent but not so loud. "We have a lot to do. We need time to do it, and order here in the county to give us that time."

"The situation may seem desperate." Pepperlake paused, a little old man in a worn tweed jacket, peering soberly into the lens through his old-fashioned glasses. "Certainly for business people. The banks are closed. Credit and transportation are cut off. Sales are down or nil.

"Yet life can go on." Hopefully, he nodded. "It will go on. The police will stay on duty. Schools will stay open. School buses will still run, so long as we have gasoline. We must ration that, as well as essential supplies left in stock. We are inviting contributions to a food bank."

He turned to his companions at the table.

"Don't forget the Rifles." Stuart smiled into the lens. "We're armed to keep order and prepared for survival. Till times get better—and we mean to make them better—we are opening a soup kitchen for anybody hungry."

Pepperlake thanked him for that.

"Speaking to you citizens of the Haven—" He tried to raise his thin old voice. "We beg to understand the task we face. Roy has given us a noble opportunity. If we make the best of it, we have the chance to frame a splendid future. If we fail, we face disaster. We beg you to let us try."

With a bleak little smile, Beth left for school. McAdam spent the day in his study, writing up his battlefield notes for the *Freeman.* On KRIF, the infonet line was dead. Looking for news, all I found was a story on nominees for Reb football queen: half a dozen slim young women, smiling in the monitor as if they had never heard of war.

For lunch, Orinda served a salad from the garden and bean soup with cornbread muffins. McAdam didn't eat, and she sat with me.

"What coming, Mr. Barstow?" She made a dismal face when I praised the meal. "I was at the market this morning, shopping for supper. Mr. McAdam likes a good pork roast, but a crazy mob was there ahead of me. People piling up their carts and standing in line to pay. Meat shelves stripped bare. I guess we'll have leftovers for dinner."

I asked for another muffin.

"Idiots!" she exploded. "Piling up the meat in deep freezes, ready to rot if the power goes out again. Ain't the whole county gone plumb mad?" She blinked unhappily at me. "Everything we need comes here from outside. Now the trains ain't running and the trucks ain't running. If this wall stays up, we'll all go hungry. Don't you think?"

I didn't know what to think.

"This Free State thing? Or the Haven, if they call it that?" Anxiously, she searched my face. "Throwing Father Garron out of the county? Declaring this independence? What about Mr. Stuart? Mr. Rob Roy? People say they ought to hang for treason. They say we'll all suffer a judgment of God if they don't open the wall and join America again. I want things back like they used to be."

"I'll stick with the Haven," I told her. "I like what Pepperlake and Moorhawk and Rob Roy are trying to do. A noble thing. It won't be easy, but I wish them luck."

"I don't—don't know." Her voice was breaking, and she had to wipe her eyes. "I been with the McAdams all my life, had a better life than most, but now I just don't know."

Back on the monitor, Ramona Del Rio said the camera was not allowed inside the shell and she would be back when she could. I tried to get a nap, tried to read McAdam's first volume, tried to imagine what the shell really meant to the future of mankind. She never came back.

Orinda's leftovers were well disguised at dinner. We ate a silent meal, all of us too anxious to make small talk. Beth and McAdam left the table early, she to grade a test, he to revise his Civil War paper. Darkness fell and I went outside for a walk in the back yard.

My room and McAdam's study were on opposite sides of the house. I paced back and forth behind it, keeping to the strip of grass between the building and the garden. In the light from McAdam's window, I saw a crouching figure. I heard the jangle of shattered glass, heard a gunshot, heard Beth scream.

CHAPTER TWENTY-THREE

STOOPING LOW, THE man ran and vanished through an open gate. I stumbled after him. A motor coughed and roared. The front yard looked empty till I came around the front of the house and glimpsed a car in silhouette against the glow of a distant street light. It raced down the drive and turned into the street, the engine thunder fading to a gentle purr.

I went back inside through my own room. McAdam had fallen forward over the papers on his desk. The back of his shirt had reddened around a ragged hole and his blood was dripping on the floor. Bent over him, Beth straightened to stare at me in mute distress. Orinda was on the telephone, calling the police.

"He's alive." I felt his limp wrist. "There's a pulse."

"Who would do this?" A faint little whisper. "Why? He had no enemies."

I knew no answer. The ambulance came screaming up the drive. The crew unfolded a gurney, laid him on it, started an IV, took him away. Beth went with him. I was left staring blankly into the dark and empty street, wishing I'd found some word of hope or comfort for her.

"The cops are coming." Orinda told me. "You go to your room. Stand in the closet till they're gone. I won't tell."

I wanted to hug her, but I had to shake my head.

"No time to run," I said. "Nowhere to hide." She let them in, half a dozen men in McAdam Police uniform. The sliver of brown plastic on the chest of the man in charge was lettered *Sgt Aaron Hawes*, Ben Coon was with them, still in his Kentucky Rifles gear, but wearing a badge that read *Sheriff*. He pushed importantly ahead of Hawes and stopped to blink at me.

"Barstow!" He stopped o get his breath. "We've been hunting you all over. Where have you been?"

"Out of the county."

"Hold him," he told Hawes. "We'll take him in. Frisk him and watch him. He's been on the run for the Starker killing."

I had to squint into the glaring light on a video camera while they searched me. Coon turned to question Orinda.

"He was there at his desk." She pointed, and a man with a video camera was sweeping the scene. "Shot in the back, through that window." She pointed. "There's the broken glass."

Hawes had turned to look at Coon, perhaps uncertain of his authority or competence.

"Get moving!" Coon shouted impatiently. "Get the camera! Get every thing! Frick and Hale, you take a look outside the window."

"Yes, sir." They stood a moment looking at each other. I saw the hint of a wink. "Of course, sir." Coon swung to me. "You, Barstow? How'd you get here?"

"Through the barrier, when Garron's people were leaving."

Peering hard at me, he raised his voice. "Come in the kitchen. You've got a lot to explain."

He grinned at me across the kitchen table with a sort of ferocious warmth.

"We're old friends, Barstow, remember? Since we met in the Jay Eye See. Looks as if things have changed, but I want to treat you fair. I don't know what all you've done, but your best shot is to come clean with me. Let's hear where you've been."

I told him what I thought he already knew, about my stay in Marion's Georgetown house and my drive back to Kentucky in her car.

"About this shooting tonight?" The false warmth was gone. He sat crouched across the table, his heavy shoulders tensed as if for a tackle. His eyes were bloodshot, and I caught whiskey on his breath. "Where were you when the shot was fired?"

"Outside, walking in the yard. I heard the shot. I saw somebody running and heard a car taking off."

"So?" His voice turned sardonic. "Somebody who?"

"It was dark. All I saw was an outline against the light on the drive."

"How come you were out of the house?"

"I've had to keep out of sight. Shut up inside all day. I've been walking after dinner, for fresh air and exercise."

He crouched farther forward.

"How come McAdam was hiding you?"

"He's my friend." I didn't mention Beth.

"A friend?" His voice fell to a grating undertone. "Barstow, would you shoot a friend in the back?"

He read me my rights.

"Rights before the rebellion," he added. "I can't speak for your rights here just now."

"Can I phone?" I asked. "Phone for a lawyer?"

"Okay," he muttered. "But you need a better lawyer than you're apt to get."

Kit Moorhawk was the only attorney I knew here in the county. Now a leader of the new nation, he wasn't likely to have time for me, but Orinda brought a phone. I was almost in shock; she looked up numbers for me. There was no answer from Moorhawk's home, none from his office.

Cass Pepperlake finally answered from the *Freeman* office.

"Clay?" He listened in silence while I told him about McAdam. "Hit in the back by a shot through a window. It seems I'm suspected. I need a lawyer."

"Dunno." He stopped to think. "Most professionals, got out of the county to wait till the dust settles, but maybe—" He paused again. "There's Luke Huron. Bright and young and maybe still in town. He has a sick mother to care for. I can call him."

"You'll have to tell him I have no money, not here in the county."

"Nobody does," he said. "Not till the council decides what to do about our legal tender. But Luke's dad used to sell ads for the *Freeman.* Hawk Huron. Claimed he was Indian, but black as the ace of spades.

"Moorhawk all but adopted the kid. Paid for his law school and hired him when the IRS got on his tail. He's a tax attorney with no criminal experience, but he's a friend. I think he'll do what he can for you. If I can find him."

Coon had listened, still grinning.

"That nigger kid!" he snorted. "The lawyer you deserve."

The cops had come back from outside to show him an automatic pistol in a plastic bag.

"Dropped on the grass right under the window," the sergeant said. "If the light was on, he had a clean shot at anybody at the desk"

"Foreign." The other was inspecting the gun under the light. "Look at it. Nine millimeter. It's one of them damned Chinese knockoffs of a Russian cop-stopper."

That gave me a shock. I recalled Cyrillic characters on the gun Stuart had left in the bedside stand in his room. Wondering, I kept silent, but Hawes called Orinda out of the kitchen. He showed her the gun in the transparent plastic bag and asked her if she had ever seen it.

"Sir, I don't know." She shot me a glance of evident distress. "I don't know guns."

"Look at it. Have you ever seen any weapon like it?"

"Maybe." She peered at it and shook her head. "I can't really say."

"Look again."

She looked and glanced unhappily at me.

"There was a gun. I seen it in a drawer when I was cleaning Mr. Stuart's room before he went away. Later it was gone. I don't know what happened to it."

"Yours?" Hawes thrust it in my face.

"No," but I had to nod. "I saw a gun like that in Stuart's room back before I was thrown out of the county. I looked in the drawer after I came back. It was gone."

"Sure, Barstow?" He glared accusingly at me. "Are you sure?"

They took me downtown, handcuffed and locked in the back of a police car. In the police station on the ground floor, I looked hopefully for Luke Huron, but he had not appeared.

"Dimwit nigger!" Hawes sneered, "Never trust 'em."

Fingerprinted, booked on charges that included the murder of Lydia Starker, arson, grand larceny, aggravated assault, and flight from justice, I was taken up to the top-floor jail. The jailer was Axel Oxman, a heavy, wheezy man in a shapeless corduroy jacket, his belly bulging over tight blue jeans. Chewing on a toothpick, he accepted a copy of my records with hardly a glance at me.

"A fresh guest for you." Hawes gave him a sardonic grin. "The missing Clayton Barstow. Worth a fortune to somebody, if you can keep him safe."

"No sweat. I'll watch him like a prize pig."

I had to strip and surrender my clothing, my watch, Alden's billfold, the cryptophone. Oxman gave me a pair of faded yellow coveralls and took me to a cell.

"Come in, sir! Welcome to the guest house."

My cellmate was a smooth-spoken young man who wore a Yale class pin on the lapel of an expensive silk suit. He shook my hand with a warmth more genuine than Coon's, and showed me the name *Hamilton Quigg* on a card embossed in gold: *Global Securities, Ltd.*

"One more victim of this tinpot rebellion?"

"A victim of something," I agreed. "I'm not sure what."

"I'm in an awkward spot myself." He seemed far more cheerful than I was. "We've been merchandising international securities over the infonet. I was here negotiating an arrangement with a Father Garron who runs a local Christian scam. We were selling shares in a Celestial City he was planning to develop on a bit of acreage out west of town.

"Hick justice." He made a face. "This Garron is a local saint, too hot for the law to touch, but the idiot cops let the Feds haul me in. They're still tangled up in all their picayune regulations written for the old paper world. Their laws make no sense in this information age, though they don't know it yet. They picked me up, but not for long.

"We have resources in offshore banks and an army of top-flight attorneys in Washington. They'd have had me out in an hour, but this silly silicon thing has cut us off. I know they're doing what they can, but all I can do is wait for my break."

"I'm not so lucky," I told him. "Accused of a dozen crimes I didn't commit. No money. No friends likely to help."

"Tough." He shrugged without concern. "Whatever you scam, you've got to look for legal cover."

He had made his peace with Jailer Oxman, an easy-going, shrewd-eyed ex-tobacco farmer, arranging with him for an infotel set in the cell and catered meals from the Bristol House. Generously, next morning, he shared his breakfast with me. Before noon, however, he was leaving.

"Thanks to a great organization. They got bail money through the barrier." He shook my hand while he waited for the jailer to let him out. "There're quick millions on the infonet," he confided. "Just keep one skip ahead of the stone-age morons who think they can control it."

An hour after Quigg was gone the jailer brought Luke Huron to the cell. He was a slim quiet brown man in a neat gray business suit. He shook my hand with a sympathetic smile and sat gingerly on the opposite bunk.

"Sorry for the delay," he said. "The woman who cared for my mother has left the county. I spent the night with her."

I asked about McAdam.

"Mr. Pepperlake says they removed the bullet last night and tried to repair the damage to his lung. A lot of internal bleeding. Cass is worried."

He listened very soberly to my problems.

"I don't know what to tell you, Mr. Barstow." He shook his head, frowning doubtfully. "Our situation here is very fluid, as they put it. A lot of our local officials have run for cover."

I asked what I might expect.

"Hard to say." He paused to study me. "I gather you can't make bail. The charges are grave. So far as I can see, you'll have to sit here till something clears up the situation." For a moment, he looked brighter. "You do have a friend close to the council. Mr. Pepperlake. But—"

He glanced into the corridor and dropped his voice.

"You know Colonel McAdam?"

"Too well."

"So do I." A rueful shrug. "As you may have heard, he's had his own legal difficulties. Five years on narcotics and conspiracy charges, though he's now out on a political pardon. The original charges included tax evasion, and I was hired on his defense team. He fired me when the case went bad. Out of temper, he called me a numbskull nigger. Which goes to show . . ."

He shrugged, with a philosophic grin, and asked me how I'd got here.

I told him my story, beginning with *Terror in America* and my murdered brother. He listened with growing concern.

"You better hope Stuart never gets the power he's fighting for.

He thinks it was your brother that set the FBI on his tail. He's convinced, in fact, that Alden was an agent."

"He was." I hated to admit the fact, but Alden was beyond harm now. "Unwilling and unpaid. A debt he felt he owed."

"I think I see why." Huron nodded gravely. "I admired him for the book." His eyes narrowed. "You say you came to look for the bombers. Find anything?"

"Nothing but riddles. This phrase, 'Acorn Three,' does it mean anything to you?"

He shook his head.

I told him about the oak acorn fragments the bomb had left in Alden's study, the acorns left with Lydia Starker and left by my head when I was dumped in the woods.

"A signature?" Silent for a moment, he stared at the scrawled graffiti on the wall of the cell. "Why anything so obvious? The boast of an arrogant fool? Or an effort to confuse his trail?"

I told him about the acorns I'd found in the McAdam house, in the room where Stuart had lived.

"Stuart?" I heard his breath catch. "Could he be the bomber?"

"He has an ironclad alibi. He was still in prison."

"He has friends." He shook his head, looking head at me. "If he suspects that you saw those acorns in his room, you could go the way your brother did."

It wasn't a cheering thought.

CHAPTER TWENTY-FOUR

THE JAILER HAD been a cordial companion to both of us so long as he was sharing Quigg's wine. Now, however, the jovial talk and catered meals were no more. When I hailed him from my cell, he paused to scan me coldly with pale sly eyes in a hard poker face.

"Critic██ ██ muttered shortly when I called a question about McAdam. ██ ██better hope he lives. Another murder rap on your book if he dies."

He walked on down the corridor.

His office and living quarters were separated from the main cell block by the elevator shaft. I remained alone in the cell next to the shaft, which I had shared with Quigg. The corridor ran on beyond to the big tank that had served as an exercise and dining room.

"Before this craziness we was full up and more," Mrs. Oxman told me. She ██ as shorter and fatter than her husband, with her gray-streaked ██ ██ an untidy knot on top of her head. More talkative than he, ██ ██d a waspish nasal voice and a habit of shrill complaint. She sweated a lot and had an odor of her own. "Hopheads or dealers, most of them. Always scheming to get another fix or raising some ruckus."

I asked what had become of them.

"That dratted council!" She sniffed, her thin lips pursed. "Damfools, hell-bent on a new name for the county. Freelandia or Free State or the Haven. Some heaven with no God in it! An oasis of freedom, they call it.

"Freedom for what? The first damfool thing they did was call drugs legal and turn that pack of devils loose on the town. All except a few Colonel McAdam drafted into his Kentucky Rifles.

"No good for me and Mr. Oxman. Our paid staff walked off the job when they heard our good American dollars ain't worth pig shit here in the county. Besides the deputy, we had a trusty janitor, a trusty cook, a trusty to help me in the kitchen. McAdam's cops turned 'em all loose to stick us up and slit our throats."

Her peevish whine took on a sharper edge.

"But we still got the hardest cases here and only Oxman and me left to do all the work. We'd be out of here in half a minute if we had anywhere to go."

Waddling behind a jingling cart, she pushed meals down the corridor to feed those few hard cases. Dinner, that day, was a bowl of beans and a slab of cold cornbread. I heard howls of protest from down the corridor.

"Pigs!" she sniffed when she brought my bowl. "Picky pigs! They'll soon be begging for good red beans."

"Budget trouble?"

"We got the budget. It's food we need."

"Food?"

"Most everything we need was trucked from outside the county. Now we're bottled up in this damn bubble. A trick of Satan, Father Garron called it, meant to cut us off from God. He said we're damned to starve and die here. Likely doomed to hell."

"That bad?" I shook my head, but nothing checked her bitter vehemence.

"Mr. Barstow, you ought to see the stores. Shelves stripped

bare. No flour. No sugar. No coffee. No cans but sauerkraut and spinach. Mr. Oxman says people won't take this rebel shit much longer. He says they'll fight before they famish. Colonel McAdam is bringing National Guard guns up to guard the building."

That startled me. "To guard it from what?"

"Mr. Oxman is afraid of a four-way war. The council on one side, the Colonel on the other, Higgins agin them both, the rest of us caught in the middle. The council wants to turn the county into their lunatic Libertarian Haven. The Colonel wants to help his militia friends spread the rebellion all over the world. Higgins is itching to break the barrier and bomb us all to hell. God help us!"

Anxiety pinched her face.

"My son tried to warn us." She shook her head, staring wistfully past me. "David. About your age, Mr. Barstow. He's a Louisville cop. He begged us to come and stay with him but of course we couldn't go. We depend on Mr. Oxman's job, but I don't know." Her troubled eyes came back to me. "Ain't nothing sure no more."

She took my empty bowl and left me alone.

That was a miserable day. Quigg had left his infotel set for Oxman, with the understanding that I might use it till I got out. I turned it on, but all I got was military music from the Kentucky Rifles drum and bugle corps and then a rerun of the last Rebel football game. At noon, a flushed and flustered young man in rimless glasses came on the tube to broadcast the local news.

"In fact," he confessed, "there's not much new. Nothing from out of the county. The council is meeting now to draft a constitution and bill of rights for the new nation. Mr. Pepperlake calls it the last citadel of liberty.

"Maybe so, but it won't last long. Not without money. Interviewing local businessmen, I found a few offering their goods and services for barter, but most have closed their doors."

He went on to read a list of closed services, canceled meetings, and social activities suspended until further notice.

A promotion film made for the Kentucky Rifles before Stuart went to prison showed men in the mud squirming under barbed wire with bullets whining over their heads. That gave way to another Rebel footfall game. I turned it off and spent the rest of the day pacing my cell and hoping for a call from Luke Huron.

It never came.

I begged Mrs. Oxman for a telephone when I saw her pushing a broom down the corridor. She grunted and pushed on, but an hour later Oxman brought a phone back to my cell and stood sneering while I dialed Luke's office and let it ring till he took the phone away.

I longed to see Beth but knew she must be at the hospital with her father. Did she blame me for that bullet out of the dark? Surely not. She had taken risks for me. I would never forget that kiss when we stumbled together in the dark. Yet she had never wanted me here in McAdam, and she must know about my fingerprints on the gun.

That long and empty night I dreamed of Beth, and Lydia, and Beth again. What finally I longed for was simply life with her. I wanted to make the breakfast coffee and hand her a towel when she came out of the shower, wanted to sit at dinner with her and plan happier days than I was expecting now.

That longing faded into darker dreams. I thought Rob Roy's shield had failed when Zeider struck with nukes. Fire and ruin rained out of the roaring sky. Searching for Beth, I wandered through empty streets and stumbled into burning buildings. I never found her.

Breakfast next morning was lumpy cornmeal mush and bitter black coffee left from the day before. Mrs. Oxman was wearing a look of grim satisfaction at the yelled obscenities from down the corridor when she brought my bowl to me.

"They'll eat worse," she muttered, "before they eat better."

I tried the infotel and found Ramona Del Rio on the tube, the silver streak in her hair now tinted azure blue.

". . . shattered hopes for peace." Nothing dimmed her perky

smile. "The Haven council opened a window in the wall last night for a teleconference with Senator Finn, spokesman for President Higgins.

"Sitting in the council chamber as a special correspondent, I was not allowed to record anything, but I can say that council members were begging again for a peaceful recognition of national independence. Finn was implacable, however. For more on that, we bring you a report from Tex Horn."

"Washintel One, with the gig from the geiger." Horn was on the tube, the bruises gone and the big white hat pulled resolutely low. "The McAdam county rebels are still defiant, crouching behind their mysterious barrier and demanding total independence. The Pentagon admits a military stalemate, but President Higgins still demands unconditional submission.

"He's determined to crush the rebellion. According to White House sources, he has ordered the National Security Agency to lead an all-out research effort to penetrate the rebel defenses. We bring you special Washintel One science correspondent, Otto Strock, to discuss what is known."

Strock was a pudgy, red-faced man with a yellow ponytail. Sloppily dressed in a worn brown leisure suit, he spoke in a curt, staccato voice.

"White house sources refuse to reveal anything they know about the rebel barrier, but the riddle of it has brought excited researchers from all over the world."

Horn had found a few of them willing to talk.

"Impossible!" in the words of Dr. Victor Venturi, winner of a Nobel in physics and sometimes called the new Einstein. "I couldn't believe it till I tried to walk through it. It is already revealing startling clues to an unknown aspect of the universe that can keep physical science busy for a dozen years. That is, if its secret is ever discovered."

"Will it be?" Horn asked.

"I'm afraid it will." Venturi frowned. "Such secrets belong to nature, after all, not to CyberSoft Corporation. Nature will surely reveal it again, to anybody clever enough to ask the right question."

"You think so?" Skeptically, Horn pushed up the big white hat. "Were you asked to join Higgins's task force?"

"I said no." Venturi shook his head.

"Personally, I can't help hoping nobody stumbles across that question. I don't like to think of what might happen if McAdam's secret is published. It could crumble nations into outlaw gangs raiding the lands round them and retreating into impregnable strongholds."

"What's your theory?" Horn pushed the hat askew. "About the nature of it?"

Venturi hesitated.

"We pick up rumors." Horn peeked at a paper on his desk. "I've heard guesses. Wave interference. Quantum effects. A space-time dislocation. Can you comment?"

"I wish I could." Venturi frowned, though a fresh interest had lit his face. "When we try to question nature, she can answer like the Oracle at Delphi. Always with another tricky riddle."

"Where would you look for an answer?"

"I'd study the barrier wall. It's transparent to light, but McAdam can make it opaque to longer-wave radiation. Radar echoes are delayed. Just a microsecond, but enough to show the wall several hundred meters farther off than it is. A tragedy for military pilots in the assault on the wall. They collided with it when their instruments still showed them safely distant."

"How can that be?" Horn persisted.

Venturi shrugged. "You night ask Ian Donegal—he was the first to pick up that radar anomaly. He's suggesting that the distorted reflections are due to a fault in spacetime."

"What could cause that?"

Venturi shrugged again. "You'd have to ask nature." He paused for a moment, frowning, and his voice fell. "I'm keeping out of any serious research, because the secret frightens me. Any man who owns it could be murdered for it. Another Stalin or another Hitler could use it to destroy civilization."

Horn blinked.

"I hope the research fails." Venturi's face was grimly set. "I hope McAdam lets his secret die with him."

CHAPTER TWENTY-FIVE

BREAKFAST NEXT MORNING was scorched cornmeal mush, scattered with black scrapings from the bottom of the pot. I heard howls of protest down the corridor, but my annoyance evaporated when Mrs. Oxman told me I had guests waiting.

"A Mrs. Kirk and two kids. Mr. Oxman says you can see them if you want, right here in the cell."

Oxman let them in. Marion wore a white uniform with *Bristol House* blue-lettered on the breast, her rust-red hair tucked under a blue-and-white uniform cap. Tim and Angela tiptoed behind her. Angela clung to her skirt, and started fearfully when Oxman clanged the steel door shut behind them.

Wide-eyed, Tim stared around the narrow cell, at the bare mattress pads, the lidless toilet and the dripping faucet above it, the obscene graffiti scrawled across the splashes of yellow-brown paint that had not quite covered older obscenities. Marion stood for a moment peering at me, her face tight and anxious.

"Oh, Clay—" Her voice caught, and she ran to hug me.

"What—" A sob checked her again. "What has happened to you?"

She stepped back to listen, but I was drowning under too much emotion. Joy that they had come, shame to be found in this dismal cell, greater shame that they were here because of me, desperation that I had no way out. Suddenly weak in the knees, I sank down on my bunk and burst into a fit of sobs I couldn't stop. Tim came silently to touch me on the shoulder.

"Mr. Oxman?" I heard Angela's small reproving voice. "What have you done to Uncle Clay?"

Still gazing through the bars, he muttered something I didn't understand. I wiped my eyes with the sleeve of the yellow fatigues and tried to pull myself together.

"Let's talk." I found Marion sitting on the other bunk, the children huddled beside her. "We have only fifteen minutes."

"Uncle Clay," Angela whispered, "we came because we love you."

"You're wonderful." I had to wipe my eyes again. "I'll be okay. It's just that I'm so happy to see you." I turned to Marion. "You got trapped here?"

"The news about you was terrible." She seemed at first calmer than I was. "Too bad to believe. We came to help if we could, but you've been hard to find. I didn't know what to do. You'd spoken of Mr. Pepperlake, your friend at the *Freeman.* He tried to help when we went to him, but we couldn't—couldn't find you."

Her voice had begun to break.

"We had to give up. Of course we had return tickets, but the airport closed. I tried to rent a car, but people getting out of the county had taken them all."

She straightened and caught her breath.

"But we're surviving." She tried to smile. "We were staying at the Bristol House. The manager has been understanding. He can't take credit cards or checks, but he's letting me clean the rooms."

"I'm working," Tim spoke up. "Bussing tables in the restaurant."

"Brave of you," I said. "I'm proud of you,"

"Clay, what—" Her voice broke again. "What do you expect?" Oxman stood close to the bars, listening avidly.

"I don't know. I'm waiting to see my lawyer."

"If you call that stinking coon a lawyer,' Oxman muttered. "If you ever see him again." He looked at a gold pocket watch and turned brusquely to Marion. "Sorry, lady, your time is up."

"If there's anything—" Marion had to gulp. "Call me at the Bristol House if there's anything I can do."

Tim came silently to shake my hand. Angela scrambled into my lap and reached her arms around my neck.

"We brought you a box," she whispered. "Fried chicken and apples and a candy bar. Mr. Oxman says he has to look in the box before he can give it to you."

"Don't you worry, kid." Oxman spoke quickly, offended. "Your uncle will get his box."

He let them out and locked the door. Angela looked back to wave me a kiss as they followed him away. I sprawled face down on the pad, breathing the faint dry scent of old piss and hating myself for what I had done to them till Oxman came back with the box.

A thigh and a drumstick. Two red apples. A chocolate-skinned candy bar. Marion had wrapped them in wax paper. Oxman had torn it off and crumpled it in the bottom of the box. I ate the candy bar, wishing Angela had kept it, and saved the chicken for dinner.

Waiting, still hoping for word from Luke Huron, I paced the narrow space between the bunks. Three steps and turn, three steps and turn, till it almost made me giddy. A program about classic Kentucky foods was running on KRIF.

"News special." The announcer interrupted a recipe for a grits casserole. "Washintel correspondent Ramona Del Rio, caught here inside the rebel shell, has given us permission to run a report prepared for transmission to her network when or if that becomes possible."

In a blue denim jacket with a red silk scarf around her throat, she looked as chipper as ever.

"Update from the Haven," her voice rang crisp as frost. "Tensions continue to increase here in the outlaw territory. Though General Zeider suffered a stunning defeat, it seems that the rebels have won a battle only to lose the war. President Higgins remains adamant in his demand that they surrender their high-tech weapon and their claim to independence.

"While the council is still debating new laws and a constitution, Colonel McAdam, their military commander, is defying President Higgins more openly. He has threatened to share the secret of the shield with other militias all across the country.

"President Higgins is promising charges of treason against every man and woman in the county unless they surrender and ask for amnesty. The council can close their so-called silicon shell, however, to prevent any mass exodus, and they seem unlikely to reveal its secret.

"General Zeider, in the meantime, has begun stringing razor wire outside the barrier. In spite of that initial victory, I think the rebels are doomed by their own success. They've cut themselves off from friends and relatives, from all the goods and services that came from outside, and they are already feeling the pinch.

"The Rotary Club and the Chamber of Commerce have petitioned the council to give up the dream of independence and reopen negotiations with the federal government.

"With disquiet increasing, a disturbing incident of violence was reported yesterday. Though the facts are disputed, it appears that a young black woman was raped and beaten by members of the Kentucky Rifles, the local militia group supporting the rebellion.

"The girl, still in her teens, is the daughter of a respected Baptist minister, Enoch Hillburn. I interviewed him. As he tells the story, his daughter is the organist at the church, only two blocks from the parsonage where they live. She was walking home after practice with the choir when three drunk militiamen in a military vehicle snatched her off the sidewalk and carried her to the park where they raped and beat her.

"Benjamin Coon, acting as sheriff and chief of police under the rebel government, tells a far different story. He says the woman hailed the men to solicit sex for money. They agreed. The violence took place after the sex, when she called their money worthless, demanded their watches instead. She threatened the rape charge when they balked at that.

"The pastor took his daughter to the hospital and reported the incident to the police. He says Coon called her a yellow nigger whore and told him the new nation is to be snow-white, no niggers wanted. A desperate situation, at least as it looks from here."

Gloomily, Del Rio shook her head at the lens.

"With the barrier still closed to wire and radio transmission, we have nothing new from the world outside, but we are standing by. When news does burst you get it first on Washintel One."

With that feeble echo of Tex Horn, her face faded from the tube.

Late that afternoon, when Luke Huron hadn't yet returned, I saw Mrs. Oxman in the corridor and begged her to let me call Pepperlake.

"The Councilor?" She looked down her nose. "He ain't got time for the likes of you."

Finally, however, she and Oxman brought a telephone and stood listening while I made the call. It was answered by a secretary who knew me from my work on the *Freeman* and said she'd leave a memo for him to call if he could. He never called.

Dinner that night was a cold cornpone and a bowl of boiled cabbage. I scraped the bowl and turned on the infotel. Ramona Del Rio was back on the line.

". . . race riot, right here in the county." Anxiety showed through her cheer. "The black pastor led a protest march to the Colonel McAdam's hadquarters in the old National Guard building. The colonel refused to see him.

"Though the facts are in dispute, guns were fired. One man was killed. Perhaps a dozen others were injured, though only seven were hospitalized. The pastor says his people carried no weapons. McAdam says his men fired only blank rounds or rubber bullets, when tear gas failed to disperse the mob—"

The door clanged open.

"I hate to interrupt your fun, Mr. Barstow." Oxman gave me a sardonic smirk, "But here's your big-shot attorney. I'll give you fifteen minutes."

He let Luke Huron into the cell and locked the door behind him. To my relief, he walked away.

"I asked for privacy."

Hardly listening, I stared at Luke. He wore a dismal face, with a puffy look around his eyes and a swollen ridge across the forehead. His left arm in a sling, he limped unsteadily to sit on the vacant bunk.

"Sorry, Mr. Barstow." He touched the sling with a painful grin. "But I've had problems. My house was torched last night, my wife inside. I cut myself on broken glass when I went through a window to save her. I'm afraid I can do nothing for you."

When I asked about his injury, he nodded grimly at the infotel, where Del Rio was summing up her report. I snapped it off.

"Nothing really serious." Ruefully, he shook his head. "A bullet wound in my arm and lacerations from broken glass. I'll be okay, but other black folks aren't. If you were listening to Ramona, there's plenty to worry about. The council may hope to turn the county into some kind of paradise, but McAdam would make it a hell for blacks. If you heard Ben Coon and his cops, they're lying about the rape that touched off the riot.

"The militiamen were drunk. I know the girl. Only fifteen, she's a gifted organist, with a music scholarship waiting for her. Her father is taking it hard. When he asked me for legal advice, I had to tell him there's no law here in the county. Not yet. Only Coon's cops and McAdam's militia till the council does more than debate what the Haven is to be.

"Anyhow, I went with the pastor to the police station. Coon sneered at us. He called the girl a two-faced nigger whore and told the pastor McAdam had agreed to open the wall 'to let the niggers out of the county.' The Haven is going to be lily-white.

"The congregation was frightened and furious. They voted to make a protest march. I walked ahead with the pastor. McAdam drove past us in his command car. We saw him park at the armory before we got there, but the guards in the sentry box outside made a phone call and said he wasn't there.

"The pastor had warned his people to bring no weapons. I saw none on them, but the guards called a dozen militia men out of the building. A sergeant with a bullhorn ordered us to drop our weapons and disperse.

"We had no weapons, and we didn't scatter. The sergeant bellowed an order and the fired something at us. Tear gas grenades, I think. They exploded behind us. The stuff choked me, nearly blinded me. I saw some kid throw a rock. They fired back with live ammo.

"They claim it was blanks and rubber bullets, but the surgeon said it was lead that hit my arm. A few of us were left lying in the road when the rest blundered away, the pastor praying over a woman who died before the ambulances got there. And that—"

He stopped, his face twisting.

"That's why I've neglected your case. I'm sorry, Mr. Barstow, but I hope you see my situation. If they do open the barrier, I'm trying to get my wife to some safer place."

I was wishing him luck when we heard Oxman's boots clacking down the corridor. He stood up and offered his free hand.

"Never mind us, Mr. Barstow." His voice fell, his stiff little grin turning grave. "You're the one in need of better luck."

CHAPTER TWENTY-SIX

THOUGH PEPPERLAKE NEVER called back, he was at the jail next morning. Mrs. Oxman came to unlock my door.

"Good news for you, Mr. Barstow." She wore a look of awed astonishment. "They are letting you out."

"Who is?"

"Mr. Pepperlake is here with an order from the council." She squinted at a paper in her hand. "Signed by Mr. Moorhawk. Mr. Oxman sure don't like it, but Mr. Pepperlake says we've got to let you go."

Dazed, I followed her out of the cell and saw Oxman and Pepperlake down the corridor, Oxman shouting angrily.

"That damfool Moorhawk! Who's he to think he can ramrod the county?"

"He's now our chief executive. Elected chair of the council."

"Chair?" Oxman snorted. "We bow down to a chair?"

Pepperlake saw me and came to shake my hand. "Well, Clay!"

He stood back to inspect me. "Still kicking, though you look a little worn. Ready to go?"

"If I can—"

"Not quite yet," Oxman shouted. "Not till I call Ben Coon. He ain't a chair of anything, but he is acting sheriff and police chief. He'll have a say."

He went back to his office to make the call, leaving us standing with Mrs. Oxman in the corridor. Pepperlake frowned when I asked about Colin McAdam.

"Still in intensive care. No visitors, but I talked to Beth this morning. He's still weak from loss of blood. They've done surgery to remove a bullet lodged near his heart. She says it's still touch and go. A hard time for her."

Oxman came back, Ben Coon behind him.

"You bastard!" Red-faced and yelling, Coon shook his fist at me. "Damn psychotic killer! If you think we'll let you out to kill again—"

He paused when Pepperlake raised a restraining hand and spoke more quietly to him. "Sir, we can't release this man. He's waiting trial for the Lydia Starker murder whenever we get a legal court. And a lot more than that."

Growing louder, he waved his fist again.

"There's the charge of homicide by arson, when he torched the Ryke clinic. There's flight to escape arrest. The FBI wants to question him about a missing agent. And he's got to be the gunman that shot the Colonel's father in the back. Another murder rap if the old man dies. He'll burn for sure if we ever get a court. Sorry, sir, but I'll have to call the Colonel—"

"Don't bother." Pepperlake reached for the yellow paper in Mrs. Oxman's quivering hand. "Your colonel reports to the council, and I have this order from Chairman Moorhawk."

Coon's jaw jutted stubbornly.

"Moorhawk and your damfool council don't command the Kentucky Rifles."

"Maybe not." Pepperlake shrugged. "But we do control the silicon shell. Could your Rifles beat General Zeider if Rob Roy lets him in?"

Coon snatched the order and peered at it grimly.

"Okay," he muttered. "The prisoner is remanded to the custody of your chicken shit council. He is not to leave the county." He scowled at me. "I think the Colonel's border guards can see to that."

"I'm sure," Pepperlake murmured blandly, and led me to the elevator. Out in bright sunlight on the parking lot, I filled my lungs with fresh air and tried to thank him.

"None of my doing. Not really. If thanks are due anybody, it's your brother's widow."

Giddy with relief, I said no more till we were in Pepperlake's venerable Ford, driving back to the Freeman office.

"Marion?" I asked him then. "What has she done?"

"She's found a car and gas to get her out to Lexington. Rob Roy is opening the shell at noon for another convoy of refugees. The car is parked in a private garage. I have the keys."

"You mean—" I stopped to stare at him. "I can leave the county?"

"Mrs. Kirk plans for you to crawl into the trunk when she picks up the car. You tough it out in the trunk till she's past the checkpoint. She'll pull off the road to let you breathe again. You'll be home free!"

I let him drive another block while I thought about it.

"I can't do it," I told him then. "I thank you. It's noble of Marion. But I don't want the risk!"

"We've considered it."

"Coon will have his guards watching the checkpoint. If they find me, Marion and the kids could be trapped here forever. And think of yourself—"

"Clay—" He paused to shake is head. "There's a lot more to think about."

He pulled off the street, parked on the strip beside an empty public playground, and turned soberly to face me.

"You've just seen a hint of the tension between the Colonel and the council, but you don't know how desperate we are."

"Desperate? I saw Coon back down when you threatened to drop the barrier."

"But suppose we had to do that?" Anxiety furrowed his weathered face. "Bad news for the likes of Stuart and Coon, but suicide for us. The end of the Haven. Treason trials for the lot of us."

"With all that at stake," I said, "how can you risk more trouble for me?"

"Not just for you." He frowned at the abandoned slides and swings on the playground beside us. "We've been eating at the Bristol House. I've gotten to know Mrs. Kirk and her children."

He gave me an odd little tight-lipped smile and went on in a slow half-whisper, almost as if to himself.

"Angela, an angel really. Your little nephew begged me to help you. I made them a promise."

"Then I think you'll understand why I can't hurt them."

"You'll be hurting them more if you make them leave you here at Ben Coon's mercy. Think it over, Clay."

I sat a moment, trying to think.

"A lot has happened to me," I said. "A lot of bad luck, or maybe something worse than luck. I've wondered if I'm not another victim of whoever killed my brother. But I am innocent, in spite of all the charges. If we get an honest government, I should have a chance in court."

He sat for half a minute staring at me bleakly.

"You're a fool, Barstow," he muttered at last. "Maybe an idealistic fool, but still a monumental fool. As I had to tell Marion, you're a dead man if you stay here."

"Could be," I said. "I hope you're wrong. It's a chance I want to take."

He dropped me on the gravel drive at the Katz House. My room key long lost, I walked in the front door and waited in the hall between *Saxon and Katz* and *Katz Guns and Ammo* till Julia Sue Katz came to the counter in a cloud of lemon scent, her hair rolled in curlers.

"Mr. Barstow!" Her black-penciled eyebrows arched in astonishment. "I thought—" She caught herself, gulped, and blinked at me. "I thought—"

"I've been in jail," I told her. "I'm out on bond."

"You are?" Her eyes narrowed. "So I guess you want your old room back?"

"I certainly do. The rent was paid through the whole semester."

"I guess it was." She nodded reluctantly. "But—" Confused, she was turning pink. "You'd better see Mr. Katz."

"I'll be glad to see him."

She rapped on the *Katz & Saxon* door and slipped inside. Sam Katz followed her back. A short thick round man in baggy pants and a tight black polo shirt, he wore old-fashioned black-rimmed glasses that gave him the look of an anxious owl.

A bundle of nervous habits when I got to know him, he was forever fiddling with the pens in his shirt pocket, fiddling with the mini-infotel on his wrist, fiddling with any object in his reach. He kept making grotesque one-sided grimaces that seemed unconscious, kept taking the glasses off to lick them with a moist pink tongue and polish them with a white silk handkerchief before he jabbed them back.

"Mr. Barstow!" He bustled to meet me. "A relief to see you free, my boy." He clapped me on the shoulder. "Come on inside."

His desk was flanked by a computer on one side and an infotel on the other, with a collection of antique handguns locked in a tall glass case across the room. He waved me toward a chair and stood shaking his head in apparent regret.

"I wish I could have seen you sooner, Clay. I might have been able to do more." He saw the question on my face. "I've been concerned about you because I knew your brother."

He smiled faintly at my shock.

"His widow told me about the kinship. She came to me for help to find you. Nothing I could do. Sit down." He gestured again at the chair. "Let's discuss your situation."

I stood blinking at him, recalling Kirk's laptop comments. A worthless windbag, to be taken with a double pinch of salt? Maybe a shyster? Maybe too apprehensive to reveal his secret self. Uncertain what to make of him, I felt desperate enough to take the chair.

He sat very deliberately and opened a silver humidor.

"Smoke?" He offered a fragrant cigar. "Cuba's finest. The gift of a grateful foreign client."

"Thanks, but I don't smoke."

Ruefully, he replaced the cigar.

"Julia Sue disapproves, but sometimes she does let me enjoy one with a client." He closed the humidor and leaned more seriously across the desk, gray eyes searching me though the black-rimmed lenses. "Clay, was your brother an agent of the FBI?"

I tried to keep a poker face.

"If he was," I answered cautiously, "he never told me."

"No matter." He shrugged disarmingly. "Just a rumor. Crazy guesswork. All we get since this damn wall went up." His shrewd eyes narrowed. "You came here to look for the makers of the letter bomb?"

I had to nod. "My brother was an investigative journalist. I was hoping to carry on his work."

"A dangerous undertaking." I saw a momentary twist of his lips. "Do you have a lawyer?"

"Not now," I said. "Not since Luke Huron was run out of the county."

"Regrettable." He made a wry face. "An ugly shadow over Pepperlake's new utopia. And on your own situation, Clay. But I'm anxious to help you in any way I can."

"I have no money."

"Nobody does." He shrugged. "Not till the council decides what to do about a currency."

Still I hesitated, uneasily wondering how he had earned my brother's comments. His face grew graver.

"You're in a hard spot."

"I know."

"It's more than just the murder raps." His voice fell confidentially. "Julia Sue knows a nurse who works at Mercy Hospital, where they have old man McAdam. She was in the room when the Colonel came to see the old man, and she says he had words with his sister."

"Beth?"

"Words about you and that shot through the window."

That took my breath.

"Beth didn't want to believe you were the gunman. Stuart raised his voice at her. Called you a conniving Yankee cocksucker. Accused her of turning soft on you. Finally stalked out and tried to slam the door.

"Stuart hates you, Clay. If you wonder why, the nurse says he's jealous. Beth has never married, so the nurse says, because he's run off every man she ever liked. He'll get rid of you, Clay, any way he can. You need all the help you can get."

"From you?"

He hesitated, blinking through the lenses. "I don't know—"

In spite of all my uncertainties, I had to beg for his help.

"If you ask." Grinning genially, he came around the desk to shake my hand and escort me to the door. Warmer now, Julia Sue took me down the hall to my room.

"There's been nobody in it," she assured me. "You'll find your things just like you left them."

Not quite true. My possessions were still there, but neatly re-arranged, doubtless after a police search. I enjoyed a badly needed shower and found clean clothes to replace the yellow fatigues. Julia Sue knocked while I was shaving and came in with a paper bag.

"That damfool wall has made food hard to find, Mr. Barstow. I brought you a snack."

The bag contained a thick ham sandwich and a ripe red apple. I devoured them and turned on the infotel. With the lines open for the moment, Ramona Del Rio was on the tube, broadcasting from the checkpoint on the Lexington road.

The refugees were creeping through it slowly. Cars whose owners had found gas, pickups stacked with household goods, now and then a yellow-painted school bus, a dragging line of people shuffling on foot, many lugging bundles or bags.

Inside the line of painted posts that marked the invisible barrier, police were peering into vehicles, sometimes searching them. Beyond it, on the federal side, uniformed immigration officials were demanding identification, searching everybody.

Once, as the camera swept the crawling line, I thought I saw Marion at the wheel of an old blue Ford sedan, Tim leaning out of the window. I wasn't certain, but a cop was gesturing for them to stop and I felt glad I wasn't suffocating in the trunk.

Del Rio's cameraman drove south, panning the base of the shell. Outside it, under the guns of a camouflaged tank, his lens caught bulldozers clearing a broad strip, uprooting trees and leveling buildings. Men with drilling machines were planting a row of posts down the middle of it, stringing razor wire.

"Tex Horn on the World Wide Web for Washintel WebWatch One." He was on the tube, the big white hat canted jauntily back, his mellow voice pealing. "The White House announced today that President Higgins is sending Rocky Gottler back to the outlaw county with a final attempt at a peaceful reconciliation.

" 'If the rebels want isolation,' the president said, 'we'll give them isolation. We can seal them in, deny them everything they are used to importing, let them imprison themselves forever in their silicon cell.

" 'But we are not without concern for the misguided rebel leaders and the innocents they have trapped. Once again we offer amnesty. Our new perimeter around the rebel position will remain open for thirty-six hours to those who wish to leave. Their American citizenship will be restored, and they will be granted immunity from prosecution. Those who remain forfeit all rights and expose themselves to changes of treason—' "

His voice stopped. His image vanished. The tube was dark for a long two minutes until Ramona Del Rio returned.

"Our Washintel feed has been interrupted. The rebels have evidently closed their shield again, but now—"

The tube went dark, and she was flushed and breathless when her image came back.

"Now our field camera has picked up something else. Something I don't understand. Just another moment—"

The tube darkened again, but her voice went on.

"The cameraman reports a curious flicker in the sky, something so brief that I missed it on the feed. He reports a momentary distortion of everything in the distance—everything outside the rebel barrier.

"And now the tank! The fencing machines! The men running!"

Her face on the tube, she fell silent, red lips parted, wide eyes staring. In an instant she was gone. Her image was replaced by the tank, wrapped in a yellow fireball. The fencing machines stood motionless, smoking. The workers were running for safety. The camera followed them till they collided with something that checked them, sent them sprawling backward.

The picture vanished. The tube stayed dark and silent for a full five minutes, before I heard a blare of military music and saw a scene I remembered: the Kentucky Rifles marching down Main, passing the *Freeman* office, Stuart McAdam on his bay Thoroughbred leading the parade.

CHAPTER TWENTY-SEVEN

THROUGH A LONG and anxious afternoon I kept checking the infotel for news. Tex Horn and Del Rio did not return. I saw bits of a Kentucky Rifles recruitment film and a glimpse of Father Garron under a huge silver sword at his new Tennessee temple, yelling defiance at the baby-killing Satans of McAdam County. When I thought time enough had passed, I called the Bristol House and asked for Mrs. Kirk.

"Gone," the manager said. "With her kids and a few other stranded guests. I saw them through the checkpoint."

"So they're safe!"

Relieved at that but also overtaken with a sudden ache of loneliness, I sat down at the desk to write letters of thanks and love and perhaps farewell to her and Angela and Tim.

"Take care of the kids," I told her, "and stay away from McAdam County, no matter what happens to me."

I sealed and stamped the letters, wondering if they would ever leave the county. I read my copy of Alden's laptop notes again and walked the empty hall for an hour, searching my mind for clues to the Acorn riddle or hints that might help Katz with my defense.

Hope was hard to find. Mrs. Starker would swear that I had killed her daughter. Ben Coon had sworn that he saw me running from the burning clinic. I had been outside McAdam's house when the bullet came through the window. My fingerprints were on the gun.

Julia Sue saw me in the hall and asked me to join her and Mr. Katz for dinner.

"Hard times." Her voice had a bitter edge. "They're trying to ration food, what little the hoarders left in the stores. We was lucky. The students upstairs all went home when trouble started. We got their ration numbers."

Dinner, when she finally called me, was boiled cabbage and bean soup seasoned with shreds of ham. Katz got home late. He didn't care for cabbage, but he seemed elated with his news.

"Old Higgins thought he had us bottled up, but Rob Roy just pushed the shield a thousand yards farther out. Blew up half a dozen armored vehicles and trapped the work crews stringing their damn razor wire.

"Men were hurt or killed when munitions and gas tanks exploded. We caught a hundred prisoners. A lot of 'em begging for a chance to join the Rifles. But that ain't the big news."

Grinning, he paused to scrape his bowl.

"Wait for later tonight. You know Rocky Gottler? Or maybe you don't. They call him the power behind Senator Finn. He slipped in while they had the shield open for the refugee convoy. He claims to have another message from Higgins, and he's meeting with the council tonight."

"Maybe things will change." Julia Sue brightened. "This craziness can't go on."

"It's only begun." Muttering into his empty bowl, Katz shook his head. "The world that was, it's gone to total hell." He stared at me through the black-rimmed lenses. "It's the breakdown into terror your brother hoped to stop."

His sudden vehemence startled me. Julia Sue had begun to clear the table, but she sat down to listen.

"Cass Pepperlake wrote about it in the *Freeman.*" He spoke slowly, recollecting. "It couldn't have happened a hundred years ago. So he says. He calls it one more curse of the information age. The electronic clamor, that's what he calls it, leaves people no time to think. Public opinion is shaped by tiny sound bites. Actual information has gone to chaos."

"My brother wrote something like that," I said.

"I read the book." Katz raised his voice as if to challenge me. "He studied all the signs of trouble coming and tried to warn the world, but he never pointed out the real cause, not the way he should."

"So?" I asked. "What is the cause?"

"It ain't what he heard from anybody here." His face was twisted for a moment with his grotesque tic. "It ain't poverty. It ain't the gangs. It ain't bad schools. It ain't loss of religion. It ain't drugs. It's the idiots that try to outlaw drugs."

"Alden didn't think much of the drug laws."

"But he never attacked the fools that make them." His face twitched again. "The self-righteous bigots who want to run over everybody else."

He stopped till I asked what bigots he meant.

"The dumbfuck racist majority that poison themselves with the legal nicotine and legal alcohol that kills them a hundred ways, while they outlaw marijuana, even to study it for medical use."

"Racist, you say?"

"Look in the prisons. A million and a half men and women, most of them Latin or black, locked up because they've chosen the wrong poison. Forced into crime and tempted into dealing because the crazy laws keep prices beyond the reach of honest men and make the profits enormous.

"Not just for the dealers." He glared through his glasses. "The authorities connive with the drug lords in a hellish partnership. Look back at history. I've talked to old Colin McAdam. He had to admit that the Volstead Act failed because people under pressure will always find relief. He likes his juleps.

"It was national prohibition that created our criminal underworld. The damfool white majority have done it all over again, double plus. Done it to minorities with different drugs of choice. They've set up a monstrous machine. That's their whole judicial system, the cops and the lawyers and judges, the prison wardens and prison guards and prison builders.

"They're a generation of smarter crooks than you can find in any foreign cartel. Every year the drug czar reports great progress and begs for more money to make greater progress, while the traffic keeps on growing and the prison builders want more money to build bigger prisons to hold more victims. They're symbionts, the drug lords and the lawmen. The laws keeps the prices up and the billions rolling in. Working together, the dealers and the narks are sucking the life-blood out of America.

"And it ain't just America. Whole nations corrupted! Look at crime in Mexico. Crime in Colombia. Asia. Africa. But we've got The worst drug lords right here at home, squandering billions fighting a war they know they'll never win, like old King Canute sweeping back the sea. Killing kids, rotting governments, poisoning the world.

"Sorry, Barstow." Katz caught himself and smoothed his strident tone. "That's how I feel, though I can't say so in public. I have to live here. But I do think your brother learned and wrote too much about it. I think that's what got him killed."

He paused, fiddling uneasily with the silver humidor on his desk as if still tempted by the cigars inside.

"Talking about it, I get carried away." He was suddenly apologetic. "Mostly I keep my head down, but that's why I'd side with Stuart, if I had to take a stand.

"As for your own case—" He paused to study me speculatively. "Could be somebody thinks you know too much."

———

Back in my room, I thought about his unexpected outburst. Alden had said some of the same things, though in more temperate language. He had even suggested that the vast sums spent on drug wars locking up offenders might better have gone for treatment and education. Had such comments led to the letter bomb? Still I had no clue, nor any reason to think Katz might be a good defender.

Del Rio came back on the infonet, profiling Gottler. Born in Argentina but brought up by a generous uncle here in McAdam, he had become a power in Washington with means to spend half his time on a yacht in the Caribbean.

"Our mysterious Mr. Big!" She rolled her eyes in mock wonder. "His dad claimed to have a bonanza, a fortune made breeding race horses on the pampas. Gottler senior disappeared when the bubble broke. Junior's now riding high on his own gravy train. International finance? Backroom politics? Gambling on the infonet? He never says."

I saw him on the tube when Del Rio covered the council meeting for KRIF. He and Stuart sat waiting like opposing lawyers in the shabby old county courtroom. The councilors filed in to sit like presiding judges, Moorhawk in a rumpled business suit, Rob Roy in a white lab jacket, Pepperlake in shirt sleeves, none of them recently shaven. They frowned impatiently at Gottler till a clerk closed the doors.

A heavy man, darkly tanned, he rose and bowed to them with an affable smile.

"Gentlemen, I speak for Senator Finn." In gray flannel slacks and a green polo shirt, he looked dressed for his yacht rather than diplomacy. Pitched high, his voice had a slight Spanish accent. "I speak for President Higgins."

"Okay." Pepperlake was curtly unimpressed. "What's your message?"

"An appeal to sweet reason." He spread his hands like a high-school orator. "Mr. McAdam, I do admire your technology." He nodded warmly at Rob Roy and turned soberly to Moorhawk.

"You've just won a trick. I grant that, but you've dealt yourselves a losing hand."

"How so?" Moorhawk bristled. "We've beaten Zeider."

"Not yet." Gottler waved that aside. "We don't know the range of your weapon, but you can't stretch your shell forever without taking in more good Americans than you can bamboozle with your crazy utopia."

Stuart was muttering, his hand impatiently raised. Gottler ignored him.

"We've got you hemmed in. If you think you can exist on your own resources, you'd best think again. How many of your good American citizens will want to eat their race horses when beef and pork run out? How many can feed themselves on the cabbage and turnips they grow in their backyards?"

He grinned at Stuart.

"If you don't want turnips, I'm here to offer you a carrot. That's total amnesty for all the legal charges that can rise from your lunatic rebellion. President Higgins has set just one condition. You must open up this silicon shell and reveal plans and specifications for it to the National Security Agency."

The camera swept them, Rob Roy doodling on a yellow scratch pad, Moorhawk scowling in anger, Pepperlake glancing at them inquiringly. Stuart snorted, his hand indignantly raised. He turned to Gottler, almost sneering, when Moorhawk let him speak.

"We've got another ace to play."

"Let's hear."

"We've got the silicon shell. What's your answer to that?"

"The armed forces of America."

"We've stopped them cold."

"What has that got you?"

"Freedom." Moorhawk shook a long forefinger at Gottler's face, a big diamond flashing. "Freedom we won't give up."

"Freedom to die here?"

"Freedom." Stuart turned grim. "Freedom for all the world."

Gottler blinked and stared. "I'm not tipping our hand. Just wait till you see."

"I'll see you on trial for treason." Gottler glanced at his watch and turned to the councilors. "Gentlemen, I've heard wind enough." His easy smile was gone. "It's now or never if you want to save your lives."

"You'll see——" Stuart was beginning. Moorhawk banged a gavel. The tube went dark till Del Rio's incandescent smile lit it again.

"Council Chairman Moorhawk adjourned the meeting," she said. "The councilors retired with Colonel McAdam to the judge's chambers. Mr. Gottler stalked out to look for a hotel.

"This is all for now, but please stand by."

I sat up late with KRIF, the only station on the air. The county agricultural agent was giving instructions for growing garden vegetables under glass or plastic, if glass or plastic could be found. The station engineer ventured into meteorology.

"Fortunately the barrier has had little effect on our weather. Though hailstones bounce off, it is now set to allow free passage to air currents and the water droplets in clouds. We forecast thunderstorms, possibly severe."

An old interview with Colin McAdam followed, about his books on slavery. Del Rio was suddenly on the monitor, interrupting a question about Daniel Boone and the Cherokee Indians.

"Urgent update from Washintel WebWatch One!" For all her air of tension, she looked heavy-eyed. "Special correspondent Ramona Del Rio, reporting Council action on the ultimatum brought by Ambassador Gottler. The meeting has ended with no communiqué. Our camera caught Colonel McAdam and the Councilors after the meeting."

Stuart came out first, and stopped to scowl into the lens.

"Here's one for Gottler and Higgins." He made an ugly gesture. "They offered us a carrot or a stick. I never cared for carrots, and I've got a bigger stick."

The councilors followed him, one by one. Tight-faced, they had no comment. The time was almost midnight. I yawned and went to bed. Half asleep, I heard sirens and what I thought was distant gunfire.

"Open up!" The order woke me. "Open to the law!"

The door crashed in before I could reach it. Men in Rifle gear burst into the room. An hour later I was back in Oxman's custody at the city-county jail.

CHAPTER TWENTY-EIGHT

"WELCOME HOME!" OXMAN greeted me with a sardonic smirk and booked me in. "Back to stay?"

I didn't know; they hadn't told me anything.

I begged for any explanation, but he locked the door and tramped on down the corridor toward the prisoners in the tank. The cell was the one where I had been, the infotel Quigg had left still on the shelf. It stayed dark and silent when I turned it on, but I heard sounds outside.

A crackle of distant gunfire. A heavy thud, perhaps an explosion far away. Steel doors clashing a little later, as more prisoners came in. I was dozing when the rattle of Mrs. Oxman's cart woke me for breakfast, scorched grits and a slab of half-cooked salt pork. She had time to talk when I asked what was going on.

"God knows!" She wrung her stringy hands. "They was fighting at the TV station. Kelly Flynn was on the air, telling about shooting on the street. Men busted in and took his mike." The station was still off the air, but Oxman had talked to the cops.

"They say it's General Stuart McAdam agin' the council—he's a general now. Mr. Oxman's sick and tired of this crazy mess with Pepperlake and Moorhawk. Too much empty wind about turning the county into some lunatic paradise. They've let Higgins cork us up like scorpions in a bottle. Stuart never fell for their idiot tricks. When they wouldn't listen to good horse sense, he just took over."

She grinned in satisfaction.

"A squad of his Rifles brought the whole dern council in. We've got 'em upstairs now, in the penthouse suites. Them's the high security cells on the top floor."

"All three members?"

"A midnight surprise." The grin went wider, showing crooked yellow teeth. "They winged Mr. Moorhawk when he tried to grab a gun. Just a scratch on his arm, but they had to take him by the hospital and get it dressed. Mr. Pepperlake was on the phone to this Washintel reporter when they got to him."

"And Rob Roy McAdam? Stuart's brother?"

"Him too. Upstairs with the others, though he don't seem upset about it. A funny thing. He had one of his high-tech cryptophones. Mr. Oxman took it when they searched him, but the general's staff called and told us to give it back, so him and the general could talk."

She squinted at the ceiling.

"They's soldiers up there now, left to watch 'em. We've got orders to feed 'em special meals, like we did Mr. Quigg. I took 'em the same chow me and Oxman had for breakfast. Buckwheat cakes with maple syrup—stuff I found on a shelf in the pantry. Too bad there ain't none left for you."

I asked if I could call my lawyer.

"Katz?" She shook her head. "Mr. Pepperlake tried. His wife said he'd call back, but he never did."

She rattled away with her cart. With nothing else to do, I paced the cell and watched the dead infotel till at last it came to life with a blare of military music. A putty-faced man in a Rifle uniform was suddenly on the monitor.

"This is station FREE." I recognized the oily tones of the florist I'd met at Rotary. "We are back on the air as the official electronic organ of the Free State of America. Stay tuned for an interview with acting president Stuart McAdam."

I watched the dead monitor till the bugles blared again.

"Ramona Del Rio." She had a fresh shine on the silver sheaf of hair and a fresh excitement in her eyes. "I'm an international correspondent for Washintel WebWatch One, speaking to the world from McAdam City, capital of the world's youngest nation.

"A historic moment!

"The Free State of America was born this morning when General Stuart McAdam took control. Formerly a militia leader, McAdam comes of a pioneer family, prominent in the county for the last two centuries.

"The former commander of the rebel military, he is now acting president of the new provisional government. Washintel WebWatch One is privileged to present his first statement to the world."

Stuart leaned alertly across a long bare table in a wood-paneled office in what had been the National Guard armory. I saw Beth in the piercing blue eyes, the shape of the bones, the wave of the light-brown hair, but all her grace grown hard in a way that wrenched me.

"President McAdam," Del Rio was crisply respectful, "can you tell us what happened last night?"

"Freedom was born again."

Through the window that framed his head, I saw the well-kept lawn, trees luminous with autumn red and gold, and the dull gray dome of the old courthouse. Consciously striking, he paused and turned to perfect his image for the camera.

"The Haven Council met last night to consider a shameful ultimatum from President Higgins, delivered by Rocky Gottler, a special mediator. The council refused, debated for hours, and finally decided to do nothing at all. That was the end of the charade they called the Haven. I speak for a group of saner and braver citizens who prefer freedom to famine.

"Early this morning, we acted to replace the unpopular and illegitimate Haven gang." Stuart straightened in his chair, right hand lifted to his eyebrow. "I salute our new government. I am proud to be speaking for the Free State of America."

"Sir, may I ask one question?" Del Rio smiled disarmingly. "What makes your new government any more legitimate than the old?"

"They were a handful of arrogant and autocratic zealots who had lost faith in democracy. They thought they saw us us sliding into chaos and terror, and they were trying to use my brother's silicon shell to save the world from its own people.

"We, however, trust the people." He looked beyond her, raising his voice for the world. "I intend to use the shell to re-store the democracy that our founding fathers meant America to be."

"Aren't you trapped like the council was?" She was coolly ironic. "Sealed up by Zeider's blockade?"

"We are not the only friends of freedom. The Rifles have sister militias scattered all over the country. They are willing to risk their lives for liberty, and we have a weapon for them."

"A weapon?"

"The silicon shell." His smile turned harder. "The ultimate weapon."

"Ultimate? When Zeider has you surrounded?"

"That's what he thinks. We have a surprise for him. We can send our friends out in small convoys, each led by a pickup equipped with a mobile unit."

"Portable shields!" The camera caught her widened eyes and parted cherry lips. "A reality?"

"And invincible!" He gestured expansively. "Nobody can touch them. New recruits will flock to join our revolution. We'll have a hundred islands of freedom set up all across the country. The Free States of America!

"But never united! Nobody can unite them, not against their will. When they want to act together, it will be in free associations.

They'll never need to fear tyrannical majorities or despotic bureaucrats. They'll never be taxed or coerced."

Elation lifted his voice.

"The world set free!"

"An exciting vision, sir." Del Rio smiled as if she had caught
his enthusiasm. "If you can make it happen."

"Certainly we'll face difficulties." He nodded more gravely.
"We have a new government to organize, new laws to write. But the
government will be our own, not far off in Washington. The laws
will be laws we like, and we can change them if we don't."

"Don't you face opposition, even from your brother? Her eyes
had narrowed shrewdly. "Isn't he in jail?"

"Rob's caught in an awkward situation." He shrugged. "He had
sworn allegiance to the council. I suppose he still feels bound by
it, but the council is out of the picture now. He'll have to face a
new reality."

Smiling again, Stuart was on his feet.

"So will Zeider and Higgins." Brimming with confident energy,
he bowed to the lens. "You must excuse me now. We have a new
world to make."

Del Rio thanked him and asked when channels to the outside
might open.

"We have the interview recorded," she told him. "Washintel
WebWatch One will be anxious to broadcast it to the waiting world.
Whenever possible."

"I'll have it arranged."

They were gone. After another blast of military music, the monitor went blank. I watched it the rest of the day, waiting for Katz,
but he never arrived.

When Mrs. Oxman brought breakfast next morning, it was biscuits
with gravy and a few bites of scrambled eggs.

"Made for the VIPs up in the penthouse suites," she said. "A
little left over."

Hopefully, I asked for news.

"Ain't none." Lips grimly compressed, she shook her head. "None that anybody knows. Mr. Oxman says General McAdam is trying to change everything, with new laws and new courts. Now he's in some kind of spat with his brother up in the penthouse. Mr. Oxman had to put him in a private room to talk on his cryptophone."

She made an impatient swipe with the back of her hand at the beaded sweat on her forehead.

"God knows what will happen to us. Mr. Oxman always got on with Mr. Hunn—he's been the boss of the county. But there's bad blood between him and the General. I'm afraid they'll throw us out of the jail with nowhere to go. The good God knows."

She came back later escorting Katz.

"I offered the conference room," she said. "But he says he ain't got time."

He stood in the corridor to speak through the bars. The big black-rimmed glasses gave him the air of a harried owl.

"Yesterday!" He shrugged in helpless apology. "Hell of a day! One crisis on top of another. We've got a new world to cope with. A madhouse, up to now. I tried to get here quicker, but I never had a minute. Today, however—"

He spread his hands in urgent appeal.

"Today—" He stopped to take off his glasses, lick the lenses, and rub them with a wrinkled handkerchief. "Well, Mr. Barstow—" Replacing the glasses, he shook his head. "I hope you'll try to understand."

"Yes?"

"You're in a hard spot. General McAdam wants to get rid of you. 'Red meat for the firing squad,' if I may quote. He blames you for trying to kill his father. And he thinks you tried to seduce his sister."

"I didn't—"

"What you did doesn't matter. It's what he thinks you did. But please, my boy, don't give up." Once more he spread his fat hands. "I'm doing all that can be done. I've even appealed to the general's father."

"At the hospital? How is

"Not well." He shook his head. "The bullet has been removed, but it carried infection into his body. I tried to phone him, to ask if he meant to press the case against you. I never got to him, but they let me speak to his daughter."

"Beth?" I saw her in my mind, sadly shaking her head. "What did she say?"

"Nothing useful. I asked her what Stuart thinks of you. She says they're no longer in touch. I told her I would be your defender when the new courts are set up." He paused, with a nervously apologetic laugh. "I probably shouldn't say so, sir, but she seemed to think your case is hopeless."

CHAPTER TWENTY-NINE

SOME TIME AFTER midnight, I was startled awake by glaring light and the clash of steel.

"Bastards!"

A big man stood swaying in the doorway, Oxman behind him. The stranger was shirtless and streaked with grime. A purple patch had spread around one eye. Blood had run down his chin. Under the thick black hair on his chest, a tattooed mermaid struggled against the coils of a lecherous octopus.

"Blazing bastards! Nailing me to the cross for things I never done!"

"Goodnight!" Oxman shoved him in and slammed the door behind him. "Sleep it off."

He staggered to the other bunk and sprawled back against the wall, blinking at me with the undamaged eye.

"Well, sir. Who the hell are you?"

I gave him my name.

"Barstow?" The eye widened. "The Fed snoop that run amuck?" He laughed at my hesitation. "No skin off my tail. I don't give a damn if you've robbed Fort Knox. Just count me in for a cut of my own."

He struggled out of his high-topped cowboy boots, collapsed on the berth, and began a raucous snore. He was on his feet when I woke again, pissing into the toilet and then gulping water out of a paper cup. The damaged eye had swollen shut. He squinted at me with the other.

"Forgive me, sir." He grinned in amiable apology. "I forget your name."

I told him again.

"Call me Rip." He gave me a scarred but muscular hand. "Rip Ralston." He cleared his throat, but his voice was still a raspy croak. "What got you here?"

"I could say bad luck."

He grunted sympathetically, scratched a naked armpit, and sat down on the other bunk.

"Luck's what you make it. Or maybe you let the other guy hex the dice?"

He sat regarding me, waiting for more. I thought he seemed unduly inquisitive, yet I felt hungry for any kind of human contact and curious to know his own story.

"I'm a stranger here in McAdam." I tried to tell a harmless bit of the truth without revealing too much. "I came on a research job for a writer who was doing a book."

"Yeah?" He bent forward, interested. "What sort of book?"

"About politics." I didn't want to link myself with Alden and *Terror in America*, certainly not till I knew him better. "A study of what to expect in the future."

"Yeah?" He grinned at my hesitation. "I'm no scholar, but I read. I think. I wonder what's ahead. Does your friend have a forecast?"

"Trouble," I said. "He was afraid of things to come and looking for signs of hope. He came here expecting McAdam County to be a peaceful bit of the rural past. It was nothing peaceful that got me here."

"The whole world's rotten to the heart." He nodded as if the observation pleased him. "Overrun with hordes of new barbarians tearing down everything we used to trust. Watch your back if you hope to stay alive."

He stopped to listen to voices down the corridor. "When's breakfast?"

"They took my watch. I don't know."

He glanced at his hairy wrist. Oxman had somehow let him keep his own heavy gold-cased timepiece, which had computer buttons and a tiny infonet screen.

"A rough night," he muttered. "I need my java." He shrugged and leaned back on the bunk. "But I've kept alive and learned to cook my luck. I'll be out of here tomorrow."

"My luck," I said, "has gone dry."

He scanned me thoughtfully. "You don't look quite fit for the hard game we've all got to play. I had to learn young. A scrawny kid with no nerve and no friends. Dad taught computer science at schools on the rough side of Louisville. I was a teach's son."

He made a doleful face.

"Kids picked on me till I learned computers and found the infonet and made friends there. Those I admired were soldiers of fortune, or claimed to be. I was happy they couldn't see what a pimply runt I was. I learned from them and invented myself a new identity."

He paused, the good eye narrowed to observe my response.

"A dozen years ago," I told him, "that lonely nerd might have been me."

"So you get me?" He grinned. "I made myself a better image. An unbeatable fighter, afraid of nobody, then found I had to make it real. I changed myself to fit the picture. Built muscle. Learned to take a fall and fight again. Bought weapons and learned to use them. Joined the Army when I was old enough. Trained for Special Forces. Got out to lend a hand wherever killing skills were wanted.

And learned to live by the new philosophy I'd learned on the in-fonet. In a world where dog eats dog, the top dog wins."

He paused to finger the swollen eye.

"You've heard about CyberSoft and the McAdam brothers?"

"Rob Roy and Stuart?" I listened more intently.

"Not that they behave like loving brothers. I knew Stuart first. Invited here to join his rebellion, I found quite a circus!"

Elation lit his battered face.

"The thrill of my life watching the fireworks that stopped Zeider's assault. Another thrill when I met Rob Roy. I was in a captured tank, out at the Lexington roadblock. He'd come out to watch his silicon shell at work, knocking aircraft out of the sky.

"We got to talking. A cordial cuss when I got to know him. Happy with the success of his wonder weapon, but afraid somebody could take it away. He looked me over, inquired about my line of work, and hired me to guard his CyberSoft plant. That's how I got the shiner."

With a wry shrug, he touched the injured eye.

"I was caught in his showdown with Stuart."

"Showdown?" I asked. "I've been out of the world."

"A brotherly quarrel." His grin was ironic. "Rob Roy and this Haven Council were trying to turn the county into a playground of perpetual peace. Stuart doesn't care for peace. He wants to share the shell with all his militia friends and turn them loose to conquer the country.

"Rob Roy balked. Stuart had his militia round up the council. I think they're all here in the jug with us. I got the shiner at CyberSoft when the Rifles came for the shell. They came twenty to one and caught us asleep."

"So Stuart seized the shell?"

"They didn't say, but he won't quit without it."

Mrs. Oxman came with grits and salt pork for breakfast. Ralston sniffed and waved it away.

"Go talk to your husband," he told her. "He tells me this cozy little apartment can be reserved for special guests like my friend Hamilton Quigg. I've arranged for special meals."

She scowled at that. Oxman was still asleep. He didn't like to be disturbed. Grumbling that we could eat grits or leave 'em, she carried the tray away and came back an hour later, looking no happier but with a generous platter of sausage and eggs, toast and jam, and a steaming pot of excellent coffee. Ralston said nothing to explain his arrangement, but he let me join the feast.

"That was the happy half of my story," he said after Mrs. Oxman had returned for the empty pot and platter. "The rest is not so pretty."

He had relaxed on the bunk, leaning back against the graffiti on the wall, but anger now edged his voice.

"There's no reason to lock up the captured guards. The Rifle medics patched me up after we surrendered. I was drinking beer with them in the club at the armory when the cops came to pick me up. I had an ugly couple of hours with Hunn and a man from the FBI before they brought me here."

"The FBI?"

"A nasty surprise." He made a face "They're the enemy now, or ought to be, and kicked out of the county, but Saul Hunn, our good city-county attorney, has managed to keep a few agents here, pals he was working with before the rebellion." He made a sneering face. "They're trying to tie me to the Frankfort bombing. You know about that?"

I nodded, but didn't want to talk about it. Certainly not to Ralston.

"Frankfort's still a thorn in their ass," he went on. "A replay of Oklahoma City. Their state headquarters. They'd tried to protect it. Traffic controls and concrete barriers to keep car bombs away."

He grinned and scratched a hairy armpit.

"The bombers outsmarted them. Bought a paint shop across the alley behind the building. Stocked it with paint buckets filled with smuggled explosives. Built their bomb in the back room of the shop behind a wall of sandbags and concrete blocks curved to focus the blast. It killed nineteen agents, there for a conference. Garlesh herself could have been there."

He shrugged as if with regret.

"A toothache had sent her to the dentist."

I wondered how he knew so much.

"Here's the case they tried to make against me."

He cocked his head to listen and dropped his voice.

"Marijuana has always been a cash crop here, bigger since the sky-high tobacco tax. The dealers branched out into harder stuff and fought the Bureau off. Their leader is a slippery figure they call Shadow Hand from a code name he's used on the infonet. A few months ago, as I get the picture, the Bureau set up an undercover operation meant to put them out of business. It was code-named Acorn—"

He stopped, the good eye squinting, as if he had seen my astonishment.

"Acorn?" I tried to cover myself. "Shadow Hand? That sounds like something out of a comic book."

"Not very comic for the Bureau. Somebody sold them out. Acorn was to be a secret cell. Clever planning, maybe, but Shadow Hand's no dummy."

He shook his head, the good eye still fixed on my face. Recalling Bella Garlesh and Botman and "Acorn Three," I stared back as blankly as I could and waited for more.

"His gang seems to have got a mole into the Acorn cell with orders to cover any trail to the Frankfort bombers. Hunn and his friends in the Bureau want to pin the blame on me."

He shrugged, the one-eyed scowl even sharper.

"That bomb's one big fish the Bureau wants to fry. Several bodies, or fragments of bodies, were found in what was left of the paint shop. The bombers, caught in their own blast. They suspect me of being the sole survivor left to talk about it.

"As if I would—" He shrugged with an air of easy unconcern.

"One more angle they badgered me about. That's the letterbomb

that knocked off a nosy reporter that came here for dirt and dug up
more than was good for him. He seems to have been an Acorn agent,
maybe fingered by Shadow Hand's mole."

He stopped with that, belched, and stood up to stretch and
listen at the corridor. I heard voices and cell doors clashing.

"Looks like a busy day for Oxman." He turned back, grinning.
"McAdam rounding up his enemies." He sat back on the bunk.
"You've heard my story. Now let's hear yours."

"Nothing like yours." I shook my head. "Just a run of very bad
luck."

"Evidently."

He grinned and waited.

"You've heard about my research job." I picked the words with
care. "I enrolled as a history student at McAdam College, meaning
no harm to anybody. A long story, but my inquiries got me involved
with the wrong people. I'm accused of killing Lydia Starker and
suspected of shooting Colin McAdam in the back—"

"The General's father?" He made a quizzical face. "That could
hang you." He studied me shrewdly. "Something else I'm wondering
about. Hunn and his Bureau friends kept badgering me for anything
I knew about another man who came here as an undercover informer
for the FBI." The good eye squinted. "Would that be you?"

Never a good liar, I had to catch my breath.

"Not that I care." He shrugged. "But I thought you'd like to be
warned."

He went to listen at the corridor.

"I know the General," he said. "I'll be out when he knows I'm
here." He shook his head at me. "I'm afraid you aren't so lucky."

"I do have a lawyer. A man named Katz."

"Katz?" He scowled. "Don't count on Katz."

CHAPTER THIRTY

HARD-HEELED BOOTS CAME thudding down the corridor. Ralston shook my hand and stood waiting at the door till Oxman swung it open, beckoned him out, and slammed it behind him.

Alone again, I tried the infotel. It was dead. I paced the floor and hoped for Katz, who never appeared. I called after Mrs. Oxman when she pushed her cart past me with dinner for the new prisoners in the tank. She shuffled on, ignoring me, but an hour later she came back with steak, asparagus, and a baked potato.

"A gift from Mr. Ralston," she muttered sourly. "He said you deserved it, the fix you're in."

That feast marked the end of Ralston's generosity. My breakfast next morning was a cold boiled potato and a scrap of cold meat that may have been mutton.

The infotel came to life with a sudden blare of military music. I saw the Kentucky Rifle fife-and-drum corps marching down

Main Street past the old courthouse and the *Freeman* office.

"Ramona Del Rio on station FREE." The silver streak shone in her hair, but her pert vivacity looked dulled from fatigue or perhaps a night on the town. "We bring you President Stuart McAdam reviewing his troops. He is preparing to address the world on his plans for the future of the Free State of America. His remarks will be recorded for rebroadcast whenever channels open."

A captured tank rumbled after the band, flying the flag of the new nation, a single blue star on a crimson field. The Rifles marched behind it, followed by a string of pickups flying the star.

Stuart received their salutes from a raw pine stand on the armory lawn. Uniformed now in crimson and blue, a bright sun-glint on the wave in his tawny hair, he made an image of dashing arrogance. When the marchers had passed, he turned to the camera.

"Friends and fellow citizen of the Free State, I thank you for your loyal support and congratulate you on your new-won freedom. The blue star in our flag is for the unity of our new nation, the red field for the patriot blood that is the price of freedom.

"I am proud to be your leader and happy to inform you that the future of our newborn nation is now secure. The so-called Haven Council is now no more. The fanatics who formed it are now safely jailed, and the last opposition is being eliminated.

"You will be happy, I know, to welcome law and order back. I promise you now—" He placed his right hand on his heart. "On my sacred honor, I promise you a fair and honest government. Delegates will be called to a constitutional convention. Democratic elections will be held.

"In the meantime—" He paused. His voice fell, and I saw ice in his eyes. "In the meantime, our new-won liberty must be defended. In the absence of any civil law, our first decree will place the entire population under military law."

Applause rattled from the speakers, though the camera had shown no listeners. In no mood for Stuart, I killed the infotel and stumbled around the cell in a blind confusion of helpless desperation and illogical relief. Desperation, because I felt the trap finally closing on me. Relief because I thought the torment of helpless waiting must now be over. Something had to change.

Waiting for it, I heard distant voices and the thud of boots. Sometimes the screech of an unoiled hinge and clang of a door. Silence again. Nothing with any meaning for me till late afternoon when Mrs. Oxman unlocked the door for Katz.

He was rumpled and careworn, a gray stubble on his jowls and sagging pouches under his eyes. With a feeble effort at cordial fellowship, he shook my hand, asked how they were treating me, and tried to excuse himself for not coming in before.

"In a world without law, you didn't need a lawyer." His hollow cheer sharpened into bitter complaint. "I'm afraid you do need help, now that the General's going to give us his own brand of law. Bad law, and too much of it."

He sat down heavily on the opposite bunk.

"I've been his attorney for years. I thought we were friends. I've saved his scalp more than once, defending him against trumped-up charges and pulling political strings to get him out of prison. But now—"

Red-faced with anger, he gritted his teeth and shook his fist at the wall.

"He's gone crazy!" The tic twisted his face into a malevolent one-sided mask. "He's obsessed with the notion that he can rewrite history and remake the world."

"I heard his broadcast about martial law." I searched his face for clues. "What does it mean for me?"

"I hate to tell you." Dismally, he shook his head. "Believe me, Barstow, I've done all any man could do. I've talked to the general's friends. I tried to talk to him, but he had no time for me." He spoke through a snarling grimace. "He's too busy planning to conquer the world."

Next morning a Rifle detachment took over the jail. The Oxmans were gone. I saw new prisoners hustled past my cell, several of them bandaged or limping. My breakfast was late, a cold boiled potato and a scanty bowl of boiled cabbage, brought by a new recruit just off a horse farm and wearing a red-and-blue armband for a uniform.

Katz was back before noon, looking no happier.

"I've done my damnedest." Muttering half to himself, he sank down on the opposite bunk. "Got nowhere."

His bleary eyes narrowed when I asked him to try again.

"Stuart and I." He shook his head. "We used to get on. I was one of his first recruits for the Rifles. He wanted me to manage the money and steer him clear of the FBI. I was his supply sergeant, dealing for guns and uniforms, till he accused me of embezzling Rifle funds.

"But not in the civil courts." An angry toss of his uncombed head. "He was afraid of all I might say about him and the Rifles. Instead he set up his own kangaroo court to give me what he called a military trial. They gave me a dishonorable discharge and fined me a hundred thousand dollars. That's what he claimed I'd stolen."

Wondering if he had, I asked if he had paid the fine.

"Had to." He shrugged, helpless anguish on his face. "His militia thugs would have beaten me to jelly."

"Now?" I asked. "What now?"

"The same dirty game all over again. Stuart has his Free State under martial law, with a special spot of honor for you." A sardonic grimace. "Our first court-martial."

What I'd half expected, yet it felt like a punch in the gut.

"You will be charged with the murder of Lydia Starker." Grimly methodical, he counted the charges on pudgy fingers with broken, black-rimmed nails. "Arson, resulting in the murder of Dr. Stuben Ryke, when you drove the firebomb pickup into his clinic. The attempted murder of the General's father, when you shot him in the back. Conspiracy and espionage against the Free State. Flight to escape justice. Even grand larceny, when you made off with the pickup.

"That enough?"

"It will do." Dazed, I sat there trying dully to recall the far-off simplicities of life in Georgetown as it had been before the letter bomb arrived. "You're my lawyer," I said when I found wit and breath to speak. "What can we do?"

"Not much." Dismally, he shrugged. "Stuart won't see me alone, but yesterday afternoon I went back to his headquarters in the old armory with another group trying to petition him for a constitution, and a convention to draw it up.

"They never let us in, but Colonel Burleigh—he's a colonel now—finally came out to talk to our spokesman, Hack Klappinger, a social science prof from the college. Hack tried to warn him that Stuart is turning off a lot of people who used to support him.

"Burleigh snorted at that and gave us their line. The general says we're standing at a turning point in history. He has this unique chance to share his brother's secret weapon with all mankind and set the whole world free from oppression forever."

Katz made a sardonic face.

"General Stuart McAdam! A great man now, or he thinks he is. And ruthless when he tries to prove it. His military cops were busy all night, rounding up people on his blacklist. And you—" He shook his head at me. He means to make an example of you.

"Your court-martial is set for tomorrow."

"Tomorrow?" That took my breath.

"No help for it, Mr. Barstow." His voice rose in anxious apology, but then he managed an uneasy grin. "A tricky situation, but I've seen Colonel Hunn and worked out a scheme to save your hide."

"Saul Hunn?" I recalled the feral fox face in its artful frame of silky silver hair. "What sort of scheme?"

"Hunn's the military prosecutor now, and here's the deal." Katz hesitated, searching me shrewdly. "I want you to plead guilty to all the charges, and throw yourself on the mercy of the court."

"Whose mercy?" Trembling, I reached to catch his sleeve. He flinched away from my hand. "Stuart's?"

He shrugged, with an air of gloomy impotence. "What else do you think I can do?"

"I don't know." His stubbled face was blank, his wary eyes almost hostile, but I plunged ahead. "I'm not guilty of anybody's murder. The FBI did send me here, if that's a charge against me. I did steal that farmer's pickup. But I didn't knife Lydia Stalker or drive that firebomb into the Ryke clinic. I certainly didn't shoot Colin McAdam in the back—"

"Who did?"

"If I could guess, I'm afraid the right guess could get me killed."

His shrewd little eyes fixed on me for several seconds. "If you're afraid to guess, let's have what you know."

I got up to look through the bars. The corridor seemed empty. Angry voices in the tank seemed far away. Speaking under my breath, I gave him a full catalogue of my misfortunes.

"I have to trust you, Mr. Katz."

"Of course!" He was alarmingly loud. I raised my hand, and he dropped his voice a little. "And this scheme with Hunn is your best chance."

"A guilty plea? I don't trust Hunn. I won't do that."

"Please, Mr. Barstow!" He caught my arm. "I am your attorney. My best judgment is that you are asking to face a firing squad. That's what Hunn will be demanding, if your case goes to trial. Think about it."

Gripping my arm, he gave me half a minute to think.

"Here's the deal. He bent so close I caught the onion and cigar tobacco on his breath. "The General would love to see you wearing a blindfold in front of a rifle squad, but Hunn and I have worked out a strategy that ought to save you."

I sat shaking my head, but he went doggedly on.

"The General's still at odds with the Haven councilors. He has them here in jail, but they've got him stalled. His bid for world power depends on his threat to arm his militia allies with silicon shells. Rob Roy balks at that.

"He'd built one of those portable units. When the General made his putsch, Mike Densky and his crew used it to wall themselves up in the CyberSoft building where nobody can get at them. That's the basis for our arrangement."

He paused, with a strained grin of satisfaction.

"The General would prefer you dead, but Hunn thinks he'd settle for a mobile shell unit. He'll ask the court to accept your guilty plea and exile you from the Free State. You will leave with an Arizona militia group, armed with one of these portable shell units.

"You ought to be happy with that."

I wasn't, but before I had time to say so, a guard was at the door.

"Time, Mr. Katz. Time to go."

CHAPTER THIRTY-ONE

THE SHEER ADVENTURE of it drew me. An unbelievable escape after all my weeks of desperate flight and hiding, the chance to set out with a tiny convoy of battered pickups and a few reckless men determined to bring down the old America.

Making history for Stuart. History for the world. A dazzling prospect, if the silicon shell could actually heal the contagion of terror that had obsessed my brother. It might free me from the stink of the jail and the promise of a rifle squad.

I lay awake half the night, imagining the push across the nation in search of a welcome and haunted by the hazards of it. Hostile mobs, battling to defend the dying past. Air attacks, tank traps set for us, bridges mined to blow up beneath us. Madly hopeful, I dreamed of victory after stunning victory as we rolled safely onward inside our moving fortress.

I woke to a breakfast of boiled turnips and fried grits, and a shock of cold reality. It could never happen. Even if Rob Roy could be persuaded to give his secret up, I had no wish to destroy America.

I sat on the hard bunk, waiting uneasily till Katz came with the guards. They manacled my hands, marched me to the elevator, took me down to the dismal courtroom. A silent crowd waited in the pew-like seats. The jury box was empty, but half a dozen of Stuart's Riflemen stood at parade rest in front of it. Katz sat down with me at a counsel table inside the railing.

Across the room, Ramona Del Rio was murmuring into a silenced mike. Her camera man was fussing with a tripod. He swung the lens to me for a moment, and then to sweep the room.

I found Beth and her father in the front row. He sat stiffly erect, but looked pinched and shrunken, his gnarled old hands clutching a cane. His deep sunken eyes were fixed on me with no expression I could read.

Sight of Beth quickened my breath and stabbed me with ache of hopeless longing and regret. Without makeup, she looked tired and troubled, yet alluring as ever, even in a simple blue business suit. She had bent to murmur something to her father. I watched till she turned to glance at me. Her eyes held mine for an endless moment, as if she tried to search my heart, till she flushed and turned very quickly away.

Hunn and Gottler came strolling in together, carrying thick briefcases. They paused for a formal handshake with Katz and a glance at my manacled hands before they settled themselves at the opposite table.

"Rocky?" Katz breathed in my ear. "What the hell's his business in the court?"

I had no idea. The room fell silent. I heard a bugle blast.

"By order of General McAdam," the Rifle sergeant bawled, "the high court of the Free State of America is now in session. All stand for the judges."

One by one, he chanted their names. Colonel James Burleigh. Colonel Benjamin Coon. Major Aaron Hawes. All newly uniformed in scarlet jackets and blue, gold-braided pants, they marched in to seat themselves behind the bar.

Burleigh glanced at me, grinned, and leaned to whisper to Coon. I remembered Hawes, the police sergeant who had arrested me the night McAdam was shot; his cold stare sent a chill through me. Burleigh banged his gavel and called for order in the court. The white-headed court reporter bent over his antique machine, and the camera lights blazed on me.

Hunn made me stand and state my name.

"Clayton Barstow, you stand charged with capital crimes against the Free State of America." He repeated the charges. Murder, arson, grand larceny, flight from justice. I heard a stir and whisper from the crowd. Burleigh slammed his gavel and turned to Katz.

"How does the prisoner plead?"

I caught my breath to speak. Features twisted with the tic, Katz gestured to stop me. He came to his feet.

"Sir, I have counseled with my client. My advice—"

I stood up.

"I plead—" Katz glared at me, muttering. I raised my voice. "I plead not guilty to all charges."

"Idiot!" A whispered snarl. "You're asking for what you'll get—"

Burleigh banged his gavel.

"The trial will proceed."

"Sir," Katz spoke louder, "I move that the case be dismissed. This is a military court. The prisoner is not in the military. The court lacks jurisdiction."

"Nonsense!" Burleigh shouted. "Until the Free State enacts a constitution, we have no civil law. General McAdam has placed the entire Free State under military law." He turned to Hunn. "The prosecution may proceed."

"Sir," Katz persisted, "we object that this is not a proper military court for the trial of a capital case. Military law would require

a general court-martial, consisting of at least five appointed officers."

"Sit down, Mr. Katz." Burleigh banged the gavel. "Until the
Free State has approved a constitution, our law here is what General
McAdam says it is. This court is duly appointed, vested with full
capital authority. Your frivolity will not be tolerated."

Flushed and fuming, Katz sat down.

Hunn's first witness was Mrs. Stella Starker, attired in a frilly
lace blouse, a purple skirt that swept the floor, and a boat-shaped
hat decorated with a tall spray of artificial ferns. Sworn, she turned
from Hunn to stab a finger at me.

"That's him!" A piercing screech. "Him that slaughtered my
precious daughter!"

I heard a gasp from the audience. Burleigh slammed his gavel
down. Katz was on his feet, objecting. Grinning, Hunn admonished
her not to speak except in answer to his questions and asked if she
had seen me at the time of her daughter's death.

"He come bustin' into my house before six that morning, lookin'
for Lydia. He had this crazy rigmarole that she'd called him to come
help her out of some trouble, but she had no trouble I knew about
and anyhow I never let her have callers that time of day, when no
decent woman would entertain a man. She wasn't even up for breakfast.

"I tried to send him on his way and saw him on his bike, but
when I looked in Lydia's room, there he was, standing over her
naked body on the bathroom floor, a bloody knife in his hand. He'd
stabbed her to death—"

Katz objected again. The witness should be advised that she
could only relate what she had seen and heard, with none of her
own conclusions. Hunn agreed, with another grin for the judges,
and kept her on the stand to testify that she had never seen me
before or heard Lydia mention my name.

She and Mr. Starker had prayed over her since the day she was
born, and worked their fingers to the bone to bring her up to fear

God and honor them. It broke their hearts that she never found Christ, but there had never been a grain of truth in all the wicked tales people told about her. She had no enemies but Satan and servants of Satan like—

She was glowering at me, pointing again, but Katz was objecting before she could go on. He had no questions for cross. Hunn excused her and had the plastic-wrapped knife entered in evidence. A police sergeant swore that the fingerprints on the blood-stained handle were mine.

A brawny black man in yellow coveralls identified himself as Fire Chief Tyson Tellmark. Keeping a wary eye on the judges, he testified that he had been on duty on the night of Dr. Ryke's death.

"The phone rang just after three. A man likely trying to disguise his voice—it was shrill as a kid's and he put on a queer accent—he told me to watch out for a hot night. He said it was going to be a hell of a night for the baby-killers at the clinic. He hung up when I asked who he was.

"The automatic alarm went off maybe thirty minutes later. I rushed over to the clinic in my own car ahead of the equipment. The pickup with the burning oil drums had rammed into the door. I got the smell of gasoline. The flames were already so high I couldn't get close, but I found a man crawling away from the fire."

"Who was the man?"

Tellmark looked at the judges, nervously licking his lips.

"Did you recognize the man?"

"Yes sir." His voice had dropped to a husky whisper. "He had stumbled on the curb and fallen in the street. Maybe knocked out. His hair was singed and his nose was bleeding. I helped him into my car and rushed him to the hospital."

"You did recognize him?"

"I—I knew him."

"What was his name?"

He glanced at the judges again and shrank down in the chair.

"He—he was Mr. Ben—Colonel Ben Coon."

I heard a gasp from the crowd but saw no change on Coon's hard flat face.

"Thank you, Mr. Tellmark," Hunn moved smoothly on. "Did Colonel Coon tell you how he had got there?"

"Yes sir." Tellmark sank back in the chair, relaxed. "He did."

"What did he say?"

"He said he was driving past the clinic on his way home from working late on the payroll at the Rifle headquarters." Tellmark kept his eyes on Coon, who nodded in approval. "He said he seen the pickup crash into the clinic and the gas explode. A man running from the blast came past his car. The headlights caught his face."

"Did the colonel know the man?"

"He says he did." Tellmark looked at me. "He says it was the man you've got right there."

"Clayton Barstow?"

"Yes sir. The colonel says he met him the day he came to town, and asked him to join the Rifles."

Smugly content with the witness and himself, Hunn asked Katz if he had anything for cross. Glumly, Katz said he had nothing. Feeling helpless, I looked at the judges. Coon looked grave till Hawes murmured something I didn't get and leaned to shake his hand. Burleigh nodded cheerfully and announced a twenty-minute recess. They left the courtroom.

"They're lying!" I told Katz. "All lying. I was in the strip-mined country out beyond the county line when the clinic burned, beaten unconscious and lying in the mud."

"If you care to tell Coon and Burleigh that, I'll put you on the stand when the prosecution rests." Katz shrugged and shook his head. "If you think anybody will believe you."

The judges returned. Hunn had a pistol entered as evidence. Officer Hyde identified it as a nine-millimeter Chenya automatic, illegal in America and known as "the cop-stopper" because it could penetrate body armor. He testified that this was the gun he had picked up outside a shattered window at the McAdam mansion on the night Colin McAdam was shot. My fingerprints were on it.

Hunn's next witness was Orinda King. Old and anxious, her thin white hair closely clipped, she shuffled to the witness box and sat peering through gold-framed glasses at him and the judges. Speaking in a breathless whisper, she testified that she had worked as a maid for the McAdam family all her life. Her time-seamed face wrinkled into an uneasy smile when he had her look at me. Yes, she knew me. I had been at the McAdam house on the night Mr. McAdam was shot.

Why was I there?

I was a friend of the family.

Did she know I was a fugitive from the law, hiding from the police?

"He never said nothin' like that."

He made her examine the pistol. Had she seen it before?

"Excuse me, sir, but I don't know nothin' about guns."

Had she seen a gun that looked like it anywhere in the McAdam house? He offered it again. She shrank as if it had been a venomous snake.

"I don't want no truck with that ugly thing."

"Do you want to go to jail?" Hunn shouted at her. "Or do you want to tell the truth? The truth you swore to tell. Did you see a gun like that in the McAdam house?"

"Maybe like it, sir. Maybe I did."

"Where did you see it?"

"In a drawer, sir." Her whisper was nearly too faint for me to hear. "In a drawer by the bed in the room where Mr. Stuart slept back when he was still at home."

"Who had been using the room since General McAdam left?" He gestured at me. "Was it Clayton Barstow?"

"He didn't—" She swayed to her feet, shouting at him and the judges in her thin old voice. "He didn't do all you say he did. He's a decent gentleman. I don't believe he killed nobody."

Trembling, crying like a hurt child, she sank back into the chair. Hunn asked the judges to have her outburst stricken, and turned to Katz with a mocking grin to ask if he had questions for her. When Katz had none, he hustled her out of the box and turned to face the court.

"Gentlemen, you have heard how Clayton Barstow killed Lydia Starker and Dr. Stuben Ryke, and how he tried to kill General McAdam's father. Our next witness will tell you why."

CHAPTER THIRTY-TWO

HUNN'S SURPRISE WITNESS was Rip Ralston, out of jail and cleaned up, the mermaid and the octopus discreetly hidden under a gray sports jacket, a neat black patch over the battered eye. At ease in the box, he raised a heavy, black-haired hand for the oath, gave me a sardonic wink, and turned to pose for Del Rio when her camera light came on.

Hunn asked what he did for a living.

"Just a soldier, sir. A professional man at arms. I work where I can. Recently I was a guard at CyberSoft."

"Prior to that?"

"Before that?" He shook his head. "My last job was confidential. I couldn't talk about it."

"Here you can," Hunn snapped impatiently. "We want the truth."

"Sorry air but too much talk about my previous employment might endanger my life."

Hunn appealed to the judges.

"The witness will answer." Burleigh scowled at him. "You're in a new country, Mr. Ralston, under new laws of life. If you need protection, you'll get it here."

"In that case—" Ralston paused, turning his eye-patched profile for the camera. "I came to McAdam County as an undercover agent for the FBI."

That caused a stir in the audience. Burleigh picked up the gavel and silence returned.

"How was that?"

"It all began with a writer named Kirk who was doing research for a controversial book." He gave me a piercing stare and turned soberly back to the judges. "His articles and infonet pieces stirred up the bureau and put them on the trail of an American *mafioso.*"

Coon nudged Burleigh, with a knowing nod.

"The gang was a hard nut to crack. It's a group of high-level nerds recruited on the infonet. They keep in touch with codes the Bureau never broke. They never meet except when they must, never learn more about one another than the work in hand requires. With no name for the kingpin, the bureau calls him Shadow Hand.

"He's keen as they come. Seems to have begun in the marijuana trade—marijuana is the big money crop here in the county—but he's gone on into more sophisticated games. White-collar crime, often international. Money laundering, infonet scams, cracking security systems to loot banks and federal agencies. High-tech tricks of his own design.

"All that put heat on Bella Garlesh. She tried to fight back with a special secret unit, code-named Oakwood. No match for Shadow Hand. Even when they caught a gang member on his Arizona ranch, with his computers hidden behind a bookcase and his loot stashed under phony names in a dozen offshore accounts, he wouldn't talk. Afraid his family would be slaughtered if he did. He killed himself—broke a cyanide tube implanted under his arm—before they could persuade him.

"But Garlesh is a tough cookie. She recruited this Alden Kirk,

who was slick enough to make a killing out of all the dirt he dug
up. Till he finally killed himself."

Ralston paused, with a long moment for the camera and a malicious grin for me.

Hunn asked, "How was that, Mr. Ralston?"

"He was acting the holy innocent, inquiring into the springs of
crime." He nodded at Hunn and winked at the judges. "Crime here
in the old McAdam County. Somehow worked his way into the gang.
Could be they had to take him in because he'd already got too much
on them. A big score for Garlesh, till he sold her out."

The impulse to slug him brought me half out of my seat. My
manacles had jingled. With a whispered warning, Katz caught my
arm. Sitting back, I took a deep breath and made my fists relax.

"Huh?" Hunn's surprise seemed almost real. "How was that?"

Happy under the searching eyes of the judges, Ralston turned
for a long glance at the camera.

"Kirk's first assignment had been to identify the ganglord. He
did, though Shadow Hand was the only name he ever reported to
Garlesh. What he did, instead, was to pass the poop the other way.
He fingered Oakwood."

"Object!" I jogged Katz's elbow. "I knew my brother. That has
to be an ugly lie. Ask Ralston how he knows."

Nervously drumming his knuckles on the table, Katz gave me
a tight-lipped, lopsided grimace.

"Order!" Burleigh brought his gavel down. "Order in the court."
He nodded at Hunn. "Your witness will continue."

"Thank you, sir." Hunn gave me a wolfish grin. "If Kirk's
brother seems astonished by this revelation, so am I. Perhaps the
witness can explain Kirk's behavior."

"Knowing what I do of him and Shadow Hand, I can guess."
Ralston paused to frown sympathetically at me. "Kirk seems to have
been fond of his wife and children. I suspect that he was swapping
lives."

"Huh?" A grunt from Burleigh. "How's that?"

"I believe he was trading his comrades on the Oakwood team
for his family—to save them from slaughter."

"Yes?" The room was hushed. "That answers the mystery?"

"Apparently sir, from what I was able to learn."

Ralston paused, frowning and rubbing at his ear, thinking for the camera. I sat trying desperately to grasp what manner of man he was. A harmless-seeming braggart with me in my jail cell, he had revealed nothing of the suave monster sitting now in the witness box.

"Oakwood?" Hunn was asking. "Are you saying—"

"Excuse me, sir." With a smile of apology, he resumed, "The Oakwood team was headquartered in the Federal Building at Frankfort. Kirk gave Shadow Hand the date when the bureau team would all be there together."

Seething with a baffled anger, I looked at Katz. Jittery now, his pale face beaded with sweat, he was removing the black-rimmed glasses. Deliberately but perhaps unconscious of the action, he licked the lenses, polished them with a white silk handkerchief, replaced them, gave me an empty stare.

"Thank you, Mr. Ralston." Beaming, Hunn waited for the judges to nod agreement. "You have answered questions that have troubled many of us. I'm sure, however, that the defendant and his attorney are anxious to know more about Kirk and Shadow Hand. Can you enlighten us?"

"Certainly." Eye-patch turned for the camera, Ralston paused to make a show of thinking. "Garlesh was just as anxious. With my evidence, she was moving to arrest Kirk till Shadow Hand beat her to the draw with the letter bomb that killed him.

"She was already setting up a new unit, code-named Acorn. Obsessed with security by then, she patterned it after the Shadow Hand gang. To guard against anything like the fate of the Oakwood team, agents were to work in secret, linked by coded signal, keeping well apart."

"You were an Acorn member?"

"Perhaps the first." Ralston nodded somewhat smugly. "She knew I had experience in military intelligence and military security. She asked me to help select and train the others."

"So you knew them?"

"True." He hesitated, frowning at the judges. "I don't want to name them all. Needless names could embarrass loyal Americans— loyal citizens who were only trying to serve their country. However, there's one man I can name."

He looked hard at me.

"Clayton Barstow. Chosen by the director herself, because he was Kirk's half brother and research assistant. She'd never suspected Kirk, and she hoped Clayton could help us nail the bombers."

With an ironic grin, he shook his head at me.

"Too bad for the Bureau—"

He stopped, looking toward the entrance. The room had fallen silent. Glittering in his new dress uniform, Stuart McAdam came marching down the center aisle, two Riflemen in step behind him. He stopped for a moment in front of the startled judges, glanced sharply across at his sister and his father, and settled himself with his guards in the vacant seats across the aisle.

Old Colin McAdam had turned his emaciated head, frowning sadly at his son. Glancing at Beth, I found her somber stare fixed on me. Our eyes met for a moment before she dropped her gaze with a look I could not read.

"Okay, Mr. Ralston." Hunn had recovered. "You were saying?"

"Barstow was a grave disappointment." Ralston continued, with a reproving headshake for me. "To the director. To all of us. He claimed to know nothing of his brother's connection to the Bureau, nothing of Shadow Hand.

"When he said he wanted to identify his brother's killers, we brought him here under cover as a graduate student at McAdam College. His actual motive, it turned out, was to defend his brother's reputation—to deny or cover up evidence of what a cunning double-dealer he had been."

"How do you know this?"

"I have his confession."

Trembling with my helpless fury, I had jingled the manacles again. Katz gripped my arm.

"You do?" Hunn assumed surprise. "How was it obtained?"

Ralston smirked at me.

"Barstow has been a guest of the county jail. I was able to join him in his cell with a fifth of Jim Beam. He drank most of it. Before daylight he was maudlin, sobbing with regret for the way Alden Kirk had wrecked the lives of his wife and his kids."

"Just what did he confess?"

"Everything." Ralston nodded soberly. "He was drunk and overwhelmed with guilt. I was a fellow prisoner. He trusted me."

"You know the charges?" Hunn was aglow with triumph. "The murder of Lydia Starker? The murder by arson of Dr. Stuben Ryke? The sneak assault on Colin McAdam?"

"I do."

"Can you tell us the circumstances of Miss Starker's death?"

I heard a muffled moan from Lydia's mother, now seated somewhere behind me. A woman hissed to hush her. Burleigh banged his gavel. After a nod from Hunn, Ralston went smoothly on.

"Starker was another member of the Acorn unit. She had met Barstow at a secret meeting of malcontents. He learned that she was in fact a double agent, recruited on the infonet by Shadow Hand. Kirk had been another member of their little secret cell. Their mission had been to save the Frankfort bombers from the Bureau investigators. Like Kirk, she died for what she knew."

He paused with that, turning to glance at Stuart.

"How so?" Hunn was impatient. "Be explicit."

"Besides the ganglord himself, Barstow believed that only she and Stuben Ryke knew that that it was his brother who had tipped off Shadow Hand. He slaughtered Lydia Starker and burnt Ryke in his clinic to save his brother's name."

"Preposterous!" I whispered to Katz. "When the fire happened—"

Rapping the table with his pen, he made a twisted grimace and shook his head at me. Burleigh scowled at him and brought the gavel down.

"Okay." Hunn was nodding, satisfied. "That wraps up the murders. There's still the charge of felonious assault, when Colin McAdam was nearly killed by a bullet fired from outside his house. Did Barstow confess to that?"

"He did."

Ralston stopped to glance at Beth and her father in their front-row seats. Colin's deep-sunk eyes were fixed on me, with no expression I could understand. Hers, I thought, were hopelessly sad.

"What, precisely, did he confess?"

Ralston eyed me with an air of mingled contempt and pity.

"He was maudlin by then, crying so hard he could hardly speak. Sorry for himself, sorry for his brother's widow and her children, sorry for all he had done. Finally, however, he got the whole story out.

"He had become infatuated with Miss McAdam. A fugitive from the law by then, he had persuaded her to hide him in her home. He said he had hoped to marry her. That may seem irrational, but no rational man would be where he is now. He believed that her father, not so gullible as she was, would oppose the marriage. With a cold brutality I can't understand—" Assuming a baffled regret, he shrugged and dropped his voice. "Standing outside in the dark, he fired though the window, hoping to put her father out of the way."

A murmur of hushed voices swept through the room. Gottler touched Hunn's sleeve and gave him a nod of approbation. The three judges bent their head together, their eyes on me.

"Very good, Mr. Ralston," Hunn said. "Very useful testimony. We thank you for it." Ralston was moving to rise, but Hunn waved him back. "One question more before you leave the stand. Can you identify the ganglord, Shadow Hand himself?"

Ralston sat back, shaking his head.

"No, sir. Not of my knowledge."

"Do you have other knowledge?"

"Only hearsay, sir. Hearsay from Lydia Starker while she was still alive."

"What was that?"

"As she told me, her association with the gang began with a call on a secure telephone. The caller was a man who asked her to join a secret group devoted to the defense of freedom. She asked who he was. He told her to call him Shadow Hand.

"She tried to balk, but his threats were convincing. Threats to expose past chapters of her private life and disgrace her family. She served in that Bureau cell with Ryke and Alden Kirk. She never was told the names of any others, even when they had joint assignments, but all her orders had come from Shadow Hand himself. She finally recognized his voice."

"And who is he?"

"You'll be surprised."

Enjoying a moment of suspense, Ralston grinned at Hunn and the waiting judges and even turned to look for a moment at Stuart McAdam.

"All of you know him. A man who'd made and lost an honest fortune before he turned to crime to make it back. A leader in the Haven cabal, he'd come close to winning all he's schemed and killed for. You have him upstairs now, in the penthouse cells. If you want his name."

He paused a moment for the camera.

"He's Kit Moorhawk."

The room buzzed till Burleigh slammed his gavel down. Hunn turned to the judges.

"Mr. Ralston is our final witness in the state versus Clayton Barstow," he said. "In light of his testimony, new charges may be filed against the Haven leaders now in our hands, but our case against Barstow is now concluded."

"Mr. Katz?" Burleigh frowned at him. "Are you ready for rebuttal?"

Katz blinked at me through the black-rimmed lenses, his face weirdly contorted, and rose to face the judges.

"No sir." He stood twisting his flabby hands together. "These accusations have come very suddenly. We have had no time to prepare any adequate defense. We must beg for a delay."

Burleigh glanced at Hawes and Coon, both impatiently stacking their notes. He glared at Katz and me.

"Have you witnesses to call if we should grant delay? Can you rebut Mrs. Starker's testimony? Or Mr. Tellmark's? If you should claim that Barstow did not fire the shot that wounded Mr. McAdam, can you tell us who did?"

"No, sir." Katz made another freakish grimace. "Not without time—"

"We have no time," Burleigh cut him off. "Not to waste on piddling frivolities or lunatic lies." He glanced at Hawes and Coon. "I believe we are ready for the verdict. Mr. Barstow will stand."

Weak in the knees, I stood. Burleigh leaned for a moment to catch the whispers from Hawes and Coon. He cleared his throat.

"Mr. Barstow, we find you guilty of the murders of Lydia Stalker and Dr. Stuben Ryke and the cowardly assault on Colin McAdam. By unanimous agreement, we sentence you to death by firing squad."

CHAPTER THIRTY-THREE

. . . *DEATH BY FIRING* squad.

The words rang loud in my head. Time had stopped. I felt a curious sense of detachment, almost as if I were already dead and beyond the need to care. The dismal old courtroom seemed suddenly strange. Looking at the judges, I saw Burleigh's thick lips half open and yellow teeth gleaming. Coon, his hand raised to cover a yawn, had tipped his head to hear a whisper from Hawes, whose hawklike features were set in a frown of angry impatience. All of them more stupid than evil, but hard, cold, with no trace of compassion for me.

Gottler was on his feet, grinning, reaching to shake Hunn's hand. Beth's face was drawn with hurt when I turned, dark eyes intent on me. Her father was staring across at Stuart, who sat stiffly, his face a masculine mirror of hers and somehow seeming to reflect her pain.

That suspended moment ended when I heard the shrill squeak of Gottler's voice, congratulating Hunn. Time swept on. I heard a muffled cough. Burleigh murmured to Coon and reached for his gavel. My own emotions alive again, I felt a shock of terror.

"Can't you—" My desperate whisper caught. "Can't you do anything?"

Wiping his glasses, staring blindly at Gottler and Hunn, Katz seemed not to hear me. I turned back to the judges.

"Colonel Burleigh?" I waited till he finally glanced at me, and raised my breathless voice again. "Sir, may I speak?"

"You have an attorney to speak for you."

I scanned the hostile faces of the other judges and found no comfort. I turned to Katz. Nervously sweating, he was replacing the glasses. With a fleeting mask of fear that seemed to mirror my own panic, he blinked and shrugged without a word.

"Please!" My voice seemed weak and broken. I caught my breath and fixed my eyes on Burleigh. "I didn't kill Lydia Starker. I didn't drive the firebomb into Ryke's clinic. I didn't fire that bullet out of the dark."

"Then who did?"

Gottler was quacking at Hunn and Ralston, who had joined them at their table. Ralston grinned and gave me a contemptuous finger. Pink with anger, Hunn surged to his feet.

"Mr. Katz!" he shouted. "Your client is out of order."

Katz made a madman's mask and said nothing.

"Colonel Burleigh!" I raised my own hollow voice. "I do know I'm not the killer. Won't you let me tell my story?"

Coon and Hawes were frowning at him, shaking their heads.

"We've had his story," Hunn was shouting again. "We've heard his confession to Mr. Ralston. We've reached a verdict. The case is closed."

I saw Beth on her feet, catching her breath as if she wanted to protest. Her father caught her arm. With a distressed glance at Stuart, she sat down.

"Saul!" Stuart was rising, his features sternly set, his voice harsh and loud. "Let him speak."

The room was startled, hushed. Burleigh sat gaping at him. Beth stared at Stuart, her face tight, pale, agonized. He looked at her and his voice rang out again, harsher, louder.

"Let the man speak."

"Thank you, General." Burleigh stood up to make a pose of rugged determination for Del Rio's camera. He took a moment to choose his words. "We are a new nation. The future we want cannot be founded on any accusation of injustice." He made an impatient gesture to silence Coon, and nodded stiffly at me. "Okay, Barstow, what can you say?"

For a moment I had nothing.

Weak in the knees, baffled by the McAdams, I glanced around the room. Gottler was on his feet again, clutching Hunn's arm. Stuart sat scowling at them, his face pale and hard. Colin had bent urgently to Beth. Listening, she shook her head.

"Speak!" Burleigh rapped at me. "If you're going to."

I heard Beth's sharp whisper, "No! No!"

Somehow, that set my mind to moving.

"My brother—" Facing the judges again, I was still uncertain how to begin. "My brother was Alden Kirk, author of *Terror in America*. I didn't know he was reporting to the FBI till after he was dead. But I do know he would never sell out to any outlaw gang."

I glanced at Hunn and Gottler. They were seated again with Ralston. He wore a mocking grin. They were muttering together, glaring at me.

"You say he wouldn't," Ralston hissed under his breath. "I say he did."

Burleigh frowned at him.

"The Bureau did send me here." I tried to ignore them. "My brother had been investigating what he called the seed of terror here in the county. He evidently found them."

I heard a muffled snicker behind me.

"I was to be working with the Bureau in the Acorn unit Mr. Ralston mentioned, though I was never really told anything about it. My contact was an agent named Botman. He gave me a telephone security device and a code name, Acorn Two.

"He was Acorn One. I called back several times, following his instructions. The last time a strange voice answered with the name Acorn Three." Watching Gottler, I saw his face stiffen, but only for a moment before he turned to listen at a murmur from Hunn.

"That was my last contact. I never called again. I heard no more from Botman or the Bureau, but I stayed here, hoping to identify the killers. And—" I stopped for a moment, searching for sane connections. "I saw more acorns than I ever understood."

Coon and Hawes were shuffling their papers and frowning at a clock on the wall. Gottler was clutching Hunn's arm, muttering at him urgently. He got to his feet.

"Sit down, Saul." Burleigh glanced at Stuart, who was staring at me with a look that chilled me. "Barstow may continue."

Lost for a moment, I turned to glance at Beth. She was watching Stuart with a look of mute distress. I stood there aching with pity for her and disturbed by his look of half-contained savagery.

"Okay, Barstow," Burleigh growled at me. "What's this about acorns?"

"A puzzle, sir." I hesitated, still with no believable answer. "The forensic lab found fibers from an oak acorn among fragments of the bomb that killed my brother. That was only the beginning. The killers used acorns to sign their work. I don't know why. Maybe to mock the Bureau. Maybe to throw it off their trail.

"Lydia Starker called me the morning she was killed. She told me to get out to her place if I wanted to know who mailed the letterbomb. She seemed frantic. I found her stabbed to death when I got to her room, lying in her blood on the bathroom floor. Three oak acorns lay in the blood around her head.

"The night of the fire that killed Dr. Ryke, I was staying in the McAdam house, asleep in the room that had been Stuart's. Sometime in the night I was kidnapped, beaten up, left unconscious by a lonely road in the strip-mined country out beyond the county line. I found three acorns placed in the mud around my head.

"The night Dr. McAdam was shot—"

"No!"

I heard that hushed outcry from Beth. Her pale hand was over her lips when I turned, her eyes on me, wide and dark with pain. She flinched away from me as if I had struck her, but in a moment she caught her breath.

"Go on, Clay." Her whisper was almost silent. "You must go on."

Burleigh's gavel fell.

"Barstow!" A sharp command. "Continue!"

I was trembling, the manacles clinking when I turned back to face him. It took a moment to recover my voice.

"My fingerprints were on the gun that wounded Dr. McAdam. Staying there at his house before I was kidnapped, I had found it in a drawer in a table beside the bed—"

"In Stuart's room?"

A cry of pain from Beth. She clapped her hand over her mouth and sank back beside her father. Stuart swayed where he stood, a glassy stare fixed on them. His look of anger faded into agonized appeal. He said something to Beth that I didn't hear and stood with his hands spread toward her, silently begging.

Her face white with pain, she shook her head.

"Sit down!" Burleigh shouted at the guards. "This is a court of law." He swung to me. "Answer me, Barstow. Do you say the General tried to kill his father?"

Looking into Beth's desolate face, I found no words.

"Do you know who fired that shot?"

"I do." Her eyes fixed on Stuart, Beth came back to her feet whispering so faintly I could hardly hear. "I'm afraid I do."

That silenced the room, people straining to listen. Gottler muttering to Hunn. Hunn shouting an objection.

"Miss McAdam!" Burleigh blinked at her. "You are not a witness. Please sit down!"

"No!" Stuart whispered hoarsely. "Let her speak. I've had too much. I've tortured her too long."

Burleigh goggled at her and caught his breath to listen.

"Bett—" Stuart's whisper was almost a moan. "Say what you know."

She stood a long time staring at him, white-faced and swaying, before she caught her breath and spoke huskily to him.

"I know too much. I know what Lydia told me."

He cringed as if from a blow.

"God forgive me!" He took a step toward her and stood there, agony on his face. "Forgive me if you can."

"Sir?" Burleigh shouted. "What do you mean?"

"I fired that shot."

Burleigh dropped his gavel. The tiny crash rang loud in the breathless room.

"Why?" Burleigh gaped and shook his head. "Tell me why!"

Stuart stared at Beth and his father, caught a long uneven breath, turned finally back to Burleigh.

"He threatened me." He had flushed, his voice gone quick and sharp. "He was afraid of what I would do with Roy's shell. He promised to stop me any way he could. I was afraid he could. Afraid of what Lydia had told him."

"General, sir—" Burleigh stood shaking his head, his voice gone sharp with incredulity. "You say you shot your own father?"

Stuart swung to face McAdam, who sat bolt upright, gripping the cane with both thin old hands, gazing at him stonily.

"You never wanted me!" Stuart's voice sharpened in bitter accusation. "I was unexpected. You already had Beth and Roy—my angel brother, so nice and fine and bright. You and Mom had your lives all planned out, you with your war between the states, Mom with her Christian missions. You left me to Orinda and set hard rules and beat me when I broke them. You couldn't wait to be rid of me, shipping me off to that military school before I was twelve years old. Nobody but Beth ever loved me."

He looked at Beth, his face working.

"I'm sorry," he whispered. "Sorry for all the hell I've given you."

She looked up at him with a sad white smile, her lips moving to words I couldn't hear. He glanced at his rigid father, made a quick angry wipe at his eyes, turned back to frown a long time at Burleigh, his lips pressed tight.

"Jim, I'm sorry for you." His voice quivering, he opened his empty hands. "Sorry for how I've let you down. And let the Rifles down. The only friends I ever had. We could have changed the world."

He stood there a moment longer, glanced vacantly around the room, and stumbled back to his seat between his Riflemen, the life gone out of him.

The judges sat for half a minute huddled together. Burleigh looked stunned. He sat motionless till Coon reached for the gavel and cleared his throat.

"A hard blow." He stopped for a long look at Stuart. "A hard blow and hard to take, but it ain't the end of the road. Nor the end of the Free State of America. We've still got the Rifles and good men to command them."

He squared his heavy shoulders. I thought he must be thinking of himself.

"We've still got the shell. We've still got a war to finish. And we've still got this rat Barstow sentenced to die for his crimes." He paused to give me a long, sardonic stare. "Unless he's got another rabbit in his hat."

I heard Gottler's high-pitched yelp. Huddled over the table with Ralston and Hunn, he was glaring across at Stuart, who was rubbing and squeezing his upper arm in an odd way.

"Sir!" Hunn stood up. "It's time to stop this outrageous nonsense. Barstow is not under oath, and I see no reason to believe a word he says."

"Neither do I." Recovering himself, Burleigh took the gavel back. "But we're making history here today. We must be fair. Perhaps our verdict must be reconsidered. Barstow, we can give you five more minutes."

I looked away from Beth's stricken face and tried to pull my mind together.

"One minute will do." Katz caught my arm to hiss at my ear. I shook him off. "I told you how the Bureau had me in that Acorn unit. The last time I called, I heard a different voice, high-pitched and oddly accented. I believe it belonged to somebody in the gang that had infiltrated the unit. Hearing it again, just now in this court-room, I recognized—"

My hand trembling, I pointed at Gottler. He was on his feet, shrilling curiously at Hunn.

"The voice of Acorn Three." I lifted my own husky voice. "Juan Diego Gottler's."

"A lie!" he snarled. "Another monstrous lie!"

White with fury, he shrugged off Hunn's clutching hand and left the room, striding down the central aisle. I heard a guard at the door ordering him to halt. He stalked on. Guns crashed, deafening in the room.

"Order! Order!"

The lifted gavel fell out of Burleigh's hand. He stood gaping at Stuart, who had pitched out of his seat and lay sprawled on the floor. One of the guards stood over him, gun drawn. The other had knelt to feel his pulse.

"The General—" He stood up unsteadily. "The General is dead."

CHAPTER THIRTY-FOUR

PEOPLE WERE ON their feet, yelling questions, crowding toward the exit where the shots had been fired, crowding forward toward the judges and the body. Burleigh shouted for a doctor. A woman who said she was a nurse slipped out of the mob, but the guards refused to let her touch the body.

Leaning on Beth, her father came limping to look down at it. She knelt to feel the wrist and close the glazing eyes. Silence around them, they went slowly down the aisle and out of the room. Medics arrived with a stretcher. Burleigh called the captain to the bar when he had examined the body.

"Stone dead, but I can't say why." He made a baffled shrug. "I'd examined him for his checkup just a few weeks ago. Found him in first-rate shape."

They carried the body away. The judges were still on the bench, watching the doors and muttering uneasily to each other. Jittery Rifle officers huddled with them and one another. Oxman bustled in to see them and bustled out. Katz went up to them, begged for his moment of attention, and came back beaming through the wide-rimmed lenses.

"Burleigh says they'll reverse the verdict and release you in my custody. You will remain at my place under house arrest, pending a final disposition of your case."

We met Pepperlake, Moorhawk, and Rob Roy McAdam at the elevator when Oxman brought them down from the jail, profusely apologetic for the unfortunate inconveniences of their stay. Awkwardly, since I still wore the manacles, they shook my hand and wished me well.

Out of the manacles and back in my room at the Katz House, I enjoyed a hot shower and clean clothing. Julia Sue invited me to dinner with them and Katz broke out a bottle of wine to toast my freedom and the future of the Harven. After the meal he asked me into his office and offered a cigar.

"Julia Sue will have to forgive me." Settling contentedly behind his desk, he lit one for himself. "I hope you will. You must blame me for the way I left you to defend yourself, but—"

He flushed and stopped, peering at the cigar in his stubby fingers as if it had been something strange. I waited, wondering at him, until at last he laid it carefully on an ashtray and took off the glasses, polished them deliberately, replaced them to blink uneasily at me.

"You see, Clay," he went on, "I'd known Lydia since she came to me for help to get away from Stuart. She'd told me a little of what came out at the trial. I'd suspected enough of the rest to make me uneasy."

Nervously, he picked up the cigar and puffed it back to life.

"Your brother spoke to me while he was here, but I had to be careful what I said. Lydia had hinted that Stuart was involved in some underground infonet gang, but she never had names for anybody. She felt she was in danger and wanted me to help her, but

she seemed to have no basis for any action I could take. And—"
He shook his head, with an apologetic shrug. "I didn't want to make
anybody's hit list."

He blinked at me, grinning.

"A lot of us feel better now."

"About Gottler's gang?"

"Lydia believed it was a one-man show. She never had a name,
but now we know he was the man. He took two bullets through his
lungs when he tried to break past the guards. He died before they
got him to a doctor. As for Stuart—"

He shook his head, his face twisted with the tic.

"What's there to say? I used to like him. People loved him.
Those who hadn't crossed him. He could be savage with those who
did. He got rough with me, but I could never really hate him. Maybe
he was born that way. Maybe his parents made him what he was,
like he said at the trial. I never knew much about what he had to
do with Gottler, but they were trying to use each other. Gottler
financed the Rifles."

I asked about Ralston.

"The cops are looking for him. A slick operator. He walked out
of the courthouse with Hunn and seems to have disappeared. Any
other associates of Gottler, whoever they are, will be taking any
cover they can."

He picked up the cigar and laid it down again.

"Stuart McAdam killed himself. When the medics looked, they
found a broken glass tube implanted in his upper left arm. It had
contained cyanide; they got the odor. It must have killed him almost
instantly."

He fired up the cigar and sat puffing on it moodily.

"You've got to feel sorry for his family. Maybe for him. I doubt
he ever was a happy man."

"His Free State?"

"Gone with him, I guess."

"The Haven's still alive?"

"And still at war with the USA. Higgins don't care what we call it. Zeider may be stalled. No guns firing now, but he's still got us bottled up."

He pulled on the cigar, exhaled blue smoke, and laid it aside.

"A crazy kind of war," he muttered. "One nobody can win. Even here in jail, Rob Roy held an ace in the hole. Mike Densky was holding out in the little safety shell around the CyberSoft building. Stuart had his Rifles surround the building, but they couldn't get inside. Pepperlake had warned them that Densky had orders to open the main shell for Zeider's army if Stuart hurt or killed Rob Roy. Stuart was stalled the same way Zeider is."

He reached for the cigar and laid it back again.

"The art of war has changed." He blinked owlishly behind the dark-rimmed glasses. "Something to think about."

He reached again for the cigar while I thought about it and finally asked, "What next?"

"Who knows?" He waved the cigar. "You might ask Rob Roy."

I lay awake till midnight, reliving the trauma of the trial. Beth's pale and agonized face ached in my heart. The image of her father stuck in my mind, a frail and saddened figure, standing bent over his dead son. And Stuart—he was still a painful riddle. I had felt his charm, seen his gift of leadership. Somehow he must have earned the love that Beth and even Lydia had spent upon him. Groping to understand him, I pitied him for the bright promise he had wasted and tried to forgive the harm he had done.

I slept late and found Del Rio on KRIF next morning.

"Bulletin! Bulletin!" Her breathless excitement seemed real. "The Kentucky rebels have captured Washington and paralyzed America. Information is fragmentary and confused, but sources in Baltimore report a barrier described as a second silicon shell that has sealed off the entire capital area from Silver Springs to Alexandria.

"It is said to have appeared before sunrise. Transparent at first, like the shell over the Kentucky county, it flickered and became a mirror surface, reflecting a distorted image of the landscape. Local police authorities report morning traffic on highways into the city backed up for many miles. Rail and air services are blocked. Electronic contact has ceased.

"President Higgins is believed to have been caught in the White House. The Vice President and most cabinet members were in the city. Congress and the Supreme Court were in session. With almost the entire national leadership trapped, the nation has been decapitated. Sporadic and conflicting reactions are reported outside the barrier. Several state governors are said to be mobilizing guard units. General Zeider is believed to be moving armor to surround the capital, though no organized and immediate response seems apparent. In the words of one commentator, the nation is flopping like a chicken with its head cut off.

"A plea for calm, however, has come from Secretary of State Margo Brooke. Somewhere over the Pacific on her way back from a mission to Beijing, she has called from an Air Force plane to assure the nation that she sees no reason for panic. 'We Americans are sane,' she said. 'Though Haven forces are reported to have invaded the capital, I am not yet aware of any violence. I expect none.'

"Secretary Brooke is next in succession to the presidency, if the President and Vice President are incapacitated. Though she has refused to announce any plans for political action, she may be expected to play a leadership role in the formation of a new government if that becomes imperative.

"At this moment, the capital is still in total isolation, cut off from all contact. In a brief interview granted to this reporter, Haven Councilor Cass Pepperlake denied any knowledge of what may be happening under that mirror shell. He did admit, however, that Councilor Kit Moorhawk is now in Washington, invested with full authority as a minister plenipotentiary to negotiate for the immediate recognition of the Haven as a sovereign nation with guaranteed unimpeded access to the outside world by road, rail and air. Pepperlake expects the barrier to remain in place until negotiations are completed."

After that, the rest of the day seemed strangely uneventful. Broadcast popular music from KRIF was interrupted with scraps of confusing news. Washington was still hidden beneath the mirror shell. A militia unit in Arizona had declared its independence, but it appeared to possess no high-tech weaponry. The county sheriff was organizing a posse to capture the leaders. Landing at Andrews Air Force Base, Secretary Brooke had answered questions about the possible formation of a provisional government with only three words, "Wait and see."

Del Rio caught Pepperlake again, sitting at his *Freeman* desk in shirt sleeves, his wispy hair rumpled and the antique eyeglasses pushed up on his forehead. He wanted to thank former Free State officials and ordinary citizens for rallying now in support of the Haven, and he expressed his sympathy for the McAdam family in their grief over Stuart's tragic life and death.

"That's another world." He laughed when Del Rio tried to press him again for news of Washington. "I imagine Kit's negotiations with the federal government are in progress. I can't predict the outcome."

"If you could?" she persisted.

"I'd expect something surprising." Pushing the glasses higher on his furrowed forehead, he squinted at her thoughtfully. "I see our stalemate as a fresh chapter in the old story of the individual and society. The individual fights for freedom. Society has to limit it. In the past, society always won the battle. It could always crush the rebel individual.

"Outcomes have to be different now with Roy McAdam's silicon shell. The individuals inside the shell may be isolated from society, a high price to pay, but they can't be crushed. They may go hungry, but freedom is a precious gift. With Roy McAdam's technology, they'll find ways to survive."

"Can you guess—?"

He shook his head and vanished from the tube.

Cooped up too long, I rode my bike around the town that afternoon. With gas tanks gone dry, pavements were empty. I saw a man raking leaves, a man putting up storm windows, people standing in line outside the Rifles' soup kitchen, people carrying bags away from the Rifle food bank.

When I stopped with a group standing on a street corner, I heard that Ralston and Hunn were missing, thought to have slipped out of the county. The Rifles had announced an election for a new commander. Ben Coon was in jail for public intoxication and disturbing the peace. Gottler's body lay in the morgue, still unclaimed. Stuart was to be buried in the family plot at the cemetery, only the family and a few friends invited to the funeral.

I found the cryptophone that Rob Roy gave me still in my room and gathered resolution to call Beth.

"Yes?" Her cool, inquiring tone made her a stranger again, and it took me a moment to speak her name.

"Clay?" The sudden warmth in her voice made an ache in my throat that kept me silent till I heard it again. "Aren't you Clay?"

"I am."

I caught my breath and tried to tell her what I felt for her and her father and her brother's tragedy. "He surprised me with what he told his father. But still he's hard for me to understand."

"He always was." I heard more sorrow in her voice than bitterness. "He could be cruel. He could have been great, but he was always reaching too far, demanding too much, ruthless when anybody got in his way."

I heard a long sigh.

"He lived his life the way he wanted, or maybe had to, in spite of everybody. He hurt a lot of people, himself most of all. He took his own way out. I loved him, but I have to be glad he's gone."

I asked about her father.

"He's recovering from the shocks," she said. "On the infonet this morning, he was looking for news and able to philosophize. He agrees with Pepperlake that we're still playing the old game of the self against the group—the need for freedom against the need for order. The joker now is the way Roy has changed the playing field. People under the shell may enjoy an unquenchable freedom, but the price may be too high to pay. The best outcome has always been some kind of compromise. Kit Moorhawk has gone to fight for that. He hopes for something we can live with."

I asked if I might see her.

"Of course," she said. "I've longed for you, Clay, in spite—" Her voice caught and came back more steadily. "Give me time. This has been dreadful for my father. For both of us. I need to be with him a little longer."

Back on KRIF next morning, Del Rio reported that the mirror shell was gone from Washington. It had caused no loss of life. National Airport was open again; trains were running, highways open. President Higgins was in Bethesda Naval Hospital. His personal physician said his sudden collapse in the Oval Office was due to fatigue and strain; he was responding magnificently to an experimental genetic therapy for a pancreatic malignancy.

Electronic communication now restored, Washintel WebWatch One was back on the infonet with the amazing tale of the rebel raiders who had seized the national capital and changed the course of history.

"Tex Horn, back on the air with the buzz that does."

He was on the infotel, the big white hat tipped her aside, booming out his inside buzz. He had just returned from a briefing from Secretary of State Margo Brooke and Haven Councilor Kit Moorhawk. Reporters had met them in the lobby of the Georgetown Towers hotel.

"Moorhawk told us the inside story of the daring commando raid that has won the Haven the freedom it has fought for. He and a few CyberSoft engineers rented the penthouse suite of the old hotel, which was just reopening after extensive renovation. They sealed the building off with a compact shield device they had brought in their luggage, allowed the other guests and most of the staff to leave, and then set up a second barrier to enclose the entire city.

"Secretary Brooke revealed details of a conversation between Moorhawk and President Higgins, who was able to speak from his hospital room. She says they found something in common; neither wanted to destroy America. Higgins is now persuaded that the silicon shell is here to stay. Without much choice that I can see, he agreed to the outlines of a preliminary truce which should end hostilities and lead to the recognition of the Haven as a sovereign nation.

"Councilor Pepperlake calls it a historic social experiment designed to test whether total freedom and stable global order can exist together. A noble compromise, in his words, and 'the only way to keep our world alive.'"

Julia Sue knocked on my door late the next afternoon to say that I had a visitor. I found Beth waiting, thin and wan from her ordeal, but her smile warmer than it had ever been. She had come to ask me for dinner. Orinda was making corn muffins and her creole gumbo. I promised to be there.

ABOUT THE AUTHOR

JACK WILLIAMSON has been in the forefront of science fiction since his first published story in 1928. Now in his seventy-second year as a published author, Williamson is the acclaimed author of such trailblazing science fiction as *The Humanoids* and *The Legion of Time*. *The Oxford English Dictionary* credits Williamson with inventing the terms "genetic engineering" (in *Dragon's Island*) and "terraforming" (in *Seetee Ship*). His seminal novel *Darker Than You Think* was a landmark speculation on the nature of shape-changing and will soon be reprinted by Tor Books.

Williamson also has been active academically. He has taught since the 1950s, and is professor emeritus at Eastern New Mexico University. Williamson recently was presented a Lifetime Achievement Award by the Horror Writers Association. He lives and works in Portales, New Mexico.